Teens and the New Religious Landscape

I0585178

Teens and the New Religious Landscape

Essays on Contemporary Young Adult Fiction

Edited by JACOB STRATMAN

McFarland & Company, Inc., Publishers

Jefferson, North Carolina

Library of Congress Cataloguing-in-Publication Data

British Library cataloguing data are available

ISBN 978-1-4766-6807-9 (softcover : acid free paper)
ISBN 978-1-4766-3099-1 (ebook)

Front cover image © 2018 Leks052/iStock

Printed in the United States of America

McFarland & Company, Inc., Publishers
  Box 611, Jefferson, North Carolina 28640
  www.mcfarlandpub.com

Acknowledgments

John Brown University is a good place to be a teacher and a scholar. I thank the administrators, my colleagues, and my students for encouragement, criticism, and support. Special thanks goes to Kelly Escarcega and Samuel Cross-Meredith for their work with copy-editing and indexing. Lastly, this book does not exist without the expertise and talents of the contributors. The essays included in this collection are important contributions to young adult literature scholarship. Editing this book was fun. Thank you.

Table of Contents

Introduction

Young Adult Literature and the Postsecular Novel

Jacob Stratman

In 2009, the *Wall Street Journal* published Katie Roiphe's intriguing summation of contemporary young adult literature, titled "'It was, like, all dark and stormy': Teenage Readers Are Gravitating Toward Even Grimmer Fiction; Suicide Notes and Death Matches." In the article, Roiphe makes the argument that while teen fiction seems bent on exploring the many variations of human depravity, much more than what she remembers as a child, "in the end, these investigations of personal disaster are much less depressing than the 'Gossip Girl' knockoffs which initially seem frolicky and fun but are actually creepy and morally bereft and leave you feeling utterly hopeless." What I appreciate about Roiphe's conclusion here is that contemporary young adult fiction is certainly not scared of tackling the difficult conversations and dilemmas that real teenagers must face each day, and while there are many titles that leave the protagonist in a state of flux, if not in total despair, there are still authors who choose redemption and reconciliation (or at least the invitation to wholeness) as appropriate and probable conclusions for their protagonists' journeys through challenge and hopelessness.

Yet, what guides these characters through these challenges? What frames their decision-making processes? In my young adult literature course, I suggest that existential philosophy is evident in much contemporary young adult literature, as the protagonist must rely, for the most part, on herself to navigate the absurd and despairing world in which she lives. In this rather meaningless world, she must strive to find some—to cultivate and define meaning in order to live authentically and free, without cause to believe in a benevolent and just designer or creator guiding her along. In this fairly big sea of existential young adult fiction, there are, however, authors who investigate how particular faith commitments encourage and support that character's discoveries and revelations. As I prepared a proposal for this manuscript, there was no book-length critical exploration of the field of young adult literature and religious belief and just a handful of peer-reviewed articles on the subject; however, I am pleased to say that during the compilation of this book, Rowman and Littlefield published Patty Campbell's *Spirituality in Young Adult Literature: The Last Taboo* (2015). My hope is that this book, as a complement to Campbell's, will be considered an important introduction to the field of religious faith and literature, namely young adult literature, spawning more books and articles on the topic.

In the initial phases of this project, I knew I needed a scholar to help readers understand the history of the term "postsecular" and its connection to contemporary young adult literature. I invited Paul T. Corrigan to write this essay for the collection, titled "Postsecular Young Adult Literature: or, Harry Potter and the New Religious Landscape," and I believe it is the best starting point for this book. All of these authors, whether they are conscious of it or not, have created characters that are participating in a new (if not always shifting) religious landscape, whether that landscape be embedded in realistic societies or the fantastic.

Instead of organizing the book around themes, sub-topics, or particular religious beliefs, in these essays I have asked each contributor to address key questions regarding fiction and religious belief. Readers will discover characters of all stripes, religious and social, struggling with life and faith. There are several questions that each essay addresses: how are the religious experiences of teenagers expressed in contemporary young adult literature? What is the relationship between the characters' religious beliefs/values and their interactions with their parents, their friends, their schools, and their societies (real and fantastic)? How do young adult authors use religious texts, traditions, and beliefs to add layers of meaning to their characters, settings, and plots? How does contemporary young adult literature place itself into the larger conversation regarding the postsecular? Essentially, as Campbell argues, the world of young adult literature has been very open to a variety of complex social issues; however, religious belief has been the last taboo of YAL. More scholarship should be dedicated to exploring how literature targeting teens showcases protagonists struggling with and navigating religious belief as a part of identity construction.

As I mentioned above, Corrigan frames this book by investigating the literary history of the postsecular. He suggests that the usual binary categories of "religious" and "secular" are not quite up to the task of unpacking literary texts—such as the Harry Potter books—that confront readers with a far messier engagement with religion than we might have expected in previous times. The concept of the postsecular has emerged within literary studies precisely to come to terms with such nontraditional, religious/nonreligious phenomena in contemporary literature. Since religion and spirituality are enduring realities in young adults' lives and enduring concerns in young adult literature, understanding these texts requires reckoning with religious dimensions. In the contemporary period, that means reckoning with messy, nontraditional religious dimensions—that is, with the postsecular. Reviewing postsecular theory and literary criticism, this essay makes a case for the significance of applying the concept of the postsecular to contemporary young adult literature.

Jeremy Larson's "Fantasy as Realism: N.D. Wilson and the Influence of Mythology" explores themes of envious warfare, death and resurrection in the stand-alone YA novel *Boys of Blur* (2014), written by best-selling author N.D. Wilson. Wilson's fiction problematizes the distinction between fantasy and reality, showing that this distinction is constructed and must be deconstructed. Such deconstruction occurs naturally in young adult fantasy. Ultimately, Larson argues that, while the modern poison of scientism destroys sacramental imaginations, the genre of fantasy holds a unique power to appropriate mythology and thereby make reality more visible for a postsecular audience.

Carrie Myers' "A Ninja, a Nun and a Knight: Christianity and Narrative Mischief in Brian Meehl's *You Don't Know About Me, Suck It Up* and *Suck It Up and Die*" uses Brian McLaren's *A Generous Orthodoxy* as a critical lens to explore teen protagonists and other central characters in Meehl's novels as they engage with Christianity's beliefs, culture, and symbols. *YDKAM* features outspokenly Christian characters wrestling with God, their identities, and Bible verses about homosexuality while they embark on a road trip that parallels the journey of Huck Finn and Jim in Mark Twain's *The Adventures of Huckleberry Finn.* In *Suck It Up* and its sequel, the immortal vampires/parental figures and teen characters are largely unmotivated by Christianity—with one key exception—yet Christian history, tropes, and symbolism are key to the novels' characterizations of good and evil, dreams and self-sacrifice, gender and sexuality, and the people and things that make life worth living.

Susan Leigh Brooks' "The Book Worlds of Nikki Grimes: An Invitation to Dialogic Reading" argues that a postsecular reading of *Dark Sons* and *A Girl Named Mister* reinforces the idea that the religious and secular have always co-existed and have far-reaching influences into the worlds of characters and readers. Bakhtin's concepts of heteroglossia and dialogism can help readers see why. This essay asserts that narrative heteroglossia—the ways that the historical and contemporary narratives interact, as well as textual heteroglossia—the ways that the books depend on intertextual understandings, create an atmosphere that invites secular readers into these religious worlds. In addition, instead of relying on simple religious assumptions, these books complicate them. Bakhtin's concept of dialogism can be helpful in negotiating the historical tensions as readers move between ancient and contemporary worlds; the cultural tensions as these characters explore and embody their religious beliefs in society; and personal tensions as readers must consider the ways in which religious beliefs and practices serve or don't serve these characters well.

Fatema Johera Ahmed's "Young Adult Fiction, Diaspora and the 'Muslim' Question: A Study on Faith and Feminism in Randa Abdel-Fattah's Novels" argues that young adult literature in the West tends to feature the Muslim diaspora where assimilation, ethnicity, and the state of being Muslim are some of the discursive frames through which migrants negotiate their new lives in unfamiliar spaces. Yet, Randa Abdel-Fattah's *Does My Head Look Big in This?* and *No Sex in the City* suggest that there are different ways in which counter-narratives challenge the cultural politics of mainstream spaces to create a third culture or a third space of liminality where creative beginnings are possible. These texts look at the implications of the status quo on young Muslim adults on a quest to belong, the search for self-validating images by which the marginalized Muslim community may reclaim its representation, and the ways in which cultural, religious, and social norms effect the formation of the multicultural community. Finally, the essay also addresses how Islam in YAL forwards feminist discourse.

Jacob Stratman's "The Customized Religion: Moralistic Therapeutic Deism, American Teenagers and Pete Hautman's *Godless*" suggests that even though these "misfits" in the novel create a separate religious reality quite outside of the center (other historical, organized religions) in an attempt to maintain order and structure in their lives, they are, according to Christian Smith's seminal work *Soul Searching: The Religious and Spiritual Lives of American Teenagers*, surprisingly in line with the majority of American teens. Smith argues that most teenagers' ideas of religion, faith practice, and theological doctrine are completely outside of the center of historically orthodox religion (Islam, Judaism, and Christianity, namely) even though they may profess one of those religions. Exploring the religious lives of American teenagers has become increasingly common and important in this post–9/11 era. How Smith's work intersects with young adult literature, namely Hautman's *Godless*, is the focus of this essay.

Patricia F. D'Ascoli's "Learning How to Be Jewish in *The Truth About My Bat Mitzvah* and *Confessions of a Closet Catholic*" explores these novels as they capture the dynamic and complex nature of Judaism through the portrayal of young adults in search of their Jewish identity. While these novels adapt and expand upon many of the themes established in Judy Blume's *Are*

You There God? It's Me Margaret, they feature protagonists whose spiritual journey culminates in an awareness of what it means to be Jewish. In their portrayal of an adolescent's search for Jewish identity, these novels accurately depict how Judaism is much more than a religion and how a search for Jewish identity must also consider the ethnic and/or cultural elements of Judaism.

Katelyn R. Browne's "'Stick up for these crazy stupid things': Emily Horner's Queer Quaker Road Trip Novel" explores the Religious Society of Friends (better known as Quakerism). She suggests that Quakers occupy a peculiar space both within the Christian tradition and in broader discussions about religion and secularism. Emily Horner's 2010 novel *A Love Story Starring My Dead Best Friend* demonstrates many of the ways in which Quakers can play an essential bridging role in a postsecular society among people of diverse faiths and people of no faith. Horner uses her main character's Quaker identity, values, and beliefs to create a positive context for adolescent individuation and the development of a queer self-concept in ways that complicate existing narratives and scholarship about LGBTQ+ characters in religious-themed young adult fiction.

Rizia Begum Laskar's "Performing God: Kiran and Krishna in Rakesh Satyal's *Blue Boy*" navigates a novel that portrays a twelve year old who is at the crossroads regarding his identity. The protagonist Kiran and his multi-faceted being is characterized by a tussle between conformity and recalcitrance. In order to integrate himself into the social circle of his school and the tense atmosphere of his home, he conceives of himself as the reincarnation of the blue Hindu god Krishna. This performance as Krishna is thus the means through which Kiran tries to prove himself and also to come to terms with his own identity. But this performance is linked to a more crucial understanding of Kiran's own revelations regarding Krishna and a coming together of the secular and the religious. How performance is a resonance and ramification of the spirituality associated with religion, particularly Hinduism, forms the basis of interrogation here, as well as the ways in which performance leads to a conflation of Hinduism and postsecularism in a diasporic setting.

David S. Hogsette's "The Way of the Fantasist: Ethical Complexities in the Taoist Mythopoeic Fantasy of Ursula Le Guin's *A Wizard of Earthsea*" explores how Le Guin engages postsecularist spiritual sensibilities and chooses to build her mythopoeic subcreation, Earthsea, upon explicitly Taoist philosophical foundations. Readers can escape into Earthsea not only to recover a sense of mystical wonderment absent from secularist perspectives, but they can also rediscover faith in the possibility of moral instruction and personal improvement. Despite some unresolved philosophical paradoxes, and because of her nuanced integration of lesser known Taoist principles, Le

Guin creates a comprehensive mythopoeic fantasy novel that both delights and edifies the postsecular imagination that is open to such fabulation and willing to explore, analyze, and contemplate the spiritual blessings and philosophical paradoxes that are Earthsea.

Erin Wyble Newcomb's "The Language of Magic and Prayer: Intercession in the Works of Merrie Haskell" examines the language used to describe both magic and prayer in Merrie Haskell's *The Princess Curse, Handbook for Dragon Slayers*, and *The Castle Behind Thorns* by illustrating the way Haskell ultimately uses her main characters as intercessors to heal the supposed rift between the natural and supernatural worlds. That healing takes place only when the characters come to understand prayer not in opposition to magic, but as its own kind of magic—neither evil nor impersonal. The relationship between magic and prayer changes as Haskell's heroes recognize that there can be bridges between the ideologies of magic and prayer, just as there can be bridges between the supernatural and the natural. The characters, through their acts of intercessory prayer and use of magic, become those bridges.

Carissa Turner Smith's "Postsecular Cosplay, Fundamentalism and Martyrdom in Gene Luen Yang's *Boxers & Saints*" centers on an interview where Yang compares the Boxers of late 1800s China to "modern day geeks" who "cosplay"; "they wanted to be these gods so badly they came up with this ritual, where they believed they would be possessed by them, get their powers." The protagonists of Yang's *Boxers & Saints*, both Boxers and Christians, dwell in what Charles Taylor has described as a disenchanted age; the modern self is the buffered self, cut off from a spiritually imbued world, but occasionally dabbling in the pretense of porosity to spiritual forces. Both cosplay and religious fundamentalism are, in part, expressions of nostalgia for the enchanted world of the past; while Yang's Boxers use embodied ritual to access the spiritual realm and thereby control or even kill others, Yang also depicts similarly disenchanted characters whose embodied rituals instead lead them to compassion. *Boxers & Saints* thus demonstrates that meaningful religious performance is possible even without fundamentalist (whether "religious" or "secular") certainty.

Shih-Wen Sue Chen's "Sight, Blindness and Identity in Gene Luen Yang's *American Born Chinese* and *Boxers & Saints*" examines the interplay between religion and identity in Gene Luen Yang's work as well, focusing on *American Born Chinese* (2006) and *Boxers & Saints* (2013). Yang utilizes both verbal and visual elements of the graphic novel format to explore identity formation. Using positioning theory and narrative theory to analyze the texts, Chen argues that by employing varying motifs of sight and blindness, *American Born Chinese* and *Boxers & Saints* implicitly advocate for belief in a monotheistic Christian God and emphasize the importance of internal transformation of the heart over a corporeal transformation. Instead of prescribing answers, Yang's texts prompt the implied young adult audience to ask questions and think about how religious faith can shape one's identity. His inclusion of Buddhist images alongside Christian ones challenges the stability of the boundaries between different religions and spiritual practices.

Postsecular Young Adult Literature: or, Harry Potter and the New Religious Landscape

PAUL T. CORRIGAN

In the late 1990s and early 2000s, when a new Harry Potter book came out every year or so, many religious people took up torches and pitchforks against the series, particularly among conservative Christians in the United States.[1] Preachers condemned the books from pulpits; parents tried to ban them from libraries and classrooms. "Harry Potter books promote witchcraft!" they claimed. Of course, even a passing familiarity with J.K. Rowling's fantastical depictions of "witchcraft and wizardry" combined with even the least bit of information about the religious traditions of witchcraft such as Wicca reveals the absurdity of this claim. Harry Potter books promote witchcraft exactly as much as those other landmark series in young adult fantasy literature from the United Kingdom—C.S. Lewis's Chronicles of Narnia and J.R.R. Tolkein's *The Lord of the Rings*, stalwart Christian tales—which is to say, of course, that Harry Potter books *do not* promote witchcraft at all. But absurdity isn't the only takeaway here. On the contrary, this controversy invites a sustained consideration of religion and contemporary young adult literature.[2]

Specifically, what is the significance of religion in contemporary young adult literature? What does engagement with religion in such texts reflect back to us about religion in contemporary society? And what does this engagement offer readers? The essays in this collection are the first to take up such questions about young adult literature in light of the concept of the "postsecular." My purpose in this introduction is to explain the term *postsecular* in the context of emerging bodies of postsecular theory and postsecular literary criticism and to make a case for the concept's salience for interpreting and understanding literature written for young adults today. But before turning to that scholarship, I want to linger a bit with the case of Harry Potter to illustrate something of the nature of the literary and religious tangles before us.

In an earlier time, such questions as I've posed about the significance of religion in young adult literature may have seemed fairly straightforward. For instance, we would not be hard pressed to read Lewis's and Tolkein's works, published some sixty years ago now, as narratives presenting for readers fairly traditional Christian theology in a fairly straightforward way. The role of religion in young adult literature today is not nearly so tidy—as a twist in the Potter controversy highlights. In comments reported in *The Telegraph* in 2007, shortly after the release of the final novel in the series, *Harry Potter and the Deathly Hallows*, Rowling herself explains the centrality of religious themes in the books, a reflection of her own lifelong religious faith: "To me," she comments, "the religious parallels have always been obvious"—so obvious, in fact, that she didn't want to "talk too openly about it" before the final book had come out because she was concerned that that might give away too much about the ending of the story (qtd. in Petre). Indeed, chapter sixteen of that final book presents the most overt religious references in the books, which hold, according to Rowling, the key to understanding the whole series. When Harry visits his parents' grave, he finds inscribed on their tombstone and another tombstone nearby two passages from the New Testament: "*Where your treasure is, there will your heart be also*" and "*The last enemy that shall be destroyed is death*" (Rowling, *Deathly Hallows*, 325, 328). For Rowling, "those two particular quotations ... sum up, they almost epitomise, the whole series" (qtd. in Petre).

Her comments here make it clear that the books are religious after all but also that they are religious in a way that should turn the conversation away from the plot devices of magical spells and toward the larger themes of justice, compassion, death, and life after death. Not only do the books not promote Paganism or Wicca, they turn out to be directly and substantially informed by Christianity—quite the plot twist in the religious controversy over the books.[3] And the complications continue. To quote Rowling further on the matter:

> The truth is that ... my faith is sometimes that my faith will return. It's something I struggle with a lot.
>
> On any given moment if you asked me if I believe in life after death, I think if you polled me regularly through the week, I think I would come down on the side of yes—that I do believe in life after death.
>
> But it's something I wrestle with a lot. It preoccupies me a lot, and I think that's very obvious within the books [qtd. in Petre].

It is ironic that Christians who reacted to the books as if they were promoting an entirely different religion clearly didn't even recognize the Christianity in the stories. But with this further explanation from Rowling, it is also not entirely surprising. While the religious perspective in and behind the books is now revealed to be undoubtedly *Christian*, it is also revealed to be just as undoubtedly *untraditional*.

We find here Christianity with a difference, including as much doubt as faith, as much agnosticism as religion. This is reflected in the books' key spiritual aphorism, which we find not in the words of Jesus to Martha ("whosoever liveth and believeth in me shall never die" [John 11:26, KJV]), as we might in a more traditionally Christian book, but instead in the words of Dumbledore to Harry: "to the well-organized mind, death is but the next great adventure" (Rowling, *Sorcerer's Stone*, 297), a statement that might easily be considered more ambiguous, flexible, open to both religious and secular interpretations. Likewise, the brief glimpses of afterlife near the end of the Potter series might easily be interpreted as being quite different from that of traditional Christianity. And though the witchcraft is incidental to the books' religious aspects, the use of magical imagery does beckon toward the religious in being supernatural *and* toward the secular humanist in being fantastical (i.e., pointedly not intended to reflect the world literally).[4] In all this, Rowling blends aspects of Christianity and aspects of secular humanism.[5] In sum, the Harry Potter books, the religious controversy surrounding them, and Rowling's own comments reveal a far messier relationship between religion and literature than we might have expected in previous times. In short, we're not in Canterbury anymore.

Rowling is far from alone in practicing literary, religious innovation in young adult literature. Ursula Le Guin's Earthsea novels reflect her Taoism while incorporating patently invented religions (and wizards of her own), whereas Philip Pullman's His Dark Materials novels reflect his atheism while making use of supernatural "daemons." Naomi Shihab Nye's *Habibi* offers a universalist theology of "Big God" in direct dialogue with her father's Islam. All of these are religious (or secular) with a difference, with a twist; the usual binary categories of religious and secular are not quite up to the task of adequately unpacking them. The concept of the *postsecular* has emerged within literary studies precisely to come to terms with such nontraditional, religious/nonreligious, and blended phenomena in contemporary literature. Since religion and spirituality are enduring realities in young adult lives and enduring concerns in young adult literature,[6] understanding these texts requires reckoning with religious dimensions. In the contemporary period, that means reckoning with messy, nontraditional religious dimensions—that is, with the postsecular.

The New Religious Landscape

In the late nineteenth and early twentieth centuries, theorists put forward the idea that modernization would, as Pippa Norris and Ronald Inglehart put it, cause religion to "gradually fade" from public life (3) and, for more and more people, from private life as well. Max Weber famously called this apparent inevitability the "disenchantment of the world" (155). This understanding that reason and science would supplant religion came to be known as the "secularization thesis" and held sway among Western intellectuals for many years. Jeffrey K. Hadden paraphrases this view as follows:

> Once the world was filled with the sacred—in thought, practice, and institutional form. After the Reformation and the Renaissance, the forces of modernization swept across the globe and secularization, a corollary historical process, loosened the dominance of the sacred. In due course, the sacred shall disappear altogether except, possibly, in the private realm [598].

Given that Hadden has the benefit of looking back in time from the other end of the twentieth century, we might sense a bit of parody in the description. But the point is that, in retrospect, the grand narrative of secularization has obviously not played out—at least not in such simple terms. Instead, as Peter L. Berger confesses, the world more or less remains "as furiously religious as it ever was, and in some places more so" (2). Cesare Merlini similarly notes that recent years "appear to have been marked by a return or revival of religion" in the world (117). Charles Taylor even proposes, "we are just at the beginning of a new age of religious searching" (535).

Yet while secularization has not panned out the way many expected it to—the world remaining religious in spite of industrialization, globalization, science, and pluralism—*the way in which* the world is religious has certainly changed. While the secular and its attendant phenomena have not displaced religion, they have certainly shaken it up. In *The Restructuring of American Religion: Society and Faith Since World War II*, Robert Wuthnow documents how cultural, social, and political changes of the past half-century have had enormous impacts on religion in the United States (322). To be sure, it is the case that "rationality, natural science, and the social sciences have all exercised a negative effect on traditional religious beliefs and practices" (301). But the key word here is "traditional." Wuthnow writes, "highly diverse religious movements and countermovements ... have characterized the nation since the 1950s" (315). Taylor sees things similarly. True, "it is obvious that a decline in belief and practice has occurred" to a certain degree and among certain demographics. But the more fundamental change has not been in *how many* but in *how* people do or do not remain religious (530). While belief has not gone away, "the conditions of belief" have changed radically. To wit, we have gone "from a society in which it was virtually impossible not to believe in God, to one in which faith … is one human possibility among others" (3). Traditional ways of being religious no longer serve as "the default option" (12). In Taylor's perspective, this condition of pluralism creates a "new spiritual landscape" (513).

In the United States, several aspects of this new landscape stand out. First, more and more people report to not believe in religion. Pew Research Center's Religion & Public Life Project reports a rapidly increasing number of people identifying as atheist, agnostic, and, especially, as believing "nothing in particular" (1). Second, reactively, religious fundamentalisms are intensifying. Even if sheer numbers of fundamentalists may be declining in some areas (Jones et al.), the energy and momentum of fundamentalism has increased and seems likely to continue to do so. The Academy of Arts and Sciences' Fundamentalism Project documents in no uncertain terms that "fundamentalisms are alive and innovative" (Marty 372). Third, perhaps surprisingly given the first two trends, progressive religion also seems to be enjoying resurgence, particularly among younger people. In a recent Public Religion Research Institute report, Robert P. Jones et al. describe a shift toward progressive religious orientation among younger generations at a rate and scale that matches the increase of nonreligious affiliation (34). Fourth, as Wuthnow writes in *After Heaven: Spirituality in America Since the 1950s*, "growing numbers of Americans say they are spiritual but not religious" (2). Fifth, still other changes are also taking place that are not so easy to label. For one, as Taylor writes, "the gamut of intermediate positions greatly widens" between belief and unbelief as those terms are traditionally understood. For example, "many people drop out of active practice while still declaring themselves as belonging to some confession, or believing in God." Inversely, "more and more people adopt what would earlier have been seen as untenable positions, e.g., they consider themselves Catholic while not accepting many crucial dogmas, or they combine Christianity with Buddhism, or they pray while not being certain they believe" (513). In certain respects it appears that instead of becoming secular the United States has become, in Paul Elie's words, "a vast Home Depot of 'do-it-yourself religion.'"

So what happened? Did secularization come and go? Did it never or not yet arrive? Is it already here but looks different than expected? To address such questions theorists such as Berger, Taylor, Jose Casanova, Talal Asad, William Connolly, Jacques Derrida, James K. A. Smith, and others have begun to develop more complex notions of modernization and secularization. Talk has turned from outright *secular* to more nuanced considerations: *late secular* (e.g., Baird), *trans-secular* (e.g., McLennan, though he does not use that term), and, most importantly, *post-secular* (e.g., Habermas).

Religious, Secular and Postsecular

Responding to the new religious landscape not anticipated by secularization theory, the term *postsecular* points to a renewed interest in religion and in matters that have traditionally been considered the domain of religion. Like many post- words (postmodern, poststructural, postcolonial, etc.), postsecular is a contested term. As Ingolf U. Dalferth points out, it's "used in very different ways" not only in different contexts but even within the same context (325). For scholars like James A. Beckford, this instability renders the term incoherent. Others have found the instability not a problem but a plus, the nature of the term reflecting the nature of the phenomenon it names. As Rosi Braidotti explains, "the postsecular condition is quite diverse and internally differentiated" (10). For James S. Diamond, postsecular is inherently "a multivocal term" (599). Kristina Stoeckl adds that the postsecular condition is one of "permanent tension" and that "the meaning of the postsecular lies in the very contestedness of the term" (3, 4). Defining the postsecular, then, calls for a certain amount of intentional looseness, purposeful ambiguity, and artful equivocation. To borrow from Zygmunt Bauman, we might say that the postsecular has to do with "a *re-enchantment* of the world" (x). To borrow from Steven M. Wasserstrom, we might say it has to do with "*religion after religion*" (51). We might use the common idiom "spiritual but not religious." Or we might revise it and say "religious but not religious" or "spiritual but not spiritual." More broadly still, we might simply describe the postsecular as *religion with a difference*.

At first glance, the word postsecular may sound positioned against the secular. On one hand, it may suggest an idea that *the historical process of secularization*—in which society becomes less and less religious—has turned and begun to go in reverse. In this case, the postsecular would be about *de-secularization*. On the other hand, it may suggest a stance that *the idea of secularism*—that religion should be kept out of the public sphere—is ideologically misguided. In this case, the postsecular would be *anti-secularism*.

While some scholars talk about the postsecular with language that could be interpreted in these ways, others specifically define the term differently. For instance, Massimo Rosati and Kristina Stoeckl define the postsecular as the sense that commonly-held ideas about secularization do not adequately account for religion in the present historical situation and as an argument for "more just ways of accommodating [the] religious" in society (3). Such a position might be seen as leaning toward de-secularization and anti-secularism. But it might just as easily be understood as qualifying (rather than repudiating) the secular. Indeed, Stoeckl specifically argues that the postsecular should not be understood as "falling back" from or coming "after" the secular, even she suggesting leaving off the hyphen to avoid overly stressing the *post* in postsecular (3, 6).

Gregor McLennan goes further, positioning the postsecular *within* the secular. He argues that certain postsecular ideas—the idea that religion can continue to exist in an otherwise secular society and the idea that religion should be able to come to voice in the public sphere—already fall within the secular. The postsecular need not replace the secular; it can improve it (11). He reasons, "it is more appropriate to regard postsecular reflexive enquiries as intra-secularist rather than anti-secularist; that is to say, they form part of the intellectual process that has been dubbed the 'secularization of secularism' itself, rather than straightforwardly extending the 'revival of religion' into the heartlands of Western theory" (4). Aleksandr Kyrlezhev also posits the postsecular as secularism becoming more secular. Likewise invoking "[t]he secularisation of secularism," he writes, "After the completion of the process of de-monopolisation of religion[,] it was time for the de-monopolisation of secularism" (29). Though Mike King sees a more significant break between the secular and the postsecular than McLennan and Kyrlezhev do, he points in roughly the same direction when he writes, "To be properly 'post' anything, the new sensibility usually incorporates something of what it goes beyond, even if it transcends many of the defining features of its precursor" (11). For most scholars, then, the postsecular cannot be described simply as *anti-secular*, *de-secular*, or *non-secular*, though it might be described as trans-secular, going beyond the secular without going against or without it.

Most scholars do seem to agree on at least one point: in some way or other, the postsecular includes both the secular *and* the religious. Where scholars differ on this is how the two relate to each, including whether they even remain distinct. Arguments are made for coexistence, dialogue, indifference, blending, and blurring of the two categories. The broadest view on this question defines the postsecular in terms of the *coexistence* of the religious and the secular. Elaine Graham describes the postsecular "as a paradoxical condition in which currents of disenchantment and re-enchantment co-exist" (236). Similarly, Rosati and Stoeckl write that the postsecular requires "the co-presence or co-existence within the same public space of religious and secular world-views and practices" (4). Taking a step further, Aleksandr Morozov proposes, "The secular and religious will continue to coexist until the end of history, sometimes in conflict, sometimes existing in parallel, and sometimes in fruitful collaboration" (44). For him, neither the sacred age nor the secular age ever happened. At all times, there have been elements of both and the apparently postsecular moment we are experiencing now, in a resurgence of religion in the public sphere, is not the undoing of secularism but the latest swing of the "pendulum" (42).

While coexisting, the religious and the secular may or may not interact in significant ways. Dalferth suggests that a postsecular society be defined in terms of their *indifference* to each other (337). He writes, "truly post-secular societies are neither religious nor secular. They do not prescribe or privilege a religion, but neither do they actively and intentionally refrain from doing so ... rather, they take no stand on this matter" (324). Similarly, Kyrlezhev offers that in a postsecular age the "conflict between rational scientific knowledge and the transcendental mysticism of traditional religion ... is no longer relevant." It's not that they will be reconciled but that they may sit side by side without the contradiction being a bother (30). But other scholars understand the postsecular in terms of a more active coexistence, not indifference but *dialogue*. In a widely cited essay, Jürgen Habermas stresses the importance of a "complementary learning process." Religious people and secular people living side by side need to learn from one another in order to coexist peacefully ("Notes"). Rosati and Stoeckl add that this complementary learning process will require reflective thinking on all sides. They write, "religious and secular views are called to live together, and to live differently" (4). Such a dialogue would promote a more truly inclusive and pluralist society.

A more involved model envisions *blending* aspects of the secular and the religious. King proposes that the postsecular contains both "the habits of critical thought which partially define secularism" and an "openness to questions of the spirit" which partially defines religion (11). Yet one deeper still proposed relationship sees a *blurring* of the very lines that mark the secular and the religious as categories. Philip S. Gorski et al. point out how traditional definitions of secular and religious already overlap: "an expansive definition of religion ... will find religion everywhere, even in putatively secular and mundane activities, such as professional sports or solitary walks," while "an expansive definition of secularity ... will find secularity everywhere, even in churches and synagogues." They consider the postsecular to somehow occupy "the liminal space between the religious and the secular" (7). Kyrlezhev takes this a step farther. "The world can no longer be divided into religious and nonreligious. Both spheres now coincide," he writes. "They mutually penetrate each other to the degree that they are indistinguishable. Today, nothing is intrinsically secular or religious. Everything can be sacred and everything can be profane" (26).

Concepts of the postsecular emerge out of, and in an attempt to understand, the new, messy religious landscape in which we find ourselves. In contrast to what the secularization thesis predicted, the world remains religious. But consistent with its understanding that pluralism, science, and other facets of modernism would exert an effect, the world is not always religious in the traditional ways. Postsecular theory works to make sense of all this; postsecular literature does as well. But in contrast to postsecular theory, postsecular literature doesn't just explore the postsecular; it also enacts it.

What Postsecular Literature Offers

Some scholars describe the postsecular neutrally. It is something happening "for better or worse," write Arthur Bradley, Jo Carruthers, and Andrew Tate (1). With the broadest definitions of the postsecular, such a stance is certainly desirable. One would not imagine that any or all engagements or reengagements with religion would be something to endorse. In some cases, Kyrlezhev suggests, the postsecular moment may prompt fundamentalism and purism (28). This caution is worth heeding. However, Habermas, even while noting the apparent increase of religious fundamentalist violence in the world, stresses what the postsecular has to contribute positively. As noted already, he makes the case for a "complementary learning process" between secular people and religious people ("Notes"). A postsecular society understood in such terms will become a more just and inclusive society. More pointedly still, Habermas argues that in this dialogue religious people can contribute "semantic resources" of the sort that religious communities have long cultivated and that are "becoming depleted" in secular societies. These include "resources of meaning, solidarity, and justice" ("A Reply," 76–77).

Many other scholars point in the same direction. Even those declining to outright endorse the postsecular tend to emphasize its positive potential—appropriately so, in my view.[7] Two areas where the potential of the postsecular is discussed are spirituality and politics, specifically feminist politics in several cases. Regarding spirituality, Diamond offers that the postsecular returns our attention to questions of "the inner transformation … in human consciousness" (584). Regarding politics, Graham proposes the postsecular allows us to consider both the "authoritarian" and the "emancipatory" aspects of the "religious *and* secular" and to consider "the ways both 'faith' *and* 'reason' might inform discourses around the construction of gender." Neither the secular nor the religious "provides sympathetic spaces for feminism, since one promotes reason, autonomy, individualism at the expense of lived experiences of contingency, embodiment and spirituality, while the other seeks to limit women's freedom in the name of obedience to traditional or 'natural' ways of life" (245, 242). Regarding both spirituality and politics at once, Braidotti argues that the postsecular offers particular opportunities to tap into "the deep spiritual renewal that is carried by and is implicit in the feminist cause" (7).

The "semantic resources" of the postsecular appear nowhere more compellingly than in postsecular literary texts. As Norman Finkelstein observes, contrary to common expectations of modernism and secularism, many contemporary writers still seek the "hidden life" (6), "participate in … 'the symposium of the whole'" (5), and engage with "agencies of desire, meaning, truth, and yes, 'Spirit, with that troublesome, rebarbative capital letter'" (141). An emerging body of postsecular literary criticism describes this emerging body of postsecular literature, particularly within contemporary fiction. In 2007, John A. McClure inaugurated this work with *Partial Faiths: Postsecular Fiction in the Age of Pynchon and Morrison,* the landmark study of postsecular literature, bringing the concept of the postsecular into literary studies from religion, philosophy, and sociology. For McClure, postsecular literature offers "new forms of religiously inflected seeing and being," ones that are "dramatically partial and open-ended" and involve "'limited gift[s]' of the spirit" (ix, 6). Other scholars offer comparable assessments. Where Habermas broadly extols the resources of the postsecular, literary scholars writing about the postsecular more concretely name and describe the literary texts and forms reflecting and enacting the postsecular's new and renewed ways of thinking, seeing, being, and loving.

For Magdalena Mączyńska, postsecular literature "promises ... new ways of thinking about the ineffable, beyond the compromised structures of traditional religious belief and the limiting binary language of modern secularism" (81). For Allen Dunn, postsecular literature gives us an opportunity for "critical 'self-reflection'" (99). For Kathryn Ludwig, postsecular literature "often articulate[s] a kind of anti-religion, in which characters engage religious possibility without affirming a single system of religious thought." In this way, we can read it to "enlarge our understanding of the religious in our age" (83). Most affirming of all, Manav Ratti celebrates what he calls "postsecular affirmative values": "love, friendship, community, art, literature, music, nature, the migrant's eye-view, hybridity, and 'newness,'" along with "[f]aith, awe, wonder, and transcendence." These enduring values are made new in the postsecular when "writers write through religion by invoking its great signifiers and great ethics, and then translate and secularize them within the contingency—and urgency—of material and historical circumstance" (xxiii, 17–18). At last, even Bradley, Carruthers, and Tate, who as I've noted decline to endorse the postsecular overtly, nonetheless describe its contributions compellingly: "literature constitutes a privileged space in which the return of the religious can take place. Literature, like religion, has always implied a challenge to strict boundaries—between fantasy and fact, transcendence and immanence, the spiritual and the material" (3). For that reason, "the 'cracks' into which religious impulses flow in a world without religion are nothing other than the space of literature itself: literature is neither an alternative to, nor a substitute for religion, but a way in which religious experience can happen" (5).[8]

Conclusion

Until now, no scholarship has sought to understand young adult literature through the lens of the postsecular or to understand the postsecular as manifest through young adult literature. This collection begins to fill an important gap. After all, the new religious landscape applies to young adults more than anyone else. Young adults today may well have faced the challenges of the postsecular from birth. They stand to gain as much as any other readers from engaging seriously in postsecular literature. Moreover, if we examine contemporary young adult literature with the old categories of religious and secular, we very well may overlook key postsecular writers of young adult literature such as Rowling, Le Guin, Pullman, Nye and others who do not appear religious (or secular) in the traditional ways. We also may fail to connect these writers to each other, because of how different they seem in perspective and background. But the concept of the postsecular allows us to see how they are indeed "religious" in important ways and do indeed undertake a certain shared project, exploring questions of religious belief and unbelief nontraditionally, in ways that reflect the postsecular society emerging in the contemporary era.

An analysis of several hundred recent young adult novels found an increase of young adult novels published with multiple narrative perspectives, alternating between characters, between points of view, between times, between past and present, between styles, and so forth. Melanie D. Koss ties the emergence of this narrative technique to changes in society, particularly the unfolding of a more pluralist world, where both the Internet and increasingly "diverse populations" surround young people with multiple voices, multiple differences, and multiple perspectives. Of course, these very changes are part of the larger changes of modernism, secularism, and now postsecularism. Thus while any given young adult postsecular novel may or may not use this particular narrative technique, its prevalence is deeply consonant with the postsecular. Such literature can help students come to understand their world and their selves in these times. As Koss writes, "Books with multiple narrative perspectives may be written as a form of bibliotherapy, or to provide teens with a picture of other teens who may be going through similar life events. These books also present different perspectives on and reactions to such events." By considering multiple perspectives and reactions within a single story, young adult readers can better consider who they themselves would like to be, what they believe, and how they would like to act. While most teachers and scholars will not want to reduce the reading of literature to "bibliotherapy," we certainly want the literature students read to affect their lives, and young adults certainly need to be able to engage multiple perspectives and voices to address the difficulties they face as they come into their own as young adults—including spiritual, religious, and existential difficulties.

In my view, those Christian parents and pastors who wanted to protect young people from Harry Potter books were mistaken on multiple levels, most obviously about the books promoting witchcraft but most deeply about the very idea of what they were protecting young people from. They likely thought they were keeping children from religious *answers* they disagreed with (i.e., "witchcraft"). But actually they were keeping children from religious *questions*, indeed, from the very process of *questioning religion*. Such questioning may also appear dangerous to the overly orthodox mind. But it is in fact essential for developing as a person and becoming adult—and, for a great number of young people, it will prove inevitable and inescapable. Regardless of what some older adults might want—whether following Franklin Graham in seeing one belief as absolute or Richard Dawkins in seeing no belief (that is, no-belief) as absolute—young people *will* work through the process of understanding their own lives, deciding for themselves where they stand in relation to the religious/secular. In the era we are in, the terms of this process will very often be quite nontraditional. We can help young adults along in their journeying by providing and promoting good books. Postsecular young adult literature not only reflects the postsecular as a contemporary phenomenon in our society but also facilitates the postsecular as a process for readers, not by giving answers but by enacting questions. Attending to the postsecular within contemporary young adult literature may help readers to navigate the present postsecular moment and to draw deeply from it, not only learning to live more justly with neighbors different from ourselves in a context of religious/secular pluralism but also making personal, spiritual, intellectual use of resources found on both sides of what is becoming for many people, both young and not so young, an increasingly permeable divide between the secular and the religious.

NOTES

1. Portions of this essay are adapted from Corrigan, "The Postsecular and Literature: A Review of Scholarship."

2. For a thorough and thoroughly-documented overview of this phenomenon, see "Religious Debates Over the Harry Potter series."

3. Another account of Rowling's comments on the religious themes in her work complicates things just a tad further. *Deathly Hallows* opens with two epigraphs on death, one from Aeschylus and the other William Penn (Rowling, xvii). Rowling confesses that she "really enjoyed choosing" these specifically "because one is pagan, of course, and one is from a Christian tradition" (qtd. in Adler). This one quotation from a classical source doesn't make her work promote Paganism, of course. But her delight in specifically quoting a Pagan writer alongside a Christian writer highlights the messy nature of the religious in her work.

4. In contrast to how the "witchcraft and wizardry" in the novels has nothing to do with past or present European religious traditions, Rowling's post-*Deathly Hallows* writings expanding wizarding into North America do appropriate and distort living Native American religious traditions (Lee). Sadly, in this, Rowling joins a long tradition of cultural colonization of Native American and other marginalized peoples by white European and American writers, a fact made all the more dismaying in light of how central a theme racial justice is in Harry Potter (e.g. Voldemort's belief in the supremacy of "pure-blood" wizards underwrites all of the evil he does). This turn does not invalidate Harry Potter but does complicate the story in ways better understood through postcolonial analysis than through post-secular.

5. The religious/secular flexibility of the books has, apparently, already been abundantly clear to some of the books' most informed and committed readers. Vanessa Zoltan and Casper ter Kuile, a humanist chaplain at Harvard University and a humanist divinity student at Harvard Divinity School (i.e., ministers for humanist, agnostic, atheist, and other non-religious people) have embarked on a chapter-by-chapter meditative reading of all seven Potter novels as "sacred texts."

6. As Robert Coles and Rickey Cotton attest, respectively.

7. Not all who write about the postsecular do so favorably. As noted above, Beckford finds the concept incoherent. Slavoj Žižek goes further, referring to "this postsecular crap."

8. The growing body of postsecular literary criticism also includes Carruthers and Tate; Coviello and Hickman; Faber; Fessenden; Haque; Huggan; Hungerford; Jones; Kaufmann; Levitt; Mohamed; Morrissey; Roberts; Slater; Watt; and Ziser, among others. Also see Corrigan, *Wrestling with Angels: Postsecular Contemporary American Poetry*; "Whispers of Faith in Contemporary American Literature"; and "The Postsecular and Literature: A Review of Scholarship."

WORKS CITED

Adler, Shawn. "'Harry Potter' Author J.K. Rowling Opens Up About Books' Christian Imagery." *MTV News.* October 17, 2007. mtv.com/news/1572107/harry-potter-author-jk-rowling-opens-up-about-books-christian-imagery.

Asad, Talal. *Formations of the Secular: Christianity, Islam, Modernity.* Redwood City, CA: Stanford University Press, 2003.

Baird, Robert J. "Late Secularism." *Social Text* 18, no. 3 (2000): 123–136.

Bauman, Zygmunt. *Intimations of Postmodernity.* London: Routledge, 1992.

Beckford, James A. "Public Religions and the Postsecular: Critical Reflections." *Journal for the Scientific Study of Religion* 51, no. 1 (2012): 1–19.

Berger, Peter L. "The Desecularization of the World: A Global Overview." In *The Desecularization of the World: Resurgent Religion and World Politics,* edited by Peter L. Berger, 1–19. Grand Rapids, MI: Wm. B. Eerdmans Publishing, 1999.

Bradley, Arthur, Jo Carruthers, and Andrew Tate. "Introduction: Writing Post-Secularity." *Spiritual Identities: Literature and the Post-Secular Imagination,* edited by Jo Carruthers and Andrew Tate, 1–8. Oxford: Peter Lang, 2010.

Braidotti, Rosi. "In Spite of the Times: The Postsecular Turn in Feminism." *Theory, Culture & Society* 25, no. 6 (2008): 1–24.

Carruthers, Jo, and Andrew Tate. *Spiritual Identities: Literature and the Post-Secular Imagination.* Oxford: Peter Lang, 2010.

Casanova, José. *Public Religions in the Modern World.* Chicago: University of Chicago Press, 1994.

Coles, Robert. *The Spiritual Life of Children.* Boston: Houghton Mifflin, 1990.

Connolly, William E. *Why I Am Not a Secularist.* Minneapolis: University of Minnesota Press, 1999.

Corrigan, Paul T. "The Postsecular and Literature: A Review of Scholarship." *Corrigan Literary Review.* May 17, 2015. corriganliteraryreview.wordpress.com/2015/05/17/the-postsecular-and-literature.

Corrigan, Paul T. "Whispers of Faith in Contemporary American Literature." *Christianity & Literature* 63, no. 4 (2014): 521–32.

Corrigan, Paul T. "Wrestling with Angels: Postsecular Contemporary American Poetry." PhD dissertation, University of South Florida, 2015. scholarcommons.usf.edu/etd/5671.

Cotton, Rickey A. "Engaging the Religious Dimension in Significant Adolescent Literature." *Literature and Belief* 30, no. 1 (2010): 81–93.

Coviello, Peter and Jared Hickman. "Introduction: After the Postsecular." *American Literature* 86, no. 4 (2014): 645–654.

Dalferth, Ingolf U. "Post-Secular Society: Christianity and the Dialectics of the Secular." *Journal of the American Academy of Religion* 78, no. 2 (2010): 317–44.

Derrida, Jacques. "Faith and Knowledge: The Two Sources of 'Religion' at the Limits of

Reason Alone." In *Religion*, edited by Jacques Derrida and Gianni Vattimo, 1–78. Redwood City, CA: Stanford University Press, 1998.

Diamond, James S. "The Post-Secular: A Jewish Perspective." *Cross Currents* 53 no. 4 (2004): 580–606.

Dunn, Allen. "The Precarious Integrity of the Postsecular." *Boundary 2: An International Journal of Literature and Culture* 37, no. 3 (2010): 91–99.

Elie, Paul. "Has Fiction Lost Its Faith?" *The New York Times*. December 22, 2012. nytimes.com/2012/12/23/books/review/has-fiction-lost-its-faith.html.

Faber, Alyda. "The Post-Secular Poetics and Ethics of Exposure in J.M. Coetzee's Disgrace." *Literature and Theology: An International Journal of Religion, Theory, and Culture* 23 no. 3 (2009): 303–316.

Fessenden, Tracy. "The Problem of the Postsecular." *American Literary History* 26, no. 1 (2014): 154–167.

Finkelstein, Norman. *On Mount Vision: Forms of the Sacred in Contemporary American Poetry*. Iowa City: University of Iowa Press, 2010.

Gorski, Philip S., et al. "The Post-Secular in Question." In *The Post-Secular in Question: Religion in Contemporary Society*, edited by Philip S. Gorski et al., 1–22. New York: New York University Press, 2012.

Graham, Elaine. "What's Missing? Gender, Reason and the Post-Secular." *Political Theology* 13, no. 2 (2012): 233–245.

Habermas, Jürgen. "A Reply." In *An Awareness of What Is Missing: Faith and Reason in a Post-Secular Age*, translated by Ciaran Cronin, 72–83. Cambridge: Polity, 2010.

Habermas, Jürgen. "Notes on a Post-Secular Society." Signandsightwww. June 18, 2008. signandsight.com/features/1714.html.

Hadden, Jeffrey K. "Toward Desacralizing Secularization Theory." *Social Forces* 65, no. 3 (1987): 587–611.

Haque, Danielle. "The Postsecular Turn and Muslim American Literature." *American Literature* 86, no. 4 (2014): 799–829.

Huggan, Graham. "Is the 'Post' in 'Postsecular' the 'Post' in 'Postcolonial'?" *MFS: Modern Fiction Studies* 56, no. 4 (2010): 751–768.

Hungerford, Amy. *Postmodern Belief: American Literature and Religion Since 1960*. Princeton, NJ: Princeton University Press, 2010.

Jones, Norman W. *Gay and Lesbian Historical Fiction: Sexual Mystery and Post-Secular Narrative*. New York: Palgrave Macmillan, 2007.

Jones, Robert P., et al. "Do Americans Believe Capitalism and Government Are Working? Religious Left, Religious Right and the Future of the Economic Debate." *Public Religion Research Institute* and *Brookings Institution*. July 18, 2013. publicreligion.org/site/wp-content/uploads/2013/07/2013-Economic-Values-Report-Final-.pdf.

Kaufmann, Michael. "Locating the Postsecular." *Religion and Literature* 41, no. 3 (2009): 67–73.

King, Mike. *Postsecularism: The Hidden Challenge to Extremism*. Cambridge: James Clarke, 2009.

Koss, Melanie D. "Young Adult Novels with Multiple Narrative Perspectives: The Changing Nature of YA Literature." *ALAN Review* 36, no. 3 (2009): 73–80. https://scholar.lib.vt.edu/ejournals/ALAN/v36n3/koss.html.

Kyrlezhev, Aleksandr. "The Postsecular Age: Religion and Culture Today." Translated by Joera Mulders and Philip Walters. *Religion, State and Society* 36, no. 1 (2008): 21–31.

Le, Guin U. K. *A Wizard of Earthsea*. Boston: Houghton Mifflin, 2012.

Lee, Paula Young. "Pottermore Problems: Scholars and Writers Call Foul on J.K. Rowling's North American Magic." Salonwww. July 1, 2016. salon.com/2016/07/01/pottermore_problems_scholars_and_writers_call_foul_on_j_k_rowlings_north_american_magic.

Levitt, Laura. "What Is Religion, Anyway? Rereading the Postsecular from an American Jewish Perspective." *Religion and Literature* 41, no. 3 (2009): 107–118.

Lewis, C.S. *The Lion, the Witch, and the Wardrobe*. New York: HarperCollins, 1994.

Ludwig, Kathryn. "Don Delillo's Underworld and the Postsecular in Contemporary Fiction." *Religion and Literature* 41, no. 3 (2009): 82–91.

Mączyńska, Magdalena. "Toward a Postsecular Literary Criticism: Examining Ritual Gestures in Zadie Smith's Autograph Man." *Religion and Literature* 41, no. 3 (2009): 73–82.
Marty, Martin E. "The Future of World Fundamentalisms." *Proceedings of the American Philosophical Society* 142, no. 3 (1998): 367–377.
McClure, John A. *Partial Faiths: Postsecular Fiction in the Age of Pynchon and Morrison.* Athens: University of Georgia Press, 2007.
McLennan, Gregor. "The Postsecular Turn." *Theory, Culture & Society* 27, no. 4 (2010): 3–20.
Merlini, Cesare. "A Post-Secular World?" *Survival: Global Politics and Strategy* 53, no. 2 (2011): 117–130.
Mohamed, Feisal G. *Milton and the Post-Secular Present: Ethics, Politics, Terrorism.* Redwood City, CA: Stanford University Press, 2011.
Morozov, Aleksandr. "Has the Postsecular Age Begun?" Translated by Philip Walters. *Religion, State and Society* 36, no. 1 (2008): 39–44.
Morrissey, Lee. "Literature and the Postsecular: Paradise Lost?" *Religion and Literature* 41, no. 3 (2009): 98–106.
Norris, Pippa, and Ronald Inglehart. *Sacred and Secular: Religion and Politics Worldwide.* 2nd ed. Cambridge: Cambridge University Press, 2011.
Nye, Naomi Shihab. *Habibi.* New York: Simon & Schuster, 1997.
Petre, Jonathan. "J K Rowling: 'Christianity Inspired Harry Potter.'" *The Telegraph.* October 20, 2007. telegraph.co.uk/culture/books/fictionreviews/3668658/J-K-Rowling-Christianity-inspired-Harry-Potter.html.
"'Nones' on the Rise." *Pew Research Center.* October 9, 2012. pewforum.org/2012/10/09/nones-on-the-rise.
Pullman, Philip. *His Dark Materials.* New York: Knopf, 2007.
Ratti, Manav. *The Postsecular Imagination: Postcolonialism, Religion, and Literature.* London: Routledge, 2012.
"Religious Debates Over the Harry Potter Series." *Wikipedia.* July 15, 2016. en.wikipedia.org/wiki/Religious_debates_over_the_Harry_Potter_series.
Roberts, Michael Symmons. "Poetry in a Post-Secular Age." *Poetry Review* 98 (2008) 69–75.
Rosati, Massimo, and Kristina Stoeckl, eds. *Multiple Modernities and Postsecular Societies.* London: Ashgate, 2012.
Rowling, J.K. *Harry Potter and the Deathly Hallows.* New York: Scholastic, 2007.
Rowling, J.K. *Harry Potter and the Sorcerer's Stone.* New York: Scholastic, 2007.
Slater, Avery. "American Afterlife: Benjaminian Messianism and Technological Redemption in Muriel Rukeyser's the *Book of the Dead.*" *American Literature* 86, no. 4 (2014): 767–797.
Smith, James K.A. "Secular Liturgies and the Prospects for a 'Post-Secular' Sociology of Religion." In *The Post-Secular in Question: Religion in Contemporary Society,* edited by Philip S. Gorski et al., 159–184. New York: New York University Press, 2012.
Stoeckl, Kristina. "Defining the Postsecular." *Institute of Synergetic Anthropology.* February 2011. synergia-isa.ru/wp-content/uploads/2012/02/stoeckl_en.pdf.
Taylor, Charles. *A Secular Age.* Cambridge, MA: Belknap Press, 2007.
Tolkien, J R. R. *The Fellowship of the Ring.* Boston: Houghton Mifflin, 1993.
Wasserstrom, Steven M. *Religion After Religion: Gershom Scholem, Mircea Eliade, and Henry Corbin at Eranos.* Princeton, NJ: Princeton University Press, 1999.
Watt, David Harington. "Losing Our Religion." *Religion and Literature* 41, no. 3 (2009): 119–126.
Weber, Max. "Science as Vocation." In *Max Weber: Essays in Sociology,* translated and edited by H.H. Gerth and C. Wright Mills, 129–156. Oxford: Oxford University Press, 1946.
Wuthnow, Robert. *After Heaven: Spirituality in America Since the 1950s.* Oakland: University of California Press, 1998.
Wuthnow, Robert. *The Restructuring of American Religion: Society and Faith Since World War II.* Princeton, NJ: Princeton University Press, 1988.
Ziser, Michael. "Emersonian Terrorism: John Brown, Islam, and Postsecular Violence." *American Literature* 82, no. 2 (2010): 333–360.

Žižek, Slavoj. "Human Rights and Its Discontents." Lecture, Bard College. Annandale-On-Hudson, NY, November 15, 1999. lacan.com/zizek-human.htm.
Zoltan, Vanessa, and Casper Ter Kuile. *Harry Potter and the Sacred Text.* harrypottersacred text.com.

Fantasy as Realism

N.D. Wilson and the Influence of Mythology

JEREMY LARSON

"History often resembles 'Myth,' because they are both ultimately of the same stuff."
—J.R.R. Tolkien, "On Fairy-stories"[1]

"[F]ar from dulling or emptying the actual world, [fairy land] gives it a new dimension of depth. [A child] does not despise real woods because he has read of enchanted woods: the reading makes all real woods a little enchanted."
—C.S. Lewis, "On Three Ways of Writing for Children"[2]

"Fantasy is hardly an escape from reality. It's a way of understanding it."
—Lloyd Alexander, *A Visit with Lloyd Alexander*

"I write fantasy because I'm a realist ... I write fantasy because I live in a magical world. I don't know how to write anything else."
—N.D. Wilson, "Night One"

Leland Ryken's edited volume *The Christian Imagination* juxtaposes a section on "Realism" with a section on "Myth and Fantasy," and "Realism" concludes with an excerpt by Larry Woiwode on "The Superiority of Realism to Fantasy." Woiwode argues that when it comes to abstract principles (e.g., honor), fantasy fiction requires readers to struggle to interpret "a vague concept of honor transmitted from the stars," whereas realistic fiction teaches readers more directly "to honor their parents" (316). Woiwode "regret[s] to report" that "the Christian community ... seems to want to live in an ideological never-never land" and "be drawn out of the life they're to attend to" (316).[3] Realism, he says, traffics "in accuracy, in the many-layered dimensions of reality, and in the importance of people over recycled Big Ideas" (316).

Despite my love of fantasy, not to mention my occasional flirtation with a Big Idea or two, I do not fault Ryken for his inclusion of this viewpoint. In fact, perhaps intentionally on Ryken's part, this viewpoint operates as an amusing transition to the next section, which is explicitly dedicated to myth and fantasy. Readers sympathetic to Woiwode's viewpoint must withstand the freight train of this section, ably manned by contributions from G.K. Chesterton, J.R.R. Tolkien, and Frederick Buechner.[4] Other books on the topic of the Christian imagination take a different approach, combining fantasy and realism. For example, in her book on children's literature, which includes a chapter on fantasy and realism, Gladys Hunt writes, "Good *fantasy* helps us see *reality* in unreality, credibility in incredibility" (56, emphasis added). As Hunt reminds us, "The word *fantasy* comes from the Greek and literally translated means 'making visible'" (58). In this essay, I argue that the best-selling fiction of contemporary Young Adult (YA) author N.D. Wilson exemplifies this combination of fantasy and reality, thereby making reality more visible.

Wilson's work has many influences,[5] but I will consider both the influence of mythology as a formative force and the re-enchanting qualities of Wilson's fantasy. I have written about Wilson's work before,[6] but in this essay I have narrowed my scope to two major themes—envious warfare and death and resurrection—in his stand-alone novel, *Boys of Blur* (2014). Ultimately, I maintain that the influence of mythology shapes Wilson's fantasy, fantasy that acts as an antidote for disenchantment,[7] or even as a "prophylactic" that helps children "[n]ot to lose innocence and wonder" (Tolkien, "On Fairy-stories" 77, 67).[8] Alan Jacobs writes that C.S. Lewis's "mind was above all characterized by a *willingness to be enchanted*" (*The Narnian* xxi, emphasis original), and I contend that Wilson's mind likewise deserves this characterization. Woiwode may be correct that the teaching of realistic fiction is more direct, but I claim that themes in fantasy fiction have more staying power for young adults.[9] Envious warfare and death and resurrection are compelling themes when employed by a writer who points YA readers to the fantastic realism of this world. Before exploring these themes in *Boys of Blur*, however, I want to look at the uses of enchantment in a postsecular age and establish my assertion that Wilson's fantasy uniquely cultivates readers who are open to enchantment.

Fantasy and the Postsecular

Nathan David Wilson—named after a storytelling prophet and the king that he confronted (Douglas Wilson, *Writers to Read* 137)—has written children's board books sold at Target, Shroud of Turin scholarship published by *Books & Culture*,[10] and nonfiction published by Thomas Nelson.[11] In addition to these worthy successes, he is also a film producer and director, a screenwriter,[12] and a Fellow of Literature at New Saint Andrews College in Moscow, Idaho. But his primary vocation at this point is writing YA fantasy novels, and one of his chief goals in writing YA fantasy is to rouse readers to the enchantment of this world.[13]

The usefulness of enchantment and mythology in a postsecular age is not always immediately evident. The title of psychologist Bruno Bettelheim's *The Uses of Enchantment: The Meaning and Importance of Fairy Tales* points to the perennial dispute regarding the usefulness of fairy tales, fantasy, mythology, etc.[14] Bettelheim obviously believes that enchantment requires a defense. C.S. Lewis also is well aware of this ongoing issue when he writes, "About once every hundred years some wiseacre gets up and tries to banish the fairy tale" ("On Three Ways" 37).[15] Just as Philip Sidney defended imaginative literature in the sixteenth century, so in our day have other literary paladins such as Lewis come to the aid of lovers of the fantastic, and a recurring theme in their defenses is the power of fantasy to re-enchant the world.

But why does the world need re-enchanting, and if we really did lose a sense of enchantment, where did we put it? Do we not marvel at nature documentaries and athletes' physical abilities? Has not scientific advancement transformed us into people who have a greater capacity for wonder? Has the magic of the world really been lost because of technology, or has it been enhanced? In April 2016, a news story reported a stunning moment, caught on camera microscopes, when ovarian biology researchers at Northwestern University observed a tiny burst of light at the moment of human conception: "The bright flash occurs because when sperm enters an egg it triggers calcium to increase which releases zinc from the egg. As the zinc shoots out, it binds to small molecules which emit a fluorescence" (Knapton). Despite the disenchanting scientific labels of elements and cells,[16] who among even the most modern of us can help but feel a thrilling sense of enchantment and wonder when reading this story?

Yes, wonder still exists, but this kind of wonder regarding the natural world, without respect for a transcendent creator who has spoken in a book and is speaking the world into being moment by moment,[17] is a secular wonder. Just about everyone, from poets to sociologists, has noticed the shift from spiritual wonder to practical calculation. Speaking of the Copernican revolution, the seventeenth-century poet John Donne writes in "The First

Anniversary: An Anatomy of the World" that "new philosophy calls all in doubt" (205). In his nineteenth-century poem *Lamia*, John Keats laments that "cold philosophy" had driven out enchantment and unwoven the rainbow (2.229–38). And twentieth-century German sociologist Max Weber describes the controlling tendencies of the modern world as "an iron cage" (*Protestant Ethic* 96)[18] and describes modernity, or at least the secularized West, as disenchanted, compared to the "great enchanted garden" of non–Western societies (*Sociology of Religion* 270).[19]

Since Weber, though, sociologists and others have noticed that the foreboding prophecy of "the secularization thesis"—the prediction that societies will become less and less committed to religious practices—has not been fulfilled. In fact, in some cases scientific advancement has led directly to an affirmation of ancient myths, in a sense.[20] What is clear is the fact that mythology and history are not always completely distinct categories; in fact, they frequently are not. The roots of mythology grow in the soil of history, and traces of transcendence linger in our postsecular age.[21]

Charles Taylor points out, however, that even if traces of transcendence yet remain in Western civilization, something certainly has changed, because "it [was] virtually impossible not to believe in God in, say, 1500 in our Western society, while in 2000 many of us find this not only easy, but even inescapable" (25). Our loss of mystery, Taylor says, means that our residual wonder is generally contained within "the immanent frame," where everything is "part of a 'natural,' or 'this-worldly' order which can be understood in its own terms, without reference to the 'supernatural' or 'transcendent'" (594). And all of us, consciously religious or not, are trapped in this immanent frame—this new way of imagining life that makes the search for fulfillment-without-transcendence a viable option.[22] As James K.A. Smith paraphrases Taylor's claim, "we are all [post]secular now" (*How [Not] to Be Secular* 28).

Peter Leithart has suggested that our being situated in an immanent frame has affected the writing of many contemporary Protestants, who, Leithart claims, "can't write" ("Protestants and Writing").[23] Leithart's hypothesis has understandably sparked a debate, and this debate rages about whether or not Protestants are to blame for publishing scourges such as the influx of "bonnet rippers" (Amish romance) in today's bookstores.[24] However, I offer N.D. Wilson as an example of a Protestant writer not only who *can* write, but also who does so in uniquely enchanting ways for a postsecular audience.

Paul T. Corrigan helpfully explains in his review of postsecular definitions and discussions that *postsecular* does not mean "non-secular" ("The Postsecular and Literature").[25] I take *postsecular* to mean more or less what Taylor means by "secularity 3" (also "secular$_3$") in *A Secular Age*[26]: "The shift to secularity in this [third] sense consists, among other things, of a move from a society where belief in God is unchallenged and indeed, unproblematic, to one in which it is understood to be one option among others, and frequently not the easiest to embrace" (3).[27] My argument here is that Wilson's work re-enchants the world *to us* by showing us that the world is always-already enchanted.

Wilson's work may be enchanting, but is it postsecular? I contend that Wilson's fantasy is not so much postsecular—his books do not include "cross-pressures"[28] of our secular age—as it is indicative of a postsecular market: the fact that secular$_2$ publishers can sell so many books with overtly Christian themes reveals the "nova effect" of postsecularism.[29] For an example of Wilson's overtly Christian themes, see the third book in his Ashtown series, *Empire of Bones*, which within roughly a seventy-page range includes references to "Yeshua" (333), a Daniel who interprets dreams (343), a lamb having been slain (388), instructions regarding a Passover-like blood-on-the-doorposts ceremony (390), and lines from a Reformation-era Scottish Psalter (405–6). Wilson's success in employing openly biblical mythology points to the postsecular cross-pressures present in the secular$_2$ publishing industry.

However, if Wilson's mythological fantasy is not postsecular in the sense that characters struggle to find transcendence amid the nova effect, then we can consider Wilson's fantasy to be postsecular in the sense that his books have the potential, in Corrigan's words, to "create a space where secular people can transform their secular way of life through increased openness toward attributes traditionally associated with the religious, such as awe, wonder, the unknown, and so forth" ("The Postsecular and Literature"). In other words, the charming quality of Wilson's fantasy also serves as a disarming quality. Fantasy holds a power to change us (Jacobs, "Fantasy and the Buffered Self" 11), and as readers are delighted by Wilson's fantasy—and many are, judging by his success with Random House and HarperCollins—they find themselves open to and taught by his enchanted worlds.[30] As I have said, because of the influence of mythology on Wilson's fantasy, his novels are uniquely suited for a postsecular age—a claim that I support by exploring *Boys of Blur*.

Boys of Blur *and* Beowulf

The influence of mythology on Wilson's work is evident, first, in the fact that *Boys of Blur* depends on mythology for its narrative structure. *Boys of Blur* is a YA novel about magic, monsters, football, and family, in which a boy must save his town from creatures who have crawled right out of Old English literature. Despite its Florida setting,[31] this fantasy novel has the bones of *Beowulf*, and it is no coincidence[32] that it is dedicated to someone named Seamus.[33] Good reasons exist to consider *Beowulf* to be mythology: *Bulfinch's*

Mythology places a summary of *Beowulf* at the end of the section on "The Age of Fable" (371–73); Richard North has called the Anglo-Saxon epic an account of "Danish myths in Christian form" (195); and the epic itself refers to biblical myths, including the flood.[34] Wilson does not hide the fact that he has appropriated the *Beowulf* myth[35]: the novel opens and closes with death (3–6, 187–92), local football teams mirror ancient feuding tribes (42–49, 160–65, 169–72, 188), large men wear and boast about their rings (17, 42–43), monsters ("Gren") depend on their swamp-dwelling "Mother" (83–89, 147–48), a severed Grendel arm hangs on a wall in a place known as a "heriot" (118–20),[36] a confrontation with a hoarder occurs in an underground cavern (180–87),[37] characters explicitly reference the epic (119, 191–92)—the list could go on. Wilson's *Beowulf*-borrowing is not the first time writers have plundered the epic, but *Boys of Blur* is a remarkable attempt to accommodate the Old English saga for a younger audience by placing it in a new form.[38] I will demonstrate the influence of Christian mythology on Wilson's fantasy by examining the two themes of envious warfare and death and resurrection in his novel.

Envious Warfare

Some critics have misunderstood the connection between *Beowulf* and *Boys of Blur*, assuming that the relationship between the two narratives is arbitrary. For example, Miriam Budin writes in *School Library Journal*, "The mythology [of *Boys of Blur*] is more a net of allusions than a fully formed cosmology. Several references to *Beowulf* are made throughout the text, though how it directly relates to this contemporary story is unclear" (110). As we will see, however, the connection between these works is essential and hinges on the theme of envious warfare.

Mythological accounts, from Homer's *Iliad* and Virgil's *Aeneid* to Milton's *Paradise Lost*, have always included a titanic amount of warfare.[39] As I noted earlier in this essay, *Beowulf*'s warring northern tribes align with *Boys of Blur*'s rival towns and football teams, whose root problem is envy (134). In *Beowulf*, the continuous cycle of killing stems from envy, and we first clearly see this festering sin in Grendel, who hates the merry singing of the scop and the warriors (Douglas Wilson, *Beowulf: A New Verse Rendering* 86–110).[40] But Grendel is not the only one who struggles with envy. "The problem is," Douglas Wilson writes, "that this warrior society, for all its emphasis on honor and fealty, had created a culture which necessarily established treachery at the heart of it" ("Beowulf" 121). These treacherous Norse warriors are no better than Grendel, a descendent of "Cain, the first fratricide" (121).[41] While modern societies have largely domesticated war through sports, envy and its destructive potential are no less present. John McMurtry has credibly enumerated multiple parallels between war and football,[42] and in *Boys of Blur*, N.D. Wilson takes the envious tribes of *Beowulf* and translates them into warring football cultures. What is unique about Wilson's treatment of envy is the way that characters combat envy through their mythological sense of gratitude. As we will see, divine forgiveness is an enchanting spell that leads the forgiven to forgive even the worst of offenders.

Envious warfare in Wilson's novel manifests itself most overtly with respect to football, but it incarnates itself in relational tensions as well. Throughout the novel, the terrible stench from the swamp monsters, the Gren, triggers envious and hateful thoughts that make the protagonist, Charlie Reynolds, and other characters want to commit violent acts against others. In *Boys of Blur*, the olfactory sense, connected as it is to memory, conjures up memories and twists them into jealousies. For example, at one point, the smell of a Gren causes Charlie's mind to flood with resentments, from his broken family situation to his lack of athletic success (156–57). On a larger scale, envy even infects the relationship of two neighboring towns via sports rivalries, leading to a full-scale town-on-town brawl at a football game in one of the final chapters (160–73).

Only through humility and forgiveness is Charlie able to avoid the destruction of envy.[43] A character named Mother Wisdom explains to Charlie that the "greatest strength [of the Gren] lies in *our* envy" (130). Earlier she says, "The Gren feel only hate and envy and rage—every other part of their human souls has been devoured. They are their own poison…. Their touch, even their stench with enough time, plants their particular curse in the soul— where no doctor could ever see it" (119–20; cf. 148).[44] The most dangerous enemy is internal, not external, and the only solution that has worked for Charlie in the past is focusing on selfless giving (130–31). Mother Wisdom also talks with Charlie about bitterness, forgiveness, and pity: "Hold no bitterness…. Forgive as you would like to be forgiven" (120). When he gets a chance, Charlie shows pity on the Gren (167–68), who have been lured into the service of the "Mother."[45] Charlie's pity and forgiveness, products of the true myth of the gospel,[46] are acts of war against the vice of envy. Wilson provides enough clues in *Boys of Blur* for us to suppose that Charlie is well aware of the Christian gospel: the pastor's funeral sermon refers to the dry bones in Ezekiel 37 (5); a football coach (Coach Wisdom, whose death introduces the novel) had urged players to "Stay right with the Lord" (23); Charlie prays for both friend and enemy alike (186); etc. Only someone influenced by the true myth of self-sacrifice and the hope of eternal reward can truly forgive his enemies, and Charlie's faith and hope in divine justice make room for loving his enemies. Charlie's good qualities are not merely the good qualities of the virtuous pagans,[47] but the uniquely theological virtues of Christian mythology: faith, hope, and love.

Charlie's ability to resist envy contributes to his ability to defeat the Gren, for the death of Charlie's envy foreshadows their demise. Charlie's heroism in this regard makes him a better hero than Beowulf, as the entire epic of *Beowulf* shows the inability of Anglo-Saxons to eradicate the envious feuding from their own culture, despite their pagan nobility.[48] Douglas Wilson writes that the fact that neither Grendel nor Grendel's mother are killed in Heorot reveals the impotency of the Norse warriors to kill envy *at home*— that is, in their own hearts ("Beowulf" 124–25). Grendel *is* envy, and the Danes cannot kill Grendel in Heorot because they cannot mortify the envy in their hearts. Further support for this claim comes from the chiastic structure of the epic, which centers on Beowulf's pursuit of Grendel's mother (Douglas Wilson, "Chiastic Structure in *Beowulf*" 131–37).[49] She had killed the Danish warrior Aeschere in *his* home, and Beowulf kills Grendel's mother in *her* home, but the hearts of the warriors remain essentially unchanged. When Beowulf dies, they are no longer safe from the threat of Swedish invasion, because envy lives on.

In *Boys of Blur*, however, Charlie recognizes that the only place that envy can and must die is at home, that is, in his own heart. If Grendel *is* envy, then Charlie can defeat the Mother of the Gren only if he digs out his own seed of envy before it can take root in his heart.[50] Heroically, he does so in the end, and he forgives his deceased father and raises a glass "to the memory of a man who had hurt most of them," yet from whom "good had come" (192). Additionally, Charlie's half-brother, Sugar, functions as an anti–Cain by uprooting his own envy and acknowledging his role as his brother's keeper.[51] Sugar and Charlie share the same football-star father, but for years Sugar resented Charlie because of their father's overt preference for Charlie and abandonment of Sugar and his mother. Year after year, Sugar "birthday-wish[ed Charlie] dead" (136), but Coach Wisdom helped Sugar to deal with his envy, and when Charlie goes missing, Sugar searches for him, finds him, and admits that Charlie is not to blame: "It's not your fault.... I have a brother.... That's why I've been out looking for you" (137). Because Charlie and Sugar avoid the fratricide of Cain and struggle against their envy, they achieve something that the characters in *Beowulf* never do: peace through humble forgiveness.

Critics such as Budin who do not understand how the *Beowulf* allusions fit with *Boys of Blur* are missing this key point on envy, and Douglas Wilson's essay on envy in *Beowulf* ("Beowulf") is crucial for understanding this connection. N.D. Wilson's mythological approach to envious warfare—showing characters who resist envy by living in light of the true myth of a self-sacrificial god who dies for his enemies—makes this theme a powerful one with the ability to enchant a postsecular readership. This dying-and-rising god detail moves us into the next theme for consideration: death and resurrection.

Death and Resurrection

Traditionally, myths have provided cultures with the stories that tell people where they came from, who they are, and where they are going, and such stories have furnished the people of these cultures with a meaning and purpose to life. Myths contain narrative threads that weave morality into a culture's fabric and, ideally, lead children and young adults on the path to virtuous citizenship. In "On Fairy-stories," Tolkien writes about the power of myths to train young people in wisdom: "[I]t is one of the lessons of fairy-stories (if we can speak of the lessons of things that do not lecture) that on callow, lumpish, and selfish youth[,] peril, sorrow, and even the shadow of death can bestow dignity, and even sometimes wisdom" (67). For Tolkien, "even the shadow of death" was not off-limits for young readers. Elsewhere Tolkien writes that while *Beowulf* is no "Nordic *Summa Theologica*," it offers wisdom nevertheless ("*Beowulf*: The Monsters and the Critics" 7). A particularly wise theme in *Beowulf* is the acknowledgment that "all men, and all their works shall die" (23), but *Boys of Blur* goes further and enchants its readers by including Christianity's mythological theme of dying *and* rising.[52]

It is true that Wilson's fantasy novel includes much about life and growth, apart from the dying and rising theme. Wilson writes about living mounds that wake and stars that pull (86), characters who draw strength from the land (86), a mythological World Tree "with roots so deep that they grew straight through the whole world and became a forest on the other side" (103), and the magical activity of staying alive by breathing air produced by trees grown by starlight (117).[53] The cosmos is alive and enchanted, although characters often need to awaken to this fact. Elsewhere, Charlie asks Mother Wisdom about a dream of his in which he seems to be made of living sparks, and she explains the magic of science, about which we know less than we think we do (110–11; cf. 102–3, 195).[54] In all of his writing, but especially in *Boys of Blur*, Wilson reminds readers of the magic of life.

Mortality receives a heavy stress as well. *Boys of Blur* opens with a warning for runners to be quick, because "[t]here's quick and there's dead" (1).[55] As I have already noted, the novel begins and ends with death, and the stones on which animals are mysteriously sacrificed are known as "death stones" (83, 100, 101). The fictional town of Taper, Florida, has experienced an alarming number of runaways (46)—who are by all accounts dead to their families—and readers later discover that more than a dozen of these boys have been transformed into Gren (109–10, 167). In addition, for all practical purposes and for most of Charlie's life, his abusive biological father has been dead to him, and he does in fact die at the end of the novel.

Wilson's emphasis on mortality, however, paradoxically leads to a simultaneous stress on resurrection and living well.[56] The swamp in Taper is "[r]ich with death," and Charlie and his cousin, "Cotton,"[57] begin to realize how much life comes from the muck (89–90).[58] Over the centuries, as the dead are buried and return to the earth, the trees that root in the muck draw life from the richness of the decomposing bodies. More significantly, the structure of *Boys of Blur* contributes to the paradoxical and mythological living-by-dying theme. Following the model of several epics and ballads,[59] *Boys of Blur* has a descent-ascent (death and resurrection) shape, seen in Charlie's near-death experience in the middle chapters (Chapters 7 and 8),[60] and in his struggle to return from Mother Wisdom's heriot (Chapter 10) and face his adversary. After his return, Charlie has grown in wisdom and is ready to die for his cousin (127) and his abusive father (187), and because of his readiness to die, he is ready to live for others.[61] Charlie realizes what the Norse warriors in *Beowulf* never do: life is not about killing; it is about dying. Norse heroism excludes self-sacrifice, which is why the long tradition of Christian appropriation of pagan myths, epics, etc., is so glorious and necessary. True mythology always tells both parts of the story: exile and return, death and resurrection.[62] And true mythology tells both parts because reality includes both parts. The fantasy of *Boys of Blur* captures this dual nature of reality even more vividly than most realistic fiction, because its mythological theme of death and resurrection is so clear.

Despite Beowulf's personal successes and despite a brief moment of eucatastrophe in one of the epic's digressions,[63] *Beowulf* does not really have joyous turns, and on the surface it does not appear to end happily.[64] However, *Boys of Blur* does end happily, as the Gren—in a type of resurrection—eventually convert back to boys and return home (188) and as Charlie's family reunites and relaxes by the sea (190). Wilson has acknowledged that writing for a YA audience makes these happy endings easier to pull off because young readers have not yet developed into cynics ("Night One"). Readers who hope to find the modern angst and nuanced pessimism that characterizes many current YA books will find much in Wilson's work to disappoint them.[65] Wilson's fiction actually pushes back against postsecular malaise—the "generalized sense in our culture that with the eclipse of the transcendent, something may have been lost" (Taylor 307). Wilson's novels do not eclipse the transcendent. They highlight the transcendent nature of our world, which includes the specter of death. But although Wilson's books, which are often intentionally scary,[66] include darkness and death, they also wisely include the joyous turn of transcendent resurrections. Wilson's books carry wisdom, but they are not "those gray books" from the 1950s and 1960s, full of "thinly disguised 'moralisms'" (Hunt 61). Wilson's fantasy teaches transcendence by delighting, and his mythological death and resurrection theme in *Boys of Blur* carries great potential for enchanting a postsecular age.

Conclusion

A constant hazard of literary criticism is the danger of all analysis: the possibility of dispelling wonder by prying into mechanics. It would be a sad irony here to have discussed the re-enchanting quality of fantasy in a way that leaves a novel sliced wide open, hemorrhaging on a surgical table. As C.S. Lewis argues, "The moment we *state* [a] principle, we are admittedly back in the world of abstraction. It is only while receiving the myth as a story that you experience the principle concretely" ("Myth Became Fact" 66).[67] Expressing an abstract, universal principle pales in comparison to reading a myth itself, and if we look *at* a myth as opposed to *along* it, we tend to lose the true benefit of the myth (Lewis, "Meditation in a Toolshed" 212–15).

Lewis, Tolkien, and others, however, were literary critics themselves, and their warning is not to avoid all literary study, but rather to study literature with the goal of appreciation, not mutilation. The popularity of the contemporary fantasy genre[68] has shown that people do not primarily desire books that idolize scientific "realism."[69] Writing about *Stranger Things*, a Netflix series featuring children, Alissa Wilkinson says, "In a modern world—where science can explain everything from depression to *deja vu* to the Aurora Borealis, where belief and devotion are sometimes reduced to a series of steps or principles that you can execute with enough willpower—even religious folk yearn for a re-enchanted world, one where fairies, or demons, or other intelligences exist just beyond what we can see" ("How 'Stranger Things' Re-Enchants the World"). As we have seen, mythology influences Wilson's fiction in such a way as to open readers' eyes to appreciate the magic of this world, and in a postsecular age, we can use as much healthy fantasy as we can get, both to ward off the scientism of modernity and to foster healthy imaginations in young adults. The "escapism" of Wilson's fantasy is "not an escape *from* reality but rather an escape *to* reality" (Larson, "Embracing" 26).[70] The literary study of Wilson's fantasy helps us to see reality more clearly,[71] and although some writers protest that too few people in our postsecular age appreciate the magical mystery of this world (Boersma 21), Wilson's fantasy helps YA readers to take steps in the right direction.

It is no stretch to say that in this postsecular age, many people are too much like Caspian and Edmund toward the end of C.S. Lewis's *The Voyage of the* Dawn Treader. Caspian is king in a world with many *fantastic* qualities, in every sense of the word.[72] Yet he wishes to escape his flat world and get into Edmund's more interesting "round world." Edmund responds, "There's nothing particularly exciting about a round world when you're there" (208). Perhaps through an inundation of fantastical reality, Caspian and Edmund have momentarily fallen under the dulling spell of over-familiarity. But Lewis writes elsewhere that while some spells can make people drowsy, spells can also rouse ("Weight of Glory" 31), and N.D. Wilson's realistic fantasy serves as such a rousing spell that keeps postsecular readers willing to be enchanted.

NOTES

1. 55. Cf. Letter 131: "I believe that legends and myths are largely made of 'truth'..." (*Letters* 147).

2. In *On Stories and Other Essays on Literature* (37).

3. Regarding this "never-never land" criticism, see C.S. Lewis's review of J.R.R. Tolkien's *The Two Towers* and *The Return of the King* ("The dethronement of power" 107–8); cf. Tolkien, "On Fairy-stories" 78.

4. For more on fantasy *and* reality, see Ryken's essay "Homer's *Odyssey* and the Value of Myth" in *Realms of Gold* (32–37) and Gene Edward Veith's *The Soul of* The Lion, the Witch, and the Wardrobe (Chapter 8, 130–35).

5. For example, see Douglas Wilson's *Writers to Read*, which mentions "three major influences" on N.D. Wilson: his storytelling grandfathers (see the dedication page of Wilson's *100 Cupboards*), "the presence of books and stories read aloud," and his classical Christian education (138–39). Douglas Wilson is N.D. Wilson's father, but he includes a disclaimer at the beginning of the chapter on his son: "[I]f the suggestion is made—as it quite possibly might be—that I am including him alongside all these other worthies out of a paternal desire to puff him up into authorial importance, I would reply that any efforts of mine in that department would be both vain and superfluous. His [*100*] *Cupboards* [trilogy] has sold about three-quarters of a million copies in North America [as of 2015] and has been translated into [more than] twenty languages. So I am actually commenting here on something that has happened and am not trying to get it to happen" (137).

6. See my essay "Embracing Popular Culture's Fascination with Mythology," where I explore Tolkien's themes of sub-creation, recovery, escape, and consolation in his essay "On Fairy-Stories," then broadly look at Wilson's *Leepike Ridge*, his *100 Cupboards* series, and two books from his *Ashtown Burials* series. As I write in that essay, "Wilson has been marinating in Protestant poetics his entire life," and "his religious background has been a primary influence in encouraging him to create new myths, as each of his YA novels is deeply rooted in mythology" (27).

7. Wilson prefers to think of his writing as a meal, not medicine. See his book *Death by Living*, where in Chapter two, "Soul Food, Paper Boats, and the Pitcher: Stories Told," he writes, "I began to see the world more like a cook than a writer" (23). See also his essay "Stories Are Soul Food": "I'm not trying to provide the mechanical children of a mechanical universe with a much needed (false) daydream. I work to imitate this world; I hunt through the jungles of history and mythology looking for spices; I dig through the stories of the prophets looking for meat. I hope to write the fantasy of here, for the future heroes of here. I do what I can, hoping to feed souls."

8. For more on "the values and functions of fairy-stories" for children, see Tolkien's "On Fairy-Stories" (57–68). Fairy stories benefit adults as well, and "a taste for them may make us, or keep us, childish" (77). Cf. Lewis's preface in *The Lion, the Witch and the Wardrobe*, written to Lucy Barfield: "[Y]ou are already too old for fairy tales.... But some day you will be old enough to start reading fairy tales again" (5).

9. Besides having more staying power, fantasy is simply older and more established than realistic fiction. Wilson writes in an introduction to Howard Pyle's *Twilight Land*, "Fairy tales and fantasies are as old as the world.... What we call realism in storytelling is a relatively new concept. It is the sapling in the wood surrounded by towering moss-covered giants as old as history, giants grown up out of myths and legends. Fantasy" (ix–x).

10. See more here: www.shadowshroud.com. A potential irony of Wilson's body of work is that perhaps his most academic work is his argument that a medieval miscreant easily could have faked the Shroud of Turin. The irony lies in the fact that Wilson has persuasively disenchanted this "icon," so labeled by Popes Benedict XVI and Francis. But Wilson's entire body of work suggests that in our always-already enchanted world, we do not need icons to *make* the world enchanted.

11. *Notes from the Tilt-a-Whirl: Wide-Eyed Wonder in God's Spoken World* (2009) and *Death by Living: Life Is Meant to Be Spent* (2013).

12. Wilson wrote and directed *The River Thief*, which debuted on October 14, 2016, and he wrote and directed *The Hound of Heaven* (screenplay adapted from Francis Thompson's poem), initially released on October 4, 2014. Wilson wrote and produced the DVD version of his nonfiction *Notes from the Tilt-a-Whirl* in 2011, and he is now working on a film adaptation of C.S. Lewis's *The Great Divorce*.

13. See the character Henry York's experience of gradually awakening to the magic of this world in Wilson's *Dandelion Fire*: "Dandelions were not magic. They couldn't be.... If they were magic, well, everything was.... *I'm normal*, Henry thought. *Normal. Normal as a dandelion*" (66–67). Eventually, Henry can see the magic of his world: "'There's so much magic,' he said slowly. 'Everything. All of it is magic'" (308; cf. Douglas Wilson, *Writers to Read* 146). Cf. C.S. Lewis's "determination to rub [his] nose in the very quiddity of each thing, to rejoice in its being (so magnificently) what it was" (*Surprised by Joy* 199).

14. As I explain in "Embracing Popular Culture's Fascination with Mythology" (29n9), I use terms broadly here, although I understand that there are significant differences among fairy tales, fantasy, mythology, etc. See C.S. Lewis's *An Experiment in Criticism* for more on myth, fantasy, and realism (Chapters 5–7). Lewis treats fantasy and fairy tales (roughly) synonymously in "On Three Ways" (32, 33), and he treats fantasy and myth as the same "mode" in "Sometimes Fairy Stories" (48). On the "extraordinary symbiotic connection" between fairy tales, myths, etc., see Jack Zipes's *Fairy Tale as Myth/Myth as Fairy Tale* (1). Also note that *Bulfinch's Mythology* includes "fables" and "legends," both of which include elements of fantasy.

15. In *The Discarded Image*, C.S. Lewis writes that fairies provide an "imaginative value" to stories by adding "a welcome hint of wildness and uncertainty into a universe that is in danger of being a little too self-explanatory, too luminous [and insufficiently numinous]" (122).

16. In Wilson's *Dandelion Fire*, Henry's father asks him, "Do you understand how the ground pulls you down, or why the earth has never been drawn into the sun, or how a crawling worm morphs into a butterfly? We can give names to these things, but that is not understanding" (462).

17. See Wilson's *Notes*: "Welcome to His poem. His play. His novel.... This is His spoken world" (8).

18. Talcott Parsons uses the term "iron cage" in his 1930 translation. Some scholars are unsatisfied with this loose translation for *stahlhartes Gehäuse* (e.g., Kalberg 245n129).

19. Weber's *die Entzauberung der Welt* ("disenchantment of the world" in some translations) appears in *Protestant Ethic* (53, 59, and 78). See also Weber's "Science as Vocation" lecture (13, 14, 23, 30). For an argument that the world never became disenchanted, see Landy and Saler's *The Re-Enchantment of the World* (2009).

20. For example, although some Greek historians such as Thucydides believed that the Trojan War was an historical event, by the 19th century, almost no one thought that ancient Trojans ever battled the Greeks on an epic scale. But since the excavation work of German archaeologist Heinrich Schliemann, many scholars have come to view the Trojan War as a real possibility, with significant differences from Homer's account. J.D. Hawkins writes, "There is every likelihood that the *Iliad* and the traditions of the Trojan War, however immortalized in epic narrative, do indeed preserve a memory of actual events of the Late Bronze Age" (40). Regarding another myth, C.S. Lewis's writes of the "supposed historical truth" of *Beowulf* in his *Preface to* Paradise Lost (16).

21. For more on "the assumption that the world is getting more secular" (Keller, *Making Sense* 4), see Part One of Timothy Keller's *Making Sense of God* (2016).

22. Taylor writes, "[W]e have...changed from a condition in which belief was the default option...to a condition in which for more and more people unbelieving construals seem at first blush the only plausible ones" (12).

23. See Leithart's essays "Why Protestants Can't Write, I" and "Why Protestants Can't Write, II" in *First Things*. For some roundups of these recent debates, see Douglas Wilson's "The 7 Real Reasons Protestants Can't Write" and Steven Wedgeworth's "The Bare Symbolism of the Late-Modern Longing: A Rejoinder to Peter Leithart."

24. See Wedgeworth's "Bare Symbolism."

25. A version of Corrigan's review now functions as the introduction to this volume.

26. I summarize the two other kinds of secularity in my review of James K.A. Smith's *How (Not) to Be Secular*: "'Secular$_1$' refers to the medieval distinction between 'secular' and 'sacred,' and 'secular$_2$' refers to a-religiosity" (62).

27. The fact that our *age* is secular (in the third sense) does not mean that every individual lives with inner turmoil about his or her ultimate commitments. Some people have described our age, not so much in terms of "secularization," but in terms of "polarization": "what is really disappearing is the ['mushy'] middle" (Keller).

28. Taylor writes, "Cross pressure [means] that virtually all positions held...define themselves at last partly in relation to these extremes [of 'orthodox religion' and 'hard-line materialistic atheism']" (676; cf. 595, 598).

29. Taylor defines the "nova effect" as "an ever-widening variety of moral/spiritual options" (299).

30. Charles Taylor calls the pre-moderns, who were open to enchantment, "porous" as opposed to "buffered," or closed-off to enchantment (27, 35–41). See Alan Jacobs's "Fantasy and the Buffered Self."

31. Multiple reasons exist for setting *Boys of Blur* in Florida. For one, Wilson, an Idaho dweller, sets his stories in the United States of America so as to contribute to an American mythology. The end of the novel features a life-giving fountain (182), which has connections to Florida and the legend of the sixteenth-century conquistador Ponce de León. In addition, actual sugarcane burning occurs in Florida, as do rabbit runs, in which youthful runners chase down flame-fleeing rabbits to sell. Some locals refer to Belle Glade, Florida, as "Muck City," and the surrounding area in Florida produces most of the country's sugarcane (Desmon).

32. N.D. Wilson, Twitter post, July 21, 2016, 5:22 p.m. twitter.com/ndwilsonmutters/status/756253037568495616.

33. Seamus is the name of one of N.D. Wilson's sons, and Seamus Heaney (who won the Nobel Prize in Literature in 1995) published a translation of *Beowulf* in 1999.

34. As C.S. Lewis reminds us, the mythical quality of a story does not necessarily negate its historical reality ("Myth Became Fact" 66–67). For more on *Beowulf* as a Christian appropriation of Germanic mythology, see Leithart's "Germanic Jesus."

35. Some critics bristle at the notion of "cultural appropriation," but as Alan Jacobs has pointed out, cultures relate to each other in "a ceaseless interchange of ideas, visions, experiences, and techniques.... Appropriation is what culture does" ("Renewing the University" 19). See also Jacobs's comment in "Children and Culture" that "culture *is* appropriation." For more on the Christian appropriation of Norse culture, see G. Ronald Murphy's *Tree of Salvation: Yggdrasil and the Cross in the North*.

36. Cf. Heorot, the mead-hall of Hrothgar, king of the Danes. *Heriot* refers to a holding for "military equipments," or the return of such equipment "to a lord on the death of his tenant" ("heriot").

37. The hoarding recalls the dragon of *Beowulf*, while the cavern recalls Grendel's mother.

38. Tolkien writes of the difficulty of writing literature "that [is] founded on an earlier matter which is put to new uses—like Homer, or Beowulf, or Virgil, or Greek or Shakespearean tragedy" (*Letters* 201).

39. To be fair, Milton's explicit purpose in *Paradise Lost* is to subvert and surpass previous heroic epics, which are full of wrath and war (9.1–47). Regarding "envie" in *Paradise Lost*, Thomas Luxon notes that "Envy is Satan's motivating force. He begins with envy of the Son (5.783) and concludes with envy of man" (note to 9.175). Satan is seized more by envy than by wonder when he sees the new world that God has created for humans (3.540–54); he envies Adam's condition (6.900); and he suggests to Eve that envy may be God's motivation in keeping her from the fruit (9.729–32).

40. Wilson's "new verse rendering" (cf. the "new verse translation" by Seamus Heaney) is admittedly not a translation (1).

41. In fact, *Beowulf*'s first reference to Grendel immediately follows an oblique reference

to Ingeld, who eventually marries Hrothgar's daughter Freawaru (Douglas Wilson, *Beowulf* 85) and whose reception could be called The Wedding Reception from Hell (2022–71): a drunk, old warrior sees across the hall a young warrior wearing the sword of a slain comrade; then the old warrior whispers in the ear of the son of this fallen comrade and incites violence at the feast, which ends in a bloody and tragically ironic fashion, as the wedding was intended to produce peace between warring factions. For another connection to Seamus Heaney, see his poem "North," in which he invokes the memory of Anglo-Saxon blood feuds to address twentieth-century Irish troubles (see Richard Rankin Russell's *Seamus Heaney: An Introduction* 72–74).

42. According to McMurtry, a former professional football player himself, football is "a warrior game with a warrior ethos," and "physical injury—giving and taking it—is the real currency of the sport" (43). "[S]ome of the more conspicuous similarities between football and war" include "languages" (e.g., *blitz* and *draft*), "principles and practices" (e.g., "absolute command and total obedience," "territorial aggression," "drills," "formations," and "training camps"), and "the virtues they celebrate" (e.g., "suicidal bravery") (42). To be fair, McMurtry's 1971 essay does not take into consideration the decades of raised awareness and adjustments in player protection. Nevertheless, many of the parallels remain.

43. See James 4.1–2 in the language of the King James Version. Envious boasting leads to wars and fighting, and because wars breed new envies, the loop is infinite. The solution to envious warfare is humility and submission (James 4.6–7, 10).

44. In *The Chestnut King*, Wilson describes envy as a soul-consuming worm (197).

45. Cf. the Witch's "fingerlings" in *The Chestnut King* (188) and Sauron's Nazgûl in Tolkien's *Silmarillion* (289). Ralph C. Wood writes in *The Gospel According to Tolkien* that pity is a Christian virtue, foreign to Nietzsche's will to power: "'The pity of Bilbo may rule the fate of many' is the only declaration to be repeated in all three volumes of *The Lord of the Rings*. It is indeed the leitmotiv of Tolkien's epic, its animating theme, its Christian epicenter as well as its circumference" (150).

46. "True myth" is how C.S. Lewis describes Christianity ("Myth Became Fact" 66).

47. For Tolkien's views on "virtuous pagans," see Tom Shippey's essays "Tolkien and the *Beowulf*-Poet" and "Tolkien and Iceland: The Philology of Envy" in *Roots and Branches*.

48. Anglo-Saxon culture was not primarily noble; it was primarily hopeless *despite* its nobility (Douglas Wilson, "Beowulf" 114–17, 124–26, 128–30; Tolkien, "*Beowulf*: The Monsters and the Critics" 22–23). James G. Williams (summarizing René Girard) writes of the uniqueness of the biblical myth in its heroes' refusal to retaliate: "Imitation in the form of retaliation can destroy a group or community" (xv). Joseph's retaliation in Genesis 45 would have resulted in the annihilation of Israel, but "he forgives [his brothers] and affirms the providence of God working through his sufferings" (xviii). Even the disciples, taught by Jesus himself, could not extricate themselves from a system of envious rivalry until they recognized Jesus as a hero who conquered by dying and rising (xxi; cf. Girard 2).

49. As a literary device, a chiasm emphasizes the importance of the central episode(s).

50. Charlie's step-father tells Charlie, "Mistakes are seeds" and must be dug out (50–51).

51. See Genesis 4.9.

52. Many writers, including C.S. Lewis, have recognized that Christianity's uniqueness resides in its reality, not in its fantastic story of a god who dies and rises. Lewis mentions other mythological gods who die, including Balder and Osiris ("Myth Became Fact" 66) and Adonis and Bacchus (*Collected Letters* 997). The Incarnation is likewise a true myth. Writing of the fantastic reality of Christian mythology, J.I. Packer says, "Nothing in fiction is so fantastic as is [the] truth of the Incarnation" (53).

53. See Wilson's *Notes from the Tilt-a-Whirl*: "Caterpillars really turn into butterflies— it's not just a lie for children. Coal squishes into diamonds. Apple trees turn flowers into apples using sunlight and air. I've seen a baby born. And, *ahem*, I know what made it. But I'm not telling. You'd never believe me" (4; cf. Wilson, *100 Cupboards* 41, *Dandelion Fire* 68, and *The Chestnut King* 50). Those who watched the 2016 Olympics in Rio de Janeiro may recall feeling a thrill of enchantment when Tom Brokaw used the common description of the Amazon rainforest as "the lungs of the earth" because of its massive production of oxygen ("The Amazon"). For more by Wilson on this topic, see "Night One."

54. The references to sparks and the supernatural quality of nature tie in well with Wilson's *Notes*, in which he mocks materialism, which smothers wonder with its scientific labels (18–25; cf. 171, 183).

55. *Quick*, of course, carries with it the sense of vitality—think of "the quick and the dead" (2 Timothy 4.1) and being "quickened" (Ephesians 2.1) in the King James Version—and this language contributes to the good/quick vs. evil/dead theme. In Wilson's *Empire of Bones*, Chapter 18 is titled "The Quick and the Doomed," and in his nonfictional *Death by Living*, Chapter 10 is titled "The Quick, the Grateful, and the Dead."

56. See *Death by Living*, *passim*: "Lay your life down. Your heartbeats cannot be hoarded.... Living well is the same thing as dying for others" (84); "Grabbing will always fail. Hoarding always fails.... Live to die.... Giving will always succeed. Bestow" (110); "Be as empty as you can be when the clock winds down. Spend your life. And if time is a river, may you leave a wake" (117).

57. "Cotton" is a nickname. His actual name is René, given to him by his homeschooling mother, who wanted him to be named "after someone famous for thinking" (51–52), viz., René Descartes. Perhaps intentionally, in a move to re-enchant the world, Wilson presents us with the conversion of Descartes, whom many blame, fairly or unfairly, for our modern, disenchanted tendency to think of ourselves as "thinking things that are containers for ideas" (Smith, *Desiring the Kingdom* 32; cf. *Notes from the Tilt-a-Whirl* 13). In *Boys of Blur*, Cotton is not "converted" in a religious sense, but Wilson gives Descartes' name to a character who believes in the magic of the world. *René* Girard's work on mimetic violence may be a factor as well. For Girard's influence on N.D. Wilson's father, see "The Invisible Mainspring of Human Conflict."

58. Cf. Seamus Heaney's poems about bog people (see Russell 63).

59. Think of the temporary visits to Hades (or a Hades-like location) in the middle of Homer's *Odyssey*, Virgil's *Aeneid*, and G.K. Chesterton's *The Ballad of the White Horse*. See Douglas Wilson's "Chiastic Structure in *Beowulf*" for a treatment of the significance of Beowulf's pursuit of and underwater cavern fight with Grendel's dam in the central fitts of *Beowulf*.

60. *Boys of Blur* has fourteen chapters.

61. Cf. Cyrus in Wilson's *Empire of Bones*: "Cyrus was ready to die. He was mortal. His life was meant to be spent" (428). The living-by-dying theme appears throughout *Empire* (314–15, 352, 389, 428) and *The Chestnut King* (240, 369, 385).

62. *Boys of Blur* uses seed imagery to convey the death and resurrection theme (5, 30, 111; cf. *Notes from the Tilt-a-Whirl* [88], *Death by Living* [xiii], and *The Chestnut King* [369, 458]). Exile and return stories are common in biblical mythology (Jeffrey and Maillet 116; see Job 14.7, John 12.24, and 1 Corinthians 15.35–38), and such "stories are everywhere" (Douglas Wilson, "Undragoned" 75; cf. 173). M.H. Abrams calls the "death/rebirth theme" "the archetype of archetypes" (13). See also Douglas Wilson's review of N.D. Wilson's *Leepike Ridge*: "Death and resurrection are built into the world.... *Leepike Ridge* has a death and resurrection theme. But the author also has ten toes, which is equally unremarkable. All stories have death and resurrection themes" ("Review of Leepike Ridge"). For a related essay, see Douglas Wilson's "The R2K Crucifix Problem."

63. Tolkien defines *eucatastrophe* as "the good catastrophe, the sudden joyous 'turn'" ("On Fairy-Stories" 85–86). Tom Shippey writes, "In *Beowulf* the nearest thing the poem has to a 'eucatastrophic' moment is the one when the demoralized survivors of Beowulf's nation, the Geats, trapped in Ravens' Wood by Ongentheow, the terrible old king of the Swedes, who has passed the night by shouting threats of what he will do to them in the morning, hear *samod ærdæge*, 'with the dawn,' the horns and trumpets of the army of Beowulf's uncle Hygelac coming to their rescue" (*J.R.R. Tolkien: Author of the Century* 215).

64. Douglas Wilson argues that "the pagan and Christian elements...were placed in tension by the poet deliberately...to accomplish a stunning apologetic for the Christian faith" ("Beowulf" 113), showing readers "the high nobility [of Northern warriors] *at the point of profound despair*" (114). Wilson argues that "the first audience knew that [the Christian conversion of England] was just *about* to arrive" after the conclusion of *Beowulf* (116). The poet thus "show[s] that without Christ, such nobility does not keep people from being utterly and

completely *lost*" (114). But because the audience was aware of what was coming in England's history just after Beowulf's death (set in the late sixth century)—i.e., the Christianization of Anglo-Saxon England in the seventh century—we can say that *Beowulf*'s conclusion is as gloomy as a Tenebrae service on Good Friday, which is to say, not really.

65. Cf. Wilson, *Notes from the Tilt-a-Whirl*, 156–57.

66. See Wilson's essay in *The Atlantic*, "Why I Write Scary Stories for Children."

67. Cf. Mark Twain, *Life on the Mississippi*, 118–21; Tolkien, "*Beowulf*: The Monsters and the Critics" 15; Tolkien, "On Fairy-Stories," 46 (cf. 33, 52–54); and Lewis, "It All Began with a Picture … ," 53–54.

68. In general, sales in the YA novel market "have been neck and neck with those of adult books in recent years" (Salyer 56). Salyer reviews Cheryl B. Klein's *The Magic Words: Writing Great Books for Children and Young Adults* (2016), whose title interestingly invokes the genre of fantasy to refer to the process of writing great YA books of any genre.

69. According to Cynthia Read, Executive Editor at Oxford University Press in New York, we may be experiencing "a pendulum swing": "[P]eople really are sort of sick of that modern, materialistic worldview, and a lot of people are looking for something else. Not necessarily something religious, but at least something that, in a sense gives back the mystery of life and that sense of there being something larger than ourselves" (*The Narnia Code*).

70. Cf. Tolkien, "On Fairy-Stories," 79–85.

71. As Douglas Wilson says, good writing helps us to see "God on the other side of the world" (*Writers to Read* 119–20). That is, we see God *through* good writing.

72. For example, Caspian's world includes talking animals, aureate pools, magicians and invisible monopods, star-fathers who grow younger by eating fire-berries placed in their mouths by large white birds that reside in the sun, purple-haired sea-folk who ride on large seahorses, sweet seawater that tastes like sunlight, and glimpses of other worlds through rainbow-colored wave-walls.

WORKS CITED

A Visit with Lloyd Alexander. Directed and edited by David Savatteri. 1994. New York: Dutton's Children's Books, 1994. VHS.

Abrams, M.H., and Geoffrey Galt Harpham. *A Glossary of Literary Terms.* 8th ed. Boston: Thomson Wadsworth, 2005.

Boersma, Hans. *Heavenly Participation: The Weaving of a Sacramental Tapestry.* Grand Rapids, MI: Wm. B. Eerdmans, 2011.

Brokaw, Tom. "The Amazon: Lungs of the Earth, Heart of Brazilian Culture." *NBC* video, 5:25, August 6, 2016. www.nbcolympics.com/video/amazon-lungs-earth-heart-brazilian-culture.

Budin, Miriam Lang. "Review of *Boys of Blur*, by N.D. Wilson." *School Library Journal* 60, no. 6 (June 2014): 110.

Bulfinch, Thomas. *Bulfinch's Mythology: The Age of Fable.* New York: Doubleday, 1968.

Chesterton, G.K. *The Ballad of the White Horse.* Front Royal, VA: Seton Home Study School, 2011.

Corrigan, Paul T. "The Postsecular and Literature: A Review of Scholarship." *Corrigan Literary Review.* May 17, 2015. corriganliteraryreview.wordpress.com/2015/05/17/the-postsecular-and-literature/.

Desmon, Stephanie. "The Less Savory Side of Sugar." *The Baltimore Sun.* April 5, 2001. articles.baltimoresun.com/2001-04-05/news/0104050240_1_sugar-rabbits-cane-fields.

Donne, John. "The First Anniversary: An Anatomy of the World." In *John Donne's Poetry*, edited by Donald R. Dickson, 120–32. New York: W.W. Norton, 2007.

Girard, René. *I See Satan Fall Like Lightning.* Maryknoll, NY: Orbis Books, 2001.

Hawkins, J.D. "Evidence from Hittite Records." *Archeology* 57, no. 3 (May/June 2004): 40. archive.archaeology.org/0405/etc/troy3.html.

Heaney, Seamus. *Beowulf: A New Verse Translation.* New York: W.W. Norton, 2001.

Heaney, Seamus. "North." In *North.* London: Faber and Faber, 2001.

Homer. *The Iliad.* Translated by Robert Fagles. New York: Penguin Books, 1991.

Homer. *The Odyssey*. Translated by Robert Fagles. New York: Penguin Books, 2006.

Hunt, Gladys. *Honey for a Child's Heart: The Imaginative Use of Books in Family Life*. 4th ed. Grand Rapids, MI: Zondervan, 2002.

Jacobs, Alan. "Children and Culture." *The New Atlantis*. December 30, 2016. text-patterns. thenewatlantis.com/2016/12/children-and-culture.html.

Jacobs, Alan. "Fantasy and the Buffered Self." *The New Atlantis* 41 (Winter 2014) 3–18. www. thenewatlantis.com/publications/fantasy-and-the-buffered-self.

Jacobs, Alan. "Renewing the University." *National Affairs* 28 (Summer 2016): 3–19. nation-alaffairs.com/publications/detail/renewing-the-university.

Jacobs, Alan. *The Narnian: The Life and Imagination of C.S. Lewis*. New York: HarperCollins, 2006.

Jeffrey, David Lyle, and Gregory Maillet. *Christianity and Literature: Philosophical Foundations and Critical Practice*. Westmont, IL: InterVarsity Press Academic, 2011.

Keats, John. *Lamia*. *English Romantic Writers*. 2nd ed. Edited by David Perkins. Boston: Thomson Wadsworth, 1995.

Keller, Timothy. "Conservative Christianity After the Christian Right." Speech, South Beach, FL, March 19, 2013. Faith Angle Forum, Ethics and Public Policy Center. eppc.org/pub-lications/dr-timothy-keller-at-the-march-2013-faith-angle-forum/.

Keller, Timothy. *Making Sense of God: An Invitation to the Skeptical*. New York: Viking, 2016.

Klein, Cheryl B. *The Magic Words: Writing Great Books for Children and Young Adults*. New York: W.W. Norton, 2016.

Knapton, Sarah. "Bright Flash of Light Marks Incredible Moment Life Begins When Sperm Meets Egg." *The Telegraph*. April 26, 2016. www.telegraph.co.uk/science/2016/04/26/bright-flash-of-light-marks-incredible-moment-life-begins-when-s/.

Landy, Joshua, and Michael Saler, eds. *The Re-Enchantment of the World: Secular Magic in a Rational Age*. Redwood City, CA: Stanford University Press, 2009.

Larson, Jeremy. "Embracing Popular Culture's Fascination with Mythology." *Pro Rege* 51, no. 3 (March 2013): 23–30. www.dordt.edu/sites/default/files/documents/imported/Pro_Rege_Mar_2013.pdf.

Larson, Jeremy. "'The Siren Song of the Secular' by James K.A. Smith: How (Not) to Be Sec-ular: Reading Charles Taylor." *Modern Reformation* 25, no. 4 (July/August 2016): 62–63. www.whitehorseinn.org/article/the-siren-song-of-the-secular-by-james-k-a-smith/.

Leithart, Peter. "Germanic Jesus." *Roman Roads Media*. July 7, 2014, romanroadsmedia.com/2014/07/germanic-jesus/.

Leithart, Peter. "Protestants and Writing." *First Things*. February 5, 2016. www.firstthings. com/blogs/leithart/2016/02/protestants-and-writing.

Leithart, Peter. "Why Protestants Can't Write, I." *First Things*. January 28, 2016. www. firstthings.com/blogs/leithart/2016/01/why-protestants-cant-write-i.

Leithart, Peter. "Why Protestants Can't Write, II." *First Things*. January 29, 2016. www. firstthings.com/blogs/leithart/2016/01/why-protestants-cant-write-ii.

Lewis, C.S. *The Collected Letters of C.S. Lewis: Volume 1: Family Letters 1905–1931*, edited by Walter Hooper. New York: HarperCollins, 2004.

Lewis, C.S. "The Dethronement of Power: J.R.R. Tolkien, the *Two Towers* (Being the Second Part of the *Lord of the Rings*) and the *Return of the King* (Being the Third Part of the *Lord of the Rings*)." In *Image and Imagination: Essays and Reviews*, edited by Walter Hooper, 104–9. Cambridge: Cambridge University Press, 2013.

Lewis, C.S. *The Discarded Image: An Introduction to Medieval and Renaissance Literature*. Cambridge: Cambridge University Press, 2009.

Lewis, C.S. *An Experiment in Criticism*. Cambridge: Cambridge University Press, 2012.

Lewis, C.S. "It All Began with a Picture … " In *On Stories and Other Essays on Literature*, edited by Walter Hooper, 53–54. San Diego, CA: Harcourt, 1982.

Lewis, C.S. *The Lion, the Witch and the Wardrobe*. New York: Harper, 2009.

Lewis, C.S. "Meditation in a Toolshed." In *God in the Dock: Essays on Theology and Ethics*, edited by Walter Hooper, 212–15. Grand Rapids, MI: Wm. B. Eerdmans, 2001.

Lewis, C.S. "Myth Became Fact." In *God in the Dock: Essays on Theology and Ethics*, edited by Walter Hooper, 63–67. Grand Rapids, MI: Wm. B. Eerdmans, 2001.

Lewis, C.S. "On Three Ways of Writing for Children." In *On Stories and Other Essays on Literature*, edited by Walter Hooper, 31–43. San Diego, CA: Harcourt, 1982.

Lewis, C.S. *A Preface to* Paradise Lost. Oxford: Oxford University Press, 1961.

Lewis, C.S. "Sometimes Fairy Stories May Say Best What's to Be Said." In *On Stories and Other Essays on Literature*, edited by Walter Hooper, 45–48. San Diego, CA: Harcourt, 1982.

Lewis, C.S. *Surprised by Joy: The Shape of My Early Life*. San Diego, CA: Harcourt, 1955.

Lewis, C.S. *The Voyage of the* Dawn Treader. New York: HarperCollins, 2010.

Lewis, C.S. "The Weight of Glory." In *The Weight of Glory and Other Addresses*, 25–46. New York: HarperOne, 2001.

Luxon, Thomas H. "John Milton Reading Room: *Paradise Lost.*" *John Milton Reading Room.* 2016. www.dartmouth.edu/~milton/reading_room/pl/book_9/text.shtml.

McMurtry, John. "Kill 'Em! Crush 'Em! Eat 'Em Raw!" *Maclean's.* October 1, 1971. archive.macleans.ca/issue/19711001.

Milton, John. *Paradise Lost.* In *The Riverside Milton*, edited by Roy Flannagan, 296–710. Boston: Houghton Mifflin, 1998.

Murphy, G. Ronald. *Tree of Salvation: Yggdrasil and the Cross in the North.* Oxford: Oxford University Press, 2013.

The Narnia Code. Directed by Norman Stone. London: Entertainment One, 2009.

North, Richard. *The Origins of* Beowulf: *From Vergil to Wiglaf.* Oxford: Oxford University Press, 2007.

OED Online, S.V. "Heriot." Accessed February 12, 2017.

Packer, J.I. *Knowing God.* Westmont, IL: InterVarsity Press, 1993.

Russell, Richard Rankin. *Seamus Heaney: An Introduction.* Edinburgh: Edinburgh University Press, 2016.

Ryken, Leland, ed. *The Christian Imagination: The Practice of Faith in Literature and Writing.* Colorado Springs: WaterBrook, 2002.

Ryken, Leland. *Realms of Gold: The Classics in Christian Perspective.* Eugene, OR: Wipf & Stock, 1991.

Salyer, Kirsten. "With a Little Help, You Too Can Write a Young-Adult Novel." *Time.* September 22, 2016. time.com/4504028/magic-words/.

Shippey, Tom A. *J.R.R. Tolkien: Author of the Century.* Boston: Houghton Mifflin, 2000.

Shippey, Tom A. *Roots and Branches: Selected Papers on Tolkien*, edited by Thomas Honegger. Zollikofen, Switzerland: Walking Tree Publishers, 2007.

Smith, James K.A. *Desiring the Kingdom: Worship, Worldview, and Cultural Formation.* Grand Rapids, MI: Baker Academic, 2009.

Smith, James K.A. *How (Not) to Be Secular: Reading Charles Taylor.* Grand Rapids, MI: Wm. B. Eerdmans, 2014.

Taylor, Charles. *A Secular Age.* Cambridge, MA: Belknap Press, 2007.

Tolkien, J.R.R. "*Beowulf*: The Monsters and the Critics." In *The Monsters and the Critics and Other Essays*, 5–48. New York: HarperCollins, 2006.

Tolkien, J.R.R. *The Letters of J.R.R. Tolkien*, edited by Humphrey Carpenter with the assistance of Christopher Tolkien. Boston: Houghton Mifflin, 2000.

Tolkien, J.R.R. "On Fairy-Stories." In *The Tolkien Reader*, 33–99. New York: Del Rey, 1986.

Tolkien, J.R.R. *The Silmarillion: The Myths and Legends of Middle-Earth*, edited by Christopher Tolkien. Boston: Houghton Mifflin, 1998.

Twain, Mark. *Life on the Mississippi.* Oxford: Oxford University Press, 1996.

Veith, Gene Edward. *The Soul of* The Lion, the Witch, and the Wardrobe. Colorado Springs: Victor, 2005.

Virgil. *The Aeneid.* Translated by David West. New York: Penguin Books, 2003.

Weber, Max. *The Protestant Ethic and the Spirit of Capitalism.* Translated by Talcott Parsons and edited by Richard Swedberg. New York: W.W. Norton, 2009.

Weber, Max. *The Protestant Ethic and the Spirit of Capitalism.* Translated by Stephen Kalberg. London: Routledge, 2012.

Weber, Max. "Science as a Vocation." Translated by Michael John. In *Max Weber's "Science as a Vocation,"* edited by Peter Lassman and Irving Velody with Herminio Martins, 3–31. London: Unwin Hyman, 1989.

Weber, Max. *The Sociology of Religion*. Translated by Ephraim Fischoff. Boston: Beacon Press, 1993.

Wedgeworth, Steven. "The Bare Symbolism of the Late-Modern Longing: A Rejoinder to Peter Leithart." *The Calvinist International*. February 4, 2016. calvinistinternational. com/2016/02/04/symbolism-modern-peter-leithart-flannery-oconnor/.

Wilkinson, Alissa. "How 'Stranger Things' Re-Enchants the World: The Netflix Show, Along with 'Midnight Special,' Frank Peretti's Novels, and Even Pokemon Go Are Trying to Fill a Void." *Christianity Today*. July 26, 2016. www.christianitytoday.com/ct/2016/july-web-only/stranger-things.html.

Wilson, Douglas. *Beowulf: A New Verse Rendering*. Moscow, ID: Canon Press, 2013.

Wilson, Douglas. "Beowulf: The Unchrist." *Beowulf: A New Verse Rendering*. Moscow, ID: Canon Press, 2013.

Wilson, Douglas. "Chiastic Structure in *Beowulf*." In *Beowulf: A New Verse Rendering*. Moscow, ID: Canon Press, 2013.

Wilson, Douglas. "The Invisible Mainspring of Human Conflict." *Blog and Mablog*. February 10 2017. https://dougwils.com/s16-theology/invisible-mainspring-human-conflict.html.

Wilson, Douglas. "The R2k Crucifix Problem." *Blog and Mablog*. August 14, 2014. dougwils. com/s7-engaging-the-culture/the-r2k-crucifix-problem.html.

Wilson, Douglas. "Review of Leepike Ridge." *Blog and Mablog*. May 21, 2007. dougwils.com/ s7-engaging-the-culture/a-review-of-leepike-ridge.html.

Wilson, Douglas. "The 7 Real Reasons Protestants Can't Write." *Blog and Mablog*. February 5, 2016. dougwils.com/s16-theology/110225.html.

Wilson, Douglas. "Undragoned: C.S. Lewis and the Gift of Salvation." In *The Romantic Rationalist: God, Life, and Imagination in the Work of C.S. Lewis*, edited by John Piper and David Mathis, 65–80. Wheaton, IL: Crossway, 2014.

Wilson, Douglas. *Writers to Read: Nine Names That Belong on Your Bookshelf*. Wheaton, IL: Crossway, 2015.

Wilson, N.D. *Boys of Blur*. New York: Random House, 2014.

Wilson, N.D. *The Chestnut King*. 2010. New York: Yearling, 2011.

Wilson, N.D. *Dandelion Fire*. New York: Yearling, 2009.

Wilson, N.D. *Death by Living: Life Is Meant to Be Spent*. Nashville, TN: Thomas Nelson, 2013.

Wilson, N.D. *Empire of Bones*. New York: Random House, 2013.

Wilson, N.D. Twitter post. July 21, 2016, 5:22 p.m. twitter.com/ndwilsonmutters/status/ 756253037568495616.

Wilson, N.D. Introduction to *Twilight Land*, by Howard Pyle. New York: Random House, 2010.

Wilson, N.D. "Night One—N.D. Wilson." *ParkRenew* video, 37:04. November 11, 2015. www. parkrenew.org/category/created-to-create-symposium/.

Wilson, N.D. *Notes from the Tilt-A-Whirl: Wide-Eyed Wonder in God's Spoken World*. Nashville, TN: Thomas Nelson, 2009.

Wilson, N.D. *100 Cupboards*. 2007. New York: Yearling, 2008.

Wilson, N.D. "Stories Are Soul Food: Don't Let Your Children Hunger." *Desiring God*. October 13, 2011. www.desiringgod.org/articles/stories-are-soul-food-dont-let-your-children-hunger.

Wilson, N.D. "Why I Write Scary Stories for Children." *The Atlantic*. April 20, 2016. www. theatlantic.com/entertainment/archive/2016/04/why-i-write-scary-stories-for-children/ 478977/.

Woiwode, Larry. "The Superiority of Realism to Fantasy." In *The Christian Imagination*, edited by Leland Ryken, 315–16. Colorado Springs: WaterBrook, 2002.

Wood, Ralph C. *The Gospel According to Tolkien: Visions of the Kingdom in Middle-Earth*. Louisville, KY: Westminster John Knox Press, 2003.

Zipes, Jack. *Fairy Tale as Myth/Myth as Fairy Tale*. Lexington: University Press of Kentucky, 1994.

A Ninja, a Nun and a Knight

*Christianity and Narrative Mischief
in Brian Meehl's* You Don't Know About Me,
Suck It Up *and* Suck It Up and Die

CARRIE MYERS

Through teen protagonists and other central characters, Brian Meehl's YA novels *You Don't Know About Me*, *Suck It Up*, and *Suck It Up and Die* engage with Christianity—its beliefs, culture, and symbols. *YDKAM* features outspokenly Christian characters wrestling with God, their identities, and Bible verses about homosexuality, while they embark on a road trip that parallels the journey of Huck Finn and Jim in Mark Twain's *The Adventures of Huckleberry Finn*. In *Suck It Up* and its sequel, the immortal vampires/parental figures and teen characters are largely unmotivated by Christianity—with one key exception—yet Christian history, tropes, and symbolism are key to the novels' characterizations of good and evil, dreams and self-sacrifice, gender and sexuality, and the people and things that make life worth living.

In order to explore Meehl's novels and their relationship to Christianity, this essay borrows a critical lens from Brian McLaren's *A Generous Orthodoxy*. McClaren is one of the most prominent voices of the emerging church (other leaders include Rob Bell, Richard Rohr, Tony Campolo, and Mark Driscoll), a post-evangelical, postcritical, largely white and middle or upper-middle class expression of Western Christianity.[1,2,3] McLaren explains the term "postcritical" by citing N.T. Wright: it's an approach that invokes the "'hermeneutic of love,' as opposed to the 'hermeneutic of suspicion'" (McLaren, footnote 6). In other words, a postcritical approach to Christian traditions (rather than one unified tradition), which includes various ways of interpreting Christian Scripture, seeks to preserve the richness and goodness of the historic

45

expressions of Christian faith, while making space for difficult questions and conversations, innovation, contextualization, and interfaith dialogue (18). It is Christianity reshaped for a questioning, pluralistic, postmodern age.[4]

McLaren's title, *A Generous Orthodoxy*, functions as a kind of tagline for the emerging church. As McLaren pursues the common ground between "post-liberals" and "post-conservatives" first laid out by Yale theologian Hans Frei, from whom the term "generous orthodoxy" is borrowed, his stated intention is to be "provocative, mischievous, and unclear, reflecting [his] belief that clarity is sometimes overrated, and that shock, obscurity, playfulness, and intrigue (carefully articulated) often stimulate more thought than clarity" (23). Although his book does construct a theological argument, its first person, conversational, often confessional style is obviously meant for an audience outside of (though not excluding) the theological academy.

McLaren's use of mischief and play reflects the emerging church's belief that the Spirit continues to work in new ways, to "tweak" old understandings of Scripture (28). Borrowing from McLaren, I want to propose the term "narrative mischief" to name several strategies employed by Meehl in his portrayal of Christians and Christianity, and his use of Christian tropes and imagery in *You Don't Know About Me*, and in *Suck It Up* and *Suck It Up and Die*. Meehl's narrative mischief is grounded in intertextual play, in an emerging church-like hermeneutic that "tweaks" old interpretations of scripture, and in a repurposing of Christian metaphors and symbols in the service of secular, humanist values. The novels poke fun at and challenge stereotypes about evangelical Christians as (among other things) sheltered, militant, fundamentalist, and socially and sexually reactionary. Their narrative mischief also propels the development of several characters away from rigid definitions and practices of Christianity towards a more fluid, questioning faith.

You Don't Know About Me

Brian Meehl's *You Don't Know About Me*, published in 2011, both anticipates and parallels the current debate among both mainline and evangelical Christians regarding gay marriage, LGBT rights, and the place of LGBT Christians in the church. Meehl has stated that he deliberately set out to address homophobic attitudes towards LGBT individuals when he wrote the book, and was inspired as well by Twain's "skewering of Christianity" in his book of essays, *Letters from the Earth*.[5] In Meehl's novel, Billy Albright, escaping from his overprotective, Christian fundamentalist mother, goes on a quest to find his freedom, his own version of Christian faith, and his father, who he has believed dead for years. Along the way, he is guided by clues his father has left in a copy of *The Adventures of Huckleberry Finn*, as well as by the events and themes in the book itself, which Billy reads together with his traveling companion, Ruah Branch, a baseball player who is undertaking his own metaphorical journey to freedom.

I want to propose several interconnected strategies of narrative mischief or play that scaffold Billy's journey away from his mother's "ninja warrior" fundamentalist faith towards a more open, questioning version of belief in God.[6] First, Meehl's deployment of intertextual play makes Billy and Ruah's camper trek into a modern day mirror of Huck and Jim's travels north, with Billy's geographical movements and character development paralleling those of Huck, and the use of the problem of racism in Twain's novel as a way to call out modern instances of racism and homophobia. Second are the images, metaphors, and allusions that Meehl uses to contrast Billy's initial, militant Christianity with Ruah's image of himself as a player for Team Jesus, and to set up Ruah as a moral authority on par with the Holy Spirit. Third, is Meehl's transformation, through Billy's conversations with Ruah, through a hermeneutic of "doubt" (110) and through "generously orthodox" exegetical strategies, of the Bible itself from an unchanging, "homophobic scripture" (178) to a text that affirms LGBT identities.

Intertextual Play

The *Adventures of Huckleberry Finn* is often read as the story of Huck wrestling with the moral evils of slavery, especially as endorsed by white North American Christianity; he comes to view Jim as a friend and companion, while still being unable to jettison the indoctrination of his pro-slavery upbringing. In parallel fashion, Billy's cross-country travels and friendship with Ruah lead him to examine his beliefs about homosexuality, and to question his fundamentalist beliefs and practices about the Christianity learned from his mother, as well as, briefly, his own heterosexuality. Both characters—Huck and Billy—are on, in Meehl's words, "a treasure hunt for freedom"[7]: Huck from the racist beliefs of his upbringing as well as a geographical journey with Jim to free territory, and Billy from his fundamentalist, homophobic beliefs.

Meehl's novel is constructed on intertextual relationships with not only *Huckleberry Finn*, which Billy and Ruah read loud as they travel together, but also with Twain's planned, never-completed sequel to *Huck Finn*, for which Twain scribbled notes inside a copy of *Thirty-three Years Among Our Wild Indians*, by Richard Irving Dodge.[8] Irving's book, with Twain's precious notes hidden inside, are Billy's prize for following a series of clues—each requiring knowledge of the plot of *Huck Finn*—sent to him in a letter by Billy's dad, who Billy has long believed dead. In finding Dodge's book / Twain's notes,

Billy also meets his father, Richard, for the first and only time, and he learns Richard's own story of faith and doubt, which Richard directly links to Twain's writings. Richard's story in turn helps Billy process his own changing view of Christianity. This deeper knowledge of his father, and an ability to incorporate his father's story and beliefs into his own for the first time are, no less than the (undoubtedly quite valuable) manuscript itself, Billy's patrimony. By making Twain and Dodge so fundamental to Billy's "treasure hunt," Richard has also inserted himself into, and taken control over Twain's and Dodge's texts (his first name is even the same as Dodge's, emphasizing his own authorial status) as he directs and shapes Billy's physical and emotional travels.

The narrative unpacks the relationship between the various texts and speakers—Huck and Jim, *Huck Finn*, the Bible, Billy, Ruah—so that Huck's growing awareness of racism and Jim as a person with agency caught in an oppressive system parallels Billy's growing understanding of Ruah as more than just his sexual orientation, and his own complicity in the religious beliefs and discourse that have been used to marginalize LGBT persons. To move Billy towards these realizations, Meehl thematically links two conversations between Ruah and Billy—one dealing with the word "nigger" and the other with derogatory terms for gay persons. Ruah, who has not read *Huck Finn*, but is aware of critiques of Twain's characterization of Jim—"how the black dude, Jim, is a step'-n'-fetch-it, bow-to-the-man, stupid nigger out of a minstrel show"—asks Billy to read him the book in exchange for driving west, because "I wanna know if it's as badass ugly as everyone says" (131, 133). While reading aloud, Billy can't bring himself to say the word "nigger" until Ruah tells him to get over it, admonishing that "you're just reading it" and "It's not the words you speak, it's how you speak 'em" (134). In contrast, when Billy learns Ruah is gay and uses offensive language towards him, Ruah draws the line, saying that he'd rather hear the read words "'my nigger' ... flying out of your mouth than 'faggot' and 'abomination to the Lord'" (206; the phrase quoted is from Leviticus 20:13). Ruah is fine with Billy reading the n-word because, in the context of *Huck Finn*, "it's just another word" (206), but he's not okay with Billy's words about his sexual orientation, because in this case, Billy is not reading someone else's words—he's saying words that reflect what he believes, and which he believes have the weight of Biblical authority behind them.

In both these scenes, Ruah asserts his control over offensive discourse meant to marginalize black and LGBT persons. By juxtaposing these two conversations—the first framing Twain's language and narrative as racist, while absolving Billy as a *reader* of a racist text and word, the second calling out Billy as an intentional *speaker* of hateful words—Meehl's narrative play uses intertextual relationships and rhetorical insight in order to educate Billy about his own prejudice, and to make explicit and challenge the power dynamics of who is allowed to wield certain words, and under what conditions. It also sets up further discussions between Ruah and Billy over whether or not the Bible's apparently homophobic discourse can be read in the same way as *Huck Finn's* racist discourse—as "just words" that can be dismissed as relics of an older and more ignorant time.

Brand Jesus: Warrior, Spirit, Lunchable, Shoe?

YDKAM's narrative mischief also extends to its humorous treatment of Christianity, from Billy's tongue-in-cheek references to his fundamentalist upbringing and suburban mega-churches to Ruah's easy assertion that what God really needs is a better marketing strategy. The humor, as well as being funny in its own right, and knowing social commentary, also draws a vivid contrast between the versions of God that Billy and Ruah begin with: Billy's angry God that punishes sinners, Jonathan Edwards–like, versus Ruah's friendlier, more personal Christ.

At the start of the book, Billy's Christian vernacular is pithy, funny, and self-aware, but also inflected with the rigidity, violence, and conflict often associated with fundamentalist Christianity (as well as with other varieties of religious fundamentalism). Although Billy does see God as a helper—asking God to "help me Son-up" (5) when his faith is wavering—he also thinks of God as a punisher, wielding his "smite stick" (3) at those who need correction. Billy and his mother, Ruth, move from town to town in search of religious battlegrounds, calling themselves the "New J-Brigade ... an army of two, her and me. We didn't just show up for big battles at abortion clinics and courthouses that married homosexuals. We specialized in the little scraps with Satan. We were ninja warriors for the Lord, playing Whac-a-Mole with demons wherever they popped up" (10). The play of words and images here shows the excitement experienced from being two little people against the world (visible and otherwise), but is also reminiscent of the militant Christianity typified by "Onward, Christian Soldiers" (Baring-Gould), in which the cross is a weapon of war, and Jesus the conquering general.

Billy finds his foil in Ruah, who is about as far from a white, home-schooled "Whac-a-Mole" Christian as it's possible to get, and who also becomes companion and guide on Billy's spiritual journey. Ruah, a devoted Christian, was almost a divinity student at Princeton Theological Seminary, and he is fluent in scriptures and their interpretations. Ruah's name is not subtle: it is nearly the same word as "Ruach," the Hebrew word for "breath," "wind," or "spirit," and he is spokesperson for a shoe company called "Pneuma," the Greek word for "spirit." His last name, Branch, alludes to John 15:15, in which Jesus provides an analogy for his followers—they are "vines" to his "branches." By twice identifying Ruah with God's spirit, or (in the New Testament) the Holy Ghost, the third person of the Trinity, as well as having him metaphorically attached to Jesus, the narrative invests him with tremendous moral and interpretive authority. Ruah reframes Christianity for Billy through classic emerging terms, as "*relationship* to Christ, not religion" (111, original italics). He also freely mixes the language of baseball and that of Christian vocation in order to frame his own journey towards identity and purpose—he thinks of himself as being on the "D.L. [Disabled List] for T.L. [The Lord]" (114) while he tries to figure out his "calling" (114), and how to respond to his agent's threat to expose his sexual orientation, as well as the coercive "don't ask, don't tell" rules that he sees as governing baseball. Ruah's spiritual metaphors, both playful and deeply spiritual, become catalysts for Billy's own move towards an emerging church mindset, in which Christian faith is not a battle, but a game played for a team owner you'd want as a friend.

The novel, while firmly siding with Ruah and Team Jesus, also allows both Billy and Ruah to comment, with varying levels of irony and awareness, on the entanglements between faith and flash, Christ and consumerism. Billy's visit to the "Feast of Faith Church" found in the "*U-S-Pray Dictionary*" (17) is a knowing send-up of a certain type of evangelical church, one in which Billy finds CCM (Contemporary Christian Music), which is routinely criticized for its vapidity and for elevating emotion over theological rigor; cameras on stage; and, worst of all, packaged communion. Billy's observation that the "The body and blood of Christ should never be served as a Lunchable" (18), paired with Ruah's sincere belief that "Brand Jesus needs a makeover" (111), skewers the mass-produced, consumerist spectacle that can be found in North American megachurches and suggests how deeply implicated consumerist mind frames can be in even genuine desires for intimacy and authenticity. That the Pneuma shoe company does not withdraw Ruah's contract after he comes out, because "Gays buy shoes too" (387), enforces the uneasy alliance between faith and money, while also suggesting that churches might do well to embrace the pithy pragmatism of a Madison Avenue marketing firm.

In setting up Ruah as the closest person to Jesus that Billy has yet encountered, the novel provides Billy with an alternate version of Christianity as well as an alternative to the God of wrath and guerrilla spiritual warfare he inherited from his mother. Ruah's Jesus, like the Jesus of the emerging church, is personal, playful, and meets Billy's desire for authenticity, as evidenced by his distaste towards "Lunchable" Jesus. And yet the novel also shows, perhaps, the limits of the American church's imagination and marketing mindset when it comes to God, gesturing towards the danger of packaging Jesus in an easy-to-swallow meal that may be, at heart, empty calories and junk.[9]

Playful Hermeneutics: Doubt, "Homophobic Scripture" and a "Zigzag" God

Throughout the novel, Billy moves from a fundamentalist understanding of Christianity towards more flexible, contextualized ideas about God and Scripture. He begins the novel relying on shaky methods of interpreting the Bible and hearing from God. The first one is proof-texting, what Ruah will later call "cherry-picking"—taking topical verses out of context and making meaning of them. For several pages, Billy tries to proof-text his status as the bastard son of a man his mom pretended was dead, only to find conflicting verses: "If God was telling me anything it was *I'm on the fence, kid. Your call*" (68). The same thing happens when he tries to employ "one of Mom's providence checks" (20): opening the Bible at a random spot and taking meaning from whatever verse shows up. In this case, he gets the message that *"The truth is like taffy, Billy; you can pull it and stretch it and fold it till it's just how you want"* (20). Later, when a dream, plus a providence check, convinces Billy that he must be gay, an unfazed Ruah introduces Billy to a different kind of textual evidence, using a pornographic magazine to show Billy that he definitely likes girls. Through his own failure to find cut and dried answers, his mother's failure to tell him the truth about his father, and Ruah's (more-profane-than-sacred) guidance, Billy learns to trust other sources than Scripture, or rather his mom's unreliable methods of interpreting Scripture, and to find and accept ambiguity in the Bible.

Early in his journey, Billy reflects, "Christ says it only takes a mustard seed of faith to make you a believer. What He didn't say was the opposite. It only takes a mustard seed of doubt to make you a doubter" (18). But the novel, which affirms ambiguity, also argues for a positive view of doubt and questioning, one consistent with the stance of the emerging church. As Ruah says,

> Jesus freaks love to talk about how powerful their faith is, but wouldn't it be full-on cool if we talked about how powerful *doubts* are? ... Faith is a two-sided coin, and we always tend to look at it believer side-up ... if we spent more time turning the coin and studying the doubt side, and not just by ourselves, but with others, our faith might get stronger. Questions don't disappear if they're ignored; they disappear if they're answered.... I call it witnessing for doubt [110].

Through his explorations of faith and doubt with Ruah, Billy finds his way to a "witness of doubt," the ability to see questions as a form of strength, not weakness.

Billy also learns the value of a good lie—first from Huck, who is constantly fibbing to protect himself and Jim, and then from his father, Richard, who believes that his open and honest rejection of Christianity caused Ruth to cut him out of Billy's life, and then lie to Billy about his death; had Richard simply lied about his atheism, and pretended to remain a believer, Ruth would have allowed him to be a part of Billy's life. Instead, Richard's insistence on the truth led to another lie: Ruth telling Billy his father was dead. Billy, though rightfully furious at his mother for her lies, eventually forgives her, because he comes to understand the reason for her lie: to protect Billy and keep his Christian beliefs intact. Through learning the truth about his father, and through his discovery that Ruth—whose name is so close to "truth," and who has been his primary source of religious truth up to this point—has been telling him a fundamental untruth for his whole life, Billy learns that doubt "in the context of love" (to return to N.T. Wright's phrase)—whether love for a parent or a friend—is a valid hermeneutical option, and that truth is a similarly contextual, flexible proposition.

In addition to the narrative mischiefs of telling a good (or not-so-good) lie, the strategic use of doubt, and the mischief of another kind found in girlie magazines, Billy comes to rely on texts and textual strategies that are explicitly outside approved fundamentalist Christian sources and practices. In another example of the novel's themes being reinforced through intertextual relationships, Ruah introduces Billy to a rabbinic story about birth, in which every Jewish child is touched by an angel on his lip before birth, causing him/her to forget everything they knew about the Torah. As a result, each child spends the rest of his life "relearning what he knew before he was born" (156). While Ruah uses this story as a metaphor for his need to un-learn "homophobic" scriptures, as well as everything he knows about baseball, Billy relates it to his own need to relearn "everything: who Mom was, who my father was, who I was" (161).

At the end of this journey, having both reconnected to his father and facing the reality that Richard is terminally ill, with not long to live, Billy also realizes that he will "spend … the rest of his life re-learning his religion" (378). He says, "[It's] like my dad touched me here, and I've forgotten everything I ever learned. How to be a Christian, how to talk to my mom, how to live, even how to say goodbye" (378). By connecting his father to Ruah's rabbinic story, Billy names his father, an avowed religious skeptic, as the bearer of the transformative angelic touch. Between the Judaic texts, midrashic interpretive methods, and having Billy touched by an atheist, the novel leaves no room for doubt that Billy has come far from his "whack-a-mole" roots, and is in the process of having his identity and faith reshaped.

As Richard helps Billy re-learn Christianity and find a more capacious sense of what the Word of God is or might be, he turns more than once to

Judaism. Richard hides his legacy to Billy, Twain's unfinished story, also known as the "Bad Book," in his *genizah,* a term that comes from "the Hebrew words for 'hiding place.' The Jews never destroy their old scrolls and religious texts when they're worn out. You don't destroy the Word of God, you give it a proper burial in a cave, attic, or even a silo. My *genizah* is a place for something that was, and still may be. That's what the bad book is: a story waiting for resurrection" (361). Billy's Dad, playing the authorial "God" role, gives him the "Bad Book"—an antithesis or alternative to the "Good Book," the Bible. This book, along with all the other books that the novel interweaves, becomes the narrative vehicle for a resurrection and revelation in this life, for Billy finding a new identity and a new kind of faith, and for the temporary resurrection of his believed-dead father. Here, some of the narrative mischief lies in how Billy notes the lines have blurred between God and his father: "It was either the spirit of my father having a little fun with me, or it was God working in His weird way. Mark Twain had put Huck on a raft with a runaway slave, and God, for whatever reason, had put me in a camper with a black dude" (86). As Billy's travels in search of the "Bad Book" lead him to a new relationship with both his fathers—biological and supernatural—even Billy seems to find it obvious that his Dads are having a blast.

In addition to Billy's discovery that God might actually be capable of fun, the narrative mischief extends to teaching Billy that God might be, as Ruah puts it, more "zigzag" than straight. When Billy attempts to "convert" Ruah, via scripture, to the idea that "It's God's will that everyone should be straight" (203), Ruah responds with disgust for "fundies [fundamentalists] like you, and everyone else from the First Church of Cherry-picking. You pick verses that support your narrow view and ignore the big picture. You cut and paste the Bible till it's as shallow as a rack of greeting cards. I mean, I keep waiting for the ultimate cherry-picker's Bible: *The Good Book for Dummies!*" (178). Ruah goes further, however, than calling out "fundie" readers of the Bible; he implicates the Bible itself, calling it "homophobic scripture" (178). This usage implies it's not just homophobic readers at fault, but that the Biblical text is inseparable from its own homophobic aims. On the other hand, Ruah is able to deconstruct every verse that Billy quotes at him, to argue either that the verse is in fact *not* a condemnation of homosexuality, or at least is only a culturally-specific one that has no contemporary validity. Ruah also explains his subsequent decision to come out by saying, "The Bible made me do it" (390), which has exactly the opposite implication, that it's the Bible that has moved him from being "a slave to silence" (390) to freedom.

Ruah also suggests, via a reading of the book of Jonah that God—at least the "wrathed up" one of the "Old Testy"—was *once* homophobic, but that "along the way, God changes his mind" and "has re-thought His homosexuals-as-abominations thing," opting to throw a "curveball of compassion" (316) instead of condemnation. Rather than giving a definite interpretation of the Bible or God as homophobic or not, Ruah seems to lean away from the unchanging Scripture and God of fundamentalist Christian thought towards a God who can grow and change, to become more compassionate, less judgmental. Although this viewpoint doesn't absolve God from initially homophobic pronouncements or their consequences, it places Ruah squarely in the camp of the emergent church, with its belief that the Spirit can "tweak" how Scripture is interpreted and applied in the world, and in placing the onus on homophobic cultures and interpreters rather than on the Bible itself.[10,11]

Ruah also links God to a fluid version of human sexuality, one currently modeled by the Kinsey Scale, which sees sexual behavior and attraction as existing along a continuum.[12] As one of his self-described "dumb theories" (347), Ruah holds that "the sexual urge is like any other human appetite: it can change over a lifetime," and that "every man and woman walking the earth has it in 'em to be a zigzag-sexual" (327). Furthermore, Ruah argues, "if we're made in God's image, and He *is* a zigzag God, then we're capable of zigging and zagging right along with Him" (347). Zigzag humans, Ruah believes, mirror God's own zigzag nature, his ability to change and express compassion in new ways. Ultimately Billy, too, comes to believe in God's "zigzag loving-kindness" (4).

After establishing God's zigzag character—in essence, queering God—Ruah further defies homophobic interpretations by positioning himself as Jesus, saying, "If Jesus can be flayed and nailed to the cross, I can endure a few extra knockdowns, beaners, and high spikes" (388) from homophobic teammates and competitors. A common strategy for proponents of LGBT inclusion in churches is to point out that Jesus strongly identified with the outcasts of society (Wink 1082). Ruah is taking that strategy even further, making himself analogous to Jesus: the innocent scapegoat for the sin of homophobia in baseball, and through which baseball as a sport may be redeemed.

In an interview, Meehl mentions pressure from "Some who were in position to influence the book as it was being written" ("Taking the 'Old'") to cut the religious discussions between Billy and Ruah. However, says Meehl,

> for the kids who might read the book who actually have a fair amount in common with Billy (especially regarding the religious beliefs they've been fed) I wanted those discussions to be there for them to maybe experience a little eyeopening [*sic*] and begin to question some of the hellfire and brimstone scripture interpretations they had been exposed to. In fact, one of the undercurrents of the book is that the Bible— any Holy Book—is a very plastic thing, open to radically different interpretations ["Taking the 'Old'"].

Meehl portrays Billy's coming-to-terms with the "plasticity" of the Bible and his distancing from his mother's beliefs as a key part of his identity formation—coming to know and being shaped by both his physical father and his "Hilarious Father" (Billy's way of expressing the sense of humor he never knew God had), while also accepting his mother for who she is, a woman who was abused by her father and a patriarchal religious system, and as a result learned "Life was to be spent trembling at the feet of a higher power" (383).

Reconciling these different parental figures—his fundamentalist, rule-bound mother and his atheist father, who believes that "God" or "gods" should be treated at best "as the most fantastic friends ever invented by humankind" (383)—with an assist from "the Spirit" in the form of Ruah, allows Billy to change from a self-identified "faith-up, born-again Christian" to a "Doubt-up-Learn-again Christian" (396), but also to believe in his own ability to "put [himself] together again" (395).[13] This suggests that for Billy, unlike for his mother, faith doesn't mean self-abnegation; instead, it goes hand in hand with a stronger sense of identity.

Billy makes it clear at the end of the novel that he hasn't "arrived" yet when it comes to faith, and the way that Billy and his father, Richard, understand the controversial end of *Huck Finn* reinforces that Billy remains a work-in-progress. Billy sees Huck as regressing at the end of his story, "totally back-slid to treating [Jim] like a 'nigger'" again (381). However, his dad argues that "'it's written that way because Twain was setting up a sequel.... You see,' he went on, 'at the end of *Huck Finn,* Jim, the slave, is free, but Huck, the boy, is still a captive, a slave to Tom's foolishness. The story of Huck and Jim isn't over until *both* of them are set free.... Twain's sequel is the story of Huck, Tom, and Jim lighting out for Indian Territory and Huck winning *his* freedom ... from Tom, 'sivilization, and Christianity'" (381–2). Richard appears to suggest that Billy will not attain true freedom—the true end to his story—until he rejects Christianity altogether.

However, Richard also seems to qualify that statement. He tells Billy, "'in our world, on the brink of a war in which the feuding sides both hold books of mass delusion in one hand and weapons of mass destruction in the other, the story of Huck's escape from the dark side of Christianity is more important than ever'" (382).[14,15] On the one hand, Christianity is a "book of mass delusion"; on the other hand, perhaps it's only Christianity's "dark side"—its tendency toward holy wars, fanaticism, and oppression of all sorts—from which we need to escape. By jettisoning certainty for compassion and a posture of learning and uncertainty, Billy is "emerging" both as a Christian, and as a person navigating his personal history and his faith on the way to a more independent identity and self.

In its very title, *You Don't Know About Me* identifies itself as a narrative about coming to new knowledge, for all the "yous" and "mes" whose journeys are recounted. Through the novel's careful use of layer upon layer of intertextual relationships and resonances, Billy gets to know himself, his mother, his biological father and his "Hilarious Father." Billy and Ruah get to know each other, and Ruah constructs an identification with Jesus that gives him the courage to come out, thus allowing his teammates and the public to know him better as well. And Ruth gets to know her changed son, who returns from his treasure hunt arguably a stronger Christian, because his faith, while missing some of the bedrock certainty he once held, is now his, able to withstand questions and doubts, and even to thrive as a result of them. Both Billy and Ruah, at the novel's close, can be read as prototypical emerging Christians, employing post-critical hermeneutics of love and doubt, embracing mystery and uncertainty, and working through theological conflicts and quandaries with humor and grace.

Suck It Up *and* Suck It Up and Die

Unlike in *YDKAM*, the main characters in the *Suck It Up* novels are not Christian, nor is the narrative overtly concerned with Christianity. Neither teen vampire Morning McCobb nor his human girlfriend Portia express any interest in religion for themselves. But, as in *YDKAM*, Meehl's vampires explore the relationship between its protagonist and his opposing parental figures: in Morning's case, both vampires, one a Christian holy warrior turned pacifist, and the other a power-mad vampire with a penchant for Satanic melodrama. Morning also has a mother figure, whose relationship with Morning is much more straightforwardly supportive and nurturing than Ruth's is to Billy, even if she is a 100-year-old vampire hiding in plain sight as a nun. All three of these parental figures come from Christian typology, even if their ultimate relationship with Christianity turns out to be one of misdirection, disguise, and revision, with Christian symbols and imagery ultimately used to support a secular, humanist critique of violence, abuse, and inequality, and socially progressive ideologies of inclusion, tolerance, and acceptance.

The *Suck It Up* novels, which follow the efforts of peaceful vampires to live openly in human society, deploy the trope of vampirism as a metaphor for gay rights, as well as for civil rights. The IV League, an organization dedicated to the "coming out" of vampires into human society who have sworn off killing, organizes their own Vampire Pride Parade and "Worldwide Out Day" (*SUD* 9); and the Leaguers argue that "Given America's tradition of welcoming all races, creeds, and colors, it followed that the United States should be the first to embrace a people of different mortality and dietary habits"

(*SUD* 9).[16] Luther Birnam, the League's leader, is a former Knight Templar who once fought in the Crusades, and his name can be read as alluding to Reformation leader Martin Luther as well as to civil rights and religious leader Martin Luther King, Jr. Birnam tells his story to Morning in a way that reinforces these associations:

> When I saw Christian knights siding with our Muslim enemies so they could fight and kill my Christian brothers, God appeared to me in a dream. He told me the Crusades were no longer a holy war; they had become, like all wars, an unholy one over land, wealth, and power. God told me to lay down my sword and become a prophet of peace. So I became a pacifist. I campaigned for peace between all the warring parties, whether they were Christian or Muslim [*SUD* 188].

Luther has actually lived what Billy's father, Richard, in *YDKAM*, warned of abstractly: the dangers of feuding sides each with "books of mass delusion." (While Richard doesn't name names, given contemporary geopolitical events, Christian and Muslim conflicts are likely candidates for his critique.) Captured during a failed campaign and condemned to die with his fellow Templars, Luther was saved by a vampire who "didn't believe in taking innocent lives," knew Luther's reputation for peacemaking, and gave him the choice to be turned or die. In response, Luther literally dies to his violent Knight Templar existence forged in the clash of religions. He instead focuses on bringing "peace between vampires and mortals" (*SUD* 189) and, in allusion to Dante's *Inferno,* on guiding "vampires from the dark wood, the *selva obscura,* and into the light" (*SUD* 14) of the League and living "out" among mortals.

As a direct result of this transformation, Luther finds his way back to mortal life, discovering through his own experience that the cure for vampirism is for a vampire to pursue the dreams he or she had as a formerly living person. In turn, regaining his mortality and facing "the long, sweet stumble to the end" (*SUD* 236) causes Luther to "acquire ... a thing called faith" (*SUD* 236). Although there's nothing to indicate that he's given up his faith in the God who once appeared to him in a dream, Luther states that his faith at this moment is in Morning and Rachel, and in a future where "somehow Leaguers, and Lifers [mortals], are going to rise above the Loners [evil vampires] of the world" (*SUD* 236). For Luther, whose identity as a Christian warrior led to unholy killing and disappointment, continuing his God-given role as a pacifist ultimately leads him to mortality and to a more humanist faith in his protégé and in the future.

Just as both God and his vampire father directed Luther towards peace and mercy, so Luther plays a paternal role with Morning, both as the head of the IV League and in handpicking Morning to carry out his mission of reconciliation between vampires and humans. In this, Sister Flora, the head nun at St. Giles Group Home for Boys, helps Luther. Sr. Flora is a secret vampire, over 100 years old. She is also "the closest thing Morning had ever had to a mother" (*SUD* 41), both as his de facto foster mother, and as the person indirectly responsible for his vampirism. (She sent him to a host family one Thanksgiving, only to have the whole family attacked.) Both Luther and Sr. Flora's construction as paternal and maternal figures, respectively, resist simplistic characterizations of good and evil. Sr. Flora, like Huck and Richard Albright, is another one of Meehl's potentially holy liars. She presides over St. Giles, a name that links her not only to the word "guile" but also to the patron saint of cripples. (Not coincidentally, Leaguers often refer to vampirism as merely another type of disability, deserving of compassion and accommodation.) Unlike with Luther, who seemed to have a genuine religious identification and experience with God, Sister Flora's "Christian" role is only a disguise, chosen because of its convenience: "A nun can look the same age for a decade or two and nobody notices" (*SU* 269). Yet her very real social activism—she is an IV Leaguer in cahoots with Luther—places her in a long tradition of ordained and lay Catholics such as Dorothy Day.

The procession of characters connected to Christian religious orders continues with Ikor DeThanatos, whose name loosely translates as "blood god of death." DeThanatos is Morning's blood sire, the one who created him by accidentally backwashing in his jugular. He leads a group of rogue vampires who are proud of their "*inhumanity*" (*SUD* 264, italics from original), relentlessly amoral and determined to kill all, vampire or human, who oppose their rule. DeThanatos celebrates his first thousand years by feeding on a "bleating lamb" transfigured from his own arm (*SUD* 262) and referring to himself as "the wolf lying down with the lamb"—a ritual that is a perversion of Christology (Christ as a sinless lamb whose spilled blood leads to new life and redemption) and a mockery of an Old Testament prophecy about peace (Isaiah 11:6). Not coincidentally, DeThanatos dresses as a Friar when he hires a hit man to kill Morning. He is Luther's opposite—the dark, Satanic, warmongering father who revels in his inhumanity and immortality, instead of the Godly, pacifist one who builds bridges across religions and finds hope in mortals and mortality. Morning—unsurprisingly, given his name—chooses to ally himself with the good father, not the homicidal "Friar."[17]

In spite of the novel's ambivalence towards the Crusades, the Maltese cross, a symbol of the Knights of St. John and their heroism and self-sacrifice in a battle against the Saracens in the First Crusade, plays an important role in Morning's journey back to mortality. The cross is a gift from Luther to Morning; it is also a reminder of a foster father, one of the heroic firefighters who died at Ground Zero on September 11th while trying to save others, and a symbol of Morning's dream to become a firefighter in his honor. An old New York City firefighter, who gives Morning the unexpected chance to join the fire academy, explains that for a firefighter, the Maltese cross symbolizes "three things. He lives in courage, a ladder rung from death. He lives knowing he may lay down his life to save others. And he lives knowing his life is protected by all firefighters. That's the code. When you live by it, you're a knight at the fire table" (SU 123). Morning's desire to join this brotherhood of those committed to Christ-like sacrifice is explicitly approved by Luther, who gives him permission to become the first vampire "to resurrect the dreams that died" (*SU 226*) along with his human life, which is the key to eventually becoming mortal again. And the Maltese cross is also what prevents Morning from fully succumbing to blood lust and killing Portia when tempted by DeThanatos; he's brought back to himself by the sight of the cross, a "silent accuser" (SU 286) covered by the "crimson splatter" (SU 286) of Portia's blood—a phrase that calls to mind traditional hymns about the crucifixion.[18] While Morning himself has no religious beliefs, the Maltese Cross' Christian origin and symbolism is important to the novel's construction of heroism, which in turn is linked to the restoration and preservation of Morning's humanity, both real and metaphorical, against the amoral inhumanity of DeThanatos and his ilk.

While freely using Christian symbolism and figures to enforce characterizations of good and evil, the *Suck It Up* books playfully deconstruct the stereotypical masculinity and patriarchy with which Christianity is often associated. Morning is a "blood virgin" (*SUD* 29) and a "hemo-intolerant" (*SU* 32) "vegan vampire" (*SU* 317) who drinks a soy blood substitute called Blood Lite. Halfway through the second novel, he wonders whether his feminist girlfriend broke up with him because he's not masculine enough. Even the way Morning was turned—his super villain vampire "parent" accidentally burping / backwashing vampire virus into Morning's neck—smacks of the opposite of virility. Then, too, vampire "life" and religion is centered around a Matriarch Tree that lives in a sacred forest of bristlecone pines that "*Mortals* call.... Patriarch Grove [but] *Vampires* call ... the Mother Forest" (*SU* 127, my emphasis). In other words, when it comes to religion, vampires are more progressive than humans.

Similarly, the *Suck It Up* novels have little use for conservative Christian tropes about virginity, sex, and gender. Portia, Morning's girlfriend, is not just a "virgin who's lost her heart to love" (*SU* 308); she's also the character "who revives [Morning from death] with her own blood, then saves [him] by staking the badass vampire" (*SU* 314) trying to kill him. Nor is Portia overly concerned with maintaining her virginity—quite the opposite, in fact, as she and Morning plan to have sex for the first time as a way to celebrate the world *not* ending in a vampire apocalypse. Portia laughingly names herself as the tempting, "sinful Eve" to Morning's Adam, waiting for him "outside the garden with a bushel of apples" (*SUD* 254). The two of them refer to Morning's trajectory of mortal to vampire to "re-mort" as a "*rise* to immortality" and "*fall* back to mortality" (*SUD* 254), with Morning having been "kicked out of the garden of immortality" (*SUD* 254) when he transitions back to human. Contrary to the expected implications of a fall, of course, both mortality and sex with his girlfriend are exactly what Morning wants. Here, Meehl riffs on a reverse-fall motif that could be straight out of Phillip Pullman's *His Dark Materials* Trilogy, which also undermined the relationship between sexual experience and a "fall" into sin as constructed by John Milton's *Paradise Lost* and C.S. Lewis's *Chronicles of Narnia*. In Pullman's novels, "Sexual love … saves the world" (Miller); in Meehl's vampire novels, sex is the reward rather than the vehicle.[19]

That sexual experience is framed as a natural and celebratory part of teen romance and life, and that Portia's virginity, once it has outlived its usefulness as a plot device, is nothing to be ossified or obsessed over, is consistent with the novels' narratively mischievous use of Christian characters, tropes, and symbols without being invested in Christianity itself. Although the novels uphold ideals with Christian roots, such as sacrifice, love, brotherhood, and reconciliation, they ultimately value not immortality or a spiritual afterlife, but a fully human morality lived in pursuit of human dreams. Christianity is used to construct a secular humanist critique of ideologies of violence, abuse, and inequality, whether religiously motivated or otherwise, as well as in service of an ethos of inclusion, peace, and acceptance among those who are different, whatever their species, sexual preference, religion, or preference in blood substitute.

Conclusion

You Don't Know About Me, *Suck It Up*, and *Suck It Up and Die* are novels full of narrative mischief, deconstructing sexist and homophobic interpretations of the Bible while deploying ninjas for Jesus, vampire nuns, Spirit-filled baseball players, murderous friars, pacifist knights, and badass virgins with sexual agency, as well as engaging with trends, language, and conversations in emerging Christianity. As Billy turns to a doubtfully loving relationship with God, and Morning basks in the light of his renewed morality, Meehl uses intertextuality and humor and subverts expectations and stereotypes in order to implicate certain kinds of Christians and modes of Christianity in life-denying, injustice-perpetuating beliefs and interpretive practices, while also making room for a more "generous" Christianity, with a hermeneutic that allows for contextualization and questioning. His novels refigure Christian tropes and symbols—resurrection, faith, doubt, witness, the cross—to create space for identity formation, love, life, and reconciliation, and to hold out the playful possibility of a "zigzagged" God with a capacity for compassion, friendship and growth.

NOTES

1. The cast of leaders, as in many movements, shifts periodically and is somewhat contested. Rob Bell is regarded in even some emerging Christian circles as no longer Christian due to controversial statements about hell (not to mention his work with Oprah), although Bell himself maintains his commitment to orthodoxy (Bell, interview with Aghapour and Schulson). Mark Driscoll was forced to step down from his megachurch Mars Hill in 2015 after a series of leadership crises and misogynistic rants, though he has since resurfaced as a church planter in Arizona (Shellnut and Lee).

2. Contemporary evangelicals in North America are characterized by "a broad unity based on commitment to the Bible as its religious authority and on the gospel of Christ's saving work" ("Evangelicalism." Dictionary of Christianity in America, 416), with post-evangelicals being those who have moved away from evangelical expressions of Christianity for a variety of reasons explored in McLaren's book. In November 2016, white evangelicals played a significant role in electing Donald Trump to the U.S. presidency, with widely reported internal rifts among evangelicals over his candidacy and election, and much debate going forward about whether evangelicalism can survive its association with Trump. For an attempt to defend and preserve the term "evangelical," see Theological Seminary's "Post Election Evangelical" (Labberton and Mouw); for an argument that "a new movement is needed to replace it," see "The Evangelicalism of Old White Men is Dead" (Campolo and Claiborne).

3. Tony Jones, author of *The Church is Flat: The Relational Ecology of the Emerging Church Movement*, says his research shows the emerging church as 93 percent white.

4. For a more comprehensive description of the Emerging Church movement, see McKnight, "Five Streams of the Emerging Church."

5. Meehl, "Behind the Story," http://brianmeehl.com/the-books/you-dont-know-about-me/genesis/.

6. Fundamentalism refers to an early 20th Century movement "to defend orthodox Protestant Christianity against the challenges of theological liberalism, higher criticism of the Bible, and other modernisms judged to be harmful to traditional faith" ("Fundamentalism," Dictionary of Christianity in America, 461). It is associated with the rise of the "Moral Majority" and religious right in American politics, and is characterized by social and religious conservatism and conformity, and an insistence on God's "'original church' described in scripture" (Ault, Jr. 207).

7. Meehl, "Behind the Story."

8. That unfinished story, "Huck Finn and Tom Sawyer Among the Indians," can be read at the *Mark Twain Project Online*.

9. This, in fact, is a common critique of the emerging church, one laid out in detail in Kevin DeYoung and Ted Kluck's *Why We're Not Emergent (By Two Guys Who Should Be)*.

10. For a wider-ranging discussion of homosexuality in light of Biblical sexual ethics as a whole, see Walter Wink, "Biblical Perspectives on Homosexuality." Wink's famous conclusion is that "*There is no biblical sex ethic*. The Bible knows only a love ethic" (1082, italics from original). For a dissenting viewpoint, see Richard Hays's chapter on "Homosexuality" in *The Moral Vision of the New Testament*, which argues for a comprehensive (i.e. not "cherry picked") Biblical witness of heteronormativity.

11. Because Meehl's book came out in 2011, it seems to anticipate arguments made in favor of LGBT-inclusion by several evangelical or emerging leaders and scholars in the time since. Two notable books in that category are Matthew Vines' *God and the Gay Christian: The Biblical Case in Support of Same-Sex Relationships*, and David Gushee's *Changing Our Mind*. Gushee is particularly concerned with the high suicide and depression rate among LGBT teens, and names their well being as a key motivation for his advocacy within the church (Gushee, "Reconciling Evangelical Christians"). For current controversies and developments in the Catholic and mainline church, see "Bishop McElroy Calls for a Practical 'Apology' to L.G.B.T. Catholics" (Clarke); "[UMC] Bishops approve plan for a sexuality panel" (Hahn); and "Welby apologizes for persecution on the grounds of sexuality" (Davies and Schjonberg). The final article, which references the 2016 Anglican Primates Meeting, gives

a sense of some country- or culture-specific differences in the Anglican Communion regarding LGBT inclusion.

12. For more details about the Kinsey Scale, as well as other complementary models, see the Kinsey Institute's website.

13. Billy's acceptance of "zigzag" sexuality also brings him in line with the growing support for same-sex marriage in the United States, primarily among the religiously unaffiliated, but also among Christians. According to the Pew Research Center, 58 percent of Catholics and 64 percent of white mainline Protestants now support same-sex marriage. Among black Protestants and white evangelical Protestants, the numbers remain lower, although they show some growth ("Changing Attitudes on Gay Marriage: Attitudes on Same-Sex Marriage by Religious Affiliation").

14. For a discussion on the ending of *Huck Finn* and Huck's "backsliding" into blatant racism, including possible strategies for encouraging productive dialogue in a classroom composed of white and African American students, see Kay Puttock, "Many Responses to the Many Voices of Huckleberry Finn." Regarding Huck's conversion to "an Indian religion" and freedom from Christianity, it may be helpful to keep in mind that most of Twain's ideas about American Indians seem to have come from Dodge's blatantly racist source text, and thus Twain was probably not the best person to comment, either positively or negatively, on their religious beliefs. (In his story fragment, Twain gives his Sioux characters names like "Hog Face" (44) and "Man-afraid-of-his-Mother-in-law" (45), and was "especially eager" to refute Fenimore Cooper's ideas about "noble savage[s]" (Explanatory Notes (50).)

15. See Thomas Weinandy's argument that *Huck Finn*, although written by a known agnostic, represents Twain's "understanding of salvation history" (41). It should be noted that even Weinandy does not appear to expect anyone beside himself to take his argument seriously.

16. Using the rhetoric of civil rights, Morning is hailed as a "vampire version of Rosa Parks" (SU156) or "the Jackie Robinson of the Vampire League" (SU 199). The IV League also wants to make marriage between vampires and humans legal, likely a commentary on past U.S. laws against miscegenation as well as on gay marriage. *YDKAM* also links LGBT rights and civil rights, though in a more nuanced way. Ruah's hero, Warren Sandel, is the pitcher who gave Jackie Robinson his first professional baseball hit. And during the press conference in which Ruah comes out as gay, a reporter asks him if he wants to be "the gay Jackie Robinson: the first active player to break the gay barrier" (388). Ruah demurs, saying "Jackie broke a real barrier: skin color. There's no 'gay barrier.' We're already in the game, hiding in plain sight" (389).

In an 2013 interview about *YDKAM*, Meehl said that the "comparison to Twain's dealing with slavery and racism in *AHF*" and the "backlash against gays that seemed to be taking place just a few years ago is a bit of a stretch" ("Taking the 'Old'"), and Ruah's statement also downplays that comparison. In contrast, recent legal and legislative controversies over LGBT issues (marriage, transgender restroom access, religious freedom laws) have been consistently framed by LGBT rights organizers as questions of civil rights on par with slavery. This rhetorical move has received pushback from political conservatives and evangelicals (Williams, June 26, 2015), as well as from leaders in African American churches. (See the May 14, 2014 Amicus Brief filed by a coalition of black pastors against efforts in Michigan to legalize same-sex marriage.)

17. Morning and Portia also refer to another, unfortunately, well-known Catholic religious type: the abusive priest. They have a tongue-in-cheek conversation about a gender-neutral word for "brotherhood" and whether re-labeling Catholic Priests as "Neuter" instead of "Father" would solve the Church's problem with pedophilia (SUD 15).

18. For example, from "Jesus Paid It All": "Sin had left a crimson stain / He washed it white as snow."

19. Christian purity culture is another area where conservative Christian cultural norms are being challenged in both liberal and conservative Christian circles. See Bromleigh McCleneghan's *Good Christian Sex: Why Chastity Isn't the Only Option—and Other Things the Bible Says About Sex*, described by the mainline Protestant author as an attempt to "make theological sense of pleasure," and a July 10, 2016 interview with evangelical relationship

guru Josh Harris, addressing critiques of his "courtship" book, *I Kissed Dating Goodbye* (interview by Martin).

Works Cited

Ault, Jr., James M. *Spirit and Flesh: Life in a Fundamentalist Baptist Church*. New York: Knopf, 2004.

Baring-Gould, S. "Onward, Christian Soldiers." *Hymnary.Org*. http://www.hymnary.org/text/onward_christian_soldiers_marching_as.

Bell, Rob. *"As Orthodox as They Come": A Backstage Conversation with Rob Bell*. By Andrew Aghapour and Michael Schulson. *Religion Dispatches*. August 14, 2015. http://religiondispatches.org/as-orthodox-as-they-come-a-backstage-conversation-with-rob-bell/.

"Brief of the Coalition of Black Pastors from Detroit, Outstate Michigan, and Ohio as Amici Curiae Supporting Defendants-Appellants." *Huffington Post*. May 14, 2014. http://www.huffingtonpost.com/2014/05/15/black-pastors-gay-marriage-michigan_n_5332496.html.

Campolo, Tony, and Shane Claiborne. "The Evangelicalism of Old White Men Is Dead." *New York Times*. November 29, 2016. https://www.nytimes.com/2016/11/29/opinion/the-evangelicalism-of-old-white-men-is-dead.html?_r=1.

"Changing Attitudes on Gay Marriage: Attitudes on Same-Sex Marriage by Religious Affiliation." *Pew Research Center*. May 12, 2016. http://www.pewforum.org/2016/05/12/changing-http://www.pewforum.org/2016/05/12/changing-attitudes-on-gay-marriage/.

Clarke, Kevin. "Bishop Mcelroy Calls for a Practical 'Apology' to L.G.B.T. Catholics." *America: The National Catholic Review*. July 7, 2016. http://www.americamagazine.org/faith/2016/07/07/bishop-mcelroy-calls-practical-apology-lgbt-catholics.

Davies, Matthew, and Mary Frances Schjonberg. "Welby Apologizes for Persecution on the Grounds of Sexuality: Anglican Primates Meeting Concludes with Commitment to Walk Together." *Episcopal News Service*. January 15, 2016. http://episcopaldigitalnetwork.com/ens/2016/01/15/welby-apologizes-for-persecution-on-the-grounds-of-sexuality/.

DeYoung, Kevin, and Ted Kluck. *Why We're Not Emergent (By Two Guys Who Should Be)*. Chicago: Moody Publishers, 2008.

"Fundamentalism." In *Dictionary of Christianity in America*, 463–464. InterVarsity Press, 1990.

Gushee, David. *Changing Our Mind*. Canton, MI: Read the Spirit Books, 2014.

Gushee, David. "Reconciling Evangelical Christianity with Our Sexual Minorities: Reframing the Biblical Discussion." *Journal of the Society of Christian Ethics* 35, no. 2 (Fall/Winter 2015): 141–158.

Hahn, Heather. "Bishops Approve Plan for Sexuality Panel." *United Methodist Church*. July 25, 2016. http://www.umc.org/news-and-media/bishops-approve-plan-for-sexuality-panel.

Hall, Elvina M. "Jesus Paid It All." *Hymnary.Org*. http://www.hymnary.org/text/i_hear_the_savior_say_thy_strength_indee.

Harris, Josh. *Former Evangelical Pastor Rethinks His Approach to Courtship*. By Rachel Martin. *NPR*. July 10, 2016. http://www.npr.org/2016/07/10/485432485/former-evangelical-pastor-rethinks-his-approach-to-courtship.

Hayes, Richard B. "Homosexuality." In *The Moral Vision of the New Testament: A Contemporary Introduction to New Testament Ethics*, 379–406. San Francisco: HarperCollins, 1996.

Jones, Tony. "How White Is the Emerging Church?" *Patheos*. May 8, 2012. http://www.patheos.com/blogs/tonyjones/2012/05/08/how-white-is-the-emerging-church/.

"The Kinsey Scale." *Kinsey Institute*. https://www.kinseyinstitute.org/research/publications/kinsey-scale.php.

Laberton, Mark, and Richard Mouw. "Post-Election Evangelical: A Statement from Mark Labberton and Richard Mouw." *Fuller Theological Seminary*. November 14, 2016. http://fuller.edu/communication/post-election-evangelical—a-statement-from-mark-labberton-and-richard-mouw/.

McClaren, Brian. *A Generous Orthodoxy*. Grand Rapids, MI: Zondervan, 2004.

McCleneghan, Bromleigh. *Good Christian Sex: Why Chastity Isn't the Only Option—And Other Things the Bible Says About Sex*. San Francisco: HarperOne, 2016.

McKnight, Scott. "Five Streams of the Emerging Church." *Christianity Today*. January 19, 2007. http://www.christianitytoday.com/ct/2007/february/11.35.html.

Meehl, Brian. "Behind the Story." http://brianmeehl.com/the-books/you-dont-know-about-me/genesis/.

Meehl, Brian. *Suck It Up*. New York: Delacorte Books For Young Readers, 2008.

Meehl, Brian. *Suck It Up and Die*. New York: Delacorte Books For Young Readers, 2012.

Meehl, Brian. *Taking the "Old" and Making It "New": Commonalities in Young Adult Adaptation Literature*. By Kaitlin Slaughter. Longwood University, April 1, 2013. www.longwood.edu/staff/miskecjm/446slaughter.htm.

Meehl, Brian. *You Don't Know About Me*. New York: Delacorte Press, 2011.

Miller, Laura. "Far from Narnia: Phillip Pullman's Secular Fantasy for Children." *The New Yorker*. December 26, 2005. http://www.newyorker.com/magazine/2005/12/26/far-from-narnia.

Puttock, Kay. "Many Responses to the Many Voices of Huckleberry Finn." *The Lion and the Unicorn* 16, no. 2 (June 1992): 77–82.

Shellnutt, Kate and Lee, Morgan. "Mark Driscoll Resigns from Mars Hill." *Christianity Today*. October 15, 2014. http://www.christianitytoday.com/ct/2014/october-web-only/mark-driscoll-resigns-from-mars-hill.html.

Twain Mark. "Huck Finn and Tom Sawyer Among the Indians and Other Unfinished Stories." *Mark Twain Project Online*. 2007–2016. http://www.marktwainproject.org/xtf/view?docId=works/MTDP10360.xml;style=work;brand=mtp.

Vines, Matthew. *God and the Gay Christian: The Biblical Case in Support of Same-Sex Relationships*. New York: Convergent Books, 2014.

Weinandy, Thomas G. "Huckleberry Finn and the Adventures of God." *Logos: A Journal of Catholic Thought and Culture* 6, no. 1 (Winter 2003): 41–42.

Williams, Joseph P. "Thomas: No Link Between Civil Rights and Gay Rights." *US News and World Report*. June 26, 2015. http://www.usnews.com/news/articles/2015/06/26/thomas-no-link-between-civil-rights-and-gay-rights.

Wink, Walter. "Biblical Perspectives on Homosexuality." *Christian Century*. November 7, 1979. www.reconcilingworks.org/wpcontent/uploads/2010/01/downloads_resources_003_Homosexuality_and_the_Bible-Wink.pdf.

The Book Worlds of Nikki Grimes

An Invitation to Dialogic Reading

Susan Leigh Brooks

After Nikki Grimes won the Coretta Scott King award in 2003 for *Bronx Masquerade*, she published a pair of novels with distinctly Christian themes. Coretta Scott King Honor Book *Dark Sons* presents the Biblical teenager Ishmael and contemporary Christian Sam in a novel in verse. Both characters are religiously devout and have been abandoned by their fathers. Ishmael lives in a household where he had been Abraham's favored son. The book follows Ishmael's experience of being supplanted by his half-brother Isaac and finally being ousted from his home, while contemporary character Sam, the only son of Christian parents, struggles as his father abandons him and his mother and marries another woman who gives birth to Sam's half-brother, David.

A Girl Named Mister, also written in free verse, is told in the voices of the Biblical Mary, mother of Jesus, and contemporary teenager Mister dealing with the implications of unexpected pregnancy. Mary the mother of Jesus is an unmarried teenager who, even though her pregnancy has occurred through the Holy Spirit, fears the repercussions of the pregnancy in her relationships and religious life. The contemporary character, Mister, also finds herself pregnant and must negotiate the reactions of her religious community. In each book, Grimes follows a similar format, writing the voices of these main characters, sometimes alternating between voices and sometimes creating short groups of poems in the voice of one character and then moving the reader to the voice of another with a new group of poems.

The plots of these stories are well-known tropes, both in young adult literature and in the collection of Biblical narratives. However, these books complicate assumptions about religion in books for young people, representing a significant historical shift. In an examination of some of the early works of American literature for young people, the 19th century Sunday school curriculum, C.A. MacGregor cited them as documents which "highlight the narrow dimensions of religiosity deemed acceptable for presentation to an audience of children" (446). The Sunday school curriculum prepared by evangelical Christians to convert children, evidenced adults (usually parents) making religious decisions for children, who were primarily viewed as wards who should be sheltered from difficulty or complexity (MacGregor 447). A century later, in the late 20th century, the opposite was often true. Religion was not favorably presented. Realistic books for teenagers often portrayed evangelical Christianity as oppressive (Trousdale 63) or as a constraint that must be shed to truly find oneself (Werner and Riga 3). These two contrasting approaches both invite a straightforward reading.

In a postsecular world, however, these one-dimensional assumptions and binaries do not serve readers. Readers must be open to the nuanced and sophisticated view of Christianity as presented in Grimes's works. They must also be willing to enter into the worlds of the characters—worlds which have been founded on long standing religious assumptions and traditions—and make an effort to understand what living in those worlds might be like. In the introduction to this collection, Corrigan discusses this pluralism as a descriptor of postsecularism, where individuals are choosing not only to embrace or not embrace particular religions but also choosing particular aspects of established religions that they reject or embrace (Section 2). A postsecular reading of these texts reinforces the idea that the religious and secular have always co-existed, and have far reaching influences into the worlds of characters and readers. Bakhtin's concepts of heteroglossia and dialogism can help readers see why, Postsecular thinking, guided by Bakhtin's concepts of heteroglossia and dialogism can help readers embrace this kind of reading, allowing them to enter into the experiences of characters who live in faith.

Heteroglossia can provide a way of understanding forces at work within a text. At times it is difficult to write about religion well because it permeates the lives of both characters and readers—so much so that it becomes transparent. Literary philosopher Michael Bakhtin's work invites readers to become more conscious of the many forces at work both in the text and the reader. In his foundational essay, "Discourse in the Novel," Bakhtin explains heteroglossia as the way in which one spoken word or concept (an utterance) is attached to all of the other ways in which this utterance has been used in the past and the future.

> The linguistic significance of a given utterance is understood against the background of language, while its actual meaning is understood against the background of other

concrete utterances on the same theme, a background made up of contradictory opinions, points of view, and value judgments—that is, precisely that background that, as we see, complicates the path of any word toward its object ["Discourse" 281].

Heteroglossia recognizes the ways that texts speak to each other and uniquely accounts for this. In his introduction to *The Dialogic Imagination*, Bakhtin scholar Michael Holquist explains why this concept can be helpful to postsecular readers, explaining "This extraordinary sensitivity to the immense plurality of experience more than anything else distinguishes Bakhtin from other moderns who have been obsessed with language" (Dialogic Imagination Intro xx). Heteroglossia, however, is not an easy explanation. The plurality of heteroglossia is in tension with the unity of the novel. Bakhtin argues that the novel is a form in which many voices are held in balance, a destructive force in a world of tidy genre packages, as Holquist summarizes:

> Other genres are constituted by a set of formal features for fixing language that pre-exist any specific utterance within the genre. Language, in other words, is assimilated to form. The novel, by contrast, seeks to shape its form to languages; it has a completely different relationship to languages form other genres since it constantly experiments with new shapes in order to display the variety and immediacy of speech diversity [*Dialogic Imagination* xxix].

Heteroglossia is certainly present in postsecular Christianity when the Bible serves as a sacred utterance, but is translated and interpreted in innumerable ways over time to incorporate languages and cultural assumptions that invoke a multitude of readings. Grimes's novels in verse illustrate both Bakhtin's heteroglossia and the postsecular tension that is present with it.

Narrative Heteroglossia

Grimes grounds each novel in a pre-existing Biblical narrative: the story of Ishmael in one case and Mary in the other. However, she does not simply retell these stories; she creates parallel narratives for contemporary characters—a very postsecular move. Kathryn Ludvig describes postsecular fiction as being "infused with the same suspicion of totalizing narratives that is expressed in postmodernism. The emphasis on dialogue and reciprocal understanding … allows postsecular thinkers to move forward in creating new religious narratives" (230). Because the stories of these Biblical figures feature prominently, the reader must make intertextual connections between the historical Biblical text and the contemporary narratives in a way that encourages thematic connections. For example, all four of the main characters experience a crisis of belief. It is a common religious narrative that people experience a crisis of belief of some sort—sometimes this crisis serves to weaken or alter belief and sometimes it results in a stronger resolve and redemption. The four main characters in these books experience significant crises, and all four come through with stronger resolve as those things and people who formerly were dependable are stripped away and dependence on God becomes more necessary.

In *Dark Sons*, both Sam and Ishmael enter this crisis through feeling abandoned by their fathers. Sam states, "What gospel is it/where a father/ leaves his son?" (*Dark Sons* 95), mirroring Ishmael's cry, "For what sin/have I been judged/unworthy?" (*Dark Sons* 156). In *A Girl Named Mister*, when Mister discovers the secret that her mother had only been fifteen years old when Mister was born, she also experiences a crisis:

> *I needed you to be my rock, Mom,*
> is what I'm thinking,
> *a hefty boulder that could*
> *bear my weight,*
> *not some small smooth stone*
> *washed up on*
> *the same shore as me* [*A Girl Named Mister* 174].

The sense of disappointment that Mister expresses in this passage is palpable. Her previous trust had been shattered. Mary, upon discovering her pregnancy, fears that Joseph, as an agent of the religious culture that she has trusted in so completely, will turn against her:

> What if, convinced I have broken
> God's holy law,
> he drags me before the priest,
> has me judged and sentenced
> to be stoned? [*A Girl Named Mister* 125].

As characters move through these crises, they emerge with firmer religious identities. As characters claim these identities, a theme emerges in which God becomes their dependable source of strength and comfort after they have been disappointed. For Mister, it begins with accepting God's forgiveness as her best friend says,

> I see. So, you're telling me
> God forgives murderers,
> but can't forgive you.
> Well, that's a new one [*A Girl Named Mister* 144].

Mister's friend demonstrates forgiveness as well, ending this scene with a hug, and shortly after, Mister gives in, acknowledging,

> God's forgiveness
> falls over me
> like a quilt,

and this time,
I let it smother
my guilt [*A Girl Named Mister* 145].

This resolution does not come through theological understandings as it might have in the days of the Sunday School curriculum, or through a rejection of faith altogether as it may have in a modernist work, but rather through a postsecular personal and emotional spiritual experience. Each character's crisis of belief is resolved, but through different metaphors which invoke textual connections. Mister is buried under a quilt of forgiveness. Ishmael feels the invisible hand of God:

When I am angriest,
His is the hand
that calms me,
the one that rests
on my shoulders invisibly,
pressing patience
into my very bones,
letting me know
it is all right
to breathe [*Dark Sons* 149].

Each of the four main characters transfers his or her trust from a parent to God after disappointment and fear. This is not a result of a miraculous act by God or an acceptance of God's absence, but rather a new understanding of God as they consider and act on their experiences. In *Dark Sons*, Sam paraphrases Psalm 27:10 by saying, "If your father and mother/forsake you,/I will take you up" (194) and later refers to Jesus as "the only one/who hasn't let me down/so far" (199). Mary echoes this as she prays, "Lord Jehovah/please be my mother/tonight" (*A Girl Named Mister* 130). Ishmael declares that God is "the one father/I could count on" (*Dark Sons* 214). Characters actively forge a new relationship with God, creating their own heteroglossia as they reveal to the reader how they merge their knowledge of sacred practices and texts with their current experiences.

Textual Heteroglossia

As readers observe characters entering into this heteroglossia, they are forced to do so themselves by considering the many existing texts that contribute to the Grimes novels. In *Dark Sons*, Hammurabi's Code of Laws is quoted (14, 139) to explain Abraham's choice to conceive his son through Hagar, serving as both a historical document but also the voice of authority. In quoting Hammurabi, Grimes invokes the Jewish tradition that places

Abraham and Hammurabi as contemporaries (Farkas 159). Even readers who view Abraham as a devoutly religious man must admit that he experienced tension between the sacred and secular as he uses a secular law to fulfill sacred purposes, reflecting a heteroglossia as well as pluralism that is echoed in the contemporary characters. *A Girl Named Mister* includes ancient quotes as well such as Virgil's words on Gossip (159) invoking an ancient word of wisdom into a contemporary setting. The Bible, of course is referenced most often, but it is always through the lenses of the characters rather than standing alone to introduce a chapter. Grimes creates literal heteroglossia, including quotes from many historical texts—Hammurabi's code of law, Virgil, the dictionary (*A Girl Named Mister* 195), Bedouin proverbs, and even the Audubon Ballroom, where Malcolm X was assassinated (*A Girl Named Mister* 149).

Although the Bible provides the base narratives for the novels, for the contemporary characters, the Bible is much more than just another text. Contemporary characters must also wrestle with the place of the Bible in their lives. It serves as an authoritative text, providing guidance and inspiration. It also serves as a symbol of the characters' acceptance or rejection of their religious traditions, elevating this text in ways that other texts are not. In *A Girl Named Mister*, Mister refuses to pick up her Bible because of her guilt (57). In *Dark Sons*, when Sam's mother returns to her morning reading, she tells Sam, "God and I are talking again" (101). As it has become a literary symbol, the Bible contributes to heteroglossia but also heightens the tension between fully embracing religion and feeling estranged from it.

Tension and Dialogism

The complexity of the voices in these novels is mirrored by the complexity of their content. For Bakhtin, the novel is the form that holds the most tension referring to it as "a diversity of social speech types (sometimes even diversity of languages) and a diversity of individual voices, artistically organized" (Discourse 262). Corrigan writes, "Other writers see the postsecular not simply as attention to the religious in the midst of a secular age but rather as the development of a third position between the secular and the religious, containing aspects of both" (Section 4). Tensions in the work and in postsecular thinking reflect the kind of tensions that the characters, and by extension, readers experience. Christians, and perhaps all religious people live in the "in between," aspiring to be "in the world, but not of the world" based on Jesus' prayer for the disciples in John 17:16 (*NIV Bible*). I Peter 2 reinforces this, calling Christians strangers and aliens, also called pilgrims, foreigners, sojourners in various translations (*NIV Bible*), emphasizing the tensions between living in a culture, but not completely embracing it because of religious demands.

This presents a challenge for religious writers seeking to engage secular readers. How can readers that haven't experienced this type of religious faith understand the ways in which characters live within it? Several critics (Hungerford, Fessendon, and Haddox) have claimed that literature provides a way, perhaps even the best way to express and explore this tension. *Dark Sons* and *A Girl Named Mister* prod readers to consider ways in which religion functions in society and in the lives of these individuals—the historical, the cultural, and the personal, moving them to another Bakhtinian concept— the dialogic reading. Bakhtin conceptualizes dialogism as being a kind of "trio" between the author, the reader/listener, and "those whose voices are heard in the word before the author comes upon it" (*Speech Genres* 121). These texts encourage, if not require a dialogic reading as they reach back to history and outward to society. However, they also reach forward to the reader, drawing readers in to see how Christianity serves as an element of identity, but also a guide to daily living for past and present characters.

Reaching Back to History— Historical Tension

Grimes walks the tightrope between both explaining Christianity and helping readers understand its personal influence by invoking strong connections between the Biblical and contemporary characters, using historical language and imagery to describe the present. Ishmael reflects,

> What a twisted story, I thought.
> Born of such a history,
> I can expect my life to be
> anything but easy [*Dark Sons* 58].

All of the characters, whether contemporary or biblical, are strongly connected to a religious heritage. *Dark Sons* (66) shows Abraham telling Ishmael the stories of Adam and Eve, Noah, and other Old Testament figures. This heritage is brought forward to contemporary character Sam as his girlfriend encourages him to "Leave the ark, Sam. / Explore the new world" (*Dark Sons* 181) in a clear reference to the biblical story of Noah. One of Sam's chapters is titled "Sabbath" (*Dark Sons* 99), which has a strangely traditional sound in the conversational style of the chapter, bringing readers in the contemporary section of the book back to the tradition of dedicating one day a week to religious observance.

The image of the knife serves as a symbol of this historical tension in

Dark Sons. In the chapter titled, "The Mark" (*Dark Sons* 36), all the males in Abraham's household are circumcised. Ishmael explains, "I creep toward the tent / where hot blades wait," (37) which mirrors Sam's reference to his parents' cold stares as "the nick of the blade" (*Dark Sons* 111). Grimes ties the two references together more directly in the Epilogue where Sam refers to the story of Ishmael, finishing the book with the comment regarding Ishmael:

> It's all good.
> You made it
> in the end
> and so will I [*Dark Sons* 216].

Mary is tied into her religious tradition as she celebrates Passover and remembers the Jews' exit from Egypt:

> those blessed ones
> whose homes were blood-marked
> for salvation,
> those faithful Jews
> who knew God was
> as good as his word [*A Girl Named Mister* 63].

As characters look back to these foundational events and stories, readers are introduced to them as well and begin to understand how and perhaps even why these characters are committed to their faith traditions, inviting orthodoxy to enter the dialogue. Orthodoxy is characterized by Thomas Haddox as an adherence to truth claims. He writes, "I maintain that to take Christian orthodoxy seriously means to entertain (if not necessarily to accept) the primacy of truth over desire, utility, and custom, and to remain open to the content as well as the forms of Christian belief" (4). Grimes's characters do embrace orthodoxy. In fact, the compulsory nature and the stability of their religious traditions sustain them in ways that reinforce this stability. This type of orthodoxy may be difficult for postsecular readers to accept as Fessendon (158) characterizes postsecularism as "offering the experience of belief with no stable and compulsory object of belief." Amy Hungerford (133) argues that Protestantism depends largely on belief, and this is true for Grimes's characters as well. If these texts were only about the orthodoxy of truth claims, they may not require a postsecular dialogic reading.

Reaching Outward to Society— Cultural Tension

However, this historical heritage and its accompanying orthodoxy lives in a contemporary cultural environment, creating yet another tension. The faith of Grimes's characters is more than historical; it also frames the cultural world in which these characters live. Both Sam and Mister are strongly rooted in African American Christian culture, which is in itself a site of tension among cultures (Frey 101) and their churches serve as the primary transmitters of this culture. Mister is very involved in the life of her church, Temple of My Redeemer, where she attends youth group and sings in the choir. In fact, both contemporary characters are church musicians, and their participation in music serves as an indicator of their involvement. Their continued participation or questioning of this culture indicates to readers how they cope with their emotions. In *A Girl Named Mister*, one chapter is named "Choir Practice." Mister states,

> I do feel weird being here
> singing about a God
> I broke my promise to.
> If everybody knew,
> maybe they'd ask me to leave,
> and maybe I would.
> And maybe I should [77].

A subsequent chapter is set during a later event, although this time the chapter is titled "Rehearsal," and Mister says,

> Before I know it
> I'm lost in the music,
> rubbing shoulders with God,
> my faith as natural and easy
> as it used to be [*A Girl Named Mister* 99].

Readers are privy to Mister's internal dialogue both during the tension as well as when the tension is resolved through forgiveness. Her religious culture has dictated a particular code of behavior, but has also offered forgiveness when that code was broken—a dialogue that takes place for believers in many cultures and traditions.

A concrete symbol of this culture is the purity ring. In some Christian churches, girls are given purity rings by their parents as a sign that they have pledged to remain virgins until married. Mister wears such a ring. It is an outward mark of her Christian culture. When that culture does not match her identity, it causes significant conflict. She throws it out the window after having sex with her boyfriend (*A Girl Named Mister* 42), telling her mom that she lost the ring. Mister doesn't shed this cultural identity, however. Her mother, still unaware that Mister is pregnant, presents her with a new ring. Purity also plays a significant role in the religious culture of Mary. She witnesses the stoning of an acquaintance about her own age that was accused of adultery in the chapter ironically titled, "Neighborly."

> I peek, now,
> from half-closed lids ...
> at this poor, crumpled girl,
> writhing in pain until death
> rescues her, a girl I knew ...
> a girl who so easily
> could be—[A Girl Named Mister 111].

This event contrasts with an earlier statement by Mary, who is looking forward to more full participation in her own religious culture Church/temple as culture for Mary. She shocks her father by saying, "Next year at the Passover/ I believe I'll enter the Court of Israel/ to witness the sacrifices first-hand" (A Girl Named Mister 66), indicating both Mary's embrace of her cultural tradition, but also her willingness to step outside her gender role. Mister, too, fears the reaction of the people in her religious community, but Grimes provides stark contrast to her expectations, as Mister explains,

> Sure I get a couple of looks,
> but mostly it's the ladies saying,
> "We're praying for you honey,"
> or 'Let me know
> if there's something I can do ... "
> Maybe it's God
> reminding me
> I'm not as alone
> as I thought [A Girl Named Mister 181].

As characters struggle with their circumstances, they accept or reject various aspects of their religious culture. Sam's mother does not attend church for a period of time and then returns to it, showing readers a progression in her cultural/religious life. Mister declines to take communion, "The silver rim all but singed my fingertips," (A Girl Named Mister 153). However, this is not an "all-or-nothing" proposition. Characters make choices in a postsecular fashion, continuing to participate in religious culture even when they understand that they may not accept (or be accepted by) the orthodoxy of the church.

In addition to the religious culture, not every character is comfortable in the larger culture. In Dark Sons, Sam, must manage cultural tension. After his parents' divorce, Sam lives in both his mother's and his father's houses, unsure of where he really belongs (112). Sam's father marries a younger, Italian, White woman, evoking Sam's response, "Please./ At least he could be/ original" (Dark Sons 84). When Sam's half-brother is born, he comments,

> What
> were you thinking, Dad?
> Bringing a kid into this world

who is guaranteed to be
marooned in the middle
of two cultures,
neither this nor that? [*Dark Sons* 125].

This invokes echoes of Ishmael's lament of being "half and half."

Half Chaldean.
Half Egyptian.
Half slave.
Half free.
Half loved.
Half hated.
Half blessed.
All me [22].

In *A Girl Named Mister*, when their unsanctioned pregnancies begin to become known, both Mary and Mister fear that they will be rejected, or, in Mary's case, killed by her religious community. They are members of that community, but their pregnancies force them to live in tension within those communities.

This ambivalence about participation is more than simple indecision. As characters struggle with their place in the religious culture, postsecular readers may see themselves. Bakhtin explains, "The distinctive qualities of a character's discourse always strive for a certain social significance" (333). Corrigan's introduction to this volume makes the case that in the current religious landscape, many are finding non-traditional ways to connect with God. The future of the organized church is in flux in society, and these characters experience this dissonance as well.

Reaching out to the Reader—Personal Tension

The books can be read for these aspects alone, but a dialogic reading is not complete without considering the personal. Bakhtin encourages this:

> The word does not exist in a neutral and impersonal language (it is not, after all, out of a dictionary that the speaker gets his words!), but rather it exists in other people's mouths, in other people's contexts, serving other people's intentions: it is from there that one must take the word and make it one's own [*Discourse in the Novel* 94].

Bakhtin's words echo the idea of postsecular embodiment. Geographer Elizabeth Olson and her team (Olson et al. 1424) argue that many of the co-existing tensions present in postsecularism reside in specific places or people. Readers can enter into this tension as they relate to Sam, Ishmael, Mister and

Mary. Through the first-person verse narration, readers enter the decision-making processes, worries, and hopes that the characters experience. At times Mister views the church as purely social—just for hanging out with her friends (*A Girl Named Mister* 20), and not necessarily for spiritual value. Her boyfriend Trey is not interested in spending time at the church with other youth group members. "No more ... lame trips (his words)/ to the local skating rink" (*A Girl Named Mister* 29). Those outside of Christian communities may view them as purely social, but these books demonstrate more than that. All of the characters have specific encounters with God that become markers of identity for them. Their religious beliefs make a real difference in their identities and decision-making.

Characters are firmly rooted in a religious identity. This identity is addressed directly in *Dark Sons* as Ishmael refers to the covenant that God made with Abraham:

> Signs that would say
> "We are God's,"
> Signs that would say
> "We believe" [35].

The characters depend on signs as markers of their religious identity. In *Dark Sons*, Sam was born as a miracle as his parents struggled with infertility, recognizing in his name that he is a gift from God. Ishmael's mother, Hagar, has a personal encounter with God (18) that converts her from her Egyptian religion to belief in the God of Abraham (19). The most obvious identity marker is Ishmael's circumcision (38), but Abraham also teaches Ishmael the protocol for presenting sacrifice to God in parallel with Sam's dad teaching him how to pray on the basketball court (91). As other identities get stripped away, the identity of being a particular father's son, or in the transition from being a volleyball player to "pregnant girl" (*A Girl Named Mister* 163), religious identity becomes more important.

Religion also provides a guide for decision-making, indicating a God who is present and personally involved in daily life, which postsecular readers will find familiar. Corrigan argues via Taylor and Smith that through embodiment (Section 3), that religion is not only a set of propositions or beliefs, but also a way of navigating through one's experience. Grimes's Biblical characters demonstrate this as God guides Mary through messages from angels (*A Girl Named Mister* 68) and guides Ishmael and Hagar through water from a rock (*Dark Sons* 162). However, the contemporary characters have similar experiences. As Sam expresses his anger toward God in Central Park a plane flies over him trailing a sign with a Bible verse:

> "I am with you always,
> even to the end of the age."

I let the truth of it in,
feel my thoughts stop spinning,
and calmly head back
to the subway [*Dark Sons* 98].

Mister pleads for this kind of Godly intervention as she contemplates whether to keep her baby or place it for adoption: "God, I want the stars for this kid./..Can you take care of him Lord?/ Take care of me?" (208). She recalls Mary's story and the angel appearing to Joseph:

At long last,
I crack my Bible open,
finger the fragile pages …
the Spirit whispered
Reread the passage
so I did.
And there it was:
a reminder that God
gave Joseph
a giant push
in the right direction [*A Girl Named Mister* 154].

She does not receive a specific sign from God. Grimes leaves the ending open for readers—it is not clear whether Mister will keep the child as the book ends, which forces the reader to enter into the decision with her and perhaps get a sense of her trust in God for guidance as well as the open question of the fate of the baby. None of the characters' stories wrap up neatly, which allows the reader to continue the dialogue, both about the plot and the role of religion.

Finally, the texts encourage the embrace of mystery. Both Bakhtin and postsecular theorists acknowledge that there is something about language and spirituality that cannot be systemized or readily explained. In "Discourse and the Novel," Bakhtin discusses the synergy of the form and the content of a novel and how the novel is a form that defies particular genre characteristics. Postsecularism has been particularly difficult to define, in part, because society's relationship with religion depends largely on what is unseen. Readers of the Grimes texts must make peace with Mary's miracle of immaculate conception (*A Girl Named Mister* 69) and God's provision in the wilderness for Ishmael (*Dark Sons* 162). Even if readers do not believe that these miracles are historically true, they must be willing to suspend disbelief as they read in order to understand the worlds of these characters.

However, simple belief is not enough. As the postsecular disrupts postmodern thinking, Viswanathan notes that "the primary ruptures are not between reason and religion but, rather, between belief and imagination" (468). Readers see evidence of both belief and imagination in the characters as they wrestle with the unexplainable. Mister reflects in a chapter called which begins by examining the predictable cause and effect of sin and its resulting punishment: "But then I think of Mary/ who God gave a baby/ just because he wanted to,/ and she didn't do anything wrong" (*A Girl Named Mister* 121). The Biblical Ishmael also accepts this as he addresses God:

> Then I remember,
> You are not a god
> Of my creation.
> Any god I fashioned
> would sure as hell
> give me what I want.
> Instead,
> you offer me
> mystery [*Dark Sons* 162].

The characters and the readers are left with a sense of awe and mystery as a result of the historical, societal and personal tensions portrayed through the poetic voices of the characters.

Conclusion

The novels of Nikki Grimes, invoking both traditional Biblical stories and imagined narratives provide opportunities for readers to embrace post-secular thinking and experience many of the tensions commonly found in religious life. Bakhtinian heteroglossia and dialogism in the milieu of the postsecular can provide some explanation of how these tensions are created and navigated. However, there is still room for characters and readers to exist within these unsolved tensions—the tensions of history, culture and identity. To embrace these mysteries, readers must bring their own ideas about God, religion and spirituality to the reading experience, using imagination and perhaps even faith.

WORKS CITED

Bakhtin, Mikhail. "Discourse in the Novel." *The Dialogic Imagination: Four Essays*. Austin: University of Texas Press, 1981. *ProQuest Ebrary*. OCLC: 704289191.
Bakhtin, Mikhail. *Speech Genres and Other Late Essays*. Austin: University of Texas Press, 1987. *ProQuest Ebrary*. OCLC: 695996374.
Bible Hub. *Online Parallel Bible Project*. 2015. http://biblehub.com/1_peter/2-11.htm.
Corrigan, Paul T. "The Postsecular and Literature: A Review of Scholarship." *Corrigan Literary Review*. 2015. corriganliteraryreview.wordpress.com/2015/05/17/the-postsecular-and-literature/.
Farkas, David. "In Search of the Biblical Hammurabi." *Jewish Bible Quarterly* 39, no. 3 (2011): 159–164.
Fessendon, Tracy. "The Problem of the Post Secular." *American Literary History* 26, no. 1 (2014): 154–167.

Frey, Sylvia R. "The Visible Church: Historiography of African American Religion Since Raboteau." *Slavery & Abolition* 29, no. 1 (2008): 83–110.

Grimes, Nikki. *Dark Sons.* New York: Hyperion Books for Children, 2005.

Grimes, Nikki. *A Girl Named Mister.* Grand Rapids, MI: Zondervan, 2010.

Haddox, Thomas F. *Hard Sayings: The Rhetorics of Christian Orthodoxy in Late Modern Fiction.* Columbus: Ohio State University Press, 2013.

Hungerford, Amy. *20/21: Postmodern Belief: American Literature and Religion Since 1960.* Princeton, NJ: Princeton University Press, 2010.

Ludwig, Kathryn. "Postsecularism and a Prophetic Sensibility." *Christianity & Literature* 58, no. 2 (2009): 226–233.

MacGregor, Carol Ann. "Religious Socialization and Children's Prayer as Cultural Object: Boundary Work in Children's 19th Century Sunday School Books." *Poetics* 36, no. 5/6 (2008): 435–449.

New International Version of the Bible. Bible Hub. http://biblehub.com/.

Olson, Elizabeth, et al. "Retheorizing the Postsecular Present: Embodiment, Spatial Transcendence, and Challenges to Authenticity Among Young Christians in Glasgow, Scotland." *Annals of the Association of American Geographers* 103, no. 6 (2013): 1421–1436.

Trousdale, Ann. "Intersections of Spirituality, Religion and Gender in Children's Literature." *International Journal of Children's Spirituality* 10, no. 1 (2005): 61–79.

Viswanathan, Gauri. "Secularism in the Framework of Heterodoxy." *PMLA* 123, no. 2 (2008): 466–476.

Werner, C., and F.P. Riga. "The Persistence of Religion in Children's Literature." *Children's Literature Association Quarterly* 14, no. 1 (1989): 2–3.

Willard, Mara. "Interrogating a Mercy: Faith, Fiction, and the Postsecular." *Christianity & Literature* 63, no. 4 (2014): 467–487.

Young Adult Fiction, Diaspora and the "Muslim" Question

A Study on Faith and Feminism in Randa Abdel-Fattah's Novels

FATEMA JOHERA AHMED

Introduction

Discourses on citizenship, cultural values, and border security have consistently been employed in the construction of a nation's Other. For states with a heterogeneous population, the sanctification of any one ethnicity is adverse to the body politic. The mainstreaming of the white community in settler states like the U.S., Canada, and Australia reiterates the power politics between the First and Third World[1]: non–Western migrants are labeled as minorities while First Nations are catapulted further away from the national narrative. The increased visibility of minority communities and the rhetoric of "unity in diversity" result in the settler state experiencing bouts of anxiety about its fantasy of maintaining a white majority. This is because the Anglo-Western community "is structurally placed in a position of power inasmuch as it is granted the active power to tolerate while minorities can only be at the end of tolerance" (Ang 39–40), and so, "the limits of tolerance are determined by how much of this toxicity can be accommodated without destroying the object, value, claim, or body. Tolerance appears, then, as a mode of incorporating and regulating the presence of the threatening Other within" (Brown 27).

For individuals of Middle Eastern origin living in the West, assimilation, multiculturalism, and being Muslim are some of the discursive frames through which subjectivity is negotiated. The creation of Muslim protagonists in young adult literature (YAL) who live in the West but look at the world with Islam as their center intertextualize these literary works with the growing political discourse on the Middle East. In most cases, the Muslim protagonist's identity is nuanced by varying degrees of Islamic, Arab, and Western culture that young adults may adopt to live normal, fulfilling lives as opposed to the confining stereotypes and broad generalizations perpetrated by Western power-knowledge that insist that an Islamic lifestyle is alien to the West. *Does My Head Look Big in This?* (2005) and *No Sex in the City* (2012), the two Australian novels by Australian-Palestinian-Egyptian author Randa Abdel-Fattah that I examine in this essay, are set in two major city centers in Australia and offer counter-narratives to the mainstream image of the Muslim girl as bearing the brunt of Islamic oppression. Oftentimes, this stereotype is encapsulated in the single image of the hijab[2] as the experiences of Amal, Abdel-Fattah's protagonist in *Does My Head Look Big in This* shows, but Esma, who wears no visible symbol of her faith in *No Sex in the City*, leaves no doubt that it is her identity as a Muslim that marks her out as a non-conformist as per Anglo-Australian standards of Australian citizenry.

In the two selected YA novels, Abdel-Fattah explores through the specter of young, believing women what it is like to be Muslim in the West, an identity that is narrativized as the "could-be terrorist" (Abdel-Fattah, "The stigmatisation") and arouses suspicion and anxiety when the clash of civilizations is daily portended by the Western war on "Islamic" terrorism. Binarized against Eastern traditionalism and epistemologies, the "self-privileging versions of Western modernity" (Huggan 753) is complicit in generating the simulacrum of what Mariam Cooke calls the "the Muslimwoman" (91). Cooke's term reflects the erasure of individual, racial, political, economic, and cultural imperatives in the homogenization of the category of "woman." Since the anonymity of the terrorist is countered by those who subscribe to Islam, I examine how Abdel-Fattah's creation of empowered Muslim female characters advances the feminist discourse and argue that the heterogeneity of the Muslim community is belied by the West's monologic focus on the hijab as "a piece of material covering the hair [that] strips a woman of the ability to communicate intelligently, pursue a career, work a remote control" (Abdel-Fattah, "Living").

The West rationalizes resistance to Eastern patriarchy by propagandizing the de-Islamization of the Muslim community through a Western brand of mainstream feminism. On the other end of this continuum, "conservative" Muslims associate the hijab with piety and as a touchstone of those women who are on a spiritual journey towards a meaningful relationship with God, and subsequently view non-hijabis as far from devout. Caught in the middle, "liberals" tend to subscribe to the Orientalist attitudes towards Islam and look upon their veiled sisters as both victims and agents of patriarchy while labeling themselves "modern" and "assimilated." Meanwhile, "moderate" Muslims protest the slippages between Islam, culture, and geopolitics even as they are repeatedly scrutinized and called upon to prove their allegiance to the Western metropole that they are residents of.

Because of this deadlock, Muslim women find religion added to the structures of oppression they must contend with alongside parental authority, gender, race, and culture in order to live in the diaspora. Abdel-Fattah proposes a vision of Islam that coheres with what Anouar Majid identifies as an Islamically progressive agenda that is democratic, anti-patriarchal, and anti-imperialist (Majid 56). Abdel-Fattah's brand of feminism underscores the necessity of finding indigenous, locally-produced solutions to the "Muslim woman" question and simultaneously address the "visceral" impact of racism which affect "people's lives and opportunities … their psychology and emotional states" (Abdel-Fattah qtd. in Chang, "Solidarity with"). The different ways in which her protagonists engage with Islam reveals that a feminist discourse that does not merely mimic Western methodologies is available to Muslim women from within Islam.

The Hijabi Muslim

Secularization, the freedom of religion, and the tabooing of religious discussion into a private matter in the West contribute to a reluctance to discuss or depict spirituality in popular fiction and canonical literature. This reticence is, however, not borne out in the literary, public, and political sphere when the trope is Islam in the post–9/11 world. In an atmosphere of heightened scrutiny, the observant Muslim girl's decision to don the hijab becomes damning proof of the female version of militant Islam and delegitimizes her Western citizenship. As the hijab does not conform to the Eurocentric model of modernity and secularism, eradicating it is believed to have the same effect as de-radicalizing the hijabi.

Set in Melbourne, *Does My Head Look Big in This?* explores sixteen-year-old Australian-Muslim-Palestinian high school student Amal Mohamed Nasrullah Abdel-Hakim's decision to wear the hijab, a cultural artifact that overlaps with religious duty and produces confusion as to its significance among onlookers and even some practitioners. This is particularly the case when debates on the "Australian" identity and values focus exclusively on the Muslim woman's attire and non-participation in Western social norms such as drinking and dating (Abdel-Fattah, "Of Middle"). The pressure to conform to an arbitrary set of social practices is party to the neo-imperialist strains in the imposition of secularism on Eastern states and the minority communities living in the diaspora. Since secularism represents a specific socio-historical moment in the West, exporting this phenomenon to the former colonies or imposing it on those who have relocated to the West is a neo-imperialist strategy that seeks "the removal of absolute values—epistemolog-ical and ethical—from the world such that the entire world—humanity and nature alike—becomes merely a utilitarian object to be utilized and subju-gated" (Al Masseri 403). The power play between the West and the rest has implications on young adults on a quest to belong and the search for self-validating images by which the marginalized Muslim community may reclaim the task of representing itself.

Amal is inspired to wear the hijab "full-time" (*Does My* 2) because of a scene from *Friends*, a popular American sitcom, where Jennifer Aniston's character summons the courage to jump on stage and sing away her inhibi-tions after an embarrassing walk down the aisle in a hideous bridesmaid dress at her ex's wedding. For Amal, becoming a "full-timer" (2) means that instead of donning the hijab as part of her school uniform when she was a student at an Islamic school, when she prays, or goes to the mosque, Amal will wear it when she is around men who are not from her immediate family. She is motivated to do so because she "want[s] that identity ... that symbol of [her] faith. [She] want[s] to know what it means to be strong enough to walk around with [the hijab] on and stick up for [her] right to wear it" (22), making the hijab an article of clothing that is fraught with the contradictory senti-ments of confidence and anxiety.

Amal admits that as an Arab Muslim from Australia she "was born an Aussie and whacked with some bloody confusing identity hyphens" (5). She further elaborates that these hyphens are a source of apprehension as "there was always somebody in the playground to tell the wogs to go home" (11). The likelihood of being singled out and being made "a prefix to terrorism, extremism, radicalism, any ism" (11) would be significantly amplified if she wears the hijab in public since the garment is viewed by a significant com-ponent of the Australian mainstream as proof of the menacing advance of a feared Islamic takeover that can "transform Muslim [and potentially Anglo-Western] girls into UCOs (Unidentified Covered Objects)" (34). Amal describes taking off the hijab the moment she would step out of her former school, Hidaya[3] Islamic College, as a gesture of unease about how fellow com-muters may respond to the hijab: the garment that covered her ironically made her feel exposed whenever she would be the only one wearing it on public transportation.

Even as the hijab appears to differentiate Amal from her predominantly Anglo-Western classmates at the elite McCleans Grammar School she has recently enrolled in by marking her as a Muslim, the hijab is an act of piety for Amal, "not a *sign* intended to communicate something but *part of an orientation, of a way of being*" (Asad 96; original emphasis). Like other acts of worship, the hijab is a conduit to a special bond with God that Amal feels she is missing out on by staying a "part-time" wearer, and so Amal is acutely aware of the politicization of the hijab and the possible staring and mean comments the hijab may bring her way when she is at McCleans or out in public because, as Saba Mahmood observes, "[n]o discursive object occupies a simple relation to the reality it purportedly denotes. Rather, representations of facts, objects, and events are profoundly mediated by fields of power in which they circulate and through which they acquire their precise force, shape, and form" ("Retooling" 130). In spite of her fear of being ostracized by her peers, the calm that Amal experiences when she prays makes her "feel like nothing can hurt [her], and nothing else matters. And that's when [she] knows [she is] ready [to wear the hijab]" (Abdel-Fattah, *Does My* 29). An exploration of Amal's psyche as the strength of her convictions outweighs external obstacles reveals that wearing the much-maligned hijab is an act of individualism.

Although the hijab has increasingly been decoded by the white mainstream as un–Australian because it performs a non–Western religious identity and appears to oppress women, the mainstream's apparent non-religiosity does not detract from the Judeo-Christian values that are embedded in the foundation of the Australian state. An examination of the semantics of Amal's decision conveys agency, which is the motif that lies at the heart of the feminist movement. This makes it ironic that Amal's list of people who may have a problem with her hijab include "[h]ard-core feminists who don't get that this is [Amal] exercising [her] right to choose" (15).[4] Amal argues that her decision is an "expression of who [she is] on the inside … [she is] sharing something with millions of other women around the world and it feels so exciting … [she] was looking and feeling good on [her] own terms, and boy did that feel awesome" (25–26). The hijab liberates Amal from the consumer culture obsession with body image and the patriarchal objectification of women's bodies. With the adolescent, porn-addicted boys in Amal's high school opining that "fat chicks should be deported, girls should starve and implants should be a civic duty" (8), Amal fears "compromising [her]self by wanting to make an impression" (26). The regimes of femininity generated by the discourse of modernity veers too close to the latest Western patriarchal fashion dictate, which adopts a "self-serving theory [that] less is more when it comes to female dress" (7). The hijab's call for dressing modestly offers the potential for epistemic disobedience against being remade in the image of the Western subject, particularly the Western notion of the woman.

Dressing modestly does not mean, however, that Amal is no longer concerned about her appearance. Abdel-Fattah presents the hijab as something akin to a fashion statement and describes multiple scenes with Amal before her mirror fussing about clothes and adjusting the hijab because there is a phenomenon referred to as the "Bad Hijab Day." Amal's desire to wear the hijab is not dichotomous with looking good and dressing well or being interested in popular culture and boys. The narrative establishes that Amal's interpretation of freedom combines wearing what she wants and the prioritization of her desire to enter into a special transcendental bond with the Creator. The hijab represents a discursive space that allows for the fusion of the public and the private selves, where "the outward behavior of the body constitutes both the potentiality, and the means, through which an interiority is realized" (Mahmood, *Politics* 159). Amal's motivations are notable for their democratic origins and enable her to emerge from a "religiously anonymous" existence (Abdel-Fattah, *Does My* 10). The hijabi's independence from male-driven fashion dictates should, therefore, make Amal a model feminist. Instead "the male yardstick for acceptable dress has now been replaced by a feminist yardstick" that presumes to tell the Muslim woman what she must wear in order to be free (Abdel-Fattah, "Living").

The hijab is, moreover, made the only label that Australian-Muslim women wear. Behind this assumption lies the supposed incommensurability of being simultaneously Muslim and Australian.[5] Abdel-Fattah recounts in an interview her experience of growing up as an Arab Muslim during the eighties when Muslims were regarded as "guests" by their Anglo-Australian "host" so that Abdel-Fattah's "Muslim and Arabic heritage was how [she] defined [her]self, but now [she has] realised that [she does not] need to define [her]self according to someone else's definition—[she does not] have to know who [she is] every day" (qtd. in Al Hakawati, "Muslim chick lit"). Amal's experiences similarly reveal that in order to belong she must creatively negotiate her identity through an awareness of the forces that participate in "various local and everyday resistances [wherein converge] the existence of a range of specific strategies and structures of power" (Abu-Lughod 53). Thus, removing the hijab symbolically to convey one's freedom is neither feminist nor liberating as it merely gestures acquiescence to the cultural imperialism of the West.

By generating simplistic formulations that equate female emancipation with the clothes she wears, the West displays an inability to consider that the hijab may offer an alternative way of life that empowers believing Muslim women. The idea that the hijab is a badge of membership in a matriarchy is realized when Amal dons the veil for the first time at Chadstone Shopping Centre and is greeted by fellow hijabis with the universal Islamic greeting of peace because she is recognized as a Muslim. The incident gives her insight that the hijab is about more than just modesty. Wearing it allows Amal to act upon what she feels within and actively identify as Muslim, and thereby derive "an amazing connection, [a] sense that this cloth binds [her] in some kind of universal sisterhood" (Abdel-Fattah, *Does My* 28) with other hijabis. Thus, the headscarf consolidates Amal's and other Muslim women's ability to enter the terrain of sorority and a sense of collective identity that mainstream Western feminism fails to foster when it does not take into account the intersectionality of race, class, sexuality, politics, and culture.

Since Amal's mother is a fellow hijabi, the conclusion drawn by most of Amal's peers and the school principal, Ms. Walsh, that Amal has been forced to wear the hijab is juxtaposed with an earlier scene in the novel depicting Amal's parents' reception of her announcement that she will wear the hijab in public. Amal's parents defy the stock image of despotic Arab Muslim parents in their concern about the socio-economic and emotional consequences of veiling in a cultural and political climate that is hostile to it, and even urge Amal to reconsider her decision. It becomes clear from their discussion that the suggestion has never been made nor do her parents implicitly expect Amal to emulate her mother and wear the hijab. Although the veil has repeatedly been labeled as confronting, the relative ease with which Amal's classmates and friends accept her new appearance is testament to the fact that the hijab is not an antagonizing piece of cloth and can be gradually accepted by those who come across it for the first time or have continually been fed negative ideas about it.[6] To persistently characterize the hijab as threatening without engaging with what this female space entails, on the other hand, is symptomatic of a stubborn refusal to accept difference and to engage with others on terms that are mutually cognizant of both ideologies.

When Amal approaches Ms. Walsh for permission to wear the hijab to school, the latter considers Amal's display of her spiritual conviction as "abandoning [the] school uniform" (35) and as a breach in discipline.[7] Ms. Walsh's bias against the hijab reveals the relevance of one's positionality when it comes to affixing connotations to the interplay between the signifier (the hijab) and signified (oppression/empowerment). Given the private nature of benefits generated from all forms of spirituality and the advent of secularization, for Ms. Walsh these trends translate into her belief that "[p]ersonal is something tucked under your shirt. Personal is rosary beads in your pocket" (36) whereby she differentiates between the hijab and other religious symbols. Ms. Walsh's narrow definition of the personal to what has been deliberately placed out of sight and, by extension, the public sphere, however, is regressive as it directly opposes the popular second-wave feminist dictum during the 1960s that the personal is political.[8] Although Amal does not seek to score politically by subscribing to the hijab, the presuppositions about the veil as oppressive and regressive to the feminist cause inevitably renders the garb into a statement, and so when Ms. Walsh agrees to allow Amal to wear the hijab to school, she also pointedly reminds Amal that she is now "under an even greater responsibility to represent [the school] faithfully. With [Amal's] veil, all eyes will be on [her] outside the school, so [Ms. Walsh] trust[s] [Amal] will not do [the school's] reputation any disservice" (61). In the transition to secularism, the policing of other communities according to the standards set by one's own is negligent of the fact that certain religions require one to "embrace one's faith openly, with independence and courageous conviction" (Abdel-Fattah, "Living").

In the escalating Us versus Them rhetoric that demarcates a fair go, egalitarianism, and racial and gender equality as inherently Western values despite the universality of these aspirations, Tia Amos, one of Amal's classmates at McCleans, humiliates Amal for her Muslim and Arab background by referring to documentaries and newspaper articles that continually probe the "Muslim" phenomenon and essentialize Arab culture as violent and inferior. When Adam Keane, Amal's friend at McCleans whom she also has a crush on, tries to excuse Tia's malice as the product of ignorance, Amal exposes the privileging of whiteness on which hinges Western misrecognition and denigration of non–European people and cultures. Amal insists that she too has "family friends who think all Anglos … sit around in their thongs and Bonds singlet, rorting the dole or chucking a sickie, sculling down VBs, watching Jerry Springer and bashing their girlfriends" (Abdel-Fattah, *Does My* 138). She questions Adam if it is reasonable for her to excuse such blatant pigeon-holing by arguing that "*Oh, they're allowed to think that. After all they've never really had a conversation with a sober Anglo*" (139; original italics). Colin Haines argues that Adam's attempt to excuse Tia's ignorance is as racist as Tia's pronouncements about Muslims (34). In this scene, Amal parodies the stereotyping of the Muslim community by turning the skewed spotlight on Anglo-Australians which then allows her to prove the extent to which any community can be misrepresented when garbled logic parades as commonsense and denies the other a voice.

In a similar scene, when Lara, the school captain at McCleans, asks Amal to present a speech on Islam and terrorism at the school's next Forum meeting, Lara's request is based on the assumption that Amal would be able to shed light on why the Bali nightclub bombing happened because she, like the bombers, is Muslim. To this, Amal responds that she will attend the Forum if Lara, who is Christian, agrees to a similar speech about Christianity that would explain the actions of the Ku Klux Klan against the African American community. It is only when an analogy is presented between the Ku Klux Klan and the Bali nightclub bombers that the outrageousness of the connections made between acts of terror and Christianity and Islam, respectively, expose the uncritical collapsing of the political with the religious and the superimposition of the Muslim identity on "nutcases who exploded bombs and killed people" (Abdel-Fattah, *Does My* 243).

Yet, the religious vilification and exclusionary rhetoric that transmute

Muslims into the Other is endlessly reiterated and exemplified by the likes of Liberal Prime Minister Tony Abbott who exhorted in 2015 that people should not migrate to Australia if they do not want to be part of "Team Australia."[9] Amal's positionality as an young adult who clearly identifies as an Australian can be drawn upon to deconstruct "the discourse of nation, nationalism, Australian identity (that is, Anglo-Celtic), and "core values" in Abbott's terror prevention speech as serving "as a coded discussion of how this game of Dealing with Minorities works. You're either on the team or you're not. You play by our rules or you're kicked off" (Abdel-Fattah, "Tony Abbott"). The unilateral focus conceals the mainstream attitude towards Muslims as aberrant bodies who are unable or unwilling to assimilate in what is the post-assimilation era of multiculturalism. Amal's experiences bring to light the muscle-flexing against the Muslim community that endlessly demands explanations and displays of condemnation from Muslims by equivocating acts of terrorism committed by a few in the name of Islam as "Islamic" (Abdel-Fattah, "Love Letter").

An examination of the inundation of hard-hitting images of Muslim men as fundamentalists who plot the downfall of the West and oppress women reveals the epistemological violence an unbalanced picture does to the Muslim community and the real dangers any community faces of being made the victim of a smear campaign. It tells us more about the state machinery that produces this discourse that has "less to do with the Orient than it does with "our" world" (Said 12) and the pet assumptions promoted by white normativity, which are concerned with maintaining power and inculcating submission into minorities. Amal recalls reacting with horror and confusion to the 9/11 news flash:

> [F]or some reason their deaths were more shocking and disgusting and numbing than all the deaths you normally read about and see on the news ... you turn on the six o' clock news and there are people starving and countries bleeding and people dying for the right to freedom from occupation and dictatorship and what do you do? You tut-tut and sigh. Most times I flip over to *The Simpsons*. That's what got me all confused and upset. Because I couldn't stop bawling, watching the towers come down and the people's terrified faces. It was a terrible thing to happen. And a terrible thing to realise that I don't sit through the night crying when such horrors happen all the time (Abdel-Fattah, *Does My* 151).

The discrepancy between the placid reception to the tragedies that unfold in non–Western peripheries and the visceral reaction to the news about the 9/11 tragedy in the American metropole reproduce the racial hierarchy where those who inhabit the non–Western locales are made "unreal ... [having] already suffered the violence of derealization. ... If violence is done against those who are unreal, then from the perspective of violence, it fails to injure or negate those lives since those lives are already negated" (Butler 33).

Amal notes how the emergent racial hierarchy brings to the forefront the forces of knowledge production that collaborate in manufacturing apathy, consent, or outrage. It begs the question, who has to be the victim for collateral damage to be catastrophic? How does the media's filtering of violence and death confirm the grand narratives about that spatial and temporal reality? How does the demonization of non–Western people collaborate with the neo-imperialist justification of pedagogical violence? Why is the narrative of Islamic feminism relatively unknown in the West? What is the link between the "war on terror," the Muslim woman, and neo-imperialism? These questions underscore the interplay between Western regimes of power and will-to-knowledge that produce and circulate "truths" about communities who have been made the Other.

Amal describes the disorienting impact of the constant stigmatization of Muslims where "[i]t feels like you're drowning in it all. Like you can never come up for air. Another headline or documentary [about Islamic terrorism] comes back and clams you under the water again" (Abdel-Fattah, *Does My* 148). In this context, it is almost presumptuous for Amal to hope that she "could find [her] place in [her] country and be unaffected by the horrors and politics in the world" (237). Amal asks, "Was I going to be incriminated for [the Bali bombers'] crimes? Was I going to be allowed to share in my country's mourning or would I be blamed?" (236) when news about the Bali bombings is disseminated by the Australian media and responded to by some of her classmates with expressions of anger against the Muslim community.[10]

Although most Western states claim to be in their neo-liberal and secular phase, the "Muslim problem" is one among other so-called "Third World"–looking problems of First World countries and paves the way to the emergence of second- and third-generation young adults from minority communities who are confident of their hyphenated identities and their claim on Australia as their country. Amal belongs to the generation that simultaneously resists the nostalgic narratives of migration and rejects the rhetoric of assimilation that negates her non–Western origins. This paradigmatic shift in the negotiation of identity to a more assured positionality by individuals from minority communities take place in the wake of the interrogation of their religious and national allegiance by the settler state in what remains a settler colony, and accelerates the transition to the post-secular phase. Distanced from Eastern patriarchy by her family's exile from Palestine, and marginalized by mainstream Australia, Amal is free from both superstructures to arrive at unmitigated conclusions about her faith and sense of belonging. She actively embarks on a personal relationship with God instead of passively accepting a prescribed Muslim identity. Amal emphasizes personal inquiry over truth claims in order to differentiate religious piety from the infringement of patriarchy on institutional Islam, making her markedly different from women who regressively defend misogynist distortions of Islamic regulations.

Regardless, the mainstream infantilizes Muslim women who pursue justice and freedom from an Islamic viewpoint. It assumes that "that freedom and Islam are mutually exclusive, or, worse, that Muslim women are brainwashed, suffering from a form of religious Stockholm syndrome" (Abdel-Fattah and Carland, "Muslim feminists"). This argument elides the Muslim woman's consciousness and agency by insisting that she is incapable of critically engaging with her situation. She is viewed as a victim of Muslim men or/and transmogrified into his accomplice in the perceived Islamic infiltration of the West. This undervaluation of the Muslim woman's voice and intellect is particularly effected when she addresses the hijab or the burqa with terminology that shifts the narrative away from the frame that is generally adopted by the self-appointed Western saviors who, as Gayatri Chakravorty Spivak famously stated, want to protect brown women from brown men (93). According to Abdel-Fattah, the brand of feminism practiced in the West is "highly particular and the denial of its particularity means it is not inclusive of feminisms 'of colour' or 'Third-World' feminisms" (Abdel-Fattah, "Brown Lives"). Since the West commands the dominant narrative on the hijab, what the West needs to do is to "abandon the discourse of rescuing women and instead listen to women on a footing of respect" ("Brown Lives").

Amal's choice or the choice made by her friend, Leila, a fellow-hijab wearer and one of Amal's best friends from Hidaya Islamic College, to embrace the hijab must be understood through the nexus of the girls' interpretation of scriptural dictates, their lived experiences, and democratic Australian values. Western interventions that interpret the hijab pejoratively or willfully seek to free Amal or Leila from its perceived oppressiveness must be examined for traces of what Leila Ahmed terms as colonial feminism,[11] which binarizes an "uncivilized," "fanatic" East against the "civilized," "secular" West. That the Muslim woman struggles on multiple fronts is further exemplified through Leila's story, which features as a subplot in Amal's narrative. Amal's engagement with Leila's struggles with her mother as well as the cross-cultural obstacles Amal herself faces as a result of becoming a hijabi takes place through an Islamic framework that allows the reader to analyze the nexus of imperial and neo-imperial geopolitics and local patriarchal, cultural, social, and economic imperatives.

Despite having a mother, Gulchin, who is more interested in getting Leila married rather than encouraging her to pursue her dream to become a lawyer, Leila does not blame Islam for her domestic disharmony. Restrictions are placed on Leila's movement because Gulchin believes the family will be disgraced if Leila is seen in public, which Gulchin fears will reduce Leila's chances of finding a husband: "*[y]ou [i.e., Leila] want career—you bad Muslim girl! You no want to marry—how you be good wife? You wear hijab, but you talk to boys at school"* (Abdel-Fattah, *Does My* 85; original emphasis). Even as Leila voices her frustrations about the way in which she is treated, she attributes Gulchin's rationale to the effects of cultural fixity on first generation migrants and their resistance to Westernization. By contrast, Leila's relatives' active participation in the living, evolving culture of Turkey is markedly different from Gulchin's reification of her memories having married young and migrated to Australia at the tender age of sixteen.

Leila knows that her maternal aunts and uncles would "have a fit if [her female cousins in Turkey] wanted to get married before they finished their [university] degrees. It's like [Leila's] Mum came [to Australia] all those days ago with the traditions of her village and got stuck in a time warp, while all her brothers and sisters progressed" (142). The diaspora often contributes to the psychic dislocation and subsequent antagonism of first generation migrants towards the cultural negotiations of the next. Meanwhile, the emergence of a powerful cultural memory discourse makes misfits of both groups in their adopted countries and their original homelands. Curiously, Western knowledge production about the hijab has maintained a similar stativity— first taken up by the colonial administration in the Middle East by insisting on the supposed inferiority of Islam for its sanction of what seemed an oppressive form of gender segregation and then by neo-imperialism in the guise of secularism and modernity—despite the amorphous nature of these unrelated concepts.

It is the unmet longing for home that generates rigid cultural practices and explains Gulchin's gender-specific treatment of her children. Abdel-Fattah argues that the oppression of Muslim women is "not *because* of Islam but *in spite* of it … [and] the distinction between personal choice (*Islamic*) and external compulsion (*unIslamic*) is crucial" particularly when it comes to wearing the hijab (Abdel-Fattah, "Living"; original emphasis). Thus, Leila does not waver in her religious belief because "[she is] going by what [she] feel[s] is right and what [she] know[s] about [her] faith; Leila further argues that she would never incorporate Islam in her life if its rulings "lock[ed] [her] in the house to cook and clean" (Abdel-Fattah, *Does My* 86). While Amal argues for Leila's right to make choices handed to her by Islam and prioritizes faith over other competing value systems, Gulchin defends her origins in Turkish culture by citing its loss as negation: "You think my culture I just throw away? … All I know is how I grow up and what my mum taught me. It is my village culture and my family culture and my home culture. If you losing your culture you becoming nothing" (312). Threatened with invisibility and irrelevance by her removal to the West, Gulchin faces imminent cultural death. She is also doubly marginalized as the culturally alienated woman practicing seclusion in Australia. While Gulchin's understanding of socially accepted behavior has no basis in the Quran, the holy book of the Muslims believed to contain the word of God, as these ideas are derived from "what her mum told her and what her mum's mum told her" (86), Gulchin's inability to interrogate the teachings she has received leads her to confuse culture with religion and eventually elevate cultural practices by vehemently believing them to be religious regulations. This further motivates Gulchin's desperate attempts to despotically raise Leila to be a carrier of her cultural teachings while her son may operate without cultural accountability in his immersion in the mainstream.

While the subplot with Leila acknowledges that the Muslim community does grapple with social issues such as forced marriages and familial enforcement of the hijab when culture masquerades as religion, it also makes a case for investigating the causes of the grievances instead of dismissing Gulchin as irrational and, therefore, unworthy of empathy. It should be noted too that sans her conflict with Leila, Gulchin attests to the existence of women who are happy to live in seclusion. Simone, Amal's Anglo-Australian friend at McCleans, suffers from a similar case of parental pressure with her mother neurotically fretting that Simone will not find a boyfriend unless she loses weight. Simone's story suggests that cultural norms that are tyrannical towards women are not exclusive to the Middle Eastern community. The plot further warns that Leila's story must not be pathologized as a "Muslim" or "Turkish" problem just like the way Simone's story is not a typical "Anglo-Australian" story as this attitude constitutes a failure to recognize the very real difference between representation and representativeness.

Amal's confidence in her cultural and religious identities rest on an awareness of the dangers of freezing any viewpoint as sacrosanct and the differences generated by specificity. Amal initially hastens to admonish Gulchin for her uncritical acquiescence to her fossilized past when Leila runs away from home after Amal, Leila, and Yasmeen are caught by Hakan, Leila's brother, celebrating Leila's birthday in a restaurant when they had promised Gulchin that they were going to spend the entire time at Amal's house. Gulchin rebukes Amal in return when she states, "I always thinking you [i.e., Amal] good girl. You wear hijab, you praying. You telling me I no know religion. Where your religion when you liar and you talking back to your friend mum?" (295). Here, Gulchin underscores the correlation between the hijab as a practice of piety and the overall moral improvement of the individual, and suggests that Amal has not achieved this because she disrespects Gulchin irrespective of the ways in which the latter is wrong, an allegation that Amal concedes as true upon self-examination.

A critical examination of the facts of Gulchin's subject position leads Amal to admit the moral high ground she had assumed, which is starkly similar to the superior cultural and moral plane Western feminists claim over

Eastern women in their narrow understanding of the forces that produce a victimized woman. This approach skews intersectionality by further eliding the history of feminism within the Islamic tradition.[12] Amal is empowered by traditional Islamic principles and identifies herself with the latter phenomenon when she asserts that "Islam is where [her] rights come from, so if some crappy cultural rule says [she has] to chuck [her] education or sit at home for life, then stuff it" (312).

Margot Badran argues that Islamic feminism locates gender equality in the Quran and the dictates of the Prophet Mohammed (PBUH) ("Islamic Feminism").[13] Amal takes up the objectives of Islamic feminism to rid Islam of the patriarchal practices that have been glossed into the religion and to reinstate gender equality through Islam's manifest expressions of human equality. She does this by extricating Islam from the distortions of misogyny and its imbrications with Eastern cultural practices to reveal a pristine form that enjoins social justice all the while inscribing a space for the hijab in the West. Amal's and Leila's stories also highlight how the differential treatment meted out by the West to the hijabi is a curious replication of the second-class citizenry that the hijab denotes when enjoined by Eastern patriarchy to keep women in a state of dependency. *Does My Head Look Big in This?* also showcases other hyphenated identities negotiating with stereotypes, revealing the different forms of neo-Orientalism in operation against minorities. Eileen, Amal's friend at McCleans, for instance, is Japanese, "[n]ot Chinese. Or Asian. Japanese. She doesn't have much patience for people who are too lazy to make the distinction" (Abdel-Fattah, *Does My* 41). Amal insists that it is the non–Western migrants in Australia who have fostered and enhanced her appreciation of her hybridity, and "inspired [her] to understand what it means to be Aussie" (339) by aiding her to move beyond constricting Anglo-Western notions of belongingness that are not available for her to emulate.

Finally, Amal has to re-assess her code of *"drool don't touch"* (97; original emphasis) when it is compromised by Adam's avowal of interest in her at his birthday. At this juncture, Amal reiterates the Islamic concept of a single soulmate that disallows dating or intimacy prior to marriage. Amal explains to Adam that she will not date casually as "[t]here's no formula to love! If [she] got with ten guys, each time will be different and each time [she will] be thinking this is a risk. And when [she] finally meet[s] someone [she is] still going to [face] ... the biggest risk of [her] life but ten other experiences aren't going to tell [her] if this guy is the right one. Each person is ... too unique to be judged by ten others" (230). It is noteworthy that Amal's justification of her motivation to obey Islam is not judgmental of other ways of finding love. Amal does not see her decision as self-abnegation as she had "the personal freedom to go out there and be with someone, to have kissed

Adam back but have *chosen* not to, that makes the decision [to be true to what she believes in] quite simple for [her]" (234; original emphasis).

Kristen Phillips studies Amal's rejection of Adam in terms of the sexual non-availability of the non–Western woman for the task of the reproduction of the white nation vis-à-vis the need to promote the idea that women are emancipated in the "free" West. Phillips suggests that turning Adam down "can be understood as provocative because it challenges assumptions within the multiculturalist discourse of integration about women and sexual availability ... invok[ing] the anxiety of Muslims remaining separate" (602). Phillips further argues that Amal's decision not to date Adam is a byproduct of her refusal to be contained by the dominant order, and rests on the implicit idea that she will only consider a Muslim when she is mature enough to marry (602–3). However, Amrah Abdul Majid argues in her PhD thesis that these interpretations limit and binarize Amal's actions as either Australian or Muslim when Amal would have refused a romantic relationship with a Muslim boy as this too would have been viewed by her as a deviation from her religion's stance towards teenage romance per se (91–100).

With blue-green eyes and fair hair, Amal's appearance meets Western ideals of beauty while confounding teachers with her foreign name by deconstructing the racialized image of the Other. This means that Amal's appearance already presents her with the possibility of being assimilated into the mainstream if she relinquishes her Islamic religion and Arab culture. Hence, her rejection of Adam is not a gesture of defiance against being subsumed into white patriarchy as much as it is Amal's determination to remain true to what she believes in. Amal reasons that "there was a bit of flirting now and again [between herself and Adam] but [she] never actually thought that [she] was inviting him to think [she] wanted him on that boyfriend/girlfriend level" (Abdel-Fattah, *Does My* 304), where attraction does not necessitate the traditional closure of the requital of love or sexual intimacy as has tended to be the typical but popular conclusion in romantic literature. It is the conjunction of a strong female-centered plot and Amal's minority status that pose a challenge to the reader's expectations because finding Mr. Right is not a prerequisite for a happy ending in this YAL about an adolescent who decides to wear the hijab in a post-9/11 world.

By avoiding the romantic angle, *Does My Head Look Big in This?* decenters the traditional love story, where even as Amal enjoys Adam's company, she does not play the victim card in her decision to abide by the Islamic preclusion of pre-marital sexuality, which is a code that exists in the other major world religions such as Christianity, Judaism, Hinduism, and Buddhism. Abdel-Fattah differentiates between desire as the pursuit of pleasure and sexuality that is independent of intimacy in her portrayal of Amal's friendship with Adam, which remains within Amal's understanding of Islamic dictates regarding the place of love and intimacy in her interaction with the opposite sex and allows her to reconcile with Adam as friends during the interschool debate where Amal leads her school to victory. The novel concludes with Amal arriving at a point where she is no longer in opposition with others, including Gulchin and Tia. During the debate, there is a moment when Tia's and Amal's eyes meet and Amal senses solidarity between them. Amal realizes that Tia too feels the mounting pressure as the opposition speaker pulverizes her teammate's argument. Amal is able to rise to the occasion once again in this scene after she recites verses from the Quran and is rewarded with a boost in confidence "[n]ot in spite of [her] hijab but because of it" (308) as she takes the podium.

No longer undermined by her identity as an Australian-Muslim but strengthened by it, Amal matures at this juncture as she declares that her tussles with identity and wearing the hijab are over and that she looks to the future as one filled with exciting possibilities. The familial and communal love and harmony with which *Does My Head Look Big in This?* ends makes romantic love extraneous to Amal's plot. The place of heterosexual love in a Muslim woman's life is explored in greater detail with Esma, Abdel-Fattah's protagonist in *No Sex in the City*, the novel I consider in the next section of this essay, when she seeks a husband from within her religious and cultural community using the arranged marriage setup. While Esma's story is not a continuation of Amal's as Esma describes herself as lazy in her observance of rituals, their similarity reside in their relative inexperience when it comes to romantic affiliations with the opposite sex as well as the ways in which they are empowered by Islam.

The Curious Case of the "Moderate Muslim"

Abdel-Fattah depicts the friendship of four Australian women from different ethnicities and their search for love in *No Sex in the City* (2012). Abdel-Fattah explains that her continuing the demystification of the Muslim woman of Middle Eastern extraction was motivated by the desire to provide an alternative to the narrative on female empowerment established by the popular HBO television series *Sex and the City*, which upheld a version of feminism that was "all white, wealthy and sexually active" in New York, which is coincidently one of the most cosmopolitan and culturally diverse cities in the world (Abdel-Fattah, "Chick-lit"). Carrie Bradshaw and her friends are posited as "ambassadors of "good" feminism"; it is assumed that their successful careers, brand-consciousness, explorations with sexuality, and search for Mr. Right cut across all forms of social divides ("Chick-lit"). Abdel-Fattah also observes that "characters with other ethnicities were very tokenistic or not strong enough to carry their own storyline" in *Sex and the City* (qtd. in Strachan, "Mr. Right"). "But what if [Carrie Bradshaw's and her friends'] experiences don't resonate?" Abdel-Fattah asks. "What if, in addition to class and lifestyle, the very search for Mr. Right plays out in very different ways, in accordance with very different norms and values? In short what if the search for Mr. Right involves no sex in the city?" (Abdel-Fattah, "Chick-lit").

With *No Sex in the City* Abdel-Fattah once again presents Islam as lending itself to multiple interpretations and to varying degrees of adherence amongst believers through the figure of what is classified as the "moderate" Muslim. The West normalizes moderate Muslims as "good" citizens and makes them integral to the multicultural ethos of the state. Set in cosmopolitan Sydney, *No Sex in the City*'s twenty-eight-year-old Muslim protagonist, Esma, is "not exactly observant" (6), but the plot reveals that this does not entail a total disregard of the Islamic faith. Esma's checklist for what she seeks in a potential partner reveals that she is not diametrically opposed to the hijab-wearer:

> Spiritual? Yes. Rituals? Quite lazy. Sure, I don't drink, I've never had a boyfriend (in fact, most primary-aged children would have more experience than me) and I'm inconsistent about keeping up with the five daily prayers … it would be nice to meet someone on the same religious level, or even a bit more observant than me. Not a totally clueless guy, or a fanatic either [6].

Here, Esma is clear that she is seeking someone who is of the same faith as herself. Abdel-Fattah examines the complexities of finding a partner when one is from "a religious belief system that's not part of the mainstream" which makes one's "pool of people who are [eligible to date] … a lot smaller" (Abdel-Fattah qtd. in Strachan, "Mr. Right"). Even as acts of piety are meant to bring the believer closer to the Creator, the novel positions the hijab as only one of the acts of a believing woman so that no single act or host of rituals can elevate one worshipper above the other in Islam for each practitioner is on their own individualized journey towards spirituality.

As a non-hijabi Esma is less visible than Amal and is, therefore, categorized as part of the silent majority of Muslims who are passed over by the Western gaze to focus on the hijabi's pronounced religious identity, but Esma's experiences are a testament to the mainstream's continuing construction of the Muslim woman as the abject Other irrespective of her "modern" and, therefore, "Westernized" appearance. Like Amal, Esma does not meet the Western narrative of the victimized woman; neither is she the quintessential Muslim woman in hijab imagined by conservative Islam nor does her lax attitude towards some of the practices of her faith typify her as secular. This is primarily because Esma still lives with her Turkish parents and is happy for them to arrange meetings with suitable men, one of whom she hopes to marry.

Esma's harmony with her parents is, however, perceived as an oddity. One reviewer, Lucy Popescu at the *Independent*, writes that Esma's "prudishness may grate with western readers"; Popescu was of the opinion that "contemporary fiction about women behaving badly is a lot more interesting than reading about dutiful daughters…. Feminists and the liberal minded may find it hard to identify with Esma's self-imposed limitations" ("Book"). This view fails to fathom the alternate storyline that may emerge when a Muslim woman is on an equal footing with her parents. Esma's reliance on the traditional model of the arranged marriage, which uses the community network to find suitable matches, may similarly be a stumbling block for some Western readers who view the setup as the loss of agency. The same reviewer concludes that Esma "stick[s] to her principles and, *without undergoing a profound psychological or emotional journey*, finds happiness" ("Book"; my emphasis). This reading is unwilling to concede Esma's journey into maturity where she negotiates the racial profiling of a client-employer in her job in a recruitment agency, her father's financial crisis which he conceals from the rest of the family, her boss's sleazy behavior, and suitors.

What *No Sex in the City* offers in essence is another pathway to find "the One" and still be Australian. Esma explains what the West would regard as a quirky self-imposition not to seek romantic love or engage in premarital intimacy as a decision that is both rational and reasonable, and one that she can wholeheartedly embrace because it is not enforced by her parents. Esma states that she "can do whatever [she] want[s]—[her parents are] not with [her] every moment of the day. Ultimately, [she is] the one who makes the choices about [her] life. [Her parents] just raised [her] in a certain way. [Esma has] embraced [her] traditions because [she] believe[s] in them" (Abdel-Fattah, *No Sex* 245). Esma's upbringing re-presents socialization as a two-way process between the individual and society where culture and religion are performative acts that are adopted, negotiated, and modified as per what the individual wishes to derive from the practices.

Similar to the hijab, the institution of the arranged marriage is another contentious issue in the West because of the simplistic deduction that the arranged marriage precludes romance and must therefore be a forced union. The novel's exploration of the process that the arranged marriage involves display the internal logic of the "lounge-room date" (Abdel-Fattah qtd. in Strachan, "Mr. Right") as the equivalent of the Western blind date. The way the extended family and the community network are involved in finding Esma a suitor is similar to self-appointed role Esma's boss, Danny, takes on when he frequently insists and even attempts to set her up with someone he approves of. The difference that nevertheless lies at the core of what may appear as parallel trajectories is that Esma welcomes the involvement of her family whereas Danny was never consulted and his involvement verges into harassment. I will explore Esma's conflict with Danny in more detail below.

Since the notion of romantic love as presented by *Sex and the City* hinges on strong female characters, it is assumed that the opposite is also true—that a woman with feminist beliefs cannot condescend to an arranged marriage. *No Sex in the City* thus reveals that Esma's "dates" with suitable men function in the same way that the Western concept of romantic love does, but with the process of trial and error geared to minimize the risk of heartache. Esma's story urges for what bell hooks describes as "the decolonization of ways of knowing" (3) and for engaging with people from other cultures through their epistemology. Hence, Esma's experience reveals that the contemporary arranged marriage is not a forced union with a complete stranger. Her quest for "the One" involves "two people getting to know each other with a mutual understanding that their 'dating' is limited to their search for a marriage partner" (Abdel-Fattah, *No Sex* 7). The meeting with suitors assists in assessing compatibility and the likelihood of achieving a secure, long-term relationship, and does away with the obsessive analyzing of every conversation and text message to decode if the relationship has a future or is just a casual fling. The premise of the meeting allows Esma to "put it out there from the beginning [that she is interested in marriage] and it just takes out the complication. You cut out the uncertainty" (46). Each arranged marriage is also unique to the individuals concerned: some people get to know each other over months, while others get engaged within weeks. This process seeks to fast forward the quest for and the probability of successfully finding Mr. Right by disqualifying all applicants who do not want to be married from the outset.

Unlike Gulchin's museumization[14] of her Turkish past in *Does My Head Look Big in This?*, innovations are made to tradition in order to keep up with the changing times in *No Sex in the City*. Esma's Turkish culture is reworked as her father invents the Rule of Six. This is an arrangement by which Esma can meet potential suitors without requiring her parents to be present: since asking another couple to go along for the meeting makes it look like a double date, Esma's father asks her to take four other family members because six people unambiguously make a group. He defends this plan by insisting "[l]et [the suitor] feel uncomfortable [for the large turnout]. [Esma is] the girl. It is all about [her] needs and [her] comfort" (63). While the narrator leaves it to the reader to imagine the awkward but humorous outcome when the suitor finds himself considerably outnumbered, Esma explains that the unsuccessful Rule of Six is gradually modified by her father until it becomes the Rule of Two where chaperones are consciously elided from the system.

Although a Muslim chick-lit may sound oxymoronic with "love at first family-get-together sight" (21) expected to happen with a suitor, the feminist agenda in *No Sex in the City* is apparent from the start as the tale revolves around friendship, family, and career, and with Esma insisting that "finding Mr. Right adds to your life rather than defines it" (30). The "No Sex in the City" club Esma forms with her three best friends from various religious, cultural, and ethnic backgrounds prove that it is possible for what is often pitted as competing value systems to coexist. Nirvana is Hindu and comes from an Indian background that is considered to be "conservative" by Western standards and also relies on the arranged marriage setup to meet suitors; Ruby hails from a Greek Orthodox family that expects her to settle down with a man who like her will be from the professional class; Lisa is a Jewish agnostic, and the only one among the four friends who does not actively seek a relationship for she finds marriage a claustrophobic institution and is decidedly against having children to fulfill her female "destiny." The four women are revealed to be simultaneously conservative and radical in different ways from the white mainstream version of femininity, feminism, family, dating, and romantic love. Abdel-Fattah insists that her characters are "not just sexy and exotic—they are normal and mainstream" (qtd. in Strachan, "Mr. Right") and, as in real life, the elusiveness of Mr. Right is countered by the overabundance of Mr. Wrongs.

In one such meeting, despite Esma's father telephonic inquiries about the suitor's age, education, family background, visa status, and English proficiency, Esma has to sit through a "date" with a suitor who barely speaks English apart from the lyrics of Celine Dion's "My Heart Will Go On." Esma decides that he is interested in her because of her Australian citizenship. No sparks fly nor does she feel "the click" with a man she can barely communicate with. Even as Esma is aware that she has a small pool of eligible bachelors to choose from given her formidable checklist and the relatively small size of the diasporic community, she nevertheless insists that she deserves to be swept off her feet by the man she will marry. Danny, on the other hand, masquerades as the archetypal enlightened Western man and as the self-proclaimed champion of the supposedly powerless non–Western woman living in the West. Armed with the classic arguments of Western feminism, Danny frequently reminds Esma of the sexual liberation movement of the 1960s as he urges her to go out with a man he approves of.

The downgrading of the Western brand of feminism into a trope that can be perfunctorily mouthed by a presumptive man is made apparent through Danny's double standards, which are exposed by his demeaning references about his own wife—"My wife married me, put on ten kilos and has been a bitch to me ever since" (Abdel-Fattah, *No Sex* 15)—and his insistence that his female employees should not think of getting pregnant in the next five years because his company has invested in them. Even as he offers to "loosen the shackles of [Esma's] stone-age faith" (43) by setting her up with his friend, Marco, who is a "top bloke" (15), Danny's married status becomes a buffer by which his intrusive probing of Esma's private life, his text messages asking her what kind of lingerie he should buy his wife to make the latter feel sexy, his machinations to see Esma alone in the office during the weekend, his suggestive comments on her Facebook wall, and his behavior in person make him an unofficial contender for Esma's attention and affection.

According to Meyda Yeğenoğlu, the Western fantasy of liberating the non–Western woman is "characterized by a desire to master, control, and reshape the body of the subjects by making them visible" (64). Since Esma does not wear the hijab and is considered as "visible" by Western standards, she can be said to meet the outward standards of the Westernized, "liberated" woman, the workings of what Judith Butler labels as "First World presumption" to dictate terms to the former colonies (41) is made evident in Danny's behavior towards Esma. At the workplace, it is Esma's Muslim identity and her acquiescence to her religion and culture that is still problematic for Danny. Despite her "progressive" appearance, she is still regarded as repressed by Danny for resisting his attempts to rescue her from what he perceives as the drudgery of an arranged marriage and for her reluctance to attend an office party at a bar. Abdel-Fattah explains her portrayal of Esma's sexual harassment as, "I wanted to look at the way people's personas can be contradictions and how they are shaped. It's surprising how so many strong women I know have been in those situations and they don't know how to stop it. They treat it as a joke, as they don't want to be known as a prude or the woman who can't take a joke" (qtd. in Al Hakawati, "Muslim chick lit").

On the flipside of this, the increased emphasis on national security places Muslim communities under surveillance by both the police state and fellow citizens, and Danny and Tia's behavior towards Esma and Amal, respectively, are lukewarm versions of the conscription of Anglo-Western "law-abiding" citizens in the "execution of nationalist practices" (Hage 27). Given that Muslim women's bodies are sites of the ideological battles between the East and the West, Abdel-Fattah opens the discursive field of the Muslim woman to include a diversity of "Muslim" experiences that together suggest that different subject positions may still yield similar decisions such that Amal may not be drastically different from Esma, and so while Amal refuses a romantic liaison, Esma too is not interested in love and compatibility until she is ready to get married. While it is evident that Esma's sense of belonging to Australia is espoused and affirmed by her hybridity—for instance, she is receptive to the idea of marrying someone from her community and faith but she will not compromise on proficiency in English since it is her first language or marry someone who holds chauvinist views—as a "moderate" Muslim, Esma continues to elicit white anxiety due to the ambiguity perceived in her ability to be under the radar even as the Islamophobic state applauds her for her "successful" Westernization and for the narrative she provides of the female Muslim success story.

For Danny, Esma is perilously situated in her liminality where despite all the ways in which she has acculturated and is similar to his Anglo-Western colleagues, Danny focuses on the ways in which Esma is different. Shakira Hussein asserts that "Muslim women success stories have reached the point where the Muslim-woman-breaking-stereotypes story has become a stereotype in itself.... According to the ever-more shrill voices of anti–Muslim scaremongering, stories such as these simply confirm the successful infiltration of Islam into Australian society" (85–6). Moreover, it is the inability to tell exactly where she *really* stands, compared to the hijabi, who has supposedly announced her allegiance with the non–Western world, who is an accomplice to the despotic Arab men and a carrier and transmitter of his culture, and must be watched for further subversions against the state, that motivates Danny to react in a manner that he feels will co-opt Esma in the biological and ideological reproduction of the white settler state.

Shelina Kassam argues that in the new "racial codification, the language of race is silenced, only to be reincarnated in the language of 'culture' and 'diversity,' a 'polite racism' that accepts difference at a surface level, but balks when the difference becomes politically charged or the Muslim body is perceived to transgress boundaries of acceptability" (625). Since Esma's "Aussieness" can never be on par with the Anglo-Australian subject, consigning her into Marco's protection and thereby, rebuilding the new Empire—this time in the total annihilation of the racialized and gendered Other in her redemptive service as a help meet to the Western man in the reproduction of the white settler state—within the confines of the West becomes the next best alternative to ensuring her de-radicalization.

Danny is thus motivated by what Iris Young proposes as the "logic of masculinist protection" (2). This is where citizens, who have traditionally been women and children, assume a subordinate position of grateful dependency in return for what they perceive as protection by the male security state. In order for the logic of masculinist protection to successfully function, the security state requires unquestioning loyalty, the limitation of its citizens' democratic freedom, and the complete censorship of what it labels as unpatriotic criticism. Danny alternates between soft and hard tactics with Esma, mobilizing an offensive that aims to suspend her say in the matter of how she should find love and whom she should marry. Casting Esma as the ultimate victim—as a prude and a nerd—enables Danny to recast himself as her protector whereby they resurrect and reinstate the racial, gender, and cultural hierarchy.

Esma's status as a so-called moderate Muslim also marks her as a potential native informant with "insider" knowledge about Islam and Arab culture.

Esma's "'rescue-ability' … [is] defined through terms that reveal how these women have become 'ours' or more like us" (Jiwani 736). Esma's supposed vulnerability is remedied with a readiness to lend her visibility and the platform to confront her sufferings in public, which will consequently validate Western claims about Islam and the Middle East. This motif is dismantled through such empowered figures as Amal in *Does My Head Look Big in This?* whose subscription to Islamic feminism enables her to take on Gulchin's oppressive plans for Leila. Abdel-Fattah counteracts the view that the hijab signifies the loss of voice or the initiation into fanaticism, by presenting Amal's feminism as a locally produced version that emerges from, and more importantly, as belonging to Australia, and tackles the mainstream's inability to accept that the Muslim woman retains her agency and the ability to critique cultural practices even when she is a hijabi. Similarly, Esma draws upon Australian and Turkish values as well as Islamic regulations to shape her identity and decisions. Esma's "arranged dates" (Abdel-Fattah, *No Sex* 308) with her Muslim suitors reveal that she is far from the helpless, sexually repressed woman who cannot negotiate for herself. Esma's interaction with Metin, who "oozes sex appeal" (232), illustrates that she is aware from the beginning that his tendency to dominate the conversation is a sign to be wary of.

Despite Metin being a catch, Esma concludes that "[she's] intelligent enough to know that because [she has] never experienced physical intimacy with a man, the intensity of sexual tension between [her] and Metin is clouding [her] judgment" (232), and proceeds to disallow herself from being overtaken by his good looks and dominating persona. However, Metin's ex-fiancée's betrayal and the resultant trust issues makes him propose that both he and Esma must cut off their friendships with the opposite sex in order to be truly exclusive to each other, a suggestion that is oddly reminiscent of the patriarchal establishment of the harem that segregated the sexes. Esma reasons with Metin that "[they] can't segregate [themselves] from the opposite sex; that's not how the world works. Each of [them] is going to be thrown into situations where [they will be] tested. Ultimately, it's about [their] character" (261). Esma's comment about integrity—or what Abdel-Fattah terms "intellectual conviction" (qtd. in Dow, "Love Match")—underscores the view that individuals from minority communities are not always forced to perform the religious, cultural, and social practices that have been passed down to them by the previous generation. Ultimately, Danny's suggestive posts on Esma's Facebook makes Metin declare that the male behavior of entitlement is encouraged by provocative women because "the way we behave gives people permission to treat us in certain ways" (332). This convinces Esma that she can no longer overlook the warning signs. Metin's expectations from Esma are also ironically another instance of male entitlement and a chauvinistic interpretation of why women are harassed.

It should be noted that Metin does not express religious motivations for his reservations on how the sexes should interact. As someone who grew up in Germany, it is neither his Middle Eastern origins nor his European upbringing that is responsible for his overbearing and jealous nature. In comparison, Esma's other suitor, Aydin, displays steadiness in the way he interacts with Esma. Esma and Aydin have similar interests: Esma volunteers at the Sydney Refugee Center and Aydin makes documentaries on social issues. Esma is clear that she will not rule a suitor out for having been intimate with a prior partner although she herself is a virgin. When Esma and Aydin openly express their interest in each other, Aydin also reveals that he had refrained from pre-marital sex, which reiterates a value that Esma personally espouses. Esma concludes, "this guy has character. I'm thinking that I don't care what the movies or magazines or society say, sex is a big deal and being with someone who 'saved' himself for me is exciting and terrifying and thrilling all at once" (358). In opting to be with Aydin over Metin, Esma proves that the system she adopts to find a partner who meets her religious and cultural expectations can give her a "happily ever after" resolution.

Of Esma's "No Sex in the City" club members, Ruby goes against her Greek family's conservatism by choosing someone who is not from her social class; traditional Nirvana courageously breaks off her engagement with Anil when he refuses to see anything wrong with his mother's overbearing attitude towards her. Esma concludes that "Nirvana got the fairytale ending because she had the sense to realize that Anil wasn't going to give it to her" (380); Lisa does not change her mind about marriage or children, opting instead to be happy for her friends and finding satisfaction in her work. The notion that marriage and romantic love can fulfill women is problematized by the four friends in their rebellion against normative expectations about finding a partner and encodes their choices as feminist. *No Sex in the City* reworks the feminist agenda by drawing upon non–Western cultures to argue that they too are capable of affirming women's rights when they are not yielded by patriarchal ideologies, which is a charge that can be equally leveled against Western values and social mores.

Re-making "Team Australia"

Multiculturalism in the West is often scapegoated for the ghettoization of minorities into their cultural and religious identities. The feared Islamization of Australia is further manifested in the "halal" food labels in supermarkets, the pregnant Muslim women engaged in "womb jihad," the construction of mosques, and the celebration of Eid festivals by the Muslim community (Abdel-Fattah, "Hate Islam").[15,16] When multiculturalism is branded a national problem and there are vituperative public opinions about deporting those who fail to meet the white "cosmopolitan" ideal, Muslims are reduced to repetitively condemning so-called Islamic terrorism and performing their fidelity to the nation. In addition, the neo–Orientalist racialization and demonization of the non–West sanctions pedagogic violence so that they can be "bomb[ed] ... into 'civilization'" (Abdel-Fattah, "Love Letter"). Consequently, when the multicultural project ceases to "manage, overwhelm or proselytise the minority can Australians of diverse backgrounds fulfil their potential as equal citizens ... [by] reimagin[ing] multiculturalism on the basis of shared civic values rather than racial or cultural ones" (Abdel-Fattah, "Australia's multicultural").

In this field of contestation, the "moderate" Muslim is rendered into an ahistorical and apolitical being who panders to and absolves the colonial guilt of the predominantly white settler state. This is because in order to get on with their lives the moderate must remain "outside of colonialism, neo-colonialism and racism ... [he/she] can acknowledge that his[/her] history and roots shaped him[/her] but ... maintain that the past is the past" (Razack 181). Abdel-Fattah resists the anti–Muslim narrative by creating embodied subjects who are radical in the way they approach and remake the mainstream. Far from being enthralled by middle-class aspirations to be assimilated into the power-yielding white mainstream through mimicry or through their identification as "moderates," Amal, Esma, and their friends in *Does My Head Look Big in This?* and *No Sex in the City* contest and transform the composition and values of the settler state by dismantling the very notion of the mainstream as well as the idea that the Anglo-Western community alone represent Australia.

Abdel-Fattah also points out the importance of moving past the inclination to define "identity in terms of resistance" (qtd. in The Powerhouse Museum, "Randa Abdel-Fattah"):

> Is a Muslim voice seen as some deviation from the norm, or can we accept that Muslim voices contribute to the mainstream space and are part of the mainstream? They are not just a sexy niche voice, an exotic other but are actually part of this "us" collective. Or are we constantly going to be referenced as "them"? [qtd. in The Powerhouse Museum, "Randa Abdel-Fattah"].

Amal in *Does My Head Look Big in This?* claims her place in Australian society by affirming its multicultural values, where "[w]henever we felt like a mishmash of identities and started to wonder what our place was here, there was Mr. Aziz [the principal at Hidaya Islamic College] telling us we didn't need to apologise for our heritage. Telling us that we weren't flat nouns, we had our adjectives, our ethnic backgrounds, which gave meaning and shape to our identity as Aussie Muslims" (Abdel-Fattah, *Does My* 212). This transition to a third culture embraces linguistic, cultural, racial, experiential, gender, and sexual categories, while leaving the damaging effect of labels behind for their proven role in the erasure of individuality. Amal's and Esma's access to a cross-section of society helps them face challenges and fosters their appreciation of Australia as the place they do belong to, because as bell hooks argues, "[a]nti-racist work requires of all of us vigilance about the ways we use language. Either/or thinking is crucial to the maintenance of racism and other forms of group oppression. Whenever we think in terms of both/and we are better situated to do the work of community building" (37).

Amal and Esma debunk monolithic ideas about Islam by adopting varying degrees of Islamic regulations that they wish to satisfy. This nuance allows Abdel-Fattah to represent the diversity and complexity that naturally exists within the Muslim community. Amal decides that she wants to undergo moral improvement by observing more religious practices, such as wearing the hijab in public and praying at each designated time rather than postponing it to when she is at home. Esma seeks a spouse who will complement her cultural and spiritual disposition. In their journey to self-realization, Amal and Esma conjugate their Middle Eastern origins with their Australian identity because their hyphenation is, in essence, the affirmation of both.

Does My Head Look Big in This? and *No Sex in the City* also point to the need to be aware of what Nigerian author, Chimamanda Ngozi Adichie, warns in her TED talk presentation as "the danger of a single story" ("The danger"). This is where grand narratives desensitize the Western public who continue to hold the Western "coalition of the willing" in high esteem, even after the visible devastation and destabilization it has wrought in the Middle East and Asia, by unilaterally focusing on violent acts that are perpetrated by "those" out "there" against "us." These narratives overwrite the ground reality, dehumanize people who are not like "us," and feed into ideologies that "they," the Islamic fundamentalists, hate "us" and "our" freedom and values. In this context, the Muslim woman is binarized as either victim or perpetrator. However, Anouar Majid argues that "whether veiled or not, women's conditions are determined not by the clothes they wear, but by the degree to which they manage to forge an identity for themselves that is not manipulated by the (often male-constructed) discourses of modernity or religious authenticity" (70).

Abdel-Fattah talks of "whistle-blowing" literature, where "the only time Muslim females appeared as heroines in books were as escapees of the Taliban, victims of an honour killing, or subjects of the Saudi royalty! I wrote *Does My Head Look Big in This?* because I wanted to fill that gap" (qtd. in Sandell, "Does My"). These native informant literature[17] need to be read as part of a larger narrative responsible for proliferating Islamophobia, and the racialization and marginalization of Muslims. The use of humor to do this humanizes Muslims and facilitates the imaginative ground for YAL readers to comprehend marginalized standpoints and engage in interfaith dialogue. Abdel-Fattah prioritizes allowing young adults to arrive at their own conclusions, and "although there are many issues in young adult fiction in particular which some people might say are inappropriate, but I [i.e., Abdel-Fattah] think we've come a long in the maturity of young adult fiction and the ability of writers to write about a whole range of topics" (qtd. in Irving, "Breaking down").

Abdel-Fattah explains her inclusion of religiosity as a theme in YAL as a "response to our neo-liberal, uncaring, profit-driven societies. People have given up expecting the state to care for them, and offer them a dignified future, and more and more people are turning to a spiritual existence as a way to understand the world and their place in it" (qtd. in Handal, "Both Freedom"). By showcasing a spectrum of beliefs in the sacred and challenging YAL readers to move beyond the narrative of the Muslim as a phenomenon to be feared, defended, or saved, the two texts examined in this essay posit Muslim womanhood as more than a phase of helpless confusion or willful rebellion. Abdel-Fattah's novels enter the daily inner lives of its characters to attest to their normalcy and place in the mainstream by pushing beyond the privileging of the hijab or the "moderate" Muslim identity to inscribe resistance into sites of interpellation like the school and the workplace. By engaging in the politics of visibility and identity through their status as protagonists, whereby those who have been previously otherized becomes speaking subjects, Esma and Amal contest the "secular" and "postsecular" descriptors where the insurrection of their subjugated knowledge reveal that they do not stop identifying as Muslim in their Australian-ness or as Australian in their Muslim-ness. The representation of Islam in YAL enable readers to investigate Anglo-Western feminism alongside Islamic and transnational feminism, and challenges presuppositions that female agency can only take one particular form.

Even though Esma may not wear the hijab, she remains within the fold of Islam, and this challenges received ideas about women who abide by traditional Islamic and Turkish values and the supposed opposition between secularism and piety. Finally, the depiction of the diaspora makes the novels different from most mainstream YAL due to the harmonious relations between Middle Eastern parents and their daughters, which reinforces the link between the individual and society, whereby the unraveling and negotiation of identity becomes an intergenerational process of discovery. In the imagined and real struggles for ascendency between religious practices and cultural engagement, the Australian citizen who is both diasporic and at home may experience an identity crisis whilst negotiating with religious ossification and cultural relativism, which Esma and Amal resolve through their hybrid identities and their informed differentiation between patriarchal behavioral codes and religious and cultural institutions like the hijab and arranged marriages. It is part of Amal's and Esma's feminism to be modern and secular in their negotiations with the modern state using the rights it bestows on its citizens to live culturally and religiously, and in their refusal to impose their worldviews on others, shattering yet another Western slogan that Muslims "hate our freedom."

NOTES

1. I use "First World," "Third World," "modern," "traditional," "secular," "conservative," "moderate," etc., loosely to register the constructed nature of these terms that is meant to convey certain hegemonized ideas.

2. Hijab in Arabic means to screen or cover, but does not specify in what manner this is to be done. It has typically been used to mean the covering of the woman's hair. Most hijab-wearers cover their head, ears, and neck and the hijab is worn by Muslim women who believe that practicing modesty is an injunction from God for believing men and women. I use the term hijab interchangeably with veil and headscarf.

3. Hidaya means "guidance" in Arabic. The suggestion is the school would be responsible for the transmission of Islamic, moral, and ethical teachings that Amal would proceed to adopt in her life. However, the plot subverts the charge of indoctrination and radicalization that is often levelled at Islamic schools established in the diaspora because it is only after Amal leaves Hidaya Islamic school where the hijab was part of the school uniform that she considers wearing the headscarf "full time."

4. In a 2005 interview, Liberal MP Browyn Bishop, for example, rejected the possibility that some Muslim women choose to wear the hijab. She insisted that she could not accept "someone who wants to be a little bit of a slave, or a little bit subservient. The fact of the matter is that in this country, freedom is defined by our laws, and that's the standard, not someone else's definition of what they think freedom might be" (qtd. in "National Interest").

5. Alia Imtoual's study (2007) revealed a trend in the mainstream to regard Australian-Muslim women as new migrants and as "non–Australians." These Australian-Muslim women's tendency to privilege their religious identity and community is understood to be a betrayal of their allegiance to the country. On the other hand, the Muslim women's negotiation with identity and belongingness reveals that there are alternative ways of belonging to the nation by "feeling" Australian where these women speak with Australian accents and idioms and view Australia as their home.

6. Liberal Prime Minister Tony Abbott, for instance, stated in 2014 that he found the burqa, which has traditionally been a black, loosely-fitting dress that Muslim women wear, but has of late accommodated colors and styles and been designed by leading fashion brands, a "confronting form of attire and frankly I wish it weren't worn" (Abbott qtd. in Bourke and Massola).

7. Liberal MP Bronwyn Bishop told the media that she saw Muslim girls wearing the headscarf in public schools as part of the forces contributing to "a clash of cultures and the headscarf is sort of being used as an iconic item of defiance." Bishop pushed the move to ban headscarfs in state schools where "[i]f people are in Islamic schools and that's their uniform, that's fine" (qtd. in AAP, "Bishop backs").

8. Feminist writer Carol Hanisch's 1970 essay, "The Personal is Political," discusses the necessity of recognizing the intersectionality of public or social issues and personal problems in order to mobilize collective action against the superstructure.

9. Liberal Prime Minister Tony Abbott argued in 2015 that "[e]very one has got to be on 'Team Australia.'" He further added that "[e]veryone has got to put this country, its interests, its values and its people first, and you don't migrate to this country unless you want to join our team" (qtd. in Griffiths, "Tony Abbott meets").

10. Abdel-Fattah argues in her article, published in the aftermath of the Lindt Café

siege in 2014 when a gunman with mental health issues and a criminal history held several people hostage, that the incident led to speculations of a terrorist attack by the Islamic State on Sydney. While questions were asked about how the legal system could allow such an individual to be out on bail, other questions pertaining to the role of the Muslim community that the gunman hailed from were voiced, such that "[t]o even express sympathy and offer condolence becomes tainted. Do we offer as human beings, as fellow Australians, as Muslims? To think that these categories are neutral is dangerously naïve. For all those many Australians who have the decency to see such expressions for what they are—sincerely felt grief as fellow human beings—there are many divisive voices operating in the structures of power in this country that will use such gestures to reinforce the idea—even implicitly, even unintentionally if you will—that Muslims must take responsibility" (Abdel-Fattah, "The Narrative").

11. The veil as a gaze inhibitor frustrated the colonizer's ethnographical viewing the "native" as a specimen in the gender-segregated Arab world. Arab women could not only not be seen by the male colonizer, but were instead seeing subjects (Yeğenoğlu 63). During the British occupation of Egypt which began in 1882, for instance, the veil worn by Arab women was made the "visible marker of the differentness and inferiority of Islamic societies" by the colonizer (Ahmed 152). The veiling and seclusion of Egyptian women were singled out by Lord Cromer as obstacles to the "attainment of that elevation of thought and character which should accompany the introduction of Western civilization" (Cromer qtd. in Ahmed 153). The Europeanization of Arab women became the final frontier to be mastered in order to ensure the colonizer's consolidation over and emasculation of Arab men. As the founding member and president of the Men's League for Opposing Women's Suffrage in Britain, Lord Cromer's championing of women's emancipation in Egypt reveals the imperial ideologies embedded in the discursive practices of colonial feminism. Hence, Randa Abdel-Fattah stated in the 2016 speech she presented at the International Women's Day breakfast hosted by Greens MP Mehreen Faruqi that feminists in the West "need to understand the link between imperialism, colonialism, western government's intervention in the third world and the destruction of civil society institutions and nation building projects that are fundamental to guaranteeing basic rights for women" (Abdel-Fattah, "Brown Lives").

12. Margot Badran traces two trajectories of feminism within Islam. While Muslim secular feminism originated in the late nineteenth century against the backdrop of modernization and the nationalist anti-colonial struggle, Islamic feminism, also known as "gender jihad," emerged in the late twentieth century as a post-colonial phenomenon and relies on the interpretation of Islam and gender as grounded in *ijtihad*, an intellectual investigation of the Quran and other exegetical texts (*Feminism* 2–9).

13. PBUH (Peace Be Upon Him) is used as a mark of respect when referring to all the Prophets in Islam.

14. Museumization suggests an artificial freezing of the evolutionary process of culture.

15. "Halal" is an Arabic term for what is permissive for Muslims to eat and do.

16. "Womb jihad" refers to what is perceived as the Muslim woman's contribution to the purported clash of civilization by engaging in the act of procreation that will increase the size of the Muslim population with the aim to outnumber the Anglo-Western community. Erica Millar (2015) studies, for instance, the pressure placed on white women to reproduce the nation vis-à-vis biopolitical strategies that discourage abortion in order to counter settler anxieties that Australia will become a Muslim nation if white women cannot be recruited to the task of procreation.

17. Hamid Dabashi (2006), for instance, responds to Azar Nafisi's *Reading Lolita in Tehran* (2003) as a comprador intellectual who "serve[d] a crucial function in facilitating public consent to imperial hubris," where he reads Nafisi's portrait of Iran as justifying the Western intervention in the Middle East ("Native informers").

Works Cited

AAP. "Bishop Backs Muslim Headscarf Ban." *The Age*. August 28, 2005. www.theage.com.au/news/national/liberal-mp-backs-headscarf-ban/2005/08/28/1125167541500.html.

Abdel-Fattah, Randa. "Australia's Multicultural Project." *Al Jazeera*. February 1, 2015. www.aljazeera.com/indepth/opinion/2015/01/australia-multicultural-project-201512183322327295.html.

Abdel-Fattah, Randa. "Brown Lives for a White Utopia: The War from the West." *New Matilda*. March 9, 2016. newmatilda.com/2016/03/09/brown-lives-for-white-utopia/.

Abdel-Fattah, Randa. "Chick-Lit for Muslim Women." *The Telegraph*. July 3, 2013. www.telegraph.co.uk/culture/books/10155944/Chick-lit-for-Muslim-women.html.

Abdel-Fattah, Randa. *Does My Head Look Big in This?* Sydney, Australia: Pan Macmillan, 2005.

Abdel-Fattah, Randa. "Hate Islam, Love Muslims? Exploring the Ambiguities of Islamophobia." *ABC Religion and Ethics*. July 11, 2014. www.abc.net.au/religion/articles/2014/07/11/4043888.htm.

Abdel-Fattah, Randa. "Living in a Material World." *Griffith Review*. February 2006. griffithreview.com/articles/living-in-a-material-world/.

Abdel-Fattah, Randa. "A Love Letter from New York: Randa Abdel-Fattah Writes Home." *New Matilda*, November 25, 2015. newmatilda.com/2015/11/25/a-love-letter-from-new-york-randa-abdel-fattah-writes-home/.

Abdel-Fattah, Randa, and Susan Carland. "Muslim Feminists Deserve to Be Heard." *The Sydney Morning Herald*. Fairfax Media, January 28, 2010. www.smh.com.au/it-pro/muslim-feminists-deserve-to-be-heard-20100127-mywf.html.

Abdel-Fattah, Randa. "The Narrative Must Shift: Randa Abdel-Fattah on the Need for a New Conversation." *New Matilda*. December 16, 2014. newmatilda.com/2014/12/16/narrative-must-shift-randa-abdel-fattah-need-new-conversation/.

Abdel-Fattah, Randa. *No Sex in the City*. Sydney, Australia: Pan Macmillan, 2012.

Abdel-Fattah, Randa. "Of Middle Eastern Appearance." *Griffith Review*. February 2007. griffithreview.com/articles/of-middle-eastern-appearance/.

Abdel-Fattah, Randa. "The Stigmatisation of Muslims as 'Could-Be Terrorists' Has Produced a Toxic Social Order." *The Guardian*. October 9, 2015. www.theguardian.com/commentisfree/2015/oct/09/the-stigmatisation-of-muslims-as-could-be-terrorists-has-produced-a-toxic-social-order.

Abdel-Fattah, Randa. "Tony Abbott's Anti-Muslim Bigotry Exposed." *Al Jazeera*. March 2, 2015. www.aljazeera.com/indepth/opinion/2015/02/tony-abbott-unambiguous-anti-muslim-bigotry-exposed-150224053709399.html.

Abu-Lughod, Lila. "The Romance of Resistance: Tracing Transformations of Power Through Bedouin Women." *American Ethnologisti* 17, no. 1 (February 1990): 41–55.

Adichie, Chimamanda Ngozi. "The Danger of a Single Story." *TED Talk* video, 18:49. July 2009. www.ted.com/talks/chimamanda_adichie_the_danger_of_a_single_story/transcript?language=en.

Ahmed, Leila. *Women and Gender in Islam: Historical Roots of a Modern Debate*. New Haven, Connecticut: Yale University Press, 1992.

Al Hakawati, Ameera. "Muslim Chick Lit, Revisited: Author of 'No Sex in the City' Shares Views." *Aquila Style*. November 4, 2014. www.aquila-style.com/focus-points/mightymuslimah/muslim-chick-lit-revisited/85026/.

Al Masseri, Abdulwahab. "The Imperialist Epistemological Vision." *American Journal of Islamic Law Scientists* 11, no. 3 (1994): 403–415.

Ang, Ien. "The Curse of the Smile: Ambivalence of the 'Asian' Woman in Australian Multiculturalism." *Feminist Review* 52 (Spring 1996): 36–49.

Asad, Talal. "French Secularism and the 'Islamic Veil Affair.'" *The Hedgehog Review* (Spring and Summer 2006): 93–107.

Badran, Margot. *Feminism in Islam: Secular and Religious Convergences*. London: Oneworld Publications, 2009.

Badran, Margot. "Islamic Feminism Revisited." *Al-Ahram* 781 (Feb. 2006). weekly.ahram.org.eg/Archive/2006/781/cu4.htm.

Brown, Wendy. *Regulating Aversion: Tolerance in the Age of Identity and Empire*. Princeton, NJ: Princeton University Press, 2006.

Bourke, Latika, and James Massola. "Burqa Debate: Tony Abbott Says People Need to Be

Identifiable in Secure Buildings." *The Sydney Morning Herald*. October, 1 2014. www.smh.com.au/federal-politics/political-news/burqa-debate-tony-abbott-says-people-need-to-be-identifiable-in-secure-buildings-20141001-10oio5.html.

Butler, Judith. *Precarious Life: The Powers of Mourning and Violence*. London: Verso, 2004.

Chang, Caitlin. "Randa Abdel-Fattah: Solidarity with Other Minorities Is Key to Fighting Racism." *SBS*. August 4, 2016. www.sbs.com.au/topics/life/culture/article/2016/08/04/randa-abdel-fattah-solidarity-other-minorities-key-fighting-racism.

Cooke, Mariam. "Religion, Gender and the Muslimwoman: Deploying the Muslimwoman." *Journal of Feminist Studies in Religion* 24, no. 1 (2008): 91–99.

Dabashi, Hamid. "Native Informers and the Making of the American Empire." *Al-Ahram* 797 (1–7 June 2006). weekly.ahram.org.eg/Archive/2006/797/special.htm.

Dow, Steve. "Love Match." *The Sydney Morning Herald*. July 8, 2012. www.smh.com.au/entertainment/books/love-match-20120706-21nbs.html.

Griffiths, Emma. "Tony Abbott Meets with Muslim Community Leaders in Bid to Sell Proposed Counter-Terrorism Laws." *ABC*. August 18, 2014. www.abc.net.au/news/2014-08-18/abbott-meets-with-muslim-leaders-to-sell-counter-terrorism-laws/5678538.

Hage, Ghassan. *White Nation: Fantasies of White Supremacy in a Multicultural Society*. London: Pluto Press, 2000.

Haines, Colin. "Challenging Stereotypes: Randa Abdel-Fattah's Use of Parody in Does My Head Look Big in This?" *Bookbird: A Journal of International Children's Literature* 53, no. 2 (2015): 30–35.

Handal, Nathalie. "Both Freedom and Constraint: An Interview with Randa Abdel-Fattah." *Words Without Borders*. April 2015. www.wordswithoutborders.org/article/both-freedom-and-constraint-an-interview-with.

Hanisch, Carol. "The Personal Is Political." In *Notes from the Second Year: Women's Liberation*, edited by Shulamith Firestone and Anne Koedt. Radical Feminism, 1970. Couldn't find publisher location

hooks, bell. *Teaching Community: A Pedagogy of Hope*. London: Routledge, 2003.

Huggan, Graham. "Is the 'Post' in 'Postsecular' the 'Post' in 'Postcolonial'?" *Modern Fiction Studies* 56, no. 4 (Winter 2010): 718–751.

Hussein, Shakira. *From Victims to Suspects: Muslim Women Since 9/11*. Montgomery, AL: Newsouth, 2016.

Imtoual, Alia. "'Is Being Australian About Being White?': Australian Whiteness, National Identity and Muslim Women." In *Taking Up the Challenge: Critical Race and Whiteness Studies in a Postcolonising Nation*, edited by Damien W. Riggs. Goolwa, Australia: Crawford House Publishing, 2007.

Irving, Sarah. "Breaking Down Stereotypes: Randa Abdel-Fattah Interviewed." *The Electronic Intifada*. May, 4 2011. electronicintifada.net/content/breaking-down-stereotypes-randa-abdel-fattah-interviewed/9912.

Jiwani, Yasmin. "Helpless Maidens and Chivalrous Knights: Afghan Women in the Canadian Press." *University of Toronto Quarterly* 78, no. 2 (2009): 728–744.

Kassam, Shelina. "'Settling' the Multicultural Nation-State: Little Mosque on the Prairie, and the Figure of the 'Moderate Muslim.'" *Social Identities* 21, no. 6 (2015): 606–626.

Mahmood, Saba. *Politics of Piety: The Islamic Revival and the Feminist Subject*. Princeton, NJ: Princeton University Press, 2012.

Mahmood, Saba. "Retooling Democracy and Feminism in the Service of the New Empire." *Qui Parle* 16, no. 1 (2006): 117–143.

Majid, Amrah Abdul. "The Practice of Faith and Personal Growth in Three Novels by Muslim Women Writers in the Western Diaspora." Master's thesis, National University of Malaysia, 2015.

Majid, Anouar. "The Politics of Feminism in Islam." In *Gender, Politics, and Islam*, edited by Therese Saliba, Carolyn Allen, and Judith A. Howard. Chicago: University of Chicago Press, 2002.

Millar, Erica. "Too Many." *Australian Feminist Studies* 30, no. 83 (2015): 82–98.

"The National Interest: 28 August 2005—Bronwyn Bishop Responds to the Aussie Mossie."

Australian Broadcasting Corporation. www.abc.net.au/cgi-bin/common/printfriendly. pl?http://www.abc.net.au/rn/talks/natint/stories/s1447773.htm.

Phillips, Kristen. "Provocative Women in the Border Zone: Articulations of National Crisis and the Limits of Women's Political Status." *Continuum* 23, no. 5 (2009): 597–612.

Popescu, Lucy. "Book Review: No Sex in the City, by Randa Abdel-Fattah." *The Independent*. July 14, 2013. www.independent.co.uk/arts-entertainment/books/reviews/book-review-no-sex-in-the-city-by-randa-abdel-fattah-8707535.html.

"Randa Abdel-Fattah." *Powerhouse Museum*. 2012. www.powerhousemuseum.com/faith fashion/women-in-profile/randa-abdel-fattah/.

Razack, Sherene. "Making Canada White: Law and the Policing of Bodies of Colour in the 1990s." *Canadian Journal of Law and Society* 14, no. 1 (1999): 159–184.

Said, Edward W. *Orientalism*. New York: Vintage Books, 1979.

Sandell, Lisa Ann. "Does My Head Look Big in This? Book Focus." *Scholastic Inc*. www.scholastic.com/teachers/article/does-my-head-look-big-book-focus-0.

Spivak, Gayatri Chakravorty. "Can the Subaltern Speak?" In *Colonial Discourse and Post-Colonial Theory: A Reader*, edited by Patrick Williams and Laura Chrisman. New York: Columbia University Press, 1994.

Strachan, Julieanne. "Mr Right's Gotta Have Faith." *The Sydney Morning Herald*. July 1, 2012. www.smh.com.au/lifestyle/mr-rights-gotta-have-faith-20120627-213fz.html.

Yeğenoğlu, Meyda. *Colonial Fantasies: Towards a Feminist Reading of Orientalism*. Cambridge: Cambridge University Press, 1998.

Young, Iris Marion. "The Logic of Masculinist Protection: Reflections on the Current Security State." *Sign: Journal of Women in Culture and Society* 29, no. 1 (2003): 1–25.

The Customized Religion

Moralistic Therapeutic Deism,
American Teenagers and
Pete Hautman's Godless[1]

JACOB STRATMAN

In the introduction to *Coming of Age in Contemporary American Fiction*, Kenneth Millard suggests that "adolescents are important because of the ways in which they are at the forefront of social change, even while they are simultaneously the products of an adult social culture that shapes their development" (1). The misfit or outcast seems to be an obvious result of a young person's desire to express his/her autonomy and individuality within a particular context that is created by the parent-world. According to Millard, "there is a struggle here between self-fashioning on the one hand, and historical determination on the other, and it is in the tension between the autonomy of the individual and the shaping pressure of history that the political ideology of each novel lies" (10). This tension is intriguing to me in the way that it involves a child's spiritual development and religious struggles and in the ways that authors create a religious ideology in their novels.

What is particularly interesting to me is that even though these "misfits" create a separate religious reality quite outside of the center in an attempt to maintain order and structure in their lives, they are, according to Christian Smith's seminal work *Soul Searching: The Religious and Spiritual Lives of American Teenagers*, surprisingly in line with the majority of American teens. Smith argues that most teenagers' ideas of religion, faith practice, and theological doctrine are completely outside of the center of historically orthodox religion (Islam, Judaism, Christianity, namely) even though they may profess one of those religions. Exploring the religious lives of American teenagers has become increasingly common and important in this post–9/11 era.[2] How

Smith's work intersects with Young Adult Literature, namely Hautman's *Godless*, is the focus of this essay.

Pete Hautman's 2004 National Book Award winning novel, *Godless,* "a semi-autobiographical condensation of my teenage journey from devout Roman Catholic to skeptic," explores the life of a young man, tired of his parents' religion, who creates his own religion and fully equips it with a sacred text, sacraments, rules and commandments, and a need for community (Candlewick Press Kit). Of course, hi-jinks ensue. Hautman dedicates his novel "for those who would walk alone." In light of Smith's work and how the novel allows a character to create a religion that flirts with orthodoxy and unorthodoxy, I want to explore how this novel reflects more accurately current trends in American teenage religious thought and practice than perhaps Hautman intended. Ultimately, calling the protagonist, Jason Bock, a misfit or outcast, as the inscription implies, is misleading.

The novel begins with big-man Jason Bock and his skinny, nerdy (and not incredibly emotionally stable) best friend Shin running into the local ruffian Henry Stagg. Jason and Shin are at the park near the town's water tower looking for snails for Shin's snail farm (Shin calls it a gastropodarium) when Henry interrupts them with shouts of ridicule and contempt. Finally, Henry slugs Jason, felling him quickly. Jason does not retaliate (which he could have done easily, since Henry is only 5' 5"); instead, he just remains on his back looking up. He says,

> I was flat on my back looking up past Henry at the silver, dripping bottom of the water tower tank, my head still scrambled, when it hit me just how important that tower was to St. Andrew Valley. It was the biggest thing in town. Water from that tower was piped to every home and business for miles around. The water connected all of us. It kept us alive. That was when I came up with the idea of the water tower being God [8].

Jason lives with his normally ineffectual parents.[3] His mother's "specialty is diagnosing rare diseases in other people" and his father's specialty is spirituality. He is an orthodox Catholic who drags Jason to mass at the Church of the Good Shepherd each Sunday and sends Jason to Teen Power Outreach every Thursday night in the church basement. Like most adolescents, Jason tries to order and structure a universe that has very little to do with his parents; he does this by starting his own religion. After recruiting his best friend, Shin; his crush, Magda Price; the good Lutheran, Dan; and eventually the ruffian Henry Stagg, the Chutengodians, as Jason calls them, begin creating a water tower-worshipping religion.

Recently, I have discovered several young adult novels that take this disenchantment with organized religion in a different direction. Instead of appropriating their parents' mainline beliefs or wholly rejecting organized religion for individual existential ideas, for example, these protagonists create their own belief system that actually mirror, and at times mimic, although in incredibly odd and bizarre ways, the belief system of the orthodox world while remaining in the margins of that orthodoxy: Cynthia Voigt's *Tree by Leaf*, Bruce Brooks' *In Asylum for Nightface*, Robert Heinlein's *Stranger in a Strange Land*, William Golding's *Lord of the Flies* Pete Hautman's *Godless*, and even Yann Martel's *Life of Pi*. These titles are representative of a subgenre of religious novels written for teens where characters create alternative universes or higher beings to help them order their universe. These characters tend to be, quite frankly, either emotionally unstable or a visitor from another planet or universe. Life's chaos and trauma drive them to madness as they attempt to work out their own religious and spiritual struggles. It seems to me that Hautman's Jason Bock is quite different than most characters in these types of plots: he's bright, insightful, witty, stubborn, a bit cynical, a lot sarcastic, a bit immature, impulsive, thoughtful, articulate, and pretty normal for an American, suburban, middle-class teenager. Insane he is not. This protagonist is in control of his own questions, struggles, and searching. Jason Bock systematically and logically creates a religion outside of mainstream orthodox religions as a way to order his normally teenage chaotic life.

Hautman's inscription, then, is intriguing and ironic at the same time. Again, he dedicates the story of Jason Bock and his newfound religion "for those who would walk alone," and he thanks a variety of people for "their water-tower stories." This dedication certainly gives power and agency to Jason's decisions to create a religious system that functions outside of the religious center created by adults. It is easy to see that Hautman likes Jason and any other kid willing to push back on orthodox religion. As Joel Shoemaker writes,

> One of the strengths of this book is the emphasis Hautman puts on the idea that Jason—and, by extension, teens in general—think and care about religion, faith, and ritual. Jason is not a "whacko"—he's a normal, smart, curious teen who finds that religion, in one way or another, is never far from the surface of his life [43].

Again, the inscription may try to set Jason apart from other kids, and while his ideas might be classified as incredibly odd and even "whacko," his motivations for creating a new religion are not.

At the end of the novel, after many problems (legal and social) have occurred due to the Chutengodians, Jason and his father argue about religion. Breaking an awkward silence, Jason exclaims, "What makes being a Catholic so special? What about Buddhism, or Hinduism, or whateriverism. Look, I admit it was a dumb idea to climb the tower. I'm sorry. But that doesn't make Chutengodianism any dumber than your religion…. It's all made up anyway" (145). And, as the readers begin to believe, as the plot synopsis on the back of the book leads us to believe, that Jason will have a change of heart and see the error of his ways, Hautman surprises all of us with the last paragraph of the novel. Jason intimates his entire religious experience: "Me? I have Chutengodianism—a religion with no church, no money, and only one member. I have a religion, but I have no faith. Maybe one day I'll find a deity I can believe in. Until then, my god is made of steel and rust" (198). Jason's sincerity (although some can argue misguided) impresses upon me that Jason is not a satirical tool or a vehicle for religious criticism; he is simply a character who genuinely creates a new religion in response to his world. Hautman's hero is the teenager who risks everything to create his own religious path instead of simply following the order and structure laid down by an adult's orthodox religion. The irony is that, although the particulars of Chutengodianism may place Jason's religion in the margins, Jason's religious thoughts and explorations mirror current trends in American teenage religious practice, namely moralistic therapeutic deism.

Moralistic Therapeutic Deism

From 2001 to 2005, the National Study of Youth and Religion, led by Christian Smith (William R. Kenan, Jr. Professor of Sociology and Director of the Center for the Study of Religion and Society at the University of Notre Dame) then at University of North Carolina Chapel Hill, surveyed thousands of adolescents around the country to better understand their religious practices and spiritual lives. The study's findings were published from Oxford University Press as *Soul Searching: The Religious and Spiritual Lives of American Teenagers* in 2005 (one year after *Godless* was published). Although the research shows that most teenagers "generally view religion as something that simply *is* and not the kind of thing worth getting worked up about one way or the other," this standard view is made possible only when the idea of religion becomes utterly subjective and personal (124). The study argues that the orthodox, mainline religions, especially Christianity, are "either degenerating into a pathetic version of itself, or more significantly, Christianity is actively being colonized and displaced by a quite different religious faith" (171). Smith and his team coin this new religion Moralistic Therapeutic Deism. It is formally defined as "a widely shared, largely apolitical, interreligious faith fostering subjective well-being and lubricating interpersonal relationships in the local public sphere" (169). Although Jason does not profess an orthodox religion (actually, he openly opposes them), I still argue that Jason's religious practices are very similar to moralistic therapeutic deism practiced by his contemporaries.

The only difference between Jason's thinking and Smith's American teenagers is Jason's cognizance. He completely understands that he is creating a religion that resists and rejects parts of orthodox religion.[4] To him, it's a game—a serious game, but a game nonetheless. For Smith's interviewees, their theological understandings seem orthodox to them. Smith argues that if we define Christianity based on American teenagers' views of Christianity, then "Christianity in the United States is actually only tenuously Christian in any sense that is seriously connected to the actual historical Christian tradition, but has rather substantially morphed into Christianity's misbegotten step cousin, Christian Moralistic Therapeutic Deism" (171). For the remainder of the paper, I want to briefly discuss moralistic therapeutic deism's major tenants and how they apply to *Godless*.

First, Smith's teens believe that "a God exists who created and orders the world and watches over human life on earth" (162). Each chapter of the novel begins with a brief epigram with loaded religious imagery. Readers discover that each epigram is a part of the Chutengodians' sacred text (called *Genesis*) written and kept secretly by Shin. Chapter one begins with, "In the Beginning was the Ocean. And the Ocean was Alone" (1). In Shin's sacred narrative, Ocean is the god-head. We learn that Ocean creates everything, including rivers, lakes, and eventually humans to safeguard the water sources. It is obvious that Shin steals verbiage from Genesis and the common, yet not theologically sound, concept that God was lonely before He created the universe. But more importantly, the sacred text, much like many sacred texts, describes and defines the god-head as one who exists and is sovereign over creation.

Another tenet of moralistic therapeutic deism is that "God does not need to be particularly involved in one's life except when God is needed to resolve a problem" (163). Shin's sacred text is helpful. The problem with Ocean's humans is that they create dams, dig canals, and pollute water supplies and the air. Chapter nine's epigram states, "And it came to pass that the lands and the waters became stained with human filth, and the Ocean became concerned" (50). In an effort to save the creation, Ocean commands the humans to create effigies where Ocean can maintain its purity. Each ten-legged god is worshipped as an intercessory for Ocean. At the end of the novel, the sacred text narrates the great war between the Faithful (those who believe in the Ten-legged gods) and the Pragmatists (those who believe that the water-towers are man-made), which ends in the destruction of all humans, creatures, and water-towers. The last chapter states, "And in the end, only the Ocean remained, and the Ocean was alone" (193). Shin's god, much like many teenagers' god, only interacts with creation when it is necessary. Like the Enlightenment's clock maker, God tends to the creation only in an effort to get it going again.

Shin's text, although bizarre to many orthodox believers and other teens, still explores theological ideas like paradise, worship, sin, salvation, and destruction. And, according to Smith, Shin and his text are not that different from many contemporary teens. Smith's study shows many examples of teens' "propounding theological views that are, according to the standards of their own religious traditions, simply not orthodox" (136). I'll give you three:

> One 13-year-old white mainline Protestant girl from Colorado told us, "I think [laughing] I kind of picture God like this man, this woman, all types of animal and I mean no real total definition, can't even see the shape or anything, this great amazing being who, one snap of his or her fingers and a human being is born, it's just amazing and really nice."
>
> A 14-year-old Hispanic Catholic boy from California said, "I kinda believe in reincarnation and I kinda don't, 'cause like my little brother totally believes in it, that he can become a hawk as soon as he's dead. Sometimes I think it's cool and then my cousin says no, so I'm all lost. So I just kinda believe in it."
>
> A 15-year-old Arabic Muslim boy from California summarized religious faith as, "I don't know, just like pretty much try to live life without regrets, try to take responsibility for what you do, 'cause I don't know, just don't be a bitch about things. Try to make things fair, that's another thing, as fair as possible" [136].

Not to overstate my claim, but Shin and Jason simply do not walk alone. They, like many American teens, create religious doctrines that may look like orthodoxy but, actually, simply reflect that particular teenager's desires and subjectivity.

The next two tenants of moralistic therapeutic deism are "God wants people to be good, nice, and fair to each other, as taught in the Bible and by most world religions" and "The central goal of life is to be happy and to feel good about oneself." Whether you believe that this type of subjectivity or individualism is a product of postmodern thinking or not, Smith suggests that "some version of individualistic subjectivism and relativism is the dominant, assumed viewpoint about religion among most contemporary U.S. adolescents" (145). Early in the novel, Jason and Shin discuss the new religion when the very pretty Magda Price interrupts:

> "Can I join?"
> "I thought you were a good Catholic girl."
> "Can't I be Catholic and Chutengodian at the same time?"
> Like I said, Magda can't stand to be left out of anything [44].

To Magda, espousing two different religions is not a problem. If a religious practice keeps one out of a social gathering, then it would seem silly not to subscribe to another religious practice, if only to be involved socially with those practitioners. It's just religion. Jason responds to Shin's and Magda's conversion this way: "Why mess around with Catholicism when you can have your own customized religion? All you need is a disciple or two. And a god" (18). This new religion feels good and maintains social relations without conflict. Religion has no authority over the believer; instead, each teen is in charge of his/her own religious design as it pertains to his/her particular need or desire.

Earlier in the novel, Jason states that he has no faith. He makes it clear in the novel that he doesn't actually believe that the water tower is omnipotent. He assures the reader that "I might be a religious zealot, but I'm not crazy" (90). Later, he even says to Shin, who is falling deeper and deeper into madness, "What do you expect? I mean, it *is* kind of a joke" (99). What he is, however, is serious about religion. He has defined religion as a community of believers that has sacraments, commandments, and worship experiences. Jason knows the basic tenants of religious practice: evangelism, worship, sacrament, and community living. He gets it. This cognizance can be quite alarming to the adult world as teenagers attempt to piece-meal a religious framework that best fits him. As Jason defines religion for the reader, he states, "There are something like ten thousand religions in the world. What makes them think that they happen to have been born into the right one? I have asked this question several times. So far, I haven't' heard a good answer. Better to start your own religion, I think. That way you get to be your own pope" (34). Jason's goal is not necessarily to walk alone but to be in charge of his own narrative.

The irony with Jason, and other teenagers portraying control, is that Chutengodianism is simply an amalgamation of other, more orthodox, religious narratives. Smith's study is clear in stating that world religions, adult religious practices, and social engagement with religion do influence the way teens think about and practice their own type of religion, as we see in *Godless*. Practice is still important, and practicing religion well is what matters in the end. Therefore, lastly, moral therapeutic deism promulgates that "Good people go to heaven when they die" (163). Chutengodianism and moral therapeutic deism are works-based theologies that focus on pleasure, fairness, and community. As a part of a working theology, the Choots come up with commandments and rules in order to create goodness and fairness. Jason speaks of the necessity for commandments in any religion. He says,

> I'm well on my way. I have a god, I have sacraments, and I have two converts—plus myself. But the Church of the Ten-legged God (CTG for short) still needs one more thing: a set of rules, or commandments. I wonder what sort of commandments the Ten-legged One might hand down. I'll have to make some up [34].

And so he tries out one on fellow followers: "Thou shalt not pollute the water supply" (62). Later, however, after a coup of sorts, Henry Stagg creates an alternative list of commandments:

1. Don't be a wuss
2. Don't forget to duck
3. Don't take any shit

4. Honor you fellow Choots
5. Don't fall
6. Don't get caught<

The rules seem to change as the group changes, but the principle is the same: create rules that order lives and practices in a way that perpetuates goodness and fairness.

Jason also attempts, like many churches and religious centers to create community through corporate worship. Following Henry's lead, the group ascends the town's water tower. Not sure what to do while they're up there, Jason suggests a "Midnight Mass." He even urges Henry, the High Priest, to create the Chutengodian Beatitudes to recite during worship: "Blessed are the climbers: for theirs is the kingdom of water. Blessed are those who reek: for they shall be cleansed. Blessed are they who thirst: for they shall drink the water of life" (95). These beatitudes, the sacred text, and the commandments all show that Jason attempts to create a religious discourse for his followers. This discourse, coupled with the practice of climbing the water tower for worship, creates community. These are not the acts of a kid who wants to "walk alone."

Conclusion

Chutengodianism is a religion; therefore, it is a part of a community. Yes, we can rightly assume that it is an amalgamation of world religions or simply an odd replica of American Christianity. However, Jason's religion is fully equipped with a sacred text that looks a lot like Genesis, sacraments, commandments and rules, and a particular interest in creating community. With enthusiasm about his new creation, Jason says, "By summer's end we might convert half of St. Andrew Valley. I could be like the guy that started the Mormon religion, or Scientology" (46). So, he is not really alone. He follows a long line of religious prophets and leaders.

Complementing the diverse and complex conversation concerning the definition of religion, Bruce Lincoln (professor of History of Religions at the University of Chicago) suggests that if we are to label something a religion then it must contain four domains[5]:

1. a discourse whose concerns transcend the human, temporal, and contingent, and that claims for itself a similarly transcendent status.

2. A set of practices whose goal is to produce a proper world and / or proper human subjects, as defined by a religious discourse to which these practices are connected.

3. a community whose members construct their identity with reference to a religious discourse and its attendant practices.

4. An institution that regulates religious discourse, practices, and community, reproducing them over time and modifying them as necessary, while asserting their eternal validity and transcendent value [5–7].

Although it might be useful and intriguing to see how the Chutengodians perform under these domains, the scope of my argument is simply to argue that the Chutengodians do perform what they consider a religion. And, according to religious scholars, they are doing just that. Where the adults of this novel (and I assume adult readers as well) misunderstand Jason and his friends is that they trivialize teenagers' exploration of the tension between orthodox religious belief and teenage life experience. During a discussion about Jason's TPO meetings, his father says, "I hear you talk about quite a number of things.... I bet you kids come up with some pretty wild stuff ... that you kids have a lot of strange ideas" (102–103). The father's use of words "wild" and "strange" place Chutengodian ideas into the margins; however, what the father misunderstands that, although this religion is not Christianity, Islam, or Judaism, it is the product, according to Lincoln's definition, of orthodox religion. It is, ultimately, one teenager's way to respond, react, resist, and struggle with orthodox religions handed to him by a seemingly ineffectual, irrelevant, and even ignorant adult world.

This is the religious landscape of Jason Bock and the Chutengodians. And, although Hautman does introduce a protagonist that creates a religion quite outside of the religious center, Smith's work convinces me that Jason's religious practices are actually quite similar with the majority of his friends and classmates. Ultimately, Jason does not walk alone; he is no misfit even if Hautman wants him to be. Young Adult literature is filled with young protagonists that struggle, resist, or even reject the adult world's orthodox religious frameworks for a more individual experience outside of mainline beliefs due to tragedy, overbearing and overzealous parents, corrupt religious leaders, etc.[6] So, if Kenneth Millard is correct in stating that "the contemporary novel of adolescence is often characterized by a concerted attempt to situate the protagonist in relation to historical contexts or points of origin by which individuals come to understand themselves as having been conditioned," then *Godless* is the perfect novel to begin discussions about the American teenager's exploration of religion in the twenty-first century (10). For both Jason and American teenagers, the tension is that they are caught between already constructed, historically orthodox truths handed down to them by the adult-world and their own desires to construct truth for themselves. *Godless* is the product of that tension.

Notes

1. A version of this article was first published in *Literature and Belief* (33.2). Many thanks to Jesse Crisler, editor, for the permission to use a revised version for this collection.

2. A Gallup poll asked the following question: "At the present time, do you think religion as a whole is increasing its influence on American life or losing its influence?" From 2002–2009, the average percentage of people who answered "increasing" was about 38 percent. Interestingly, in 2001, 58 percent of those polled answered that religion is increasing its influence on America.

3. In Patricia Campbell's *The Last Taboo: Spirituality in Young Adult Literature* (2016), she writes about parents in religiously themed novels: "Parents in books of this church-negative type are usually either gullible fanatics or unbelievers who are obstacles to their children's religious interests" (xv). In *Godless*, however, the Bocks, while a bit out of touch with Jason, seem thoughtful and supportive of Jason's explorations. Actually, they seem quite normal.

4. This might be a plot fault. If Smith's studies are accurate, then Jason thinks much more articulately and analytically about religion than most teenagers. This can be true of course, but Jason could also be the voice of an adult author.

5. First, I would like to thank Dr. Robert Moore (Associate Professor of History, John Brown University) for introducing me to Lincoln's, Geertz's, and Asad's work. It should be noted that Lincoln's careful suggestions are a part of a large, complex conversation about the definition of religion. His four domains are a product of and in response to, in particular, Clifford Geertz' "Religion as a Cultural System" (1966) and Talal Asad's *Genealogies of Religion: Discipline and Reasons of Power in Christianity and Islam* (1993).

6. There are several published lists of religious-themed Young Adult novels. Start with Janet Hilbun's "The Role of Protestant Christianity in Young Adult Realistic Fiction" (*Journal of Religious and Theological Information*, 7 (2009): 181–201) and "I Believe It, I Doubt It: Young Adult Fiction for Questioning Christians" in VOYA: *Voice of Youth Advocates* (June 1998).

WORKS CITED

Asad, Talal. *Genealogies of Religion: Discipline and Reasons of Power in Christianity and Islam*. Baltimore, MD: Johns Hopkins Press, 1993.

Brooks, Bruce. *Asylum for Nightface*. New York: HarperCollins, 2000.

Campbell, Patricia. *Spirituality in Young Adult Literature: The Last Taboo*. Lanham, MA: Rowman & Littlefield, 2016.

Geertz, Clifford. "Religion as a Cultural System." In *The Interpretation of Cultures*. New York: Basic Books, 1973.

Golding, William. *Lord of the Flies*. London: Penguin Books, 2003.

Hautman, Pete. Candlewick Press Kit, 2014.

Hautman, Pete. *Godless*. New York: Simon Pulse, 2004.

Heinlein, Robert Anson. *Stranger in a Strange Land*. New York: Ace, 2006.

Hilbun, Janet. "The Role of Protestant Christianity in Young Adult Realistic Fiction." *Journal of Religious and Theological Information* 7 (181–201): 2009.

"I Believe It, I Doubt It: Young Adult Fiction for Questioning Christians. *VOYA: Voice of Youth Advocates*. 1998.

Lincoln, Bruce. *Holy Terrors: Thinking About Religion After September 11*. Chicago: University of Chicago Press, 2003.

Martel, Yann. *Life of Pi*. New York: Harcourt, 2001.

Millard, Kenneth. *Coming of Age in Contemporary American Fiction*. Edinburgh: Edinburgh University Press, 2007.

Shoemaker, Joel. *Pete Hautman: Speaking the Truth to Teens*. Lanham, MA: Rowman & Littlefield, 2016.

Smith, Christian. *Soul Searching: The Religious and Spiritual Lives of American Teenagers*. Oxford: Oxford University Press, 2005.

Voigt, Cynthia. *Tree by Leaf*. New York: Aladdin Paperbacks, 2000.

Learning How to Be Jewish in *The Truth About My Bat Mitzvah* and *Confessions of a Closet Catholic*

PATRICIA F. D'ASCOLI

Young adult novels featuring characters who engage in an exploration of their spiritual identities have much to offer young adult readers who are questioning their own religious beliefs. Novels such as Norah Raleigh Baskin's *The Truth About My Bat Mitzvah* (2008) and Sarah Darer Littman's *Confessions of a Closet Catholic* (2005) are especially useful for Jewish readers, as they capture the dynamic and complex nature of Judaism through the portrayal of characters in search of their Jewish identity. Both of these novels draw heavily upon Judy Blume's 1970 novel *Are You There God? It's Me Margaret* in their portrayal of a young girl seeking to discover her own spiritual identity whose parents are of different faiths. *The Truth About My Bat Mitzvah (Truth)* and *Confessions of a Closet Catholic (Confessions)* both adapt and expand upon many of the themes established in *Are You There God? It's Me Margaret (Margaret)*, although they differ from Blume's novel in a significant way. Unlike *Margaret*, in which the central character's search for a religious identity remains unresolved at the novel's conclusion, *Truth* and *Confessions* feature protagonists whose spiritual journey culminates in an awareness of what it means to be Jewish. "Being Jewish" is a multi-faceted identity, as it must also consider the ethnic and/or cultural elements of Judaism; therefore, reading about a fictional character's search for a Jewish identity can offer young adult readers a perspective on how to navigate this complex spiritual journey.

Are You There God? It's Me, Margaret

It is important to understand how *Margaret* serves as a model for *Truth* and *Confessions* in its representation of a girl's journey toward religious self-discovery because 1) for many years it was one of the few novels that recognized how young adults think seriously about organized religion and 2) it was the first young adult novel to represent interfaith marriage. The rate of interfaith marriages in America has been increasing steadily over the past several decades. According to a 2013 Pew Research survey, 60 percent of Jewish person marriages today are interfaith, compared with approximately 30 percent when *Margaret* was published. The novel, therefore, provides a kind of benchmark for examining how fictional representations of a young adult's spiritual journey (arising from an interfaith family) have evolved in the intervening years. Those familiar with the novel will recall the story of 11-year-old Margaret Ann Simon whose parents do not practice any religion; her mother was raised Protestant, her father Jewish, and they have elected to allow Margaret to choose what religion she wants to be when she grows up. The title of the novel is particularly relevant to its theme, as it is about questioning whether Margaret has any connection with a higher power. In other words, she is unsure if any God (not a Jewish God or a Christian God), is listening to her. Through a series of unstructured prayers that begin with "Are you there God? It's me, Margaret," Margaret seeks above all, an answer to the issue most pressing in her life: is she a Christian or a Jew?

Margaret knows that this choice will have consequences not just for her, but especially for her parents, and that is why it is so difficult. She does not quite understand the circumstances of her parents' interfaith marriage, but eventually, she learns that her maternal grandparents disowned their daughter when she married a Jewish man. This no doubt accounts for the parents' decision to forego religion entirely. The novel does not, however, explore the issue of anti–Semitism, and this sets *Margaret* apart from *Truth* and *Confessions* in important ways. As her own parents' method for resolving their religious differences was to abandon their respective faiths entirely and raise their daughter in a secular household, Margaret has received no formal training in either religion. She does, however, share a close relationship with her grandmother Sylvia, who is Jewish. The Jewish grandmother is an important trope that also appears in *Truth* and *Confessions* as it provides a foundation upon which the central characters can build their Jewish identity.

Margaret's interest in exploring religion is triggered by the Simon family's move from New York City to suburban New Jersey, as she makes new friends who identify themselves as belonging to a particular religion. Margaret tells her friends when asked, "My parents are nothing" and "I'm not any religion" (Blume 34). It is Margaret's increasing awareness of this religious "nothingness" that motivates her quest to discover her own religious identity. Later in the novel she tells God, "I'm the only one without a religion—let me be like everybody else" (Blume 101). Margaret looks to God for the answer, as she is afraid to discuss the issue with her parents and believes they won't understand. Her mother even tells her, "I think it's foolish for a girl of your age to bother herself with religion" (Blume 56). The idea that an adolescent's quest for religious identity is, by necessity a private endeavor, is central to Blume's novel, and both Baskin and Littman embrace the concept in their novels as well. In "Those Kinds of Books: Religion and Spirituality in Young Adult Literature," Margaret Auguste discusses this notion:

> Adolescents are sometimes uncomfortable or inarticulate in their expression about religion and spirituality as it relates to them even though they are curious. This occurs because they aren't asked their opinions about it often enough. This creates an atmosphere where teenagers may feel embarrassed that their questions are silly or that it is not appropriate to care about religion [39].

That Margaret overcomes this embarrassment reveals the strength of a young adult's need to explore a religious identity.

Such need is borne of the religious climate established by one's parents; in Margaret's case, this climate is secular. She decides to act upon her curiosity by attempting to experience different religions. She tells God, "I think it's time for me to decide what to be. I can't go on being nothing forever" (Blume 53). So Margaret attends a Protestant service with her friend Jamie and goes by herself to a Catholic church to confess, but can't go through with it. She asks Sylvia if she can go to temple with her, following which her grandmother replies delightedly, "I knew you were a Jewish girl at heart! I always knew it!" (Blume 55). Margaret remains adamant that she just wants to see what it's all about. After her visit to temple, she prays: "Are you there God? It's me, Margaret. I'm really on my way now. By the end of the school year I'll know all there is to know about religion. And before I start junior high I'll know which one I am" (Blume 61). Margaret wants very much at this point to choose one religion over another but eventually decides to choose neither, because it is too difficult to make the choice.

Margaret learns, just as many young adults do, that there are no simple answers, and deciding which religion to be is not only difficult but painful. It is a task which is, however, central to an adolescent's spiritual identity formation. Conflicts arise during the process, as they do for Margaret who witnesses an angry discussion that reveals her maternal grandparents' assumptions about her religious identity:

> "We hoped by now you'd changed your minds about religion," Grandfather said.
> "Especially for Margaret's sake," Grandmother added. "A person's got to have religion."

"Look," my mother explained, "we're letting Margaret choose her own religion when she's grown."

"Nonsense!" Grandmother said. "A person doesn't choose religion."

"A person's born to it," Grandfather boomed.

"Margaret is nothing!" my father stormed. "And I'll thank you for ending this discussion right now."

"Stop it!" I hollered, jumping up. "All of you! Just stop it! I can't stand another minute of listening to you. Who needs religion? Who! Not me.... I don't need it. I don't even need God!" [Blume 134].

While Margaret may not ultimately "need" religion, she does need God, and it is this spiritual connection that trumps a religious identity for her.

Religious identity is not self-evident for a young adult, especially one whose parents practice no religion. Grandparents and other family members who believe religious identity is predetermined can impede a young adult's spiritual quest. This is the case for Margaret. When Sylvia insists that Margaret is a Jewish girl, she shouts, "'No I'm not! I'm nothing, and you know it!'"(Blume 140). Following this exchange, Margaret asks a poignant question that reveals the central point of Blume's narrative: "As long as she loves me and I love her, what difference does religion make?" (Blume 141). Margaret comes to realize that it shouldn't matter whether someone is Jewish or Christian. She ultimately decides not to decide, and this is made clear when she turns in her school project on religion in the form of a letter to her teacher:

I have conducted a yearlong experience in religion. I have not come to any conclusions about what religion I want to be when I grow up—if I want to be any special religion at all.... I don't think I'll make up my mind one way or the other for a long time. I don't think a person can decide to be a certain religion just like that [Blume 143].

In this passage Blume seems to suggest that it is not possible (or perhaps not necessary) for an adolescent to undertake a quest for religious identity that results in identification with a specific religion, especially when she has been raised by interfaith parents who have not provided her with *any* religious foundation.

Margaret's many communications with God throughout the novel do, however, reveal that despite her lack of affiliation with any particular religion, she is a spiritual being who feels connected to a higher power and will no doubt continue to experience this as she progresses on her spiritual journey. Whether she chooses to be a Christian or a Jew is beside the point. While the narrative clearly conveys the significance of such a journey in the life of an adolescent, it fails to offer readers a final resolution. That Baskin and Littman depart from this outcome points to a significant difference between their novels and Blume's. *Truth* and *Confessions* both portray a young adult's search for a *Jewish identity*, which is, as will be seen, a complex identity.

Jewish Identity

Before examining how *Truth* and *Confessions* consider an adolescent's search for a Jewish identity, it is important to understand the concept of Jewish identity. David Arnow, Clinical Psychologist and Research Fellow at the CUNY Center for Jewish Studies, defines Jewish identity as "the inner experience of the self in relationship to the religious, political, ethnic and/or cultural elements of Judaism, the Jewish people and Israel" (30). Arnow considers how Jewish identity is developed and shaped through four different approaches: Psychodynamic, Functional, Structural and Developmental. The Psychodynamic Approach acknowledges how early experiences within the family impact Jewish identity formation. Parents play an important role as transmitters of Jewish identity and can either strengthen or weaken this identity. The Functional Approach considers how an individual with a weak Jewish identity is not likely to embrace the Jewish world, but can do so with the help of a "provider/gatekeeper" who can provide the seeker with "an atmosphere that inspires a sense of confidence and security" by responding to the seeker's needs in a nonjudgmental manner (33). The Structural Approach offers a perspective on how it is difficult to build a Jewish identity in a society where conflict exists between Jewish and American identities associated with practices that are "not closely rooted in a serious expression of Jewish religious practice" (35). Such conflict, Arnow notes, has ultimately resulted in increased secularism in America. Finally, the Developmental Approach analyzes how a Jewish identity changes and grows throughout one's lifetime. Central to this approach is the idea that a strong Jewish identity is built during childhood and adolescence. Jewish identity, as reflected by a 2013 Pew Research Center study is, for the majority (62 percent) of American Jews, more a matter of *ancestry, culture, and values* than of religious observance. The survey revealed that "Jews of no religion" have grown as a share of the Jewish population. Fewer than 15 percent of Jews believe that being Jewish is mainly a matter of religion; 23 percent say that being Jewish is a matter of religion as well as ancestry and/or culture. Although many Jews say religion is relatively unimportant in their lives, eight-in-ten Jews say *being Jewish* is either very important (46 percent) or somewhat important (34 percent) in their lives (Pew).

What it means to "be Jewish" is clearly complicated; that Jews identify to a greater extent with Judaism as a *cultural construct* rather than a religious construct is in fact in accord with the postsecular nature of contemporary society, as it offers opportunities for new ways of thinking and believing. Such ways, as explored in young adult literature, are evidenced in the narratives created by Baskin and Blume, in which young adults investigate a spiritual identity that is ultimately defined, by necessity, as one in which the religious and the secular coexist.

The Truth About My Bat Mitzvah

The development of a Jewish identity as represented in *Truth* can be best understood through the Psychodynamic approach that "analyzes the formative relationships and ethnocultural and religious experiences within the family that shape an individual's Jewish identity" (Arnow 30). Baskin, like Blume, examines the spiritual quest undertaken by the child of an interfaith marriage. Caroline Weeks is the 12-year-old daughter of a Jewish mother and a Christian father, who considers herself half Jewish, half Christian, having grown up with some exposure to both traditions. Her understanding of Christianity and Judaism is limited, however. According to the Psychodynamic perspective, her parents have accordingly *weakened her Jewish identity*. Caroline's decision to explore her religious identity is precipitated by the death of her Jewish grandmother, who leaves Caroline her Star of David necklace. As a symbol of Judaism and a reminder of her nana, this necklace takes on a special significance for Caroline as she ponders whether she is a Christian or a Jew. Her quest is also motivated, in part, by a friend's upcoming bat mitzvah, the traditional Jewish coming-of-age ceremony. Caroline's search for religious identity is therefore established as an inquiry that is *focused on Judaism*.

Tradition and family history are important elements of the Jewish faith, and Caroline comes to learn painful truths about anti–Jewish attitudes within her own family. She learns that her maternal great-great grandparents who were Jewish disowned their son for marrying a woman (Nana) they considered to be "the wrong kind of Jew." Caroline overhears her parents talking about the story, which she later relates to her friend Rachel: "I guess my nana's family was an embarrassment to my grandfather's family," I said. "They thought she was *too Jewish*" (Baskin 14). There are, then, degrees of "Jewishness" further complicating the Jewish identity which Caroline must grapple with as she forms her own identity.

Caroline is confused about what this means: "Nana how could you be too Jewish when I am barely Jewish at all?" (Baskin 16). Thus far Caroline has considered Jewishness only in a religious sense. Here she learns for the first time that there is another dimension to being Jewish; it is a religion *as well as* a culture and an ethnicity. Baskin reveals an important distinction that complicates the question of Jewish identity for Caroline and, no doubt, many American Jews. As noted in the Pew study, Jewish identity has a significant secular component; therefore, Caroline's quest for a religious identity is far from simple. Caroline has been designated half-Jewish, half-Christian. It is, no doubt, confusing to subscribe to two different systems of belief. Caroline's choice is made more complicated by the fact that in the Jewish tradition, if the mother is Jewish, the child is Jewish. Caroline does therefore understand herself to be Jewish on a *basic* level: "Rachel's mother said I was Jewish because my mother was Jewish, and my mother was Jewish because my grandmother was, my nana (Baskin 25). In other words, she is "technically" Jewish, but not "actually" Jewish, and therein lies the conflict. Her weak Jewish identity as represented here clearly reflects a failure on her mother's part to properly convey "deeply held convictions of why Jewish tradition is worth passing down and learning about" (Arnow 31).

Caroline's mother, like Margaret's, does not recognize her daughter's need to explore her religious identity, despite the fact that her desire to examine her Jewishness is strongly connected to her grandmother. Caroline has not told her mother about the Star of David necklace: "I guess I could have told my mother about the necklace right then, but I was afraid she'd think it was silly. Or she'd say something like she said to Rachel's mother, that it was hypocritical" (Baskin 46). Caroline believes that by wearing the necklace she can prove to herself and others that she is, in fact, Jewish: "If I wear this, will people think I am Jewish? Is that what I want to be? Will I be?" (Baskin 53). The idea of having a bat mitzvah begins to grow in Caroline's mind, and although she wants to broach the subject with her mother, she cannot. It occurs to Caroline that if she wears the necklace when she asks her mother, it might somehow prove that she sincerely wants to be Jewish. She wonders, "What would Mom think? Would she think I was trying to be someone I wasn't?" (Baskin 69). Baskin, like Blume, emphasizes here that parents often fail to take their child's religious inquiries seriously, and as a result, the child is left to explore an important subject alone. When Caroline receives the invitation to her friend's bat mitzvah, Caroline ponders the question; like the Star of David necklace, the bat mitzvah ceremony serves as a powerful symbol of Judaism.

Baskin moves beyond the significance of these symbols in respect to a Jewish identity, however, to examine the subject of anti–Semitism in her novel. Deciding whether or not she wants to be Jewish takes on new meaning when Caroline finds herself having to confront how Jews often experience discrimination. In what appears to be an innocent conversation, Lauren, a girl who has been invited to Rachel's bat mitzvah notes, "Rachel doesn't even look Jewish" (Baskin 78). In response to Caroline's building anger, Lauren says, "It's a compliment, for Pete's sake, Caroline. Lighten up" (Baskin 79). Caroline realizes that something's not quite right about this: "If not looking Jewish was a compliment, then what was Lauren saying? It didn't feel good. It was scary" (Baskin 79). Her recognition of anti–Jewish attitudes reflects how "the symbolic importance of anti–Semitism is so widespread that it is one of the few measures that cuts equally across religious denominations or level of affiliation" (Arnow 31), thus adding another dimension to the Jewish identity.

When Caroline makes the bold decision to wear her Star of David necklace for picture day, thus announcing to everyone that she is Jewish, she suffers a moment of weakness when she sees Lauren coming toward her. Here we see how vulnerable she is and how conflicted she feels about being Jewish: "I reached up to try and tuck it into my shirt.... I didn't want to be different or stand out. I didn't want her to know who I was. And maybe have a reason to not like me even more than she already did" (Baskin 96). Knowledge of anti–Semitic attitudes does, therefore, impact the decision to embrace a Jewish identity. Caroline accidentally breaks the necklace during her attempt to hide it and later realizes it is missing. When she finds it, she understands how the necklace had made her think about things she never would have. Shortly thereafter she has an epiphany about being Jewish: "If that's what I wanted, I didn't have to convince anyone. The only person doubting it was me.... I didn't need to prove anything to anyone, not to anyone but myself. I could be whatever I wanted, even Jewish" (Baskin 100). Word choice here is significant; "even" as a qualifier emphasizes that embracing a Jewish identity is somehow outside the norm. This highlights Caroline's confusion about her emerging Jewish identity which is, as Arnow explains, a product of parental ambivalence (31).

It is, in fact, hard to be Jewish as Caroline learns when her great-aunt, Gert, confirms the family story about her grandfather being disowned. In this telling, Caroline sees that being Jewish is much more complex than she might have imagined: "A Jew couldn't make it in the business world. Doors were shut to us.... So my family just kept their Judaism to themselves. Hoffman is a German name. It didn't have to be Jewish. We were Jewish; we just didn't wear our Judaism on our sleeves." Being Jewish came at a certain cost (Baskin 121). Disavowing one's Jewish identity as a means of survival is a harsh concept for Caroline. But her grandfather's love was, in the end, more powerful than his sense of allegiance to a family that was essentially afraid to be Jewish. And when he was later faced with his daughter's decision to marry a non–Jew, he chose to embrace his son-in-law, thus strengthening the family's Jewish identity.

We come then, at last, to the "truth" of the bat mitzvah—that one does not "have" a bat mitzvah, one "becomes" a bat mitzvah. Caroline is Jewish because her mother is Jewish, and by virtue of this, when she turned 12, she became a "daughter of the commandment." No religious ceremony is necessary for this to occur. Her journey, then, comes full circle. In exploring her Jewish identity, she comes to understand that there was no question at all about whether or not she was Jewish. While Caroline appears to "choose" to be Jewish rather than Christian, it is easy to recognize this as a foregone conclusion. Despite her mother's ambivalence, other family members and friends provide the necessary support to Caroline, enabling her to embrace her Jewish identity. Her ability to do so is reflective of the Functional Approach to Jewish identity; through her interactions with other Jews (gatekeepers)—Rachel's mother and her great Aunt Gert—Caroline has been able to discover this identity in a positive and nurturing way, thus allowing for a smooth transition into an adult Jewish identity.

Confessions of a Closet Catholic

Confessions further develops important issues examined in *Truth*, such as anti–Semitism as well as the ways that those with different interpretations of Judaism engage in their religion, further exemplifying the complex nature of a Jewish identity. As such, the novel has much to offer young readers seeking to understand what it means to be Jewish. As K.L. Mendt notes, "young adult books with spiritual themes can be particularly useful as a way for young adults to gain access to the information they need to "assuage the loneliness of their passage as they make their way through the process of identity definition in relation to spirituality" (1). *Confessions* is such a book, as the very *process* of gaining information in order to comfortably create a religious identity is central to the narrative. This also reflects key aspects of the Functional perspective of Jewish identity formation that addresses how Jewish identity can grow dramatically when adolescents seek out "providers or gatekeepers to the Jewish world of resources" (Arnow 33). This is, in fact, how the central character comes to discover her Jewish identity.

Confessions is narrated by 11-year-old Justine Silver whose parents practice different forms of Judaism. While her paternal grandmother is a Holocaust survivor who keeps kosher and observes the Sabbath, her mother's parents are what might be considered "casual" followers of Judaism. Justine describes her own parents as "twice a year Jews." Justine has a close relationship with her paternal grandmother "Bubbe" with whom she has frequently attended synagogue. From the outset, we learn that when it comes to practicing Judaism, Justine's family dynamics are complicated. As reflected in the Psychodynamic approach to Jewish identity formation, Justine's weak Jewish identity is a result of parental ambivalence (cite name 31). Worse than ambivalence, however, are the conflicting messages she receives about the right way to be Jewish. Justine is "stuck in the cross fire between Bubbe wanting me to be Jewish the Orthodox (or what my other grandparents would call the "old-fashioned") way, and Grandma Lila and Grandpa Leo wanting me to be Jewish but not too Jewish" (Littman 7).

Justine's confusion about her Jewish identity is reflected in her reaction to her parents' unwillingness to recognize her need to fully explore Orthodox traditions and rituals. When her family ridicules her desire to keep kosher like Bubbe does, Justine tells the reader, "I decided that if my family was going to make fun of me for trying to be Jewish, I might as well try something else" (Littman 6). From the outset, it is clear that Justine is not particularly happy being Jewish. So she decides to give up being Jewish for Lent and to "try out" Catholicism (her best friend Mary Catherine, or Mac, is Catholic). Giving up being Jewish for Lent is an ironic gesture on Justine's part, as Lent is a time of sacrifice. Whether she knows it or not, Jewishness is important to Justine; being Catholic is never really an option for her.

The fact that she experiments with a religion completely at odds with her own religious upbringing reflects what Paul Corrigan describes in the introduction to this collection as a non-traditional exploration of religious belief in a way that reflects today's postsecular society. Embracing one's Jewish identity by way of Christianity clearly exemplifies this tendency. Justine's knowledge of Catholicism is naturally limited, however, as it is largely predicated on the fact that she gets to celebrate Christmas, she enjoys the music, and she likes the idea of doing confession every week rather than saving it up all for Yom Kippur. Although she has no real sense of what confession entails, she nonetheless endeavors to secretly engage in the practice by creating a secret "closet confessional" in her room. Her confessions are juxtaposed against a family environment that does not encourage an exploration of the Jewish faith, and as Arnow explains, a lack of positive Jewish memories and the absence of affirmative parental reinforcement have a negative impact on an adolescent's developing Jewish identity.

Justine feels like an outcast in her own family, entirely unsure of what a healthy, Jewish identity might be. Her interest in Catholicism is, in fact, reactionary, as she associates Mac's warm and loving family with that religion. Reflecting the non-traditional exploration of religion presented in the narrative, Justine learns the first of many important lessons about being Jewish not by speaking with her own mother, but by talking with Mac's mother who helps her understand Judaism better:

> "Being Jewish is all about suffering," I argue. "People hate us, try to kill us, and don't want us to join their country club...."
>
> "All religions have persecution in their history," she says. "Take the Huguenots in France, Catholics in Northern Ireland, Muslims in Bosnia or the Kurds in Iraq." "But your heritage is so rich with tradition...."
>
> "Be proud of where you come from, Justine." Mrs. McAllister says. "If you aren't happy with who you are, then the grass will always look greener somewhere else. But when you get there you won't be any happier, because you've taken your insecurities with you" [Littman 44–45].

The focus here is on the cultural rather than the religious aspects of Judaism, a perspective Justine has not considered in her exploration of an alternative religion. This too is indicative of deficits in Justine's Jewish identity formation.

The cultural aspect of Jewish identity is reinforced when Justine goes to mass with Mac's family. As she sits nervously in the pew, she reflects upon her "secret alter ego" Sister Teresa Benedicta, the only Jewish saint, who although converted to Catholicism, still ended up being killed in Auschwitz. This makes Justine think: "I guess to some people, if you are born Jewish it doesn't matter if you've given up being Jewish for Lent, like me, or for good, like Edith Stein. You can even become a nun and be made a saint, but they still think the world is a better place without you" (Littman 47). Here and elsewhere in the novel, we see that Justine's central understanding of what it means to be Jewish is to be part of a culture that is despised. Her grandmother's family perished during the Holocaust, and Bubbe, whose arm bears the numbers tattooed on it at Auschwitz, is a living reminder of anti–Semitism. As such, Justine's Jewish identity has been built on the idea that being Jewish is problematic at best and dangerous at worst.

Alan Dershowitz discusses this attitude about Jewish identity in *The Vanishing American Jew*, arguing that Jewish history has created a Jewish identity "far too dependent on persecution and victimization" (18). To counter this negative sense of Jewish identity, he suggests that American Jews must adopt an identity that is founded on "a 3,500-year-old tradition of education, scholarship, learning, creativity, justice, and compassion" (18). Dershowitz notes that many Jews are ignorant of this rich tradition, and this lack of awareness makes assimilation easy because most Jews generally associate Judaism with "inconvenient rituals and rules that have no meaning to them" (18). We see that Dershowitz himself blends the religious and secular natures of Judaism in his discussion, further demonstrating the complex nature of a Jewish identity. Making sense of these coexistent aspects of a Jewish identity is particularly challenging for an adolescent; hence, Justine spends a great deal of time in a state of confusion.

Her confusion, compounded by parental disconnect, comes to a head when Justine finally admits she's given up being Jewish for Lent and receives a tongue lashing from her mother: "HOW CAN YOU DO THIS TO POOR BUBBE, WHO SUFFERED IN AUSCHWITZ JUST BECAUSE SHE WAS JEWISH?" That her mother perceives Justine's actions in this manner exemplifies her inability to take her daughter's interest in exploring her religious identity. Bubbe, however, defends Justine: "Adele. Leave her," she interjects gently. "It's not such a big thing. All children go through a time of questioning. It's natural. Actually, I think questioning is a sign of intelligence" (Littman 104). Questioning is, in fact, central to the search for a religious identity; it is a critical process that enables young adults to understand who they are.

Justine cannot really *give up* being Jewish, however, without learning more about what it actually means to *be* Jewish. Bubbe's death acts as a catalyst for her investigation into Judaism:

> I have to figure out what being Jewish is all about. Grandma Lila and Grandpa Leo see it one way.... I get the impression that for them, being Jewish is more about community than spirituality. For Bubbe it was different ... being Jewish for Bubbe wasn't just about observing rituals. She seemed to really believe in God [Littman 145].

Here, Littman emphasizes the multi-faceted nature of a Jewish identity—that it is both secular and religious. We see that the real issue for Justine is to learn about Judaism in order to choose *how* she wants to be Jewish. She only realizes this, however, when she reads a letter Bubbe has left for her: "Check out your Jewish heritage before you make a final decision. If you aren't proud of who and what you are then changing the name of the person you pray to won't make you feel any better" (Littman 151). This gives Justine confidence to figure out what Judaism is all about.

This "figuring" out is an important factor in the Functional perspective to Jewish identity formation, as the "seeker" (Justine) endeavors to come to a greater awareness of Judaism by consulting a "gatekeeper" (rabbi). It is at the Jewish Center for Understanding where Justine receives valuable lessons about what it means to be Jewish. Justine sees that a Jewish identity can incorporate the religious and the secular, thus revealing that her grandparents' differing perspectives on what it means to be Jewish are not, in fact, mutually exclusive. When Justine asks Rabbi Freeman, "How do I know which is the right way to be Jewish?" he replies, "I have a feeling that if you keep learning you'll figure out what's the right way for you to be Jewish" (Littman 166). Learning about Judaism is a life's work, he tells her; and she has only just begun her journey.

While Justine has taken the bold step to visit the Jewish Center for Understanding, her search for religious identity is not complete until she "confesses" to her family that must follow her heart and continue to explore what it means to be Jewish. While thus far her journey has been unconventional, she ultimately returns to her initial inclination, that is, to experience Judaism by engaging in traditional practices such as keeping kosher. Justine's journey also comes full circle, returning her (albeit in a roundabout, unconventional way) to the place from which she began her spiritual quest. The resolution to this spiritual identity crisis reflects her newfound understanding of what it means to be Jewish.

Conclusion

In their portrayal of an adolescent's search for a Jewish identity, *The Truth About My Bat Mitzvah* and *Confessions of a Closet Catholic* accurately depict the difficulties associated with learning how to be Jewish. Readers who may have suspected that being Jewish is complicated learn that this is indeed true. Judaism is much more than a religion; a search for Jewish identity must consider, as Arnow notes, the ethnic and/or cultural elements of Judaism, as well as a connection to the Jewish people and to Israel. Jewish identity formation is very much contingent upon attitudes and beliefs conveyed by parents; this task is more difficult when parents come from different religious traditions. These novels serve an important purpose for young adults struggling to understand their Jewish identity. Reading about a fictional character's search for a Jewish identity can go a long way to help young adult readers see the relevance of such an inquiry and also understand the intricate nature of such a quest.

Works Cited

Arnow, David. "Toward a Psychology of Jewish Identity: A Multidimensional Approach." *Journal of Jewish Communal Service* (1994): 29–36.

Auguste, Margaret. "Those Kinds of Books: Religion and Spirituality in Young Adult Literature." *Young Adult Library Services* 11, no. 4 (2013): 37–40.

Baskin, Nora Raleigh. *The Truth About My Bat Mitzvah*. Simon & Schuster: New York, 2008.

Blume, Judy. *Are You There God? It's Me Margaret*. New York: Random House, 1970.

Dershowitz, Alan. *The Vanishing American Jew*. New York: Touchstone, 1997.

Littman, Sarah Darer. *Confessions of a Closet Catholic*. New York: Penguin, 2005.

Mendt, K.L. "Spiritual Themes in Young Adult Books." *The Alan Review* 23, no. 3 (1996). https://scholar.lib.vt.edu/ejournals/ALAN/spring96/mendt.html.

"A Portrait of Jewish Americans." *Pew Research Center*. October 1, 2013. http://www.pew forum.org/2013/10/01/jewish-american-beliefs-attitudes-culture-survey/.

"Stick up for these crazy stupid things"

Emily Horner's Queer Quaker Road Trip Novel

KATELYN R. BROWNE

In children's and young adult literature, as in the public imagination, Quakers are the stuff of historical fiction. Religious exiles,[1] early American colonists and revolutionaries,[2] conscientious objectors and draft dodgers,[3] and particularly abolitionists[4]—these are the characters who populate the majority of recent Quaker-themed fiction for young people. Even the humorous "Quaker Problems" meme, created by four Earlham College students, encapsulates the limited public understanding of the Religious Society of Friends in early entries like "History teacher thinks I'm extinct" and "No, not like the oatmeal" (Satterthewaite).

Modern-day Quakers have appeared in war-centric stories like Kathryn Erskine's *Quaking* (2007), in which a teenage girl learns about her Quaker foster family's peace activism, and Rosanne Parry's *Heart of a Shepherd* (2009), whose Catholic main character copes with his father's deployment to Iraq while living on his Quaker grandfather's ranch.

Into this literary context came Emily Horner's *A Love Story Starring My Dead Best Friend* (2010), which explores the beliefs, values, and experiences of a Quaker teen through a cross-country bicycle trip, a covert school musical about a ninja death squad, and the cautious blossoming of love between two teenage girls who were once nemeses. *A Love Story Starring My Dead Best Friend* (henceforth "*Love Story*") is only rarely a novel about Quakerism— some fundamental values are explained when they are central to Cass's identity—but it is thoroughly a novel about a Quaker teen, and about the ways her religious identity defines her self-understanding and her understanding of the world.

First, a few words about Quakers. Also known as the Religious Society of Friends, Quakerism began in England in the 1650s as a movement seeking more thorough Protestant reform and an inward Second Coming of Christ (Dandelion 8).[5] Today, Quakers are a relatively small religious group: in 2012, the Friends World Committee for Consultation counted 377,055 Friends worldwide, about .005 percent of the world's population ("Finding Quakers Around the World"). That count included 76,360 Friends in the United States, about .024 percent of the 2012 U.S. population. American Friends' experiences are diverse. Some Quakers belong to programmed, churchlike meetings that more closely resemble mainline or evangelical Christian denominations, while other Friends attend silent, unprogrammed meetings with broad theological diversity. North Carolina Yearly Meeting (Conservative) captures the complexity of pinning down a noncredal faith based on individual revelation in their Faith & Practice statement, explaining, "Quakerism can be described but not defined, since it is an inner vision and outward lifestyle rather than a theological world view."

So let me describe what we know of the Quakerism in which Cass, *Love Story*'s main character, has grown up. We know that Cass lives in the suburbs of Chicago, and that she describes her religious community as a "meeting" (rather than a church) that meets in a "small and house-shaped" meeting-house (Horner 8). Given this vocabulary and geography, it's almost certain that Cass's monthly meeting (that is, the group that meets weekly at the meetinghouse for worship and conducts business once a month) shares unprogrammed, or "silent," worship, in which attenders sit together and await messages from the Spirit. It's similarly almost certain that Cass's monthly meeting is a part of Illinois Yearly Meeting (that is, a larger collection of monthly meetings that gathers once a year to conduct business, and which publishes some procedures, guidelines, and testimonies for its constituent meetings).[6] Cass's meeting thus would be situated well within the tradition of Liberal Friends described by Pink Dandelion in *The Quakers: A Very Short Introduction* by their "don'ts":

> Belief is plural but also marginal. Ask a Liberal Quaker what they believe and the answer typically includes a list of statements about worship, such as "we don't sing hymns, we don't have a separated priesthood, we don't have outward sacraments." It can feel like an evasion to the eager enquirer, but these Friends are simply answering the question on their own terms: this is what is central to our faith, that is, the way we worship—the means to experience [70].

Supporting this plural-yet-marginal approach to both belief and practice, Illinois Yearly Meeting notes in the introduction to their *Faith and Practice* that "the ongoing life of our meetings is shaped to an extraordinary degree by each meeting's members" and their experiences with the Spirit ("Concerning this Book of Faith and Practice"). While the emphasis on Christ, the Bible, and even theism has changed over time in Friends' traditions, the central emphasis on individual revelation and waiting for truth has not.

Quakers occupy a peculiar space within the Christian tradition, as well as in larger society. *Love Story* demonstrates many of the ways in which Quakers can play an essential bridging role in a postsecular society among people of diverse faiths and people of no faith. A subgroup of Quakers, known as Convergent Friends, even takes engaging with postsecular culture as a particular avenue to renewing their Quakerism (Daniels). Quakers are religious without being credal; in some cases, individual Friends—including Cass—are atheist or agnostic without being secular. Cass is actualized in her own religious and social identity without evangelizing her friends; she is also able to participate in the religious and secular rituals of her friends without abandoning her own values. Indeed, she frequently uses her core Quaker values to make decisions about her own actions and choices.

In this essay, I will use those core values to trace the ways in which Cass's Quaker identity creates a positive context in which she individuates herself as a young adult, makes decisions about appropriate actions, and integrates her attraction to women into her self-concept. This positive concept of identity places *Love Story* on Claire Gross's list good coming-out novels; Gross specifically explains that in Horner's novel, "the protagonist's process of coming to terms with her identity[…] is integral to the book, but it is not all of the book; her life's borders aren't defined by this one aspect of her identity." Yet Cass's faith is rarely mentioned in articles such as Gross's that focus on queer texts, though she is clearly a religious character and clearly a queer character. After looking specifically at the ways Quakerism affects Cass's life, I will look at the ways her multifaceted identity complicates existing narratives and scholarship about queer characters in religious-themed young adult fiction.

The plot of *Love Story* unfolds in alternating chapters from two different timelines. The earlier timeline, "Then," takes place the summer after the death of Cass's best friend, Julia. Cass attempts to ride her bicycle from Illinois to California to scatter Julia's ashes. She gets sidetracked by everything from the weather to a long-term hook-up with a young woman named Maggie. Eventually, Cass realizes that she's not going to reach her destination, and she has to call her friends (including Julia's ex-boyfriend, Ollie) to come pick her up. The other timeline, "Now," takes place the subsequent school year. Cass and several of Julia's other friends work together in secret to put on *Totally Sweet Ninja Death Squad*, the musical Julia had written before she died. Meanwhile, Cass's middle-school nemesis, Heather, has returned to public school after a stint at a Catholic school, and she and Cass discover that they have romantic feelings for each other. In both timelines, Cass and her friends work through their grief over Julia's sudden and unexpected death when her bicycle is hit by a car. In this mourning, as well as throughout the cooperative production of *Totally Sweet Ninja Death Squad* and Cass's earlier solo bike trip, Cass's Quaker identity, beliefs, and values define her character and shape her relationships.

The common American Quaker acronym "SPICES" provides a concrete framework through which Cass's religious identity and values shine. SPICES represents six major testimonies[7] that, for many, describe Quaker priorities: Simplicity, Peace, Integrity, Community, Equality, and Stewardship.[8] The testimonies of integrity and equality are most central to my arguments about Cass's total integration of her religious identity and her sexual orientation, and they will be discussed last. Simplicity, community, and stewardship are mostly implicit in Cass's decision-making, while peace is a frequent reference point on which Cass and other characters hang her Quakerism.

Peace

Peace is the most visible of these testimonies in Cass's self-description and in the way her friends and classmates perceive her. At the very beginning of the book, when Heather reappears in Cass's life, she uses Cass's longstanding participation in anti-war demonstrations to critique her behavior at school, observing, "I've seen your glitter-painted anti-war signs. Aren't you supposed to be the kind of person who'd make peace with Satan himself?" (9). Later, Cass specifically relates a memory of painting those glittery signs when "the war started" when she was twelve (166–7). Pacifism is a repeated part of Cass's self-identity and identification of her parents' values (73).[9] However, Cass is also quick to notice Quaker strengths in her non–Quaker friends (particularly Julia and Heather, the two classmates she has developed crushes on): "I was the pacifist one, at least in theory. But she [Julia] was the one who actually knew how to cool tempers and smooth rough bits over and smack people and tell them to grow up when they needed to hear that. Not me" (34). Cass recognizes that her Quaker upbringing has given her more experience with the performative pacifism of protests, but Julia's pacifist disposition serves as an aspirational example.

Quakers are encouraged to live their testimonies in all aspects of their lives, whether major (an ongoing war) or minor (everyday social decisions). The peace testimony, which often includes an absolute embrace of nonviolence and a rejection of weapon-like toys for children, also comes into play with the production of *Totally Sweet Ninja Death Squad*. Cass, who prefers to work behind the scenes, is asked to build weapons for the musical, and she gives the question serious consideration before agreeing to take part. Her friends note that Julia must have written catapults into the musical because Cass, a skilled math student, could do the math and physics necessary to set them up. Cass initially complains: "'I don't know if I should be building weapons,' I said, not so much because it was true as because I was a little overwhelmed" (17). Weighing her concern for peace with the opportunity to be included in a community production, Cass agrees to participate, if not to actually use the catapults herself. (Her decision is bolstered by her vegetarian friend Lissa, whom she consults for advice.) Later, while testing the catapults with Heather, Cass hesitates again when asked to "return fire," but decides that "it was just stuffed animals. Small stuffed animals. That does not even count as violence" (107) Whether Cass is guided primarily by her pacifism or by her desire to play along with Heather's games, reconciliation with the peace testimony is essential before she can act.

These considerations not only demonstrate the nearly absurd situations in which Cass feels connected to her testimonies, they point to the centrality of individual revelation and conscience in the Quaker tradition. Cass does not consult with a religious leader, a parent, or even a peer to locate her own moral compass; rather, she relies on her own consideration and, presumably, leadings from her Inward Teacher.[10] Cass's mother does eventually express her concerns that the play is glorifying violence, but she ultimately respects Cass's assessment of the situation (122–3). That assessment isn't assumed to extend to others—when the play finally goes up, Cass's parents deliberate about whether they should attend the play, and then ultimately decide to show up (253).

None of these pacifist quandaries rise to the levels seen in Quaker historical fiction, where Friends must devise nonviolent means to endure world wars and defeat oppressive systems like slavery. But these ongoing dialogues with pacifism, and each character's unique interpretation of their obligations, ground Cass and her parents in their faith and in this literary tradition. The Quaker peace testimony admonishes Friends to do whatever they can to remove causes of war and violence in the world, and these local, personal, almost trivial examples are an equally important representation of a typical Quaker life.

Community

Cass's participation in *Totally Sweet Ninja Death Squad* also reflects the lived testimony of community. Illinois Yearly Meeting's approved explanation of their testimonies explains that "Friends' orientation toward community stands in stark contrast to the individualism that characterizes our contemporary secular world." Their explanation of the value of community focuses primarily on the community of Friends who gather in worship and in support of one another, but they note that a foundational Friendly community influences the way Quakers participate in other communities as well. While individual theologies and priorities may differ, Friends in Illinois Yearly Meeting and around the world gather together because of a shared belief in the power of human community.

While the violent nature of a story about murderous ninjas, however musical, presents some potential conflicts for Cass's religious values, she never questions the production's value in uniting Julia's left-behind friends in their grief. Cass's religious community appears only in casual asides and references; the reader never follows her to the Quaker meetinghouse, but the influence of Friends can be seen in Cass's insistence on togetherness and communal emotional processing. Because of past conflicts between Cass and Heather, she's particularly offended when Heather is cast in a major role—not because Heather can't act, but because "it was about loyalty. It was about sticking up for one another" (41). Soon after the group starts rehearsing, the school attempts to squelch the musical in favor of a production of *Our Town*. With some help from a sympathetic teacher, the cast and crew are able to rehearse and produce their show as an act of civil disobedience, group bonding, and thorough processing of their communal grief at Julia's death. Cass is able to regain her place among her circle of friends, which she had disrupted the previous summer by taking off with Julia's ashes; simultaneously, the community opens up to include Heather for the first time.

Simplicity and Stewardship

While the *Totally Sweet Ninja Death Squad* plot provides an entry to Cass's peace and community testimonies, her bike trip the previous summer is rooted in the testimonies of simplicity and stewardship. Cass is an experienced bicycle rider and knows how to repair her own bike. It also becomes her means of transportation for this cross-country journey because her parents enforce rules that include "no car for me until I'm eighteen and have the money to pay for it myself, because of global warming and smog and how I have two legs that work just fine" (26). This explanation efficiently combines Cass's parents' concerns for stewardship and simplicity. "Global warming and smog" may be international issues, but Quaker testimonies insist that individual decisions and actions matter, and that "each of us is called to consider what changes we can make in our lives, lifestyles, and relationships to better support the earth and all its creatures, and then to make those changes as best we can" ("Testimonies"). In addition to environmental concerns, the car restriction reflects an understanding that, since Cass is physically able to walk and bike, a car is an unnecessary material possession.

Simplicity and the right use of resources come through in many of the rules that make Cass's parents seem strict: she's not allowed to wear designer clothes or make-up (56, and "usually Mom just raised her eyebrows if I picked up something with rhinestones or sequins or anything she called a ridiculous fad" (42). Illinois Yearly Meeting connects the testimony of simplicity back to the Quaker tradition of dressing plainly and without adornment to reduce vanity. Plain dress is a rare practice among liberal Friends today, but a rejection of make-up and faddishness carries on this tradition. Yet even here, the primacy of personal agency and revelation comes through; Cass later explains to Heather that even though she learned these rules from her parents, if she really wanted to wear eye shadow, she wouldn't have to sneak around to do it (180).

Integrity

This deep parental trust relies on a shared belief in integrity, which Illinois Yearly Meeting calls "perhaps the most fundamental testimony of Friends" ("Testimonies"). Cass's parents trust that her visible choices will reflect spiritually-led decision making, and that she will treat them, and everyone, with respect and honesty. Heather, whose family is Catholic and has different expectations for her life, had earlier expressed her jealousy that Cass has "parents who don't mind you doing your own thing for a while" (169). The extent to which Cass's parents "don't mind"—and, indeed, value her independence—becomes clear as she describes their support for her cross-country solo bicycle trip. Their esteem for her integrity in relating her individual leadings and convictions is clear:

> My parents were Quakers, and beyond being pacifists and not allowing makeup and cable TV, this was what they believed in. When the Spirit tells you to do something, you had better be listening. Even if it seems crazy, even if it seems dangerous, you had better be prepared to take a step outside what is safe and sane.
>
> I didn't believe that God told some guy, however many years ago, "Hey, build a ginormous boat in this desert over here." I liked it as a story, though, because it seemed like the kind of thing God ought to say. There were crazy stupid things that needed to get done, or turned out to be wonderful when they did get done. And maybe, if God ever did tell people what to do, it was to stick up for these crazy stupid things that no one in their right mind would ever do otherwise [73].

The importance of direct revelation in Quaker integrity is seen clearly in Cass's explication: instructions about right action are received from Spirit, not from religious leaders or holy texts. Cass openly questions the historicity of the Bible and is not even certain that God *does* give direct instruction, and these questions are not heretical in her religious context. The idea that a person can be individually allegiant to religious instructions while uncertain about the precise theology of their origins (and untroubled by that uncertainty) fits thoroughly into liberal Quakerism.

Integrity influences minor choices as well during Cass's road trip. For example, she stops in at a church while on the road and participates in their service, but she doesn't recite their creeds "even though the girl next to me held out her binder so I could see them. Quakers don't, because it's too easy and too dangerous to turn God into a series of logical propositions" (127). Again, the novel demonstrates the peculiar place Quakers occupy in the religious landscape: Cass dogmatically adheres to a requirement not to be dogmatic, even as she takes solace in sharing religious experiences with non–Quaker Christians.

When Cass is at her lowest point—off-schedule with her bicycle journey, passing time with Maggie and ignoring her gnawing grief—she also experiences separation from her integrity. She sinks herself completely into her nascent relationship with Maggie and surrenders her sense of self: "I just wanted to be who she wanted me to be, and do what she wanted me to do, because it was better than being miserable and trying not to think about Julia" (193). While Maggie is a distraction, Cass's romance with Heather blossoms only after Cass has started to come to terms with the jealousy and anger that haunted their earlier friendship. Along the way, Cass worries, "because I liked her [Heather] and I wasn't saying anything" (178)—a tiny, split-second crisis of integrity. The reader knows that Heather is a good partner because Cass's integrity is one of the things she loves. When Heather confesses her attraction to Cass, she admires that "you're so … awkward, and scruffy, and fearless, and *just intensely yourself*" (204, emphasis added). Many romances in young adult fiction focus on finding a partner who can accept your true self, but Heather's admiration of Cass's self-certainty carries even more import because this integrity in the face high school social conformity is a core value of Cass's Quaker identity.

The Quaker understanding of integrity and emphasis on lived experience can lead Friends to give exceedingly specific responses to questions as they are careful only to reflect that which they personally know to be true. In the example of an old joke, it leads a pair of Quakers to observe that a certain farmer has shorn his sheep—at least, on the side they can see! In Cass's experience, this specificity leads to an achingly long coming-out process. After Julia's death, but before Cass plans her bike trip, she realizes that Ollie has been jealous of her crush on Julia, and that her friends have all decided that she's a lesbian. Yet Cass is unsure. She's never been attracted to any boys, but neither has she been attracted to girls, with one exception: "except there was Julia, and I still had no idea what to think about Julia" (57). At the end of the summer, after her fling with Maggie, as her friends drive her back home to Illinois, Cass confesses that she's still not sure she's gay. "How am I supposed to know," she asks, "whether I like girls in general, or only girls, or this one girl who rescued me from a flash flood? One is a terrible sample size to get any meaningful data from" (234). Eventually, Cass does decide that she's comfortable being a person who likes girls, but she continues to describe her attraction one girl at a time. Pervasive heteronormativity may have conspired with Cass's quest for identity to create her initial hesitance describing or acting on her homoromantic feelings, but those feelings were never the source of a religious crisis in and of themselves. To better understand why, it is necessary to understand the Liberal Quaker view of equality as Cass experiences it.

Equality

Equality is a particularly useful tool to contrast Cass's adolescence with the experiences of the novel's other gay teen characters, Heather and Jon, as each negotiates the relationship between their homosexuality and their religious values. Heather assumes that Cass's parents, who are so strict about sequins and fast food, will also be "strict" about homosexuality and forbid Cass to date girls. Cass confirms that her parents were strict about things like television consumption and make-up because they "didn't want me getting my moral compass from people who are only interested in selling me something. But love is different. If two people care about each other, and take care of each other, they wouldn't ever say a word against that. And there were usually gay people around at our meeting, and they always just treated it like something normal" (180). This behavior, and these beliefs, would be supported by their broader religious community: Illinois Yearly Meeting approved a minute[11] in 1974—probably fifteen years before Cass's birth[12]—that read

> llinois Yearly Meeting is aware that there is great diversity in the relationships that people develop with one another. The worth of these relationships must not be judged on the basis of conventionality but rather to the degree that the relationship contributes to the growth of love in those affected.
>
> Homosexual and bisexual people in this society are subject to serious discrimination in many areas: in employment, housing, medical care, family life education, parental rights, and the right to worship. We believe sexual acts in private between consenting adults should be removed from all criminal sanctions. Civil rights should be extended to protect homosexual and bisexual people just as they now protect other groups which suffer discrimination. We urge Friends and Friendly organizations to work for appropriate legislation.

> Friends encourage everywhere the development of love and trust in human relationships. In this light, we urge Friends to explore and examine their knowledge and assumptions about sexuality, with special reference to homosexuality, with a view to achieving awareness of the possibility and potentials for growth, love, and trust in these and other intimate relationships.
>
> [The minute] was approved, with expressions from Friends that discussion on the topic should continue ["Collected Marriage Minutes"].

Several Quaker testimonies make themselves evident in this minute alongside a clear conviction about the equality of bisexual, homosexual, and heterosexual people. Friends are encouraged to bring about change by peacefully advocating for supportive legislation, but are also asked to examine their own beliefs, with an understanding that integrity will underlie this process—and, potentially, some changes of opinion.

Queer YA: Abandonment, Reconciliation and a Third Way

Previous work on YA literary depictions of religion and queer teens often focuses on the tension between religious communities and non-normative sexual orientations and gender identities.[13] Whether queerness is seen as antithetical to religious belonging, or whether queer characters are able to facilitate a reconciliation between their community's beliefs and their personal identity, that tension is assumed to be present. Our dominant understanding of religion in the United States is that of generic, quasi-evangelical Protestantism, and that faith is assumed to struggle with homosexual attraction and transgender identities. These faith traditions are predominant in young adult literature of the early twenty-first century, which children's literature scholar Robert Bittner describes as novels of abandonment and/or reconciliation. These novels follow characters as "a personal spirituality is formed, in which pieces of theology from a religious background are kept and then molded into a workable belief system that allows for a more liberal understanding and acceptance of queer sexuality" ("Queering Christianity" 8). While Cass's Quaker journey is free of this tension between theology and attraction, these dynamics are central to the stories of her friends Jon and Heather.

Jon's story typifies the narrative of abandonment, fitting more squarely with typical young adult depictions of queer characters in rigid, oppressive Christian settings. He is a longtime friend of Cass's who grew up in the same church as Julia, where he was a particularly enthusiastic member of the choir (29). Through Cass's eyes, the reader understands Jon and Julia's church as a place that makes her feel nervous, where "everything was dark, old wood, impossibly solemn" (28). It's a church with pews and a pastor; a church with an organ and a choir and hymnals, where Julia and Cass once sang Christmas carols; a place with haunting stained-glass windows featuring "saints and martyrs and apostles in jewel colors" (29). The precise denominational affiliation of the church is never revealed. Rather, it's developed in contrast to the comfort Cass feels with her own meetinghouse. At Julia's funeral, she sits with Jon, observing that *"He* belonged here, even if he didn't, really. He knew this church" (29).

Jon has restored the bleached tips of his hair to their natural color, and he has broken a promise to himself and the pastor never to return to the church. A year before Julia's death, Jon had come out as gay and "everything got very tense for a while" (30):

> Whether he quit or got kicked out, he was out of the church choir, out of church altogether. He flew his Gay Pride flag high and made lewd comments about Bible study club. There was a weird atmosphere when we went over to his place, like he would spontaneously combust if he stayed around his parents for any longer than absolutely necessary [31].

Jon has come to Julia's funeral to grieve and to sing. He briefly rejoins the choir, later explaining, "I'm still trying to figure out if I believe in God or I don't believe in God or believe in a God I don't want anything to do with, whether I'm even supposed to hope against all the hope in the world that there's still a place for Julia somewhere. I thought it was that complicated. But it's not. I just can't not sing for her. I can't" (34). Whether the estrangement began with Jon or his church community, his abandonment of his faith community (and their abandonment of him) was necessitated by his desire to live honestly as a young gay man.

Meanwhile, Heather's storyline hews more closely to the idea of reconciliation. Heather has recently transferred out of a Catholic high school, where she had a secret girlfriend. Heather explains to Cass that she struggled with their closeted relationship and the knowledge that her girlfriend, Gianna, would be seriously harmed by coming out (94–5). At the same time, Heather did not understand Catholic debates about homosexuality as pertaining to "my own real life and my future and whether I would ever kiss someone on the mouth," not just "obscure points of theology," (179) until she was dating Gianna.

While Heather understands the cultural dissonance between the world of Catholic school and her desire to live openly as a lesbian, she has theologically reconciled her concerns about lesbianism with reflections on her own lived experience. Catholicism also remains an important source of culture and community in her life and her family. She describes the idea of "cafeteria Catholicism" to Cass and explains that "there are times I would rather be complaining about my [metaphorical] lettuce and tomato than going somewhere else where I can eat what I want. So—that's hard to explain, and I guess it doesn't make much sense. The part that's easy to explain is that as long as I am in that house I am going to Mass on Sunday, young lady" (179). While Gianna's family, also Catholic, were "so conservative that she isn't even allowed to kiss a *boy* until she's practically married, and she really and truly bought into it" (95), Heather's family seems to be more accepting, and she looks forward to having a girlfriend she can introduce to her nephews. Heather continues to participate in the social community of her church, and her parents enforce that participation; dating girls hasn't pushed her into exile. She knows that her coreligionists will continue to find her sinful and disobedient, but her personal theological reconciliation is enough.

Cass's experience is markedly different from either Jon's or Heather's. Its presentation troubles the easy dichotomy of abandonment and reconciliation, each of which assume a fundamental gap between a queer identity and full acceptance in a religious community. Cass never has to negotiate a gap between her religious identity and her sexual orientation. For Cass as a human being, this seems to be a healthy and positive situation. One 2013 study found that

> being involved with religious or spiritual belief systems that cast rejecting or disapproving messages about sexual minorities is associated with more internalized negative self-messages, as well as greater challenges in developing and accepting one's sexual identity. ... While religiosity tends to favor positive outcomes for youth, LGB youth may actually experience psychological maladjustment when religious beliefs cause stress due to being a sexual minority [Page et al. 673–4].

For Cass as a fictional character, however, this lack of conflict prevents the cathartic and dramatic closure of a reconciliation or abandonment plotline. To fulfill this plot function, Cass seeks this closure through both reconciliation with, and abandonment of, Julia's memory.

Near the end of the book, Cass's relationship with Heather—and the impending musical, in which Heather has a lead role—experiences a major crisis in the form of Cass's lingering feelings for Julia, and Cass finds herself compelled to visit Julia's grave. At long last, Cass is able to verbalize her crush on Julia as well as her interest in Heather, and that "maybe I'm going to have a girlfriend now. If we can get past this. If we can work it out" (248). Laying a lily on Julia's headstone, Cass confesses, "ever since third grade, I've loved you. But I think I have to love somebody else too" (249). Reconciled with her long-suppressed crush, and abandoning the supremacy of her relationship with Julia, Cass is finally able to move forward—she and Heather make up on the very next page. As Heather and Cass negotiate the mostly-public nature of their relationship, Heather quickly clarifies: "if we ever happen to run into one of the nuns from St. Joseph's we're not together, but ... everywhere else is okay..." (251). Cass never has to make a similar request.

Her religious belonging, and her religious self-identity, have never been threatened.

In a further dismantling of the usual reconciliation vs. abandonment framework, in which a character either believes in God (and thus uses that belief to reconcile their identity with their community) or abandons belief in God (and thus no longer needs the religious community), Cass comments that she "believe[s] in God sometimes," but living in a nonviolent and compassionate world is more important to her belief system (181). It is a thoroughly Quaker thing to say, but it is unusual for religious-themed young adult literature. Moreover, Cass discusses this fluid theological outlook with Heather as a way of contrasting her own beliefs with her father's. Cass's dad does believe in God, and that "we're only seeing a tiny sideways glance at all the things that are working themselves out for the best in the end" (180). Even as Cass finds her father's more teleological worldview useful and worthy of explanation, she rejects it in her own understanding of the world—yet the reader is never led to believe that this fundamental shift in religious understanding has caused any interfamilial or community conflict. Cass is not required to reconcile herself with, or abandon, the specific religious beliefs of her parents, because it was never assumed that she would inherit them. While her parents' strictness has sought to shield Cass "from fast food, advertising, and the military-industrial complex," their shared religious values and testimonies—including the equality and integrity that support Cass's theological self-development—always take precedence over creeds or doctrine. To Heather's surprise, it is *exceedingly* difficult for Cass to truly "rebel" in such a family environment.

A Love Story Starring My Dead Best Friend is crucial to any theorizing about postsecular youth and their literature because it so clearly lays out the life of a teenager who is an engaged participant of a religious community, but a community that strives to be non-dogmatic and non-credal. Liberal Quaker teens, so often written off as "basically not religious" or as historical relics in plain dress, have a rare chance to see their experiences validated and their values displayed in the life of a contemporary teen. For the remaining majority of teen readers, Cass's story exists in a space often left unconsidered: one where homosexual and homoromantic attraction are totally accepted, but the struggle to be adequately pacifist permeates Cass's life and the lives of her parents. Characters freely discuss their religious convictions and those of their family and friends. Yet for Cass, there is no crisis of faith, no serious divide between the religious self and the secular self, and no question about converting friends or neighbors. Cass is thoroughly agnostic and thoroughly Quaker. *Love Story* demonstrates that a faithful, godless existence doesn't need to be a source of tension; faith communities exist where agnosticism sits permanently and fully-accepted in a religious community of believers.

The common values and testimonies that are borne out in the lives of Cass and her parents are not contingent on a shared, fixed idea of God and scripture. Yet they serve a religious community well and have served as foundational ideas for Quakers for centuries. As literature and teens from other traditions look for postsecular places to stand, they could do worse than to read and consider this book.

Notes

1. See Turnbull for an example of a book about religious persecution and exile.

2. Books about early American Quaker colonists/revolutionaries include novels by McGahan and Abbott.

3. Historical fiction about Quaker conscientious objectors in the 20th century includes Kerr (set during World War II) and Jocelyn (set during the Vietnam War).

4. Children's fiction about, or at least featuring, Quaker abolitionists is relatively abundant, averaging about a title a year in the 21st century. See Baxter, Brenaman, Carbone, Grifalconi, Krisher, Lagos, Lees, LeSourd, Lovejoy, McCully, Morrow, Rinaldi, Russell, Stowe, and Stroud for examples of this predominant Quaker archetype. Naturally, some of these books also cover other historical Quaker issues, such as the peace testimony and gender equality.

5. The first two chapters of Dandelion give a more thorough overview of Quakerism's history and evolution.

6. Bales and Watts's map of ILYM meetings shows many in suburban Chicago; no other yearly meeting has similar claim on the area.

7. To borrow an explanation from New York Yearly Meeting, "collectively, 'testimonies' are public statements about how we are to live based on our collective experience of revelation in meeting for worship. Individually, we Friends believe that we are to "let our lives speak" as testimonies to Truth, that we are to bear witness with our lives to the truths revealed inwardly to us about how we should live, how we should minister to the suffering of others, and how we should strive to bring God's love, peace, and justice to the world" (*Glossary of Quaker Terms & Concepts*).

8. See Connecticut Friends School for an example of the implementation of Quaker testimonies in one American Friends school. Some Friends only use SPICE, and others do not refer to this specific acronym at all. In their "Testimonies," Illinois Yearly Meeting explicates the six testimonies listed here as fundamental to their belief and practice.

9. "My parents were Quakers, and beyond being pacifists … " (Horner 73); "On the list of things that I was, I could've put...pacifist and Quaker" (76).

10. The "Inward Teacher" is one of many Quaker terms for the Light, or the "still, small voice," or the spark of the Divine that is believed to be present inside every person. For a discussion of various interpretations of Inward Teacher and the origin of leadings, see *Quaker Faith and Practice* 29.17.

11. A "minute" carries some weight among Friends. New York Yearly Meeting explains in their *Glossary of Quaker Terms & Concepts* that a minute is "a statement of an item of business approved by those in attendance at a given meeting for worship with a concern for business"; it is typical for minutes to be discussed and reworded at business meetings until those present can approve them with a sense of unity.

12. This was calculated based on the assumption that when Cass says she was 12 when the war started, she means the War on Terror in 2001, and thus was born in or around 1989.

13. Bittner and Jones serve as examples of this scholarly theme.

Works Cited

Abbott, E.F. *Sybil Ludington: Revolutionary War Rider*. New York: Feiwel and Friends, 2016.
Bales, Micah, and Jon Watts. "Illinois Yearly Meeting." *QuakerMaps.Com: Mapping the Religious Society of Friends*. www.quakermaps.com/illinois-yearly-meeting.

Baxter, Jean Rae. *Freedom Bound*. Vancouver: Ronsdale Press, 2012.

Bittner, Robert. "Faith and Spirituality in YA Lit: GLBTQ YA and Issues of Faith." *School Library Journal*. February 16, 2015. www.teenlibrariantoolbox.com/2015/02/faith-and-sprituality-in-ya-lit-glbtq-ya-and-issues-of-faith-a-guest-post-by-robert-bittner/.

Bittner, Robert. "Queering Christianity: The Journey from Rigid Doctrine to Personal Theologies in a Selection of YA Literature with LGBTQ Content." Master's thesis, Simon Fraser University, 2011.

Book of Discipline. North Carolina Yearly Meeting (Conservative). 1983. ncymc.org/fpframes.html.

Brenaman, Miriam. *Evvy's Civil War*. New York: Putnam-Penguin, 2002.

Carbone, Elisa. *Night Running: How James Escaped with the Help of His Faithful Dog: Based on a True Story*. New York: Knopf, 2008.

"Chapter 29 > 29.17." *Quaker Faith & Practice* (5th ed.). Yearly Meeting of the Religious Society of Friends (Quakers) in Britain. 2013. qfp.quaker.org.uk/passage/29–17/.

"Collected Marriage Minutes." *Friends for Lesbian, Gay, Bisexual, Transgender, and Queer Concerns*. November 16, 2015. http://flgbtqc.quaker.org/minutes.html.

"Concerning This Book of Faith and Practice." *Illinois Yearly Meeting*. 2008. http://www.ilym.org/drupal/sites/default/files/files/Publications/FaithandPractice/ConcerningthisBook ofFaithandPractice_as_approved_2008.pdf.

Connecticut Friends School. "S-P-I-C-E-S: The Quaker Testimonies." *Friends Journal*. September 20, 2010. www.friendsjournal.org/s-p-i-c-e-s-quaker-testimonies/.

Dandelion, Pink. *The Quakers: A Very Short Introduction*. Oxford: Oxford University Press, 2008.

Daniels, C. Wess. "Convergent Friends: The Emergence of Postmodern Quakerism." *Quaker Studies* 14, no. 2 (2012): 236–50. digitalcommons.georgefox.edu/cgi/viewcontent.cgi?article=1430&context=quakerstudies.

Erskine, Kathryn. *Quaking*. New York: Philomel Books, 2007.

"Finding Quakers Around the World." *Friends World Committee for Consultation, Section of the Americas*. 2012. fwccamericas.org/find_friends/images/2012_map/FINAL_map_123 012.pdf.

Grifalconi, Ann. *Ain't Nobody a Stranger to Me*. New York: Jump at the Sun, 2007.

Gross, Claire. "What Makes a Good YA Coming-Out Novel?" *The Horn Book Magazine*. March/April, 2013. 64–70.

Horner, Emily. *A Love Story Starring My Dead Best Friend*. New York: Dial Press, 2010.

Jocelyn, Marthe. *What We Hide*. New York: Wendy Lamb Books, 2014.

Jones, Caroline E. "'Jesus Loves Me, This I Know': Finding a Rainbow God in Contemporary Adolescent Literature." *Children's Literature in Education* 43 (2012): 223–241.

Kerr, M.E. *Slap Your Sides*. New York: HarperCollins, 2001.

Krisher, Trudy. *Uncommon Faith*. New York: Holiday House, 2003.

Lagos, Alexander. *The Sons of Liberty*. New York: Random House, 2010.

Lees, Stewart. *Runaway Jack*. Hauppauge, NY: Barrons Educational Series, 2004.

LeSourd, Nancy. *The Personal Correspondence of Hannah Brown and Sarah Smith: The Underground Railroad, 1858*. Grand Rapids, MI: Zonderkidz-Zondervan, 2003.

Lovejoy, Sharon. *Running Out of Night*. New York: Delacorte Press, 2014.

McCully, Emily Arnold. *The Escape of Oney Judge: Martha Washington's Slave Finds Freedom*. New York: Farrar Straus Giroux, 2007.

McGahan, Mary. *Raid at Red Mill*. New York: Silver Moon Press, 2001.

Morrow, Barbara Olenyik. *A Good Night for Freedom*. New York: Holiday House, 2004.

Page, Matthew J.L., et al. "The Role of Religion and Stress in Sexual Identity and Mental Health Among Lesbian, Gay, and Bisexual Youth." *Journal of Research on Adolescence* 23, no. 4 (2013): 665–677.

Parry, Rosanne. *Heart of a Shepherd*. New York: Random House Children's Books, 2009.

Quaker Glossary. New York Yearly Meeting. 2012. http://www.nyym.org/content/quaker-glossary.

Rinaldi, Ann. *The Education of Mary: A Little Miss of Color, 1832*. New York: Jump at the Sun, 2000.

Russell, Krista. *Chasing the Nightbird*. Atlanta: Peachtree, 2011.

Satterthewaite, Taylor Mary. "Quaker Problems." *Friends Journal*. August 2014. www.friendsjournal.org/quaker-problems/.

Stowe, Cynthia. *The Second Escape of Arthur Cooper*. Singapore: Marshall Cavendish, 2000.

Stroud, Bettye. *The Patchwork Path: A Quilt Map to Freedom*. Somerville, MA: Candlewick, 2005.

"Testimonies: Approved 2014–2015 for a Provisional Period Ending 2017." *Illinois Yearly Meeting*. 2015. http://www.ilym.org/drupal/sites/default/files/files/Committees/FaithandPractice/PresentedSections/Testimonies%20-%20as%20approved%202014–5.pdf.

Turnbull, Ann. *No Shame, No Fear*. Somerville, MA: Candlewick, 2004.

Performing God

Kiran and Krishna in
Rakesh Satyal's Blue Boy

RIZIA BEGUM LASKAR

Luca Mavelli and Erin K. Wilson in "Postsecularism and International Relations" have argued that Habermas' understanding and analysis of post-secularism does not take into consideration "religion as (a) tradition, practice, and lived experience" (252) and also that Habermas understands religion, and by extension postsecularism, in a disembodied and cognitive nature only. Habermas, in his division between "informal public sphere" and "institutional public sphere," says that the former allows all forms of religious discussions while the latter restricts itself only to secular discussions. The content of the "informal public sphere" can find a place within the "institutional public sphere" only when it is "translated" to suit the language of secularism. The two spheres should remain separate, and any transition can take place only through the medium of translation where religious sentiments and notions are subjected to the questioning and logical reasoning of secularism.

Habermas' postsecularism thus prioritizes secularism over religion and the fact that religion can find its place in society only if its language matches that of the secular sphere thereby relegating religion into a merely semantic product and also that religion is reduced to "to a set of cognitive choices and a function in broader processes of social production, where religion's main (and somehow paradoxical) task is to address the crisis of instrumental secular reason" (254). In the examples of postsecularism given by them, they have showed that one of the ways in which the neat division between the secular and the religious can be overcome is by understanding this schism as more of a product or tussle between power and knowledge instead of being a "natural divide." Kim Knott in "Cutting Through the Postsecular City: A

Spatial Interrogation" similarly argues for "knowledge-power relations" where "religious, secular, but also postsecular positions were coproduced and contested" (21).

This view that the secular can be conceptualized within the religious and vice-versa in the locus of the knowledge vis-à-vis power structure will be explored in the context of Rakesh Satyal's *Blue Boy* through a performance. Performance forms the basis of Kiran's experience of religion in an embodied form which takes place through his conceptualization of the Hindu god Krishna and the literal use of his body to portray his identity. He performs in quest for self from the perspective of an outsider who moves towards the center of power and this movement marks his journey from the profane to the religious, from the secular to the postsecular. My usage of the term postsecular, *not* in its hyphenated form, will therefore be more in the lines of Kristina Stoeckl's definition of postsecular as "a condition of conscious contemporarily/co-existence of religious and secular worldviews ... a condition of permanent tension."

Rakesh Satyal's *Blue Boy* is characterized by the constant tussle of identity between a confused twelve-year-old boy and a society that is at conflict with his chosen form of being. Kiran, Satyal's protagonist, is placed in a moment and milieu where he is already an outsider and can display neither his affiliation to the western society of his school nor to the Indian society of his origin. His whole existence is marked by a performance, a ubiquitous presence in his interactions with everyone else, so much so that he starts believing in the performing self rather than his original self. Kiran's narrative is marked by two specific references to performance. The first reference to it is as such: "'Mom, I'm Krishna!' I say. 'I'm Krishnaji!' I style my hands next to my mouth, miming a flute and trying very hard to smile gracefully" (13). The second instance is a more elaborate one where he says,

> The mere mention of the show has potential acts running through my mind, acts that are several stories and worlds above that talentless circle of lip-synching. I know that my act will involve dancing and singing. Singing for real. I will dance and sing so well that I will forget splinters and swings and gravel and the whispers, whispers, whispers [25].

Performance therefore forms the crux of Kiran's initiatives to prove himself and come to terms with his own identity.

But this performance is linked to a more crucial understanding of Kiran's own revelations regarding Krishna and a coming together of the secular and the religious. How performance is a resonance and ramification of the spirituality associated with religion, particularly Hinduism, forms the basis of interrogation here and the ways in which performance leads to a conflation of Hinduism and postsecularism in a diasporic setting. The basic concept of performance, especially a religious one, is that of *līlā*, particularly that of Krishna *līlā*, how Kiran bases his performance on the age old tradition of Krishna *līlā*, and his own appropriation of the art form to gain popularity and acceptance in a society which increasingly considers him an outsider.

The Outsider and Performance

Blue Boy begins with the twelve-year-old protagonist experimenting with his mother's makeup on the sly in the master bedroom. While his mother repeatedly calls him down for dinner, Kiran ignores her for what he is engrossed in. Eventually, when his mother comes to fetch him and finds him made up blue, she is at a loss to understand Kiran's behavior. And at this precise moment, he tumbles upon a brilliant idea to appease his mother. He says that he is the god Krishna who is always represented in blue colors. The relief that his mother feels is apparent in the way she hugs him and prays. But the real predicament starts with Kiran thinking that he possibly might be Krishna, a reincarnation of the blue god and thereby endowed with power and superiority. In some ways similar to his life at home, life at school is one long process of torment and humiliation. In a predominantly white school, Kiran is aberrant not only because of his skin color but also because of his queer sexuality. Precariously positioned at an age where children start to question and ponder over their burgeoning sexual identity, Kiran finds himself to be neither here nor there.

The narrative of his school life begins with two big events that determine his behavior for the rest of the novel. The first is the announcement of the school's "Fall Talent Show," and the second is the sexual taunting that he gets at the hands of his two classmates, Melissa and Sarah, and his eventual fall from the balance beam in the playground. Both of these events have a strong impetus on Kiran's future course of action and, subsequently, they are the cause that determines his character and what he ultimately turns out to be. Kiran formulates a plan for performing at the talent show that will reconcile his inner conflicts as well as his precarious identity. Performance, in a literal sense, therefore, becomes the means of liberation, but in a metaphorical sense, it is also Kiran's identity; his visualization of himself as Krishna is a constant performance that he internalizes and merges into his identity.

Richard Schechner in *Performance Studies: An Introduction* gives a broad and all-inclusive definition of performance:

> Performance must be construed as a "broad spectrum" or "continuum" of human actions ranging from ritual, play, sports, popular entertainments, the performing arts (theatre, dance, music), and everyday life performances to the enactment of social, professional, gender, race, and class roles, and on to healing (from shamanism to

surgery), the media, and the internet.... Along the continuum new genres are added, others are dropped. The underlying notion is that any action that is framed, presented, highlighted, or displayed is a performance [2].

Both Victor Turner and Erving Goffman interpret the individual in society as a performer who acts out a role meant to have an effect on others and the others will in turn analyze the role played by the individual. Turner says that these social roles or "social drama" arise out of a schism or "breach" in the normal functioning of life and the result is the damage-control measures that the individual engages in for the return to normalcy. Performance thus can be conceptualized not only as means of regaining control but also as means of defining one's social status.[1] Goffman's main argument is that social interaction like a theatrical performance is a staged one and there is a "front" which people carry in their interactions. These interactions are contrived in the "backstage" and are then enacted on the stage. But he, at the same time, emphasizes that such performances present a "contrived illusion" and despite the actors' reputations being at stake, in actuality it is all a setup.[2] Both of them therefore have taken out performance from the stage to the realms of normal day-to-day life.

The crisis is precipitated in Kiran's life by the severe betrayal of both Melissa and Sarah on the playground. Added to it is Kiran's own understanding of the importance of the talent show as the means through which he can regain or rather attain social splendor and superiority. The first person narrator Kiran presents a picture of school politics that upholds the generalized notions of it being a space marked off into territories of belonging and not belonging. His classmates constantly nag him at and there is relentless and merciless taunting because of his peculiar penchants and behaviors. In this self-proclaimed "social jungle," his only solace is Krishna whom he sees as an embodiment of all that is good and powerful, a solution to his daily problems. At the same time, embedded deep within his psyche is not so much a religious inclination or a spiritual makeover but rather a very innate tendency to show-off, to make others feel that he is superior to them. It is this very tendency that propels him towards reinventing himself as a reincarnation of the blue god and the showdown with all his internal and external demons will take place in his performance as Krishna at the school talent show.

At the same time, Kiran is fascinated by the character of Krishna and therefore he wants to know him more, to understand him in a better way than the snippets of information he gathers from his mother and at the temple. He thus sets out to find books in the library regarding Hinduism and particularly about his favorite deity. The only problem with such an endeavor is that he keeps his actions completely under wraps unable or rather unwilling to confide in anybody. The shock effect is what he is aiming for when he ultimately reveals his true form to everybody including his parents. The figure of Krishna thus becomes an obsession for him and he tries to emulate many of the idiosyncrasies of the god's character like eating butter, playing the flute and other activities. In the process of doing so, he reinvents himself, and though not yet completely, comes to terms with his peculiarity and uniqueness in small ways.

The primary reasons why Kiran is perceived as the other in a white school are not only his skin color, but also his queerness. The fact that he is born of immigrant parents and forms part of a diasporic identity is known to everybody and, as divulged later on in the narrative, it is his parents more than Kiran who have struggled in the process of assimilation within American culture. He is brought up in Cincinnati and goes to Martin Van Buren Elementary School and is part of much the same upbringing as other American children. In fact, the narrative does not emphasize Kiran's alienation because of his Indian identity. He feels the same sense of an outsider in all Indian gathering and faces much the same disdain as in his school. For Kiran, his deviant behavior brings in a double sense of alienation that contributes to his finding an outlet through other means. In *Disidentifications: Queers of Color and the Performance of Politics* (1999) José Esteban Muñoz succinctly pinpoints the predicaments of the likes of Kiran who are both racialized and queer: "I always marvel at the ways in which nonwhite children survive a white supremacist U.S. culture that preys on them. I am equally in awe of the ways in which queer children navigate a homophobic public sphere that would rather they did not exist. The survival of children who are both queerly and racially identified is nothing short of staggering" (37). The way out of this brutal space for Kiran or the "armament" is a defiance of the norms that define the "normal" world around him and to establish his authority.

The school talent show becomes the ideal platform for performance, a means through which Kiran intermingles the religious and the secular, his culture with his religion, and tries to showcase the uniqueness with which he finds himself endowed. Kiran is extraordinary in this sense because he is not cowed by the factors that alienate him but rather uses those very factors for his liberation. At the same time, he is not magnanimous in his outlook towards those who treat him badly and his religious underpinnings do not deter him from seeking revenge against them. The problematic stance that the author takes in the novel is by *not* using religion as a liberating force for the protagonist. Satyal, in fact, posits Kiran's inclination towards Krishna merely as a means through which he can project himself as a larger than life figure, somebody who, despite his acute awareness of being an outsider, wants to position himself at the center. Performance, therefore, becomes the means through which he negotiates the political spaces of his school to outperform every other contender. Dylan McCarthy Blackston aptly summarizes that after all, queer is not just about one's sexuality or one's defiances of heteronormative life narratives; rather, queer is political in multiple manners, which is to say that queer performance, like many other queer participatory spaces, is engaged with politics. These political acts may or may not be intentional; however, they contain potentiality and imaginings that shift or create anew a plethora of ways of being in the world [1].

The fact that Kiran should display his capabilities before everyone becomes the main focus of his life and there can be nothing grander than choosing to be the reincarnation of a god. At the same time, that this god is Krishna also emphasizes his necessity to concentrate on a god who does not fit into the quintessential normative molds of being and is yet revered and worshipped.

The young Kiran might also be drawn to the fact that very often, Krishna is represented in flashy dresses as if he incorporates both feminine and masculine aspects of being. His desire to assimilate himself with the god is reflected in his intense curiosity to know why Krishna is blue. At the temple, he asks the pundit's wife again and again this question, but is unable to get a satisfactory answer. This particular aspect of Krishna endears him more to Kiran, and thus he says, "The only thing that keeps me going as the class ends is the realization that I am even more like Krishna than I thought. He was blue and different but had no real explanation of why. I am so different from everyone and yet there doesn't seem to be an explanation of my oddity, either" (36). But Kiran, at some truly candid and therefore excruciatingly painful moments, also realizes that despite his bravado he will always be perceived as the other, looked down upon and shunned by everyone, including his father. His choice of god does not make him like Krishna, and the god, despite his oddities, is worshipped as one of the favorite gods in Hinduism. In fact, it is precisely the eccentricities of Krishna's character that make him loveable and venerable. On the other hand, Kiran is always despised for his eccentric nature and more so by his own father than anyone else. In a telling moment, when he sees his father huddled up in the temple, he feels laughter arising inside him. And then he realizes that probably his father also visualizes him as a ridiculous figure, which makes him immediately feel that something is wrong with him.

As a second generation Indian born of immigrant parents, Kiran bears the responsibility of performing exceptionally well in his studies so that he can establish himself in life, and more importantly, in a foreign land. His parents have struggled to secure their position in American culture, and this is a fact that is ingrained into his psyche. The necessity to outperform their American counterparts forms the core of most diasporic searches for identity, at least those from South-East Asia. This zeal to be excellent in all fields, especially academics, is the basis of diasporic conception of life though assimilation into American culture. In fact, religion and culture are at most times segregated from the American dream of success, and there is always an underlying angst and fear among parents that children will adopt the American way of life. Culture and religion often gets submerged into a single entity, and, for most Indian immigrants, Hinduism as a religion and Hindu culture become subsumed into the same notion of Indianness, which they should uphold at any cost. In their research among young South Asian Muslim women in Britain Kim Knott and Sadja Khokher reflect that these young women are trying to bring in a schism between the single entity existence of religion and culture. The sustained exploration of a given religion which is strongly intermeshed with culture, and therefore, what is cultural is also religious and vice versa, is symptomatic of the changes being brought about by these young women in defining both religion and culture as opposed to their parents' generation (596). This dichotomy between religion and culture and subsequent analysis can equally be applied to children of immigrant parents in America, especially Indians and Hindus.

In India, the cultural has for long been merged with the religious to justify the functions of both the perpetrators of culture and religion. As such, despite having some dissimilarities in culture across different religions, culture by and large remains a prominent marker of religion in India. Interestingly, there being a large number of religions in India, there is also a large number of cultures across the country. Hinduism provides numerous deities to be worshipped, allowing people from different states of India to follow a particular god or goddess and worship according to their local culture. But such differences are kept at bay when formulating a diasporic conception of religion or culture. The problem of identity is one that most second generation American Indians face in trying to cope with their dual identity as both Indians and Americans. As Rodney Moag says, first generation immigrant Indian parents always visualized themselves "as Indians in America, rather than Indian Americans" (251). For the majority of first generation Indians, the overwhelming fact is just to sustain themselves in the new land. The notion of assimilation with an alien culture or religion has never been their priority or their intention. It is in fact more of resistance to their new culture that forms their identity.

On the other hand, it is the children who, being brought up in a different culture, face the problem of what to choose and what to discard in the process of identity formation. In her analysis of diasporic Indian English children's literature, Michelle Superle terms the conflict of positioning oneself within a particular culture as "syncretic biculturalism" and the concept of self that emerges out of this conflict as "masala" self (143–44). In this construction of a "masala" self, not only culture but also religion plays a major role. But the powerfully loaded terms of culture and religion can be used to mean diverse things for diverse people. In constructing an Indian self, first generation immigrant parents would more often than not identify themselves as Bengalis or Tamils or Gujratis and also demarcate amongst themselves by their preference of certain gods and goddesses over others. But in the construction of an American-Indian self, the hyphenated self merges the differences of language and modes of worship to create a homogenous identity that encompasses within itself all the diasporic Indians as Hindus and as Indians.

As Kiran describes the various people whom they meet in their weekly sojourn to the temple, they are a motley group not belonging to the same parts of India. However, their differences are mitigated in etching out a unified but rather ambiguous concept of Indian identity. This "homogenous" identity conceptualizes itself on certain accepted features of Indian culture and religion and one of the primary features involves a covert rejection of western or American values and beliefs. The irony of the situation arises from the fact that the children are expected to excel in all American things but are led to hold onto an imagined notion of identity that abhors the American way of life. The parents are strictly vigilant of the "amorous" lifestyle that they believe most Americans follow and prohibit their own children from following it through subtle but continuous preaching about culture and religion that strongly condemns such behavior.

Kiran and other Indian children like him are also subjected to the same cultural teachings, be it in their own family or at the temple where they receive religious education. The wry humor of the situation is apparent when Kiran describes one of the kids of Indian-style Sunday school, Shruti Gupta. He says, "Her parents are so conservative—they conserve so much—that Shruti, though born and raised here, has the same Anglo-accented English they do. The Guptas really do construct the perfect paradox: they practically keep their daughter locked up in a (gold-plated) cage, and yet they practice very progressive forms of medicine, her father being an internist, her mother is a cosmetic surgeon" (32). Kiran's father is unsympathetic towards his son for what he terms to be his girlish attitude, something that is abhorred and something that he feels is detrimental in the process of his son's success in America. It is important to understand that this is Kiran's father's angst and torment at seeing his son not turn out the way he expects him to be. In a supreme moment of bonding and confession, he tells his son about his own modest upbringing in India and the travails of life in America that he and his wife had to face. The child becomes the agency through which the parents try to fulfill their own hopes and expectations of a better life. Childhood, and by extension, children, are subjected to an external idea and conception of conformity, rules and regulations which establish incorporation of the child into the timeless tradition of parents. The child becomes the site of continuation as well as change, continuation of what has been deemed right throughout history, and change of those values that history, tradition, and culture have found to be wrong in the long run. The child can thus be conceptualized as an experiment in itself, an experiment that, through trial and error, determines the divisions between right and wrong. In the process, the child becomes a repository of both individual and societal norms and values, very often denied any agency to act or react on its own.

In traditional societies where religion is held in high esteem, despite the state being termed as secular, most people follow some sort of religion and conformation to an affirmed faith is tantamount to following societal rules. In such societies, religion forms *the* way of life, and in a diasporic setting it assumes all the more importance because here religion helps in upholding a preconceived notion of identity. The relationship between religion and performance becomes more attuned then since it is performed on a daily basis before an audience (presumably both westerners and Indians) to project a certain stage presence, an identity "made up" by the circumstances.

Religion and Performance

As the chapter "Choosing My Religion" signifies, Kiran is in the process of choosing what his religion means to him and especially which aspects of it he will keep and which he deems unimportant for him. Hinduism is presumably one of the few religions in the world that allows its followers to choose from an array of gods and goddesses. As Kathleen Taylor says, "Almost every human activity and every local area or group of people has its patron deities. These are all woven together in a complex web. One deity can be revealed in many different forms; conversely, different deities can merge into each other, by sharing epithets or myths" (167). When Kiran first encounters his mother while wearing make-up, he is anxious to find a solution to his dilemma, and his eyes fall on the display of deities on the altar. There are Vishnu, Lakshmi, Shiva, and Krishna, and out of them he chooses Krishna to pray to, thereby instantly finding an answer to his predicament. As is evident from the way Kiran uses Krishna as a ruse to hide his ulterior motives, it can be surmised that the religious is juxtaposed with the secular. But at the same time, he is shrewd enough to transport his ruse to a higher level, of imagining himself as Krishna, and thus embarking on the long and difficult journey of at once performing his self as the reincarnation of Krishna and hiding this knowledge from everyone else to lead to a grand revelation. Hiding also acts as another form of performance that is more important to maintain in order that the "other" performance can be performed.

Kiran is anxious to model his act for the performance as perfectly as possible, and for this he needs to know more about his religion, more than the meager and patchy ideas he has regarding Krishna and Hinduism. The library provides him with reading material to explore the richness of one of the oldest religions in the world. Despite the fact that the Eastern Religions section of the library is rather small, Kiran sets about his task with method and accuracy. He begins with *A Journey Through Hinduism* and flips to the index, looking up his favorite entry, Krishna. He learns about the ten incarnations of Vishnu, one of the gods of the trinity of Brahma, Vishnu, and Shiva. According to Hindu myths, Brahma is the maker, Vishnu is the preserver, and Shiva is the destroyer. Out of all these incarnations, Krishna is the most memorable of figures, even more so than Rama, the hero of Ramayana. He also learns that the 10th incarnation of Vishnu, the *Kalki avataar*, is yet to come. Kiran visualizes himself as the tenth incarnation despite having hardly any similarities with what the myths describe about the characteristics of this incarnation of Vishnu.[3] He also learns about the battle between good and evil, the story of the struggle between Devaki and Kamsa and how Krishna was born.[4]

Kiran does not simply gather knowledge; he moves a step further by discussing his newfound knowledge with his friend, Cody. But Cody rejects the stories of the *Upanishads*, the ancient Indian texts, by telling him that these are actually stories from the Bible. Kiran is both amused and distracted too because he is unable to make Cody understand his viewpoint. While he assumes that Hinduism is much older than Christianity, and the Bible copies many Hindu texts, he is also appreciative of the fact that the stories of the Bible and the Hindu holy books are much the same. This tussle is important not only from the perspective of the narrative but also from a wider understanding of religion. Kiran's choice of words is also very intriguing because, in apparently simplistic terms, he codifies the struggle and the obvious resolution to the eternal problem of superiority of one religion over the other. He first tells Cody, "I have to use the words of your religion to explain mine to you" (100), and then, "Hinduism did come before Christianity, but why separate the two anyway? In terms of vitality and spirit, isn't Hinduism Christianity and Christianity Hinduism? Our houses of worship may be vastly different, but there is a shared movement toward life, light, jubilance" (101). Richard Falk summarizes it as a "uniting feature of religious consciousness, the oneness of human family that can give rise to an ethos of human solidarity, the unity of all creation, and, with it, the sense of both the wholeness of human experience and the dignity of the individual" (196). Kiran does not distinguish between religions, at least not between Hinduism (a religion he is trying to absorb in a renewed way) and Christianity (a religion which surrounds his social and political existence). But Kiran's heightened sense of acceptance is neither the product of extensive study regarding different religions, nor does it signify his actual knowledge regarding Hinduism itself.

His struggle with religion and especially Hinduism is his own simplistic (albeit twisted) way to gain recognition, and more importantly, acceptance. At the same time, Kiran is fixated on a single god, Krishna, with whom he shares certain affinities rather than delving into the vast repertoire of the myths and texts associated with Hinduism.[5] Krishna is represented as blue in color, which immediately sets him apart from other gods. This peculiarity of Krishna's nature is what attracts Kiran to him, who also finds himself in a peculiar mold, unable to adjust or mingle with those surrounding him. Kiran's ultimate aim remains in absorbing Krishna in body and spirit and in performing an aspect of his religion that will showcase his superiority.

Hinduism and Performance

In *Lived Religions: Everyday Hinduism,* Joyce Burkhalter Flueckiger says,

Hinduism is primarily an oral and visual tradition; Hindus know their stories primarily by hearing them performed and seeing them through a wide range of visual mediums. Religious narratives are sung or recited by performers in village squares and temple courtyards or dramatically enacted at particular festivals; they are danced in classical dance and dramatic forms such as Bharatnatyam, Kuchipudi, and Kathakali; they are painted on scrolls and carved into the outside of temple towers, walls, and gateways [46].

In fact, Hinduism as a religion is a demonstrative one that, through various public performances, attracts people to its mythological grandeur, the best examples being the Ram *līlā* and the Krishna *līlā*. Both these forms of performances exemplify the obvious connection between Hinduism and the overt importance of narratives. At the same time, dance forms like those mentioned above also go a long way in establishing a relationship between the religion and its followers. Hinduism is perhaps one of the few religions that extensively uses performances to engage with its followers and stimulate devotion. As Flueckiger emphasizes, the audiences of such performances do not necessarily attend them to know the stories that are being narrated. They already know them and are rather a part of it to "gain merit, as an act of devotion, and/or to participate in a social event" (47). The fact that such performances are also social events is demonstrated in none other events more forcefully than in the very public dance performances like Bharatnatyam or Kathakali. The public spaces are appropriated for religious performances and are thereby induced with a secular nature. In the context of the analysis here, I will take up the specific case of Krishna *līlā* or Ras *līlā*, its performances all over India and Kiran's appropriation of the art form at his school.

The term Ras *līlā* simply refers to the dance performance depicting Radha and Krishna's love for each other and also various scenes from Krishna's childhood. As D. L. Swann describes, the performance can be divided into two parts—the "first part is called the *rās* and it expresses the lovemaking of Rādhā and Kṛṣṇa," (177) and the second part termed as *līlā* "deals with some incident out of the early life of Kṛṣṇa, such as stealing the butter, holding up the milkmaids and demanding a toll payment, going to Rādhā in disguise, or leaving Gokul for Mathura" (180). Just as Graham M. Schweig says that the performance of ras *līlā* is "the eternal soul's loving union with the supreme deity" (1), Joanne Waghorne in the larger context of Hinduism says that "the embodiment of divinity" is the "central feature of Hinduism *and* ... a central feature in the study of religion" (qtd. in Valpey 2). The manifestation of divinity or the presence of god in the human or inside the human body is an aspect of its conception that Hinduism has often endorsed, and the ras *līlā* performance presents this overt manner. The audience not only perceives a young child enacting the role of Krishna on stage but also sees an earthly incarnation of the godly figure of Krishna. The religious and the theatrical merge in the active participation of the audience, and the performers transform the performance into a visual and sensual perception of god in the material world. The two Krishnas present on the stage—Krishna the actor and Krishna the deity—have a great impact on the conceptualization of the performance. Krishna the actor is a means through which the performance depicts the narrative of Krishna the god. But the additional presence of Krishna the deity is posited at the border of credibility and faith of the audience or perceived devotees who understand the stage as the material manifestation of the divine and the actor as god incarnate. This aspect of divinity and the material reality of a visible, accessible, and to an extent, communicable god in Hinduism is often at a crossroads with the western perception of god and worship.

Waghorne, speaking in the context of the meaning of god, says that for the west,

> The real issue was not the nature of god but rather the nature of the *meaning* of god. *God* was to be understood as a kind of language by which humanity expressed its deepest concerns.... The problem with (the) twentieth century two-step around concrete divinity is that it denied the possibility that devoted Hindus, themselves, ever actually thought that god had an embodied reality. It was assumed that in making an icon of god, the Hindu was simply making meaning. (emphasis in original) [qtd. in Valpey 161].

Diana Eck carries this idea further and says that in India, what matters more than the simple act of worship is *darśan* that is the auspicious act of seeing the divine in the seemingly mundane idol (3). While idol worship is an integral part of Hinduism, it would be wrong to assume that the apparently innocuous idol "made" from stone, mud, or even straw can sustain within itself a god who is powerful and all encompassing. It is rather the devotee engaging in a belief that "sees" the reflection of the god in the idol and who worships it as an embodiment: a material manifestation of the divine or the concrete rendition of the spiritual. Therefore, Hinduism believes in the incarnation of gods in earthly forms, as human beings who perform many miraculous things and are often upheld as the ideal of mankind in general.

Kiran's, and by extension Satyal's, understanding of him being a reincarnation of Krishna is slightly off-track, but both of them still perceive and conceive means to make this make-believe come true. Kiran, in his extensive (at least in his restrained circumstances) study of Hinduism and particularly Krishna, tries to understand the idiosyncrasies of his character as the means through which he can be more Krishna-like in his being. He even sees a blue streak in his skin that others cannot see, so he considers himself to be becoming more and more like Krishna each day. At the same time, he conjures up various images of Krishna through his drawings and tries to imagine himself to be like those drawings. The clash between the world of his imagination and the world of reality happens when Mrs. Goldberg, his language arts teacher, sees them and considers them to be brilliant. She wants to display them in the school. But the drawings are abruptly and categorically refused to be displayed by Mrs. Buchanan, the art teacher, primarily because they fall under the ambit of religious drawings, and the principal has forbidden any religious drawings to be assigned or displayed. While Kiran is at a loss to understand why Mrs. Goldberg does not press the matter, his friend Cody explains that the teacher is Jewish and, being an outcast like him, she does not want to emphasize religion in a secular school, but at the same time, she wants a school that makes the demarcations of religion clear to everyone. Kiran, probably for the first time, understands that he is not the only outsider in the school, and there are others, too, who have felt the pain of rejection. This incident makes him firmer in his resolve to prove his mettle in the talent show and thereby get accepted by the very society that he at times despises and rejects.

The notion of acceptance, albeit a convoluted one, forms the primary basis for Kiran's initiatives, and it runs throughout the narrative. He knows from the beginning that he exhibits deviant behavior, right from his affinity for his mother's makeup, his liking of dolls and ballet, his inability to mingle with others, and his queer sexual behavior. In the midst of all this is the overwhelming desire to be one with his surroundings, so when this is not happening, he comes up with a plan to be something more than average, to be a god who is deviant. This merging of the mundane and earthly (Kiran) with the ethereal and divine (Krishna) can only happen in a situation where he can showcase the best of his culture and religion, the talent show. But Krishna is a relatively unknown figure in Martin Van Buren Elementary School, a Hindu god whom very few in his school can relate to or understand.[6] So Kiran chooses a Whitney Houston song, "How Will I Know," to accompany his dance, a choice that reflects on choosing yet another outsider like Mrs. Goldberg to emphasize his fight for survival. For Kiran, the song also represents his own particular situation, his need for love and a "listening ear." But at the same time, he also has his moments of doubts as to how his whole existence came to be distilled down to "this one measly performance," and more importantly, why "Krishna decide to set his circus" in Ohio of all places.

Performing God or Performing Human Desires?

A recurring aspect of the narrative is Kiran's naïve but at times shrewd conceptualization of himself as a reincarnation of Krishna. But who is who? Is Kiran Krishna or is Krishna Kiran? More importantly, who is performing—a god who deigns to be a human or a human who aspires to be a god? Throughout the narrative, Kiran is at odds with his identity, trying to etch out a distinctive personality based on Krishna, perhaps erroneously or perhaps correctly. It is more important to understand that Kiran's anguish in choosing to be a god, to be above others, is also a desperate attempt to be commonplace, to be like everyone else. And the only way to be commonplace is to be exceptional. Despite his own queer leanings, he is repulsed at seeing Rodney, the ranger, making out with a male friend. This incident pushes him to the limits of his identity crisis. Does he really want to be like Rodney, or does he want to be like everyone else? If he cannot digest the apparent raw sexuality that Rodney displays, can he adjust himself to being "normal" like everyone else? It is here that Kiran probes himself by questioning, "But if I make myself too normal, I lose my godlike presence. If I renounce my individuality, I make myself as vulnerable as all those other babies were to King Kamsa. If I renounce my singular power, I am no longer that one blue boy protected by his own powers. Which will I choose—conformity or delectable deformity?" (191). The dilemma of choosing between being extraordinary or simply an ordinary mortal agonizes Kiran, yet his choice remains to be Krishna.

At the same time, he knows that in choosing to be Krishna he is just another incarnation of Vishnu. His affiliation is more with Krishna rather than with the incarnations of Vishnu; he longs for Krishna almost as a lover. As he justly says, he is smitten by Krishna. For a long time, Kiran has visualized himself as a reincarnation of Krishna, but probably for the first time, he accepts that he is in fact a lover of Krishna. The ability to love Krishna and ascend to a god-like status is a tradition that is prevalent in Krishna worship. Klaus Klostermaier says, "perhaps the most subtle and detailed system of gradual ascent to God by means of love has been developed in the Caitanya

School of Vaishnavism" (765). David Haberman also elaborates on this concept; that in the Chaitanya School, love forms an important and integral part of assimilation with the divine.[7]

The Chaitanya tradition is based on the principle of "achintya bheda abheda," the concept of oneness and difference with god existing at the same time. The two terms, *bheda* meaning "difference" and *abheda* meaning "non-difference," combined mean being different and not different simultaneously. The main ideology of this school of worship emanates from the view that the individual soul, or *jiva*, is *abheda,* or not different from the Supreme Being. At the same time, the divine is different from the individual in its supremacy and powers (Jones and Ryan 83). This form of worship conceives of god and his creation to be linked together as well as separate from each other. In this school of worship, Krishna is the ultimate self who is accessible to all *jivas*, or souls, if they love him unconditionally. Sri Chaitanya himself was engaged in a frenzied love for Krishna through singing and dancing. Chaitanya was later on believed to be an incarnation of Krishna himself.

Kiran, in his misplaced love for Krishna and his belief to be Krishna himself, also subverts the very notion of incarnation, or *avataar*. The Sanskrit *avatara* comes from two root words—the prefix *ava* meaning coming down and the verb *tr* meaning to pass by. The word signifies the passing or coming down of god from the realms of divinity to the human world. On the other hand, a variant of *avataar* is *avatarana,* which means to make an entry into the stage, the god as man marking his entry onto the world or stage (Bassuk 3). Kiran's *avatarana* is rather of a man making his entry as god, which he wants to justify through his performance as a god. This performance is positioned at the crucial juncture of self-discovery and self-portrayal, the point of revelation where Kiran not only learns the truth of his own twisted religious ideology but also discovers that his knowledge has propelled him towards a more powerful position of self-worth, too. The postsecular position that Kiran occupies allows him to reconstitute his identity.

Performance of a Lifetime

Kiran's ultimate test or showdown is in the talent show, which proves to be almost an ordeal by fire. He tries to channel all his hard work, anguish, dissatisfaction, hopes, and tears into this one performance. This one performance is to be his transforming miracle too, which will change his image forever in the eyes of everyone around him: "Tonight, the people out there are not so much an *audience*—something that hears—than they are an *experience*—something that senses and feels" (232). When the show begins, Kiran is not fully dressed because he knows that Mrs. Nevins, his teacher, will oppose it as being religious or too Indian, which amounts to the same thing for her. The cultural and religious merge together once again to present an instance where the overt secular nature of the public space, the school auditorium, refrains any exhibition of private religion or beliefs. But Kiran, for once, is not inhibited to perform to his heart's content and he wants "to show these close-minded people what true Indian panache is" (232). He realizes that perhaps it is necessary to "dance the hell out of time and space to make a mark on the world" (233). The performance no longer remains just an innocent dance but becomes a "me against the world" kind of means to uphold one's identity.

Interestingly, at this point in time, Kiran no longer displays any anger towards the Indian community which shunned him. Rather, it is more of a lashing out against the American school community that has always made fun of him. There is a fire raging within him, fuelled more by reminding himself constantly that this is a last go at truly finding himself. While he is applying his makeup, he realizes that his true self is this identity of his that strives for individuality, which does not want to find an exotic self but rather is "just as great, just as godly, just as genius as Krishna because he never settles for the mundane.... Kiran settles for nothing but a Krishna–worthy Kiran" (252). His identity is no longer merged into Krishna but rather one where he defines himself to be like Krishna, to emulate the greatness and uniqueness of the god who is known for his extraordinary powers. This realization helps Kiran formulate an identity *outside* Krishna, which makes his world a weird one.

Kiran, when he ultimately performs on stage, feels that his fusion of ballet and kathak might mortify the teachers who taught him dancing, but it has a liberating effect on his body. He has almost an out-of-body experience where he is both the performer and the audience, the Kiran in the mirror and the one who sees the reflection in the mirror as well as the reflection itself. This freedom that the performance allows him to indulge in allows him the possibility of realizing the fluidic nature of his being which can change and yet be constant like his every movement on stage. His conception of self is put to question through his performance, and the knowledge is revealed to him that his being and the world itself can be a capricious one, which thoroughly questions his fixity and rootedness to ideas and notions. His complete immersion in the dance culminates in his fainting on the stage, or rather losing his sight while being conscious of everything else occurring around him. He also knows that his parents have started the applause that is resounding in the gymnasium, and thus he has gained recognition in their eyes.

Kiran regains consciousness in the hospital surrounded by his parents and a doctor. He is concerned about the reaction from his parents after his exploits on the stage. But the actual bolt from the blue is not from his parents, but rather from the doctor who reveals the cause of his blue tinted skin. The doctor says that his skin has started turning blue because of the large dosages of silver supplement that his mother used to administer to him. This bit of information strips Kiran of his remnant of resemblance with Krishna and relegates him to the status of a mere mortal. In a moment of rare illumination, Kiran realizes that the mirage of Krishna has been his own creation and that mirage has never been a part of his identity. It has in fact been his imagination that he has willingly submerged himself to create a god-like being. But Kiran has no regrets regarding his decision for he realizes that his delightful fancy has brought out his talent, notwithstanding the fact that he has to face so many hurdles.

Kiran realizes that he is no longer Krishna; probably he was never Krishna, and his attempt to be like Krishna is mired in his struggle for recognition and power. But this knowledge that he can never be god-like in identity is in many ways redemptive, for it frees him from his quest to be extraordinary. At the same time, as he acknowledges himself, he has gained in a grudging manner what he set out to accomplish: acceptance. For a child like Kiran, who needs to be disguised like a god in human form to be accepted by his parents and schoolmates, the truth that he is not one does not shatter him. Deep within him he has probably always known that it is a ruse, a garb to contrast his religiosity in the apparently secular world.

The "Post" in the Secular

Kiran's performance allows him to reconcile his personal demons, but it is not enough for him to totally reconstitute his familial and social presence. His parents, particularly his father, have come to a tacit understanding regarding his sexual and mental orientation, but that does not translate into an open acceptance of him. Neither do his schoolmates regard him to be the extraordinary person that he initially set out to project. The school authorities have not been able lodge their protest over his blatant religious display on the stage because of his fainting, and thus a disease, a very secular aspect of life, saves him. Religion becomes subservient to a secular aspect of life for its presence in society, at least in the gymnasium of Martin Van Buren Elementary School. Kiran's struggle or performance is relegated to the background, and the only person who shows any pride in his feat is Mrs. Goldberg, his language arts teacher, who silently applauds him with a sticker made of two blue triangles overlapping each other for his spelling test. This almost secretive act of a display of her own religious sentiments reinforces the fact that religion needs to be or can be enacted only outside Habermas' "institutional public sphere."

Kiran achieves some sort of popularity in his school for his pain-defying act in the gymnasium, "a little bit of immortality" added to his persona, which he feels makes himself a god. However, Kiran's ultimate postsecular moment does not emanate from his godlike status but rather from the knowledge that he gains about himself and those around him. He understands that his need to conform has been the cause of his deviant behavior, and he no longer feels the urge to conform. He is neither a god nor a failed god; the constraint of religion he feels would liberate him to enjoy the secular nature of his school has been a failure. The secular aim of being uniform, subscribing to similarity rather than dissimilarity, has been the beginning of his whole exercise in being a god. Neither religion nor secularism has allowed him to know himself in entirety; he chooses non-conformity in order to conform but he realizes through his ultimate understanding of Krishna that he needed to celebrate his difference rather than lament it. This in itself might be a reductionist approach to his complex and complicated problems, but it allows him to revisit his personal god and religion without the angst of his earlier self. At the end, he experiments with the rhythm of the cymbals in the temple, basking in his self-knowledge, and in a befitting imagery, he invokes the gorgeousness of the all-consuming fire, which purifies him. The Gita (compilation of Krishna's teaching to Arjuna during the war in the *Mahabharat*) too talks about the fire that leads to self-knowledge:

> *yathaidhāṁsi samiddho 'gnir*
> *bhasma-sāt kurute 'rjuna*
> *jñānāgnih sarva-karmāni*
> *bhasma-sāt kurute tathā*

"As the blazing fire turns firewood to ashes, O Arjuna, so does the fire of knowledge burn to ashes all reactions to material activities" (Swami Prabhupada 236). Kiran's ultimate salvation lies in his acceptance of his being, a knowledge that eventually bestows him power.

NOTES

1. See Victor Turner, *From Ritual to Theatre: The Human Seriousness of Play* (New York: PAJ Publications, 1982).

2. See Erving Goffman, *The Presentation of Self in Everyday Life* (New York: Anchor Books, 1959).

3. Vishnu has a total of ten incarnations, or *avataar,* and Kalki is the last one of them who is yet to come. The onset of Kalki would bring an end to the first cycle of ages that the world goes through. Hinduism conceives of four main ages or *yuga—Satya, Treta, Dvapara,* and *Kali,* and at the end of each *yuga,* one *avataar* has come to this earth. The end of *Satya yuga* is marked by the coming of Parashurama, *Treta* by Ram, *Dvapara* by Krishna, and *Kali* by Kalki. *Srimad Bhagavatam* 12th Canto and Brahmanda-purana gives details about the birth of Kalki, who his parents will be and where he will be born. He will be born at the cusp of two *yuga,* the end of *Kali yuga* and beginning of *Satya yuga. Kali yuga* will be one of chaos and anarchy, religion and spiritualism will be on the decline, and the world will be marked

by destruction and wanton killings. Kalki *avataar* will bring an end to this chaos and herald in the *Satya yuga*, thereby the cycle of ages will recur again.

4. The narrative does not take into consideration the fact that Devaki is Kamsa's own sister. It might be Satyal's own oversight or an indication of the fact that the books Kiran has gone through are deficient in their understanding of Hinduism.

5. Hinduism, being a polytheistic religion, has a multitude of gods and means of worship. There are various sects like Vaishanava, Shaiva, Shakta, and numerous schools of thought. At the same time, according to the variance of culture, tradition, and place the forms of worship change completely. This act in itself makes the same religion alien to its own adherents who subscribe to the difference and varied nature of it.

6. Dr. Shiva Bajpaia Acharya and Arumuganathaswami, in a paper titled "Teaching of Hinduism in the California State School System: Evaluation and Recommendations," elaborate on the problems of teaching about Hinduism in American schools, particularly in California. They look at the limited ways in which textbooks represent Hinduism, thereby making the whole process of teaching about religion a triviality in itself.

7. Haberman, in *Acting as a Way of Salvation: A Study of Rāgānūga Bhakti Sādhana*, emphasizes the importance of devotion or *bhakti* as a means to attain salvation in Gaudiya Vaisnava tradition, which is primarily associated with the Bengali saint Caitanya. In this process acting or imitation forms an integral part of it, and thus the life of the devotee is a stage who imitates the god to attain redemption.

WORKS CITED

Bassuk, Daniel E. *Incarnation in Hinduism and Christianity: The Myth of the God-Man*. London: Palgrave Macmillan, 1987.

Blackston, Dylan McCarthy. "Queer Feelings, Political Potential: Tracing Affect in Performance Spaces." Master's thesis, Georgia State University, 2012.

Bose, Buddhadeva. *The Book of Yudhisthir: A Study of the Mahabharat of Vyas*. Translated by Sujit Mukherjee. Hyderabad, India: Sangam Books, 1986.

Eck, Diana. *Darśan: Seeing the Divine Image in India*. 3rd ed. Delhi, India: Motilal Banarsidass Publishers, 1998.

Falk, Richard. "A Worldwide Religious Resurgence in an Era of Globalization and Apocalyptic Terrorism." In *Religion in International Relations: The Return from Exile*, edited by Fabio Petito and Pavlos Hatzopoulos, 181–208. London: Palgrave Macmillan, 2003

Flueckiger, Joyce Burkhalter. *Lived Religions: Everyday Hinduism*. Hoboken, NJ: Wiley-Blackwell, 2015.

Haberman David L. *Acting as a Way of Salvation: A Study of Rāgānūga Bhakti Sādhana*. Delhi, India: Motilal Banarsidass Publishers, 2001.

Jones, Constance A., and James D. Ryan. *Encyclopedia of Hinduism*. New York: Facts On File, 2007.

Klostermaier, Klaus. "*Hṛdayavidyā*: A Sketch of a Hindu-Christian Theology of Love." *Journal of Ecumenical Studies* 9, no. 4 (Fall 1972): 750–775.

Knott, K., and S. Khokher. "Religious and Ethnic Identity Among Young Muslim Women in Bradford." *New Community* 19 (1993): 593–610.

Knott, Kim. "Cutting Through the Postsecular City: A Spatial Interrogation." In *Exploring the Postsecular: The Religious, the Political and the Urban*, edited by Arie Molendijk, Justin Beaumont and Christoph Jedan, 19–38. Leiden, Netherlands: Brill Publishers, 2010.

Mavelli, Luca, and Erin K. Wilson. "Postsecularism and International Relations." In *Routledge Handbook of Religion and Politics*, edited by Jeffrey Haynes, 251–269. 2nd ed. London: Routledge: 2016.

Moag, R. "Negative Pressures in the American Educational System on Hindu Identity Formation: Part Two: The Effects of Tertiary Education." In *Hindu Diaspora: Global Perspectives*, edited by T.S. Rukmani, 237–285. New Delhi: Munshiram Manoharlal, 2001.

Muñoz, J.E. *Disidentifications: Queers of Colour and the Performance of Politics*. Minneapolis: University of Minnesota Press, 2009.

Phillips, A. *The Beast in the Nursery: On Curiosity and Other Thoughts*. New York: Vintage Books, 1998.

Richmond, Farley P., Darius L. Swann, and Phillip B. Zarrilli, eds. *Indian Theatre: Traditions of Performance*. Delhi, India: Motilal Banarsidass Publishers, 1993.

Satyal, Rakesh. *Blue Boy*. New Delhi: IndiaInk, 2011.

Saunders, Ben. *Do the Gods Wear Capes?: Spirituality, Fantasy, and Superheroes*. London: Continuum International Publishing Group, 2011.

Schechner, Richard. *Performance Studies: An Introduction*. London: Routledge, 2002.

Schweig, Graham M. *Dance of Divine Love: India's Classic Sacred Love Story*. Princeton, NJ: Princeton University Press, 2005.

Stoeckl, Kristina. "Defining the Postsecular." February 2011.

Superle, Michelle. *Contemporary English-Language Indian Children's Literature: Representations of Nation, Culture, and the New Indian Girl*. New York: Routledge, 2011.

Swami Prabhupada, A.C. Bhaktivedanta. *Bhagavad-Gita as It Is*. 2nd ed. Alachua, FL: Bhaktivedanta Book Trust, 1989.

Taylor, Kathleen. "Deities." In *Encyclopedia of Hinduism*, edited by Denise Cush, Catherine A. Robinson, and Michael York. London: Routledge, 2008.

Thomson, Iain. "Deconstructing the Hero." In *Comics as Philosophy*, edited by Jeff McLaughlin, 100–152. Jackson: University of Mississippi Press, 2005.

Valpey, Kenneth Russell. *Attending Krsna's Image: Caitanya Vaisnava Murti-Seva as Devotional Truth*. London: Routledge, 2006.

The Way of the Fantasist

Ethical Complexities in the Taoist Mythopoeic Fantasy of Ursula Le Guin's A Wizard of Earthsea

DAVID S. HOGSETTE

Introduction—Postsecular Fantasy

The grand narrative of secularism and its promise to expunge the public sphere of religious expression has not lived up to its modernist expectations. Interest in orthodox religion, heterodoxy, spirituality, and mysticism thrive in this postsecular age. As J.P. Moreland discusses in *Scaling the Secular City*, the various presuppositions of materialism and the logical consequences of methodological naturalism at the very heart of secularism are too reductive and logically self-defeating to satisfy the longings of the human heart and to fuel the aspirations of the imagination (185–224). Moreover, contemporary philosophers and thinkers such as William Lane Craig, Alvin Plantinga, and Marilynne Robinson argue that the supposed irreconcilable division between secular naturalism and religious faith is pure myth, noting that reason and faith, science and religion, physics and metaphysics complement each other, opening up diverse ways of comprehending this complex universe and our places in it.[1] In short, pure secular materialism is intellectually narrow, strips the world of wonder, diminishes and even denies spiritual appreciation of beauty, and reduces the awe-inspiring human being to an accidental complex of molecules in motion. Such a spiritually bankrupt, aesthetically vapid, and imaginatively void perspective is unsatisfactory because, among other things, it is ultimately unsatisfying. For many, it is unlivable.

Where secular methodological naturalism and scientific materialism disappoint, religion and mysticism invite those postsecularists who want

171

more than mere pragmatism and physicalism into wider realms of spiritual reality and imaginative possibilities. Although many definitions of postsecularism exist, generally speaking, postsecular perspectives seek to unite religious and secular thought, to discuss how secularist and religious perspectives can complement each other, and to explore ways in which the secular and the religious coexist such that there is both disenchantment and re-enchantment of our world.[2] Some postsecularists who find materialism spiritually lacking and aesthetically uninspiring do not necessarily wish to return to traditional religious orthodoxy. Instead, they seek satisfaction in alternative spiritualities for the deeper longings of their hearts and the desires of their imaginations, often by embracing Eastern mysticism through appropriating select elements and revised versions of such religions as Hinduism, Buddhism, and Taoism.

Master storyteller Ursula K. Le Guin is one such postsecularist, choosing to build her mythopoeic subcreation, Earthsea, upon explicitly Taoist philosophical foundations. The Earthsea fantasy series abounds in Eastern mysticism, indeed rising to the level of Taoist apologetics. According to J.R. Wytenbroek, "Taoist ideas, rather than becoming the subject of her novels, become deeply interwoven with and form a basic element of many of her themes, characters, and even the structures of the plots and novels themselves" (173). Le Guin's Taoist religious perspective and dualistic moral worldview are just as fundamental to her mythopoeic writing as the doctrines, morality, and narrative structures of Christianity are for the artistic expressions of other such mythopoeic writers of children's and young adult fantasy literature as George MacDonald, C.S. Lewis, and J.R.R. Tolkien.

Much like these other religiously inspired fantasy writers, Le Guin experienced her own spiritual journey, starting when she was an adolescent observing how the *Tao Te Ching* brought her secular father much comfort and provided some satisfaction to his deeper spiritual longings. Like her father, Le Guin found a spiritual and moral home in Taoism, and this religious worldview shapes her Earthsea books and informs much of her other speculative fiction (MacCaffery and Gregory 83). In her Earthsea saga, Le Guin is overtly Taoist, and, just as Lewis's intellectually rigorous Christianity created a rich imaginative soil from which his fantasies grew, Le Guin's embracing of Taoism and Eastern mysticism provides an intriguing and imaginatively challenging foundation upon which she builds a beautifully sustained subcreation. Le Guin adopts specific Taoist spiritual, philosophical, and moral principles to craft this *bildungsroman* fantasy, offering a convincing fantasy subcreation. Readers can escape into Earthsea not only to recover a sense of mystical wonderment absent from secularist perspectives, but they can also rediscover a faith in the possibility of personal moral instruction and improvement.

Several scholars have outlined specific ways in which Le Guin integrates Taoism in her literary craft, yet they have left unaddressed some important philosophical contradictions and narrative complications associated with her selective appropriation of Taoist concepts. Even though Ged, the central character in *A Wizard of Earthsea*, raises existential questions regarding the Taoist-inspired notions of Equilibrium that govern magic and morality in the novel, Le Guin ignores the troubling philosophical paradoxes and moral ambiguities associated with Taoist dualism. Moreover, scholars have overlooked some other fascinating elements of Taoist belief that Le Guin works quite subtly into her fabulation. Despite some unresolved paradoxes and because of her nuanced integration of lesser known Taoist principles, Le Guin creates a comprehensive mythopoeic fantasy novel that both delights and edifies the postsecular imagination that is open to such fabulation and willing to explore, analyze, and contemplate the spiritual blessings and philosophical paradoxes that is Earthsea.

Le Guin's Taoism

Mythopoeic writers typically create fantasy worlds out of some religious, spiritual, and/or mystical perspective. For example, George MacDonald, J.R.R. Tolkien, C.S. Lewis, Madeleine L'Engle, and Michael Ende build their fantastic realms upon Christian theological principles. However, as Susanne Reid observes, Le Guin follows the lead of Lord Dunsany and attempts something a bit different (5). Instead of subcreating upon theistic cosmological concepts and theological principles, Dunsany chose polytheistic paganism as the foundation for his Pegana universe. Similarly, Le Guin chooses another non-theistic worldview upon which to construct Earthsea: Taoism.[3] The very name of her fantasy world, Earthsea, involves a balancing of apparent opposites: land and water or earth and sea. Le Guin prefaces her novel with a mysterious epigraph, taken from the fictitious Earthsea book of lore titled *The Creation of Ea*, which foregrounds Eastern mystical dualism common to Taoist writings like the *Tao Te Ching*:

> Only in silence the word,
> only in dark the light,
> only in dying life:
> bright the hawk's flight
> on the empty sky.

Vivid examples of Taoist principles and Eastern mysticism abound in the book, giving it a unique charm that fits neatly into the fantasy genre, at least for the average Western reader. Most Western readers are, at best, superficially familiar with Taoism and Eastern philosophy, and so a whole world and universe grounded in Taoism feels fantastical. Wizards who discourse cryptically about maintaining the Equilibrium, mysterious sages speaking inscrutable riddles, and robed wizards who, like Eastern monks, act and speak as little as possible and only when necessary lend the text a magical, fantastical, and other-worldly quality. Yet, such qualities are not otherworldly at all, for they come from the heart of Eastern religious and philosophical expressions.[4]

Le Guin's Eastern inspiration comes most directly from her life-long reading, study, and application of basic Taoist principles. As with any worldview, Taoism comprises many sects and schools of thought. For some, Taoism is a full-fledged religion, complete with mythologies, traditions, rituals of worship, and various ceremonies tied to cultural festivals. For others, Taoism is a philosophy of life that provides guidance on morality and instruction on how best to perceive reality and interact with its dynamic elements.[5] Le Guin belongs to this latter group, and she gains her understanding of Taoism from reading one of its core texts, the *Tao Te Ching*. She even produced her own edition of this classic work, drawing from many other English translations and paraphrases.

From her understanding of Taoism, Le Guin constructs the mythos and ethos of Earthsea. Taoism posits the existence of an invisible, unknowable, infinite, eternal, always existent, impersonal absolute sometimes referred to as the Absolute Tao. This dualistic understanding of reality presupposes that the Absolute is comprised of eternal opposites, like good and evil, which must be maintained in an eternal balance. Nature, humanity, the world, and the created universe are all incomplete expressions of the Absolute. Taoist principles suggest that visible processes in nature can teach astute observers about important qualities of the Absolute, particularly the significance of maintaining balance. Taoism embraces the mystical and the metaphysical as true realities existing alongside the created, material world, and Taoist principles and practices seek to provide spiritual balance for the individual, who is tasked with living in harmony with nature, the self, and others (Koller 283; Oldstone-Moore 23–24.). In Le Guin's Earthsea, these core Taoist beliefs and concepts are transformed into the wizards' teachings about maintaining the Equilibrium.

Earthsea's Equilibrium and the Taoist Way of Nature

The concept of maintaining balance within the self and between self and nature is foundational to Taoist teachings. According to John M. Koller, Taoism teaches that the human being and society should be governed by the same principles that govern nature: "Life is lived well only when people are completely in tune with the whole universe and their actions are the actions of the universe flowing through them" (284).[6] The wizards in Le Guin's Earthsea govern their use of magic according to various principles of maintaining what they call the Equilibrium, an operating principle that comes right out of Taoism's concern with maintaining balance. In fact, as Wytenbroek explains, the Earthsea novels are "structured by Ged's need for and pursuit of balance, and the search for the essential wholeness of being of both individual and world so that balance can be achieved" (174). In other words, Le Guin structures Ged's *bildungsroman* around Taoist principles of maintaining harmony and balance within nature.

Bildungsroman is a central, if not defining, element in mythopoeic high fantasy. Narratives about the moral and intellectual development of a main character are also defining aspects of children's books and novels written for adolescents or young adults. Before writing *A Wizard of Earthsea*, Le Guin had not written specifically for children or young adults, and when the publisher of Parnassus Press asked her to write a novel for older children, she decided to revisit her Earthsea world that she originally created in various stories during the mid 1960s (Reid 32). Much like MacDonald, Lewis, Tolkien, L'Engle, and Ende, Le Guin does not consider children's literature a lower form of art, and along with her mythopoeic counterparts, she would not dream of condescending to children in her books. When it comes to fantasy, children are in many ways more grown up than are adults, and Le Guin treats all her readers like adults, with respect.

Indeed, there are some readers, critics, and academics who dismiss fantasy, especially children's fantasy, as simplistic, naïve, and childish. Le Guin rightly bristles at such a view, but admits, "The most childish thing about *A Wizard of Earthsea*, I expect, is its subject: coming of age" (*Language of the Night* 50). Though her novel is grounded in the adolescent *bildungsroman* tradition, Le Guin indicates that coming of age is not merely a childish literary device, because many people, herself included, take a rather long time to mature: "Coming of age is a process that took me many years; I finished it, so far as I ever will, at about age thirty-one; and so I feel rather deeply about it. So do most adolescents. It's their main occupation, in fact" (*Language of the Night* 50). Le Guin takes adolescent readers seriously, and she treats their main concern—growing up and learning how to be an adult in world that expects them to be adults while living in contexts that demand they still be children—with great care and sensitivity.

Early in the novel Ged struggles to negotiate this liminal adolescent position, as he shirks the responsibilities of learning to be a blacksmith like his father and, instead, learns magic from his aunt. However, his instruction is misguided, precisely because his aunt, being a woman and thus not allowed access to the higher understandings of magic and wizarding theory, does not know and cannot teach the principles of Equilibrium (Taoist balance): "being an ignorant woman among ignorant folk, she often used her crafts to foolish and dubious ends. She knew nothing of the Balance and the Pattern which the true wizard knows and deserves, and which keep him from using his spells unless real need demands" (Le Guin, *Wizard* 5).[7] Initially, Ged's instruction merely serves his selfish desire for knowledge that he can horde, feeding his arrogance and desire to lord power over others—he liked "to know and do what [his playmates] knew not and could not" (4)

In Le Guin's Earthsea, it takes an experienced and knowledgeable wizard to teach Ged the true ways of magic that are informed by understanding the significance of Equilibrium. Ged's first wizard instructor is Ogion, a quiet, patient, and mysterious figure right out of Taoist myth, speaking in duplicitous riddles and behaving in humble yet self-assured ways. In his youthful exuberance, Ged wants to learn spells to gain power, but Ogion has other plans: he teaches him the names of various herbs and plants, and he explains that true wizards act only when necessary, because any action may upset balance or Equilibrium. For example, when it rained, Ogion simply let it rain and never tried to change the weather patterns, even though he had knowledge and power to do so: "But Ogion let the rain fall where it would. He found a thick fir-tree and lay down beneath it. Ged crouched among the dripping bushes wet and sullen, and wondered what was the good of having power if you were too wise to use it" (18). Ogion is very much like a Taoist priest, teaching his young apprentice that all action should be considered and executed in terms of maintaining the delicate balance of the natural world.

A key element of Ged's *bildungs*, not only as a morally grounded human being but also as a socially responsible wizard, is to understand Earthsea Natural Law theory, that the world is designed and operates according to Equilibrium, or what Taoists call balance. True wizards must recognize that humans are not masters over nature, nor are they created to have dominion over the earth, as in the Judeo-Christian understanding. Rather, according to notions of Equilibrium, humans are created to be one with nature, co-equal with all aspects of the natural world, and thus should operate in balance with the created order. Therefore, Ogion tries to keep Ged in nature, to teach him to see reality in its natural condition, untouched by human civilization and regulation and operating freely according to basic natural laws that guide all natural processes toward balance or equilibrium.

The Insufficiency of Necessary Moral Regulation

The core ethical guiding principle in Taoism is that of balance—one should strive to act in ways that do not upset the balance of nature and the self, nor disrupt the harmony between individuals in community. According to Taoism, if everyone were equally attuned to the delicate balance maintaining reality, then life would be much more peaceful. Yet, as idealistic and naïve as this principle of balance is, Taoists are not themselves so undiscerning as to think that moral regulation is unnecessary. Given that Taoism seeks to regulate without regulation, to embrace reality and all things in their natural condition, it may seem as though Taoism has no use for moral codes. However, Lao Tzu was not opposed to moral regulation. Koller explain that Lao Tzu recognized the social necessity of moral codes and institutional regulation of individual action to provide maximum potential for people to satisfy their desires (286). He presupposed individual desire to be the root cause of all human behavior, and if there were limited resources and scarce opportunity to satisfy human desire, then competition would cause conflict, division, strife, pain, and suffering. To reduce conflict that necessarily follows from competition, Lao Tzu recognized the necessity of moral and institutional regulation. However, he also noted, quite rightly, that moral regulation is insufficient to end strife, conflict, war, pain, and suffering. Moral regulation deals with the symptoms but not the root causes. For Lao Tzu, the only way to address the root cause of immorality, pain, and suffering is to pursue the way of the Tao or, in the world of Earthsea, to abide by the principles of Equilibrium.

The wizarding school on Roke Island indeed is governed by basic Taoist principles where maintaining Equilibrium informs all instruction, from the fundamentals of crafting spells to the ethical mandates behind the proper use of magic. Yet, the Archmage and the other wizards running the academic institution recognize that principles of Equilibrium are in themselves insufficient to govern the young students, and so they maintain order and discipline through codified moral regulation. On the one hand, Ogion's apprenticeship of Ged illustrates the Taoist ideal that understanding balance should be the central (and exclusive) moral principle. Ogion presents Ged with no written rules or regulations; the master mage simply instructs Ged through the existential imperatives presented each day. Ogion assigns tasks, like collecting herbs and medicinal plants or studying sets of runes, and Ged completes the tasks, receiving corrections, warnings, and rebukes as Ogion sees fit. The most dramatic admonishment comes when Ged foolishly plays into the hands of the witch's daughter, reads runes far beyond his skill level, and temporarily releases a shadow from the dead into the realm of the living. Ogion rebukes him for his pride and for not yet learning to act only out of necessity as opposed to personal gain or pride (22–24). Ogion's words are moral instruction in the ways of Equilibrium or balance, but they are not codified moral law or regulation.

In the larger community of the wizarding school, on the other hand, the administration enforces a variety of moral regulations to govern the behavior of students, teachers, and mages. For example, initiates are limited to certain areas within the school, gaining access to other areas containing higher magic as their skills develop, and they can take only certain courses before advancing to other subjects. One of the most important moral rules at the school is the prohibition of students challenging each other to magic duels. As the war of pride and arrogance escalate between Jasper and Ged, culminating in a challenge of magical power, Vetch, out of love for both young men, reminds them, "Duels in sorcery are forbidden to us, and well you know it. Let this cease!" (57). Though the Taoist principles of maintaining balance and acting only out of necessity inform the moral center of practicing magic in Earthsea, the wizards recognize, as do Taoist priests and philosophers, that some moral regulation is indeed necessary for the proper governance of human behavior and communal interaction.

However, the mages also recognize that moral regulation is insufficient to bring about a moral society, because it is human nature to violate moral codes in service of selfish, prideful desires. Le Guin reveals the practical insufficiency of moral regulation through the horrific consequences of the wizarding duel between Jasper and Ged. The great wizards of the Roke School for Wizards recognize that as the boys and young men study the ways of magic and the principles of Equilibrium (the Tao), they may still be motivated by selfish pride, and their competitiveness may lead to great harm. Therefore, they create moral regulations to keep the students in line. Unfortunately, such regulations are not sufficient to keep Ged and Jasper from trying to humiliate each other through prideful displays of magic that eventually lead to the death of the Archmage Nemmerle (59–63). According to Lao Tzu, moral regulation is necessary, but it is not in itself sufficient to address the root causes of evil, immorality, and pride in human nature. Drawing from Taoist teachings, Le Guin suggests that true moral development comes by moving beyond following moral codes and deciding to abandon selfish desire in service of balance.

Abandoning Desire in Taoist Moral Development

According to Taoism, the only way to deal with the very heart of evil is to move beyond moral regulation and to seek the way of the Tao, which is to abandon desire as the underlying motivation for action. Koller explains, "Since acting to satisfy desires brings about the conditions requiring morality, morality cannot be abandoned until desires as a source of actions are abandoned. The reason why acting out of desires leads to evil is that it is contrary to the Way, for the great *Tao* is always without desires. The good is accomplished not by action driven by desire, but by inaction inspired by the simplicity of *Tao*" (287).

Le Guin centers her moral universe upon this basic Taoist principle; however, scholars of her integration of Taoism avoid addressing the significant paradox of this moral philosophy. By nature, humans are naturally, necessarily, and unequivocally motivated by desires, be they good or evil. In Taoist philosophy, the Tao is an impersonal, uncaused causal agent and thus has no desire nor intentionality whatsoever. Ultimately, it is impossible for the personal human to pursue the way of non-desire exemplified by an impersonal causal agent. This notion of seeking the path of non-desire, as theoretically appealing as it may be, is existentially impossible to achieve, because humans can never abandon desire, as that is their very nature. The way of Taoism seeks the natural condition. Thus, it is paradoxical, if not contradictory, to suggest that humans should seek that which is natural by denying in themselves that which is natural to themselves—desire. The young Ged is a perfect example of the impracticality of this paradoxical moral teaching. Ogion frequently warns Ged against acting from prideful personal desire, yet his main motivation for learning magic is to have power and to bring glory unto himself: "For he hungered to learn, to gain power" (18). Ged's first major magical mistake, one that foreshadows his most tragic misuse of magic, is to allow his emotions to be manipulated by the witch girl into reading advanced runes to release a shadow of death into the world of the living (22–24).

Despite the paradoxical nature of this Taoist teaching, Le Guin presents readers with a flawed, and thus realistic and believable, protagonist who gradually learns to abandon his prideful desire for power, to follow the way of balance or Equilibrium, and to act only out of true necessity. The great test of Ged's character that ultimately solidifies his willingness to abandon his own desires in service of the Equilibrium comes when he faces the Stone of Terrenon (115–19). It seems Ged is given another chance to prove himself by confronting the temptations of prideful power and selfish gain. Serret, who he later realizes is the same witch girl who manipulated him into reading the summoning spell in Ogion's home so many years prior, once again tempts Ged to use magic for the wrong reasons, namely to satisfy personal desires. Serret claims the stone can give Ged the name of the shadow tormenting him. This time, Ged applies the wisdom he has gained over the previous years of studying, training, and suffering many mistakes. He realizes the Terrenon wishes to work evil through him, that these deeper powers were not meant for men to have, and in the hands of men, terribly evil things would be committed with that power. His wisdom also leads him to repudiate pragmatism as a moral system, for he rightly notes, "Ill means, ill end" (118).

Serret tempts him not only with knowledge of the shadow's name but also with power over all men, urging that by using the Terrenon, he would become king of all men, and she would be his queen and rule along with him (119). In his youth, this temptation would have appealed to him, because he desired knowledge of magic to satisfy his cravings for power over others. Now this temptation has lost its appeal, for he knows that, in human hands, absolute power corrupts absolutely. Ged is growing spiritually, morally, and intellectually. He is learning the Taoist moral principle that abandoning personal desire and rejecting quick emotional responses lead to the way of proper action. As Joel J. Kupperman explains, "The watchful, cautious [T]aoist will tend to avoid quick emotional responses. Someone who is mindful of the dynamic of the world, also, will be most unlikely to have emotions of anger, resentment, or for that matter fear" (104). Ged has finally begun apprehending the Taoist wisdom developed through the years of training, knowledge, experience, pain, and suffering. He realizes that one must act with clear purpose and that purpose must serve moral ends and interests greater than oneself. Ged is becoming a responsible and wise young wizard who will go on to become the greatest wizard of Earthsea.

Self-Sacrifice as Taoist Moral Development

Abandoning personal desire is central to Taoist morality, and the most effective and challenging means for abandoning desire is to practice self-sacrifice. Lao Tzu taught that a "simple life is one which is plain, wherein profit is ignored, cleverness abandoned, selfishness minimized, and desires reduced" (Koller 284). The best way to accomplish this type of simple life is through humiliation and self-denial, and it is one of the most difficult lessons Ged learns through his *bildungsroman*. Ged's journey toward sincere humility begins after his sorcery duel with Jasper releases the shadow and results in the death of the Archmage Nemmerle. Ged faces a freewill choice either to leave the island or stay. He chooses to remain and learn within the community of mages, having been humbled and chastened by the disastrous consequences of his arrogance and selfish pride. As horrible as this experience is, Ged finally begins his progress toward humility, and he begins to establish community: he becomes the friend of Vetch by exchanging true names (68–69). Ged risks vulnerability while also accepting the responsibility of knowing someone's true name. This is true communion and real friendship, and it marks an important step in Ged's moral development and personal growth.

As Ged gains a degree of community via friendship with Vetch, he experiences isolation when he is sent to be the wizard for Low Torning. One main purpose for this stage in Ged's personal development is to learn humility through experiencing humiliation. He who would become the greatest of all

Earthsea wizards is tasked with being a mere fishnet repairman and simple healer for farm animals and village folk. This is an important, necessary step in his development, because he must continue to be humbled and to act not out of pride but out of humane concern for others. Indeed, the village called for a wizard to protect them from the Dragon of Pendor and its nine offspring, but his day-to-day life as a wizard is deeply humbling, if not humiliating. (76–77). Additionally, Ged's humble position presents him with many opportunities to develop relationships and community based on kindness, service, and self-sacrifice. For example, Ged befriends a fisherman and puts a charm on the small boat he is making for his son. The man asks him this favor, noting it would be a "mighty kindness and a friendly act" (79). This is exactly what Ged needs to start building his character, learning to overcome his arrogance and pride, and striving to be more charitable to others.

The most important lesson Ged learns from his time as Wizard of Low Torning is self-sacrifice in the service of others. The first key instance of Ged's self-sacrifice at Low Torning comes when he tries to save the fisherman's sick and dying little boy. This episode recalls the time Ged overspent his powers to save his own village when he was a boy, and it marks an important step forward in Ged's willingness to sacrifice his own best interest for the good of others. Struggling with knowing when to act out of necessity and to serve the Taoist Equilibrium, Ged decides to risk his own life by going deep into the spirit world trying to retrieve the dying boy. On the surface, this impetuous act seems like a typical prideful Ged decision, violating commonsense and doing simply what he wants to do. He knows the first lesson of healing, which is "Heal the wound and cure the illness, but let the dying spirit go" (80). Of course, Ged ignores this lesson and dives into the realm of the dead to save this boy.

However, an important difference with this particular defiance is motive: in the past, Ged's pride, arrogance, and jealousy drove him to defy reason and authority. This time, a genuine concern for the boy and his family motivates his seemingly impulsive act. Ged has grown to love them, and he sincerely wants to protect them from illness, pain, and heartache. This harrowing experience also affords him another opportunity to grow: he could succumb to the call of the shadow and simply die. Seemingly, that would be the easy way out. However, he chooses life, he chooses to return to the land of the living and to face the darkness he has released into the world. That choice shows courage, strength, and nobility of character.

The second opportunity at Low Torning for Ged to develop in wisdom and sacrificial love is when he faces the Dragon of Pendor and its nine offspring. The dragon offered to tell Ged the name of the shadow that is chasing and terrifying him. If he knows its name, he can control it, and his troubles with the shadow would be over. However, to learn the name of the shadow and to save himself, Ged would have to betray the humans of Low Torning to the trickster dragon (92). This moral dilemma represents a grave temptation and is a true test of Ged's developing virtue. For the good of the humans he swore to protect, Ged expresses the very heart of self-sacrifice and rejects the dragon's offer, forever binding the dragon to the original deal: he is never to harm the villagers, or Ged would use his true name to destroy him. This sacrificial act is another key step in Ged's growth in wisdom, mercy, love, and nobility. Ged's moral *bildungsroman* begins with his learning about the cosmic governing principles of true wizardry found in acting only when it is necessary in service of maintaining Equilibrium. His moral knowledge deepens through humiliation and self-denial, leading to humility and self-sacrifice, all key Taoist principles governing the individual's path toward ethical enlightenment and moral behavior.

The Existential Problem of Wu Wei and Taoist Ethics

Maintaining balance, abandoning desire, and practicing self-sacrifice are central elements of the foundational Taoist principle known as *wu wei* (Koller 284–89; Kupperman 103–08; Oldstone-Moore 54). This principle is popularly expressed as the action of inaction, or acting without acting, and it is rooted in classical Taoist dualism. In her essay "Dreams Must Explain Themselves," Le Guin claims that true moral laws are not created by God (or a personal divine being) but, rather, are derived from the impersonal Absolute: "The Taoist world is orderly, not chaotic, but its order is not one imposed by man or by a personal or humane deity. The true laws—ethical and aesthetic, as surely as scientific—are not imposed from above by any authority, but exist in things and are to be found—discovered" (*Language of the Night* 44). Thus, according to Le Guin's understanding of Taoism, the moral law is somehow built into the fabric of an orderly universe, which was created by an impersonal, unthinking, amoral Absolute, and the observant, seeking person will discover the moral law and will know how to act morally. In her essay "The Child and the Shadow," Le Guin further develops her dualistic view of morality, fusing Taoist principles with Jungian psychological theory:

> Evil, then, appears in the fairy tale not as something diametrically opposed to good, but as inextricably involved with it, as in the yang-yin symbol. Neither is greater than the other, nor can human reason and virtue separate one from the other and choose between them. The hero or heroine is the one who sees what is appropriate to be done, because he or she sees the *whole*, which is greater than either evil or good. Their heroism is, in fact, their certainty. They do not act by rules; they simply know the way to go [*Language of the Night* 62].

Whereas fantasy writers such as MacDonald, Tolkien, Lewis, L'Engle, and Ende present a Judeo-Christian ethical view that posits the good as a pre-existent, monist reality and that evil is defined as the privation of the good or that which militates against the eternally pre-existent good, Le Guin embraces the dualistic view that good and evil are eternally co-existent and must be maintained in balance. Moral action, according to Le Guin's Taoist dualism, is contingent upon balancing the whole and integrating both good and evil, instead of fighting against evil in the service of good.

Taoism encourages followers to seek unity, order, and balance with all of nature, to be in harmony with creation, and to seek oneness of being. The main way such balance and unity can be achieved, Taoism teaches, is through the practice of *wu wei*, striving to return to a natural state which is unformed, fluid, and naturally unaggressive (Wytenbroek 173–74).[8] The main problem, though, is that in this dualistic system in which equilibrium must be contemplated and balance maintained, any action, be it good or evil, upsets cosmic balance (what Le Guin calls Equilibrium in her novel). Thus, with all action, there is a cost, which is the potential unbalancing of the natural order of things. Moreover, there is the added challenge of trying to figure out if one's action is restoring a prior imbalance or causing new imbalance within that context.

Le Guin is fully committed to this dualistic ethical system and builds her mythopoeic subcreation upon the principles, assumptions, and logic of Taoist ethical dualism. A critical reader may ask if this dualistic system is sufficient for sustaining the mythos of the novel. Indeed, Le Guin claims that human reason cannot separate good and evil from their eternally existent balance, and thus we cannot choose between the two but, rather, must accept them both as equally valid and necessary to the balance of existence and the wholeness of the person (*Language of the Night* 62). Yet, if we think carefully about this dualistic model, we can see that it is logically contradictory, an important critical point Le Guin scholars have not addressed. A thing is defined in relation to something else, and things are different from each other due to lack: one thing is different from another because it lacks something the other thing has, or it has something that the other thing lacks. A thing cannot be eternal and absolute if it lacks something, which leads to the logical question: how can we have two different eternal absolutes? Good and evil (two different moral things or metaphysical substances) are different from each other because one lacks something of the other, and thus both cannot be eternal and absolute. Both good and evil can be contingent upon something beyond themselves (thus disqualifying both from being eternal absolutes), or one can be defined in terms of the other (thus making one of them absolute and eternal and the other contingent—in theism, good is the eternal absolute and evil is contingent upon good, being defined as the privation of the good). In short, both good and evil cannot be eternal and absolute at the same time and in the same way as Taoist dualism claims.

Additionally, Le Guin scholars have not discussed ways in which her Taoist ethical dualism relies upon problematic assumptions about the nature of reality. Note that the Absolute Tao is impersonal, unthinking, and amoral (Oldstone-Moore 23–24). Yet, according to Le Guin and Taoism, this Absolute Tao gave rise to an orderly universe. The critical mind asks how a non-rational, unthinking entity could ever give rise to anything at all without the ability to reason or to express intention, let alone create an orderly universe complete with reasonable natural laws that govern the interactions of matter and energy. Also, another reasonable question asks how an unthinking, impersonal, amoral absolute could ever anticipate the eventual emergence of thinking, personal, moral beings like humans and then devise a moral law for them to discover and use. Lastly, morality is by nature personal. Individuals feel guilty because of a broken relationship with other persons. Even when violations are not caught, there is a personal sense that immoral action has transgressed personhood, be it that of other humans or that of a personal divine being. There is a deeply personal dimension to moral actions which is not adequately accounted for in dualism that asserts morality is simply the maintenance of an impersonal, absolute balance.

Finally, these above logical and philosophical questions give rise to serious existential concerns with Taoist dualism. Le Guin scholars have not addressed the ways in which these existential questions are raised in the novel yet left unresolved. If all actions, both good and evil, lead to an imbalance that must be corrected by some other necessary action, then any action of inordinate good must be counterbalanced by inordinate evil. Consequently, there is no moral incentive to act in good ways just for the sake of acting for the good of another, because that unexpected act of goodness will invite a corresponding evil to balance the good. Similarly, there is no incentive to act against evil. How does one know that the evil being fought is not a necessary corrective to balance some prior act of good? If one acts against some evil that was intended to balance a prior good action, then that confrontation may further disrupt the moral balance. Ultimately, moral hands are tied, and no one knows when and how to act. Indeed, Taoism does acknowledge this difficulty and tries to address it with principles of *wu wei*, and Le Guin asserts throughout the novel, without explanation, that individuals will know how to act if they simply contemplate the whole. The contemplative person will somehow do that which is necessary.

However, it would require omniscience to know the beginnings from the ends, to know if it is truly necessary to act in any given circumstance, and to know all possible prior causes and later consequences of that action. Humans are not omniscient, and those following *wu wei* struggle to know whether or not to act in any given situation, if at all. Furthermore, as much as Le Guin values love as a human virtue, her critics have not discussed how the theory of *wu wei* is ultimately and necessarily devoid of genuine love. The individual cannot act righteously or compassionately for the sake of these virtues or for the good of another person, because such action may not, in that context, be necessary. In Taoist *wu wei*, blind duty to necessity supersedes devotion to the good of an individual. There is no true love here, because a person is not acting in the best interest of the beloved but, instead, out of devotion to the necessity of preserving a mystical and unknowable balance. Ultimately, the good of impersonal balance displaces the good of persons.

Le Guin's novel is full of moral dilemmas, and Ged struggles to learn when, if, and how to act in various situations—he struggles with understanding *wu wei*. These situations raise more questions and problems for Ged and discerning readers, yet the narrative provides no satisfactory answers. Two key scenes illustrate such unresolved moral confusion: the Karg attack on Ged's village and the threat of the dragons of Pendor. Early in the novel, Ged works powerful magic to hide his village in a mysterious fog, thus protecting the villagers from the violently aggressive Kargs (10). Ged proactively uses magic to counteract an impending and horrific evil—the potential genocide of his village. Ged seemingly acts properly out of need, following *wu wei*. But how can Ged be sure that there is real need here? Indeed, the Kargs are violent, and they are threatening to destroy his village. On dualism, however, how can he know with any moral certainty that the Karg violence should be thwarted? Why *must* he act in *this* instance? Could it be that this Karg aggression is necessary to reset a prior moral imbalance in Earthsea? If so, stopping the violence would cause further imbalance. How is Ged to know when to act and when not? That is the central question he rightly asks throughout the novel. Unfortunately, it is the very question that is never answered, for in the Taoist, dualistic perspective, it never can be answered with any moral or existential certainty.

Another thrilling example is Ged's battle with the dragons of Pendor (87–89). In many ways this is one of the most exciting and dramatic scenes in the whole book. Yet, it is reasonable to ask why Ged acts with such wild abandon and dramatic violence. Sure, the dragons pose a threat to the small fishing village Ged is assigned to protect, but why is this dragon threat *necessarily* a bad thing at this time in Earthsea history? Could it be that this specific threat is necessary to maintain broader Earthsea Equilibrium? Why *must* Ged act to destroy them in *this* case? This crucial existential question is not even raised, let alone answered, by the text. Yet, given the worldview upon which the novel has been constructed, and given the extent to which the doctrines of Equilibrium and acting only out of necessity have been foregrounded by the text, it seems quite reasonable to ask why Ged *must* act in this ultra-violent way. The text, and indeed the dualistic Taoist worldview upon which it is constructed, offer no clear and existentially satisfactory answer.

Conclusion—Postsecular Escape, Recovery and Consolation

Much twentieth-century mythopoeic fantasy literature is indeed postsecular. As literature, art, philosophy, and even theology to varying degrees became more secular in response to the horrific incongruities, paradoxes, confusions, and contradictions of two world wars, mythopoeic writers such as Lord Dunsany, J.R.R. Tolkien, C.S. Lewis, Charles Williams, Madeleine L'Engle, and Michael Ende staunchly rejected the philosophical materialism surging in the tides of secularism. Eschewing literary realism and philosophical materialism, these writers built literary worlds of wonder, magic, mysticism, love, beauty, and grace founded upon a firm belief in metaphysical reality. Le Guin is one such postsecular fantasist, but instead of drawing from Western paganism and Christian theism, she builds a wondrous fantasy world upon Taoist foundations that introduce many Western readers to the mysticism, paradoxes, incongruities, and unresolved perplexities of *wu wei*.

Like her theistic counterparts, Le Guin fashions a subcreated fantasy world that encourages compelling discussion of religion, spirituality, philosophy, theology, and the relationship between reason and faith. For readers who are philosophically and theologically minded, these works encourage lively and important discussions of the relationships between religion and science, faith and reason, and logic and emotion, within both traditional religions and alternative spiritualities. Good mythopoeic literature sparks such dialog, and if read as openly as possible, readers can escape into Le Guin's wondrously magical land of Earthsea, encounter these perplexing issues, and then return to the real world prepared to examine, discuss, change, and reshape reality into a more tolerant world grounded in reason, maintained by faith, and sustained through love. While this may not be comforting to everyone, especially those secularists who distrust metaphysics and those materialists who are suspicious of anything not sustained by pure naturalism, it is still altogether true that postsecular fantasy has the power to bring the beauty, love, and light of Truth into the darkened spirit of a desolate world, thus providing much needed consolation in this dire hour of need.

NOTES

1. For example, see Craig, "What is the Relation between Science and Religion?"; Plantinga, *Where the Conflict Really Lies*; and Robinson, "Humanism."

2. For overviews of the emergence of postsecular reactions to materialism, re-valuing of religion and spirituality, and analysis of a secular and religious co-existence, see Bauman vii–xi, Carruthers and Tate 1–8, Graham 236, Kaufman 68–73, McClure 1–25, and Ratti 1–32.

3. For excellent overviews of Le Guin's use of basic Taoist principles in her science fiction and fantasy work, see Bain, Barbour, Galbreath, and Wytenbroek.

4. Taoism is largely attributed to Lao Tzu; however, there were many other seminal thinkers contributing key texts that lay the foundation for Taoism: *I Ching, Book of Chuang Tzu, Book of Huai Nan Tzu*, and *Book of Lieh Tzu*. See Oldstone-Moore, 14.

5. For discussions of Taoism, its history and central tenets, see Koller 283–302, Kupperman 93–112, and Oldstone-Moore. Two key primary Taoist texts are Lao Tzu, *Tao Te Ching* and Chuang Tzu, *Book of Chuang Tzu.*

6. See also Kupperman, 94.

7. All subsequent references to Le Guin's *A Wizard of Earthsea* include page numbers only.

8. Wytenbroek and other literary scholars who analyze Le Guin's appropriation of Taoism take these principles for granted and do not critically examine their assumptions and implications. For example, we know from empirical analysis and personal experience that the natural self is far from unaggressive and unformed. Rather, there are inborn qualities and behaviors that are natural to the self but which are contrary to moral behavior and virtue: namely, selfishness and a propensity to sin. Christian theology explains this reality through the doctrine of original sin, understanding that humans are sinful by nature. This notion of seeking what is natural in the human is a movement toward evil, sin, selfishness, and aggression, all of which are contrary to the ultimate aims of Taoism and all other major ethical models of virtue and notions of the good.

WORKS CITED

Bain, Dena C. "The *Tao Te Ching* as Background to the Novels of Ursula K. Le Guin." *Extrapolation* 21, no. 3 (1980): 209–22.

Barbour, Douglas. "On Ursula Le Guin's 'A Wizard of Earthsea.'" *Riverside Quarterly* 6 (1974): 119–23.

Bauman, Zygmunt. *Intimations of Postmodernity*. London: Routledge, 1992.

Caruthers, Jo, and Andrew Tate. *Spiritual Identities: Literature and the Post-Secular Imagination*. New York: Peter Lang, 2010.

Craig, William Lane. "What Is the Relation Between Science and Religion." *Reasonable Faith with William Lane Craig*. www.reasonablefaith.org/what-is-the-relation-between-science-and-religion.

Galbreath, Robert. "Taoist Magic in the Earthsea Trilogy." *Extrapolation* 21, no. 3 (1980): 262–68.

Graham, Elaine. "What's Missing: Gender, Reason and the Post-Secular." *Political Theology* 13, no. 2 (2012): 233–45.

Kaufman, Michael. "Locating the Postsecular." *Religion and Literature* 41, no. 3 (2009): 68–73.

Koller, John M. *Oriental Philosophies*. 2nd ed. New York: Charles Scribner's Sons, 1985.

Kupperman, Joel J. *Classic Asian Philosophy: A Guide to the Essential Texts*. Oxford: Oxford University Press, 2001.

Le Guin, Ursula K. *The Language of the Night: Essays on Fantasy and Science Fiction*. New York: HarperCollins, 1989.

Le Guin, Ursula K. *A Wizard of Earthsea*. New York: Bantam Books, 1975.

McCaffery, Larry, and Sinda Gregory. "An Interview with Ursula Le Guin." *The Missouri Review* 7, no. 2 (1984): 64–85.

McClure, John. *Partial Faiths: Postsecular Fiction in the Age of Pynchon and Morrison*. Athens: University of Georgia Press, 2007.

Moreland, J.P. *Scaling the Secular City: A Defense of Christianity*. Grand Rapids, MI: Baker Publishing Group, 1987.

Oldstone-Moore, Jennifer. *Taoism: Origins, Beliefs, Practices, Holy Texts, Sacred Places.* Oxford: Oxford University Press, 2003.

Plantina, Alvin. *Where the Conflict Really Lies: Science, Religion, and Naturalism.* Oxford: Oxford University Press, 2011.

Ratt, Manav. *The Postsecular Imagination: Postcolonialism, Religion, and Literature.* London: Routledge, 2014.

Reid, Suzanne Elizabeth. *Presenting Ursula K. Le Guin.* Woodbridge, CT: Twayne Publishers, 1997.

Robinson, Marilynne. "Humanism." In *The Givenness of Things*, 3–16. New York: Picador, 2015.

Tzu, Chuang. *The Book F Chuang Tzu.* Translated by Martin Palmer. New York: Penguin, 1996.

Tzu, Lao. *Tao Te Ching.* Translated by D.C. Lau. New York: Penguin, 1963.

Wytenbroek, J. R. "Taoism in the Fantasies of Ursula K. Le Guin." *Contributions to the Study of Science Fiction and Fantasy* 39 (1990): 173–80.

The Language of
Magic and Prayer

Intercession in the Works of Merrie Haskell

ERIN WYBLE NEWCOMB

Merrie Haskell's *The Princess Curse, The Handbook for Dragon Slayers*, and *The Castle Behind Thorns* are non-serialized books, each set in a fantasy world richly interwoven with magic and Christian imagery. All of Haskell's protagonists wrestle to some degree with the relationship between magic and faith. I analyze the language of incantation and of prayer used in these three texts, where magic and prayer both call upon supernatural intervention in the natural world but are assigned different meanings and intentions. These different conceptions of the supernatural blur together in Haskell's novels, often working better in tandem but also causing confusion and anxiety for characters whose worldviews evaluate magic and prayer as antitheses.

By examining the language used to describe both magic and prayer in these three texts, I illustrate the way that Haskell ultimately uses her main characters as intercessors to heal the supposed rift between the natural and supernatural worlds. That healing takes place only when the characters come to understand prayer not in opposition to magic, but as its own kind of magic—neither evil nor impersonal. The relationship between magic and prayer changes as Haskell's heroes recognize that there can be bridges between the ideologies of magic and prayer just as there can be bridges between the supernatural and the natural; the characters, through their acts of intercessory prayer and use of magic, become those bridges. I use theories of language, magic, and prayer to demonstrate the ways these fantasy texts, like the magic within them, can operate in the real world—to heal and to transform through relationship with the supernatural.

Practicing Prayer

I begin by illustrating the relationships of each text's main character with prayer, while also providing brief summaries of the novels for those readers unfamiliar with them. In *The Princess Curse* (2013), protagonist Reveka grows up in a convent, but she leaves to join her soldier-father at a castle under a mysterious curse; each night the twelve princesses wear out their dancing shoes, though no one knows where or how. The curse causes catastrophe if the princesses are removed from the castle, and anyone who tries to discover their secrets ends up in an enchanted sleep.

Reveka, a gifted apprentice apothecary, wants to root out the curse and win the dowry so she can join a convent and establish her own herbary. When Reveka explains her motivation to fellow apprentice Didina, her friend answers, "'I'm sorry, I didn't realize you had a spiritual calling'" and Reveka muses, "I was ashamed to admit that I didn't so I skipped answering that" (21). She doesn't miss the lack of religious devotion in her position at the castle, noting, "I'd expected to have to keep the night watches for prayer again when I was apprenticed to a monk, but Brother Cosmin's lax monkishness didn't demand prayer even the night before an important saint's feast" (73). Still, Reveka accepts religious devotion (or its appearance) as a fair exchange for professional freedom, acknowledging, "the convent was the best choice for me. A place where I would have all the time I was supposed to be devoutly praying to think about herbs. I didn't really care for all the silence and singing and obedience—but my own herbary!" (22–23). Reveka regards religion and prayer as a means to an end, less unpleasant than marriage and more likely to fulfill her desire to study. The book's conclusions suggest that she does have a kind of spiritual vocation, though not one that fits the predefined roles of her world; her work as intercessor ultimately positions her as both Christian and pagan, with an herbary of her own (unrestricted by convent life) to heal both worlds.

The main character of the 2013 novel *The Handbook for Dragonslayers* shares many of the same attitudes as Reveka. Princess Mathilda (Tilda) longs to spend her days copying manuscripts and composing her own works, but her royal responsibilities interrupt her studies. She runs away from home after escaping from her evil cousin Ivo, who threatens to take over her principality. Tilda is easily encouraged to abscond, believing herself to be feared and disliked among her people because of her disability, a leg injury that impairs her mobility and inspires her subjects' superstitions. Tilda takes off with handmaid Judith and friend Parz to hunt dragons, and, for the princess, ostensibly, to write about them. When the friends rescue a pair of magical horses, they feel better equipped on their mission. Tilda admits, "[w]e woke to a cloudy morning and the tolling of church bells. We felt obligated to go to mass, but as soon as that duty was done, we returned to the stables and loaded the horses up again" (129).

Despite her desire to live in a convent where she can write, her response to being cared for in one after an injury lacks enthusiasm: "Sister Hildegard smiled. Her white veil and wimple were almost blinding. 'The cloister received word that you had gone missing. We have been praying for you daily, that you did not fall into villainous hands.'" Tilda responds, "'That's nice,' [she] said feebly, all good manners abandoning [her]" (174). A few weeks into her treatment, Tilda's lack of enthusiasm morphs into regret:

> I no longer dreamed of a peaceful cloister life. It turned out that at Saint Disibod's I had no more time to attend to the *Handbook* than I would have had at Alder Brook—in fact, I had less time, between my treatments and the daily work of the cloister. And the interruptions to pray were near constant. I had made the mistake of telling Hildegard I was contemplating a life of religious devotion. Judith and Parz, as secular patients of the infirmary, were not expected to follow the nuns' schedule. I was awakened in the middle of the night to pray and read scripture. Then I was sent went [*sic*] back to bed, only to wake at dawn and begin needlework, which was hourly interrupted by prayer [175].

Tilda regards prayer and religious participation as duty but also distraction, an interruption from her scholarship and less interesting than magical objects like the horses or the elusive dragons. Tilda's transformation into a dragon at the end of her text challenges the binaries she's established between responsibility and freedom as well as between good and evil.

The most devout of Haskell's main characters is Sand, the blacksmith's apprentice in *The Castle Behind Thorns* (2014). Indeed, he is drawn into the curse of the Sundered Castle (a decrepit, uninhabited castle surrounded by thorns) after praying at the shrine of his patron saint. Sand sets to work cleaning and repairing the castle, including taking a hand in the resurrection of its heir, Perrotte. He is clearly uncomfortable with the suggestion that his mending is magic, seeing that supernatural power as at odds with his religious convictions. He prays to the saints and trusts in their power to intercede on his behalf. Early during his time in the castle, he prays "to Saint Eloi, who watches over blacksmiths: 'Please don't let me die here, alone. I don't even know why I came to be here—but it can't have been to let me die, can it?'" (21). He prays "to his name saint to watch him through the night" (23), and again "to Saint Eloi, to send his stepmother a sign. 'Let her know I am safe. Let her know I am well. And if you have time, let her know I require rescue! Let her look to the smoke here at the Sundered Castle and worry on it'" (42). He visits and repairs the relics of Saint Trifine and Saint Melor in the castle's chapel (48). Sand also bargains for his freedom: "Sand crossed himself and prayed to Saint Eloi and his name saint and to the Seven Founder Saints of Bertaèyn: 'If the Lord grants me the gift of leaving this place, if I ever rejoin my family, I will not gainsay Papa again. I'll go to university, as he wants. I will obey him in all things" (54). Unlike Reveka and Tilda, Sand seems sincerely devoted to his faith, not as a means to an end but as fulfilling in and of itself; yet that same devotion opens Sand up to the role of intercessor, where the saints provide him with magic because of his faith that causes him discomfort because of that same faith.

Each of these characters lives in a context where religious devotion (at least on the surface) is taken for granted, yet each also resides within settings where magic is commonplace. Their stories require them to navigate the relationships between prayer and magic in much the same way that Christian thinkers have done for centuries. In *The City of God*, for instance, Augustine proposes a distinctive hierarchy: "[f]or if such marvels are wrought by unclean devils, how much mightier are the holy angels! and [*sic*] what cannot that God do who made the angels themselves capable of working miracles!" (772). Religion and magic, according to Augustine, are opposed because one calls upon good spiritual forces and one calls upon evil; the supernatural realm itself never comes into question, and this holds true for all of Haskell's novels as well. C.S. Lewis asserts "[a]ll theology would reject the idea of a transaction in which a creature was the agent and God the patient" (48) in his *Letters to Malcolm*. Yet he also concludes,

> the magical element in Christianity is this. It is a permanent witness that the heavenly realm, certainly no less than the natural universe and perhaps very much more, is a realm of objective facts—hard, determinate facts, not to be constructed *a priori*, and not to be dissolved into maxims, ideals, values and the like. One cannot conceive a more completely 'given,' or, if you like, a more 'magical,' fact than the existence of God as *causa sui* [104].

Here Lewis rejects the idea that humans can direct God through their prayers yet maintains the supernatural realm with God as its head, not in opposition to magic but as a kind of magic that points to a great Magician. Webb Keane, meanwhile, states "[p]rayer often seeks to bring about interaction between human beings and other kinds of beings that would (or should) not otherwise occur" (50). This position emphasizes supernatural communication as the fundamental tenant of prayer, though, of course, it can apply to magic as well. In my next section, I discuss the ways that Haskell's characters negotiate with magic within the context of faith-based traditions that assume a supernatural premise but establish hierarchies and taboos of supernatural powers.

Practicing Magic

Although she doesn't want to join a convent because of a religious vocation, Reveka of *The Princess Curse* still sees tension in the relationship between prayer and magic. In her efforts to find a cure for the enchanted sleepers and the cursed princesses, she consorts with a witch. When Reveka's attempts to use herbs to turn invisible and follow the sleepers fails, the witch Marjit explains, "'You've no *intentions*. You've not called on any Holies. There's nothing to spark the magic" (120). Marjit goes further, pressing Reveka, "'You'll be good enough. You'll make up your cap, I think with a prayer to the Big Lady" (121). Reveka expresses reluctance to trust Marjit's haphazard instructions:

> When I was slow to move, she grabbed my hands and plunked the ferns into the water, then waved her hands over the bucket and muttered in the church language. I could make out only a few words, mostly numbers. My eyes glazed. "I'm calling on the Big Lady now," Marjit told me. "And to Athena, the goddess, who stole the Lord of Hell's own cap of invisibility and gave it to Perseus. I figure her for your best patron. Not so much Hades, given what you've said." "All right," I said. Pagan nonsense, I supposed, calling on dead gods instead of ever-living saints, but I still suppressed a shiver. At least it wasn't the Devil. I closed my eyes and muttered a prayer for intercession to Saint Hildegard [135].

Reveka wants to use magic, but the mixture of paganism and her own church tradition frightens her. Marjit comfortably conflates the two, calling upon the supernatural figures of both belief systems and using the church language as part of her incantation. Reveka goes along with this fusion of faiths in hopes that it will achieve her desired ends, though she counters Marjit's spoken spell with a private prayer to a Christian saint. The same character who daydreams of life in a convent where she can use prayer as a cover for contemplating her herbary still feels fear at pitting pagan deities against Christian figures. It's enough to provoke her to pray.

Tilda also struggles with language issues as her own faith collides with magic in *Handbook for Dragonslayers*. During her quest to slay dragons, Tilda slowly realizes that not all dragons are evil, a belief confirmed by her interactions with a dragon who gives her aid and shelter. Returning to the dragon, Tilda "crossed [herself], remembering that all the saints did that first, and frequently subdued the dragons just through the holy gesture or prayer" (248). When the dragon is not visibly weakened by Tilda's act, the princess concludes, "This was not an evil dragon" (248). It's telling that Tilda does not doubt the power of crossing herself or prayer; instead, she changes her perspective on dragons. At one point during her speech with the dragon, Tilda sees, "So was this just dragon language? In the stories, the few dragons who spoke all knew human speech. But maybe that was because they were always talking to saints, who had power beyond regular folks" (238). It does not occur to Tilda here that she may be saint-like or that she, too, may have extraordinary power, yet her understanding of her faith's relationship to magic is that Christianity can subdue magic; her interactions with the dragon require her to reconsider the hagiographies and question the presumed evilness of an entire species. And, like Reveka, Tilda too resorts to prayer in the face of magic, though she often sees religious devotion as a duty and a distraction.

Sand of *The Castle Behind Thorns* faces the greatest challenge of Haskell's protagonists in coming to terms with the relationship between faith and magic, perhaps because his own faith seems the strongest. As he evaluates his mending, he sees "that some sort of magic was at work in the castle" (82), and he and Perrotte argue about the nature of his abilities. She concludes, "It was obvious, wasn't it? He was gifted in ways that a normal boy would not be" (120). Yet Sand considers the consequences of his magic in light of a Christian upbringing hostile to competing supernatural forces. He thinks: "How could he say that he was afraid he was a witch? Because admitting that meant admitting [Perrotte's] awakening was unnatural and wrong. It was all to the good that they were trapped in a castle surrounded by impenetrable thorns—it saved them both from interrogation, accusation, trial, and possibly even burning" (127). These fears, likely drawn from his own experience within his community, haunt Sand's movements throughout the text. It is Perrotte who presents the possibility that Sand's work is not magic but miracle, that he is "someone blessed by a saint" (166), a belief that fits the patterns of Sand's practice of intercessory prayer. The relationship between prayer and magic in this text blurs the boundaries between the spiritual realms that these characters, at times, attempt to keep distinct. Perrotte's idea suggests that perhaps the distinction does not matter as much as the effects, but Sand still struggles to accept that his prayers prompted his magical mending.

H.S. Versnel brings up a similar point to Perrotte's in his cross-cultural study of the relationship between magic and religion, in which he claims, "[m]agic does not exist, nor does religion. What do exist are our definitions of those concepts" (177). He says the term "magic" gets used "to stigmatize illegitimate or undesired (religious) behavior of socially or culturally deviant groups" (177). In other words, whether a practice gets labeled religious or magical depends on the power of the person or group acting. In *A General Theory of Magic*, Marcel Mauss makes a like claim, noting that "[w]ords such as religion and magic, prayer and incantation, sacrifice and offering, myth and legend, god and spirit are interchanged indiscriminately. The science of religion has no scientific terminology" (7). Robert Markus agrees, citing in antiquity that "[t]here is not, then, as with us, a sphere of magic in contrast to the sphere of religion" (253). It is one common, supernatural sphere.

Other scholars illustrate that religion often supersedes magic as a kind of better magic; as Keith Thomas points out, "[c]onversions to the new religion, whether in the time of the primitive church or under the auspices of the missionaries of more recent times, have frequently been assisted by the belief of converts that they are acquiring not just a means of other-worldly salvation, but a new and more powerful magic" (25). Richard Fenn indicates the same phenomenon working the other way around, where "the need for magic increases as the religious framework of a society becomes palpably weak, shaky, and ineffective in allaying the worst anxieties of death" (78). That magic and prayer can be used interchangeably or together shows up in each of Haskell's texts, and in each novel, the characters seek out or employ magical means because prayer is (or seems) insufficient on its own. For Haskell's characters, the distinction between prayer and magic matters within the social context, but the ultimate merging of the two supernatural systems is pragmatic.

That is not to say that the efficacious use of magic is without conflict, either in Haskell's texts or the history of Christianity. Indeed, in the article titled "The Attitude of Origen and Augustine Toward Magic," Lynn Thorndike explains the concept of magic as evil and antithetical to religion "because it employed the services of spirits who were hostile to God" (64). Fritz Graf depicts the same binary within antiquity but muddies the waters by introducing intentions: "the actual Christian spells (which never enlist the help and intercession of demons, but rather of Christ, the Virgin, or the Saints), [have] to rely on the concept of intention in order to distinguish magic and religion. An invocation to the Virgin is religious when made with good intentions, but magical when used with evil intentions" (104). Yet, clearly, for Haskell's characters as well as Christians throughout history, intentions are not always clear-cut even when Christian figures are called upon. Reveka and Marjit call upon Christian and pagan figures alike with the goal of rescuing the enchanted sleepers; Tilda reconsiders dragons as an evil species once she learns their language; Sand and Perrotte try to reinterpret magic as miracle as they mend the broken castle. All of these characters' intentions can be regarded as good, but at the same time, their disruptions of the natural world and the social order can (and there is historical precedent here) also be regarded as evil. Speaking of the Middle Ages, Richard Kieckhefer writes, "[o]pposition to magic came partly from a sense that it posed an alternative to Christian prayers. It was a competing system of practice, a rival to Christian ways of coping with adversity" (39). Herein lies the problem, for Haskell's characters as well as history: definitions and intentions can be murky, but both magic and prayer recognize supernatural systems that, for social and political reasons, are often placed in a false binary.

The editors of *Prayer, Magic, and the Stars in the Ancient and Late Antique* explain that "[t]hough many of these rituals have traditionally been placed under the rubric of 'magic,' others could just as easily be called religion" (12–13). Specifically discussing The Prayer of Mary, Marvin Meyer argues, "miracle and magic, prayer and magic, meet. Expect for the politics and the polemics, the ritual power of the magical spell becomes practically indistinguishable from the ritual power of the Coptic Church, and Christian prayer and Christian invocation of ritual power seem to be two sides of the same coin. Or maybe even the same side" (67). It's difficult to leave aside Meyer's "politics and polemics," but at the same time, it's difficult to differentiate between magic and prayer or determine the source of the supernatural power. Haskell's characters discover this difficulty and transcend it by becoming intercessors within their supernatural worlds. By the end of each of her texts, the supernatural is ascendant, but the hierarchies of supernatural systems are discarded by characters who embrace the roles of mediators.

Practicing Intercession

Reveka solves the mystery of The Princess Curse, summarizing "[t]his was the secret the princesses protect with poison and with lies: They came to the Underworld nightly to feast and dance with a demon, because it was that or marry him" (159). Reveka concludes that the princesses' "immortal souls were in peril. Consorting with demons, even unwillingly, was a sin" (159), somewhat justifying poisoning those who attempted to rescue them. Following the tradition of the Persephone myth, Reveka eats a pomegranate and stays in the Underworld, agreeing to marry the demon Dragos and be queen of Thonos. Her training as an herbalist helps her to save the enchanted sleepers and gives her hope that she can heal Thonos and the world above. As the nymph Alethe informs her, "[s]ouls disappear on their journeys and gain neither the Heaven nor the rebirth they have earned. It will be your task, as Queen, to stop this, to heal the land" (230). This conversation highlights the traditional role of Queen as mediator, yet it combines the Christian afterlife with the pagan belief in reincarnation, and Reveka will intercede equally on behalf of both systems. Also like Persephone, she balances her time between the earthly kingdom and the Underworld, serving as intercessor between worlds as well. Regarding the shift in her plans, Reveka concludes, "[i]t wasn't as if I could have used the dowry to join a convent now anyway, not when I'd become, essentially, a pagan goddess. Well, I didn't know if I was a goddess. I tried consulting with Brother Cosmin about the situation obliquely, but that sort of thing can't really get answered in the hypothetical" (315). Despite her initial unease about Marjit's incantation combining both Christian and pagan elements, Reveka mirrors a pagan queen and seeks counsel from a Christian monk. She intercedes for souls from supposedly opposing belief systems and moves between worlds that turn out not to be rivals but reflections of each other; her movement between supernatural systems does not threaten her immortal soul but empowers her to heal and restore both worlds. Marrying Dragos frees the princesses (which eases the strain of political conflict in the world above) and gives Reveka the power to rejuvenate the forests of the Underworld that mirror the political conditions of Sylvania. By rejecting the binary of Christian/pagan, Reveka embodies a supernatural framework that encompasses and benefits all the characters of Sylvania and the Underworld.

Tilda also transcends the spiritual divide in her world of *Handbook for Dragon Slayers* by transforming into a dragon. Captured by an evil sorcerer on her return to her principality, Tilda fights magic with magic. Like Reveka, Tilda calls upon the aid of a pagan goddess, using "[t]he words of the dragon summoning ... from *The Sworn Book of Hekate*" (270). Instead of calling another dragon, she becomes one herself, escaping from the sorcerer and shocking her companions. Her handmaid and best friend Judith faces her as a dragon, urging her to return to her human form. Tilda thinks, "I can see inside of her, can see her thoughts racing. I see her fear and revulsion for the dragon shell that surrounds me. I see the love and compassion for the whole world, which she has carried around with her entire life. The whole world, including me" (289). It is Tilda's sacrifice that defeats the evil sorcerer and it is the love she and Judith feel for each other than transcends self and species. Where once Tilda sought to slay dragons (or at least write about the slaying of dragons), following in the footsteps of the saints, instead she calls upon pagan powers to become a dragon herself. She ultimately chooses her human life instead of a dragon one, and she agrees not to use the magic again even in hopes of a magical eternal life (310). By the book's end, the divide between the pagan and Christian worlds, between the supposedly evil and good, has disappeared. As Tilda muses, "sometimes dragons are not dragons at all—but human girls (or boys), trapped within scales and claws. If you can overcome your fear and show these trapped creatures kindness and love, you may just discover the truth inside them" (324). Like Reveka, Tilda's sacrificial love breaks down the barriers between creatures and between supernatural belief systems; perhaps this is the working out of their good intentions, and perhaps it is the potency of a supernatural continuum that existed all along.

Sand's social position or species does not change as he intercedes in *The Castle Behind Thorns*. When he and Perrotte confront the rulers who come to investigate the castle and its diminishing thorns (the work of Sand's miraculous mending magic), one knight calls him "evil sorcerer" (247). Yet as Sand faces his family, he learns his father's role in Perrotte's downfall, and understands that he's been chosen as intercessor: "[i]t answered why Saint Melor had chosen him. His family owed a debt, for the sins of his father" (251). Sand explains the situation publicly as follows: "'[a] saint kidnapped me from his shrine and put me into a fireplace here. So I guess the answer is, a miracle of Saint Melor. Or so I think. He has not told me'" (245). It's clear that Sand sees himself as embodying his father within the castle, as taking on the role of intercessor to right the wrongs that created The Sundered Castle and nurtured the thorns. His intercession is viewed as sorcery, and he expresses discomfort and fear about the role his prayers have provided for him.

For the most devout of Haskell's characters, though, Sand's transformation is the least dramatic—no pagan deities or species transformations. And instead of demonstrating the reach of his power and influence, his conversation with the patron saints of the castle illustrate his limitations; they tell him "*Some things are not meant to be mended*" and "*Some things are not for you to mend*" (original emphases 258). Part of his role as intercessor is revealing the community's responsibility for the thorns around the castle, as illustrated when Perrotte's stepmother Jannet (the woman partly responsible for her stepdaughter's untimely death) enters the castle and the thorns regrow. As Saint Melor explains, "'[t]he thorns are not one person's magic. Do not read intention in the thorns. They are a wilderness created by rage and sorrow'" (264). Sand and Perrotte leave the castle with the saints' blessings, and without punishment, because Sand, through the saints' intercession, mediates between those within the castle and those outside it. Saint Trifine says, "'we brought Sand to this place and we enhanced certain of his abilities—we gave him mending magic'" (264), which shows their direct intercession to use Sand as intercessor, a blending of prayer and magic that resonates throughout Haskell's work. In all three texts, prayer and magic work most effectively in concert.

This merging of supernatural systems speaks to the transcendence found throughout Haskell's work; it needn't be prayer or magic. It can be both. As Carissa Turner Smith writes in her analysis of *The Princess Curse*, when Reveka "opens herself to the possibility of other narratives, the darkness—and the fear accompanying it—is transformed" (193). In my own examination of disability within *Handbook for Dragonslayers*, I discuss the breakdown of binaries as well, where Tilda's choice to be human and not dragon "is informed by the opportunities available to her as a princess; neither wholeness nor transcendence can fully exist outside of the material world" (Newcomb 218). The intercessory work that Haskell's characters execute, and sometimes embody, disrupts ideologies that posit religion and magic as rivals.

Turner Smith, writing this time about *The Castle Behind Thorns*, indicates that particular characters have their own unique needs regarding prayer and magic, too; she says, "[w]hile Perrotte needs to see her story's connection to the saints, Sand, as the possessor of mending magic, needs to see the ways in which he should not appropriate divine power to himself" (227). Such a reading is supported by practice throughout the history of the Christian church. Despite Augustine's avowal that "the things done by magicians and by saints are often alike; but in fact they are done for different ends and by different rights ... for the magicians do them seeking their own glory, the saints seeking God's" (Markus 258), people's practice often elided those distinctions. Says Markus, "[a]lmost any object associated with ecclesiastical ritual could assume a special aura in the eyes of the people. Any prayer or piece of the Scriptures might have a mystical power waiting to be tapped" (45). Like centuries of practitioners before them, Haskell's characters access the supernatural world through the means available to them, blending the Christian and the pagan to suit their situations, often with less concern than theologians express for the distinctions between the two. Augustine (though not exclusively him, of course) refers to Christ as "the true Mediator" in *The Confessions*, yet the belief in Christ's mediation between heaven and the world accepts the premise of supernatural and natural mediators. That Christ is the foremost is standard to mainstream Christian theology, but it's also within the realm of religion for humans to intercede, too. In the case of Haskell's characters, those intercessory roles enable the characters to mediate between the religious and the magical, and, in doing so, to broaden the supernatural possibilities of their fictional worlds.

The relationships Haskell's characters develop between prayer and magic dovetail with the trend Paul T. Corrigan reviews in "The Postsecular and Literature." He defines the term as follows: "In postsecular literature religion, nonreligious spirituality, and secularism converge and diverge and are transformed around questions of human meaning, transcendence and immanence, pain and joy, and the reality and unreality of life in the twentieth- and twenty-first-century world." By situating her stories within fantasy realms reminiscent of the Middle Ages, Haskell hearkens back to a time when religious thought dominated society and politics, and accusations of magic could be dangerous indeed. Yet the fantastical elements of Haskell's tales weave together fairy tales and myths, incantations and prayers, pagan figures and Christian deities, and ultimately embrace the kind of transcendence that Corrigan describes as definitive of the postsecular. Haskell's characters do not eschew religion or magic; in each case, the protagonists take religious faith (or at least religious duty) somewhat seriously, whether by vocation or cultural conditioning or a bit of both.

Just as Corrigan points to opposites within his definition of the postsecular, Haskell's characters embrace and transcend binaries: the Christian apprentice and pagan goddess, the faithful princess as dragon, the mending sorcerer who doesn't want his magic. As C.S. Lewis asserts, "*this* universe with its determinate character—exists; as 'magical' as the magic flower in the fairy-tale" (104). Magic can be a matter of perspective where supernatural elements recognize humanity as, meaningfully, more than the natural or material world. Haskell's novels depict a similar theme to the pop-holiday anthem by Dar Williams, "The Christians and the Pagans." Williams sings,

So the Christians and the Pagans sat together at the table,
Finding faith and common ground the best that they were able,
And where does magic come from, I think magic's in the learning,
Cause now when Christians sit with Pagans only pumpkin pies are burning [17–20].

For Haskell's characters, and perhaps Haskell's readers, Williams's line that the "magic's in the learning" might just mean that the boundaries between belief systems might be blurry, after all. Curses can be broken and rifts healed. Species can be transformed from enemies to friends. Thorns can spring up and draw back. What Williams's song and Haskell's tales offer is "faith and common ground" within a world imbued with supernatural magic that doesn't need to eliminate the competition to be meaningful. Haskell's protagonists serve as intercessors between Christian and pagan, between fantasy and reality, and demonstrate the ways that the supernatural can heal and transform the natural for those willing to look beyond the binaries.

WORKS CITED

Augustine. *The City of God*. Translated by Marcus Dods. New York: Modern Library, 1993.
Augustine. *The Confessions of Saint Augustine*. Translated by E.B. Pusey. *Project Gutenberg*. May 16, 2013. www.gutenberg.org/files/3296/3296-h/3296-h.htm.
Corrigan, Paul T. "The Postsecular and Literature." *Corrigan Literary Review*. May 17, 2015. corriganliteraryreview.wordpress.com/2015/05/17/the-postsecular-and-literature/.
Fenn, Richard. "Magic in Language and Ritual: Notes on Augustine's *Confessions*." *Journal for the Scientific Study of Religion* 25, no. 1 (1986): 77–91.
Graf, Fritz. "Theories of Magic in Antiquity." In *Magic and Ritual in the Ancient World*, edited by Paul Mirecki and Marvin Meyer, 93–104. Leiden, Netherlands: Brill Publishers, 2002.
Haskell, Merrie. *The Castle Behind Thorns*. New York: HarperCollins, 2014.
Haskell, Merrie. *Handbook for Dragon Slayers*. New York: HarperCollins, 2013.
Haskell, Merrie. *The Princess Curse*. New York: HarperCollins, 2013.
Keane, Webb. "Religious Language." *Annual Review of Anthropology* 26 (1997): 47–71.
Kieckhefer, Richard. *Magic in the Middle Ages*. Cambridge: Cambridge University Press, 1990.
Lewis, C.S. *Letters to Malcolm: Chiefly on Prayer*. San Diego, CA: Harcourt, 1963.
Markus, Robert. "Augustine on Magic: A Neglected Semiotic Theory." In *Christianity in Relation to Jews, Greeks, and Romans*, edited by Everett Ferguson, 253–66. New York: Garland Publishing, 1999.
Mauss, Marcel. *A General Theory of Magic*. Translated by Robert Brain. New York: W.W. Norton, 1972.
Meyer, Marvin. "The Prayer of Mary in the Magical Book of Mary and the Angels." In *Prayer, Magic, and the Stars in the Ancient and Late Antique World*, edited by Scott Noegel, Joel Walker, and Brannon Wheeler, 57–67. University Park: Pennsylvania State University Press, 2003.
Newcomb, Erin Wyble. "Deconstructing Disability: The Dragons and Girls in Ursula K. Le Guin's Earthsea and Merrie Haskell's *Handbook for Dragonslayers*." In *Lessons in Disability: Essays on Teaching with Young Adult Literature*, edited by Jacob Stratman, 200–20. Jefferson, NC: McFarland, 2016.
Noegel, Scott, Joel Walker, and Brannon Wheeler. Introduction to *Prayer, Magic, and the Stars in the Ancient and Late Antique World*, edited by Scott Noegel, Joel Walker, and Brannon Wheeler, 1–17. University Park: Pennsylvania State University Press, 2003.
Smith, Carissa Turner. "Relics and Intersubjectivity in the Harry Potter Series and the *Castle Behind Thorns*." *Literature and Theology* 30, no. 2 (2016): 215–32.
Smith, Carissa Turner. "Reading in the Dark: Narrative Reframing in the *Unheimlich* Underworld of Merrie Haskell's *The Princess Curse*." In *The Gothic Fairy Tale in Young Adult*

Literature, edited by Joseph Abbruscato and Tanya Jones. Jefferson, NC: McFarland, 2014.

Thomas, Keith. *Religion and the Decline of Magic*. New York: Charles Scribner's Sons, 1971.

Thorndike, Lynn. "The Attitude of Origen and Augustine Toward Magic." *The Monist* 18, no. 1 (1908): 46–66.

Versnel, H. S. "Some Reflections on the Relationship Magic-Religion." *Numen* 38, no. 2 (1991): 177–97.

Williams, Dar. The Christians and the Pagans. Razor & Tie. 1997. Compact disc.

Postsecular Cosplay, Fundamentalism and Martyrdom in Gene Luen Yang's *Boxers & Saints*

CARISSA TURNER SMITH

On July 26, 2016, jihadists proclaiming allegiance to ISIS entered a church in a small French town and slit the throat of Fr. Jacques Hamel, a priest in the act of officiating mass. Amid calls for immediately launching Fr. Hamel on the path to canonization, Paul Vallely penned a *New York Times* op-ed titled "Leave 'Martyrdom' to the Jihadists," in which he argued that applying the label of "martyr" to Fr. Hamel "feeds the idea of retaliation— our martyr for yours—that gives the jihadists the war of religions they seek." According to Vallely, the concept of martyrdom must be disavowed because of its associations with religious extremism. The 19-year-old terrorists who committed this act would consider themselves martyrs for being killed by French police outside the church; therefore, Vallely reasons, we should not seek to apply the same "extremist" label to Fr. Hamel, who was simply going about his daily business. To do so would be to contribute to the narrative of the "clash of civilizations." However, Vallely reinscribes this very narrative with his argument, by classifying any religious fervor for which one would be willing to lay down one's life as "extremism," and failing to distinguish between religious zeal one would die for and religious zeal one would kill for. By making religious extremism the culprit, Vallely holds up a false and outdated notion of the "secular West"—or at least a West in which religion is an attenuated, privatized matter.

The problems with Vallely's op-ed are similar to the problems with much "postsecular" fiction and criticism. Postsecular fiction is skilled at identifying unacknowledged fundamentalisms; Zadie Smith's *White Teeth* powerfully aligns the fundamentalism of "secular" scientism and "religious" Islamic fundamentalism, showing how similar they truly are. In postsecular fiction, zeal is a cardinal sin, whether "religious" or "secular." As Magdalena Mączynska writes in her analysis of Smith's *Autograph Man*, "postsecular engagement with religion is the opposite of fundamentalism, valuing messiness over order and ambiguity over certainty" (81). While postsecular fiction goes a long way toward acknowledging the possibility of the supernatural in everyday life and toward undermining the enclosed narratives of secularism, it reserves its positive affirmations for "the rearticulation of a dramatically 'weakened' religiosity with secular, progressive values and projects" (McClure 3). Such a stance still has little to say to religious fundamentalism—or even any firmly held religious commitment—other than "get over it and be like us." Yet, as John McClure argues, an alternative response to resurgent fundamentalism can be to "imagine vigorous forms of spiritual life disarticulated from the will to 'power and grandeur'" (20). Indeed, what could be farther from "the will to 'power and grandeur'" than going about one's daily business in a quiet French town, celebrating a sparsely attended mass and—unprepared, unexpecting—meeting death for one's faith?

Gene Luen Yang's two-part graphic novel *Boxers & Saints* (2013), while resonating with many aspects of postsecular fiction, goes beyond most postsecular fiction in the attempt to make religio-political fundamentalism comprehensible to young, primarily English-speaking readers, as well as to ultimately draw a distinction between fundamentalist violence and the perhaps "extremist," but non-violent, religious performance that would lead one to suffer martyrdom.[1] Even though Yang's two protagonists—Bao, who joins the nationalistic Boxer Rebellion and kills many in its service, and Vibiana, a Chinese Christian convert who ultimately is martyred—are living in a late nineteenth/early twentieth-century China very unlike the disenchanted "West" delineated in Charles Taylor's *A Secular Age* (2007), Yang depicts these characters' situations in ways that resonate with twenty-first-century young readers. Most notably, Yang, in an interview, describes trying to come to terms with Bao's character by viewing him as a teen participating in cosplay. Yang compares the Boxers of late 1800s China to "modern day geeks," "powerless kids who really had no position in life," who "turn to their pop culture" for "stories about magic and super powers and colorful clothing" (qtd. in Rozema 6). In Yang's words, they "cosplay"; "they wanted to be these gods so badly they came up with this ritual, where they believed they would be possessed by them, get their powers" (qtd. in Rozema 6).

Cosplay, or "costume play,"[2] in which fans dress up and perform as characters from another text, is an appealing practice in what Charles Taylor describes as a disenchanted, buffered world. Taylor famously describes the pre-modern "enchanted world" as "the world of spirits, demons, and moral forces which our ancestors lived in" (*Secular* 26). In the enchanted world,

> there is a whole gamut of forces, ranging from (to take the evil side for a moment) super-agents like Satan himself, forever plotting to encompass our damnation, down to minor demons, like spirits of the wood, which are almost indistinguishable from the loci they inhabit, and ending in magic potions which bring sickness or death.... [T]he enchanted world, in contrast to our universe of buffered selves and "minds," shows a perplexing absence of certain boundaries which seem to us essential [Taylor, *Secular* 33].

In an enchanted world, the self is "porous," "vulnerable to a world of spirits and powers" (*Secular* 27). The modern, "buffered" self, by contrast, lives in a disenchanted world in which no rituals are necessary to separate one off from spiritual forces; meaning resides in the self, not in the outside world, and this discrete self emerges through inwardness and self-discipline. In Taylor's framework, we no longer have to secure the boundaries between ourselves and the spiritual forces that inhabit the world. The modern buffered self may occasionally like to dabble in the pretense of porosity: as Alan Jacobs writes, "Fantasy, in most of its recent forms, may best be understood as a technologically enabled, and therefore safe, simulacrum of the pre-modern porous self." Cosplay is another of these practices, a kind of nostalgia for a richer past—not entirely unlike the nostalgia of modern fundamentalism.

While a real peasant boy in turn-of-the-century China would have still inhabited a porous world, Yang uses the analogy of buffered cosplay for Bao so that the "porous" past is not so distant from ours and so that readers can see the ways in which, in our increasingly globalized world, porous and buffered selves really coexist. As Taylor himself acknowledges, "An 'essential feature of our divided age,' is that that many secular-minded persons find themselves drawn back toward the religious by inchoate inner promptings 'beginning intimations and intuitions that [they] feel bound to follow up'" (qtd. in McClure 9).[3] Yet these seekers are "products of a culture in which many people remain almost completely unschooled in religious beliefs and practices. Religiously illiterate, they are drawn by vagrant promptings into the obscure countries of the spirit, where they find themselves ... without even those rudimentary maps that have helped mark the way for earlier, better schooled, predecessors" (McClure 9). Both Bao and Vibiana are equally ignorant, at least at a cognitive level, of their own faiths, despite receiving direct apparitions from spiritual beings; yet Yang shows possibilities for performing those faiths through embodied imitative action, both for good and for ill. For its young readers, *Boxers & Saints* challenges the view that global conflicts are between religion and secularism; we all worship, especially through our embodied actions, and much of what we worship—including "the nation"—may have a spiritual dimension.

Bao: Performing the Unknown God in a Disenchanted World

While Bao and Vibiana—as well as Bao's love interest Mei-wen—dwell in a culture in which spiritual forces are perceived as real entities, they enact rituals in order to *open* themselves up to the spirits; in other words, Yang's portrayal of them as somewhat buffered allows for more connection with primarily buffered readers. All three "put on" spiritual identities in order to make their buffered selves feel more significant or better suited to address the expectations put upon them. However, neither Bao nor Vibiana has complete control over the spiritual beings they encounter—beings who are presented as realities, rather than as mere fantasies of lonely teenagers. The combination of these porous and buffered characteristics places *Boxers & Saints* in postsecular territory. While Katherine Ludwig claims that "the postsecular shows up as the recognition that we are and always have been porous, despite our claims to modern autonomy" (85), I would argue that a framing more consistent with Charles Taylor would involve the acknowledgment that we can never return to full porosity or enchantment; rather, the postsecular involves the recognition of the possibility of porosity. By depicting characters whose world is becoming increasingly buffered through the encounter with Western colonialism, as well as characters who gain new spiritual possibilities through this encounter, Yang highlights the mixture of enchantment and disenchantment that characterizes contemporary life.

Bao, at the beginning of *Boxers*, lives for spring, the season when operas are performed in his village. Even after the performances end, "the operas linger," he says: "Sun Wu-kong, the Monkey King, comes with me to fetch water" (Yang, *Boxers* 6); "Guan Yu, the God of War, tends crops with me" (7); and "the Lady in the Moon sings me lullabies as a drift off to sleep" (7). "The Gods of the Opera stay with me until the cold winds of autumn carry them away," Bao narrates. "After that, there is nothing to do but wait until the next spring" (7). Bao thus dwells in a partially disenchanted world, at least in autumn and winter. But there are hints, too, that he feels disconnected from a more glorious, meaningful past redolent with "hero[es] of old ... hero[es] they could compose operas about" (14).

Encounters with Western colonial forces increase Bao's sense that the world of his ancestors and their spirits is diminished. He witnesses his father, who he thought might be like one of these heroes of the past, beaten into submission and silence when he attempts to stand up to a British constable, and he sees a French priest smash the statue of the local earth god, Tu Di Gong. The village potter subsequently shapes a new Tu Di Gong, but the potter is "a gambler and a drunk." A panel showing the malformed, lopsided Tu Di Gong concludes with the wry caption, "He [the potter] is not as skilled as his ancestors" (30). "Things just aren't the same," Bao laments (30). Yang thus demonstrates how a sense of disenchantment and nostalgia can lead young people to embrace fundamentalism, an attempt to bring back what one perceives to have been a purer and more faithful past. This particularly becomes the case when Bao encounters a guru, "Master Big Belly," who tells him that "even the air has changed" because the foreigners "blemish our skies with smoke and build metal railroads across our dragon lines," "incit[ing] the land's anger" (85).

The idea that the land itself is angry—an idea that is made concrete in a panel with a thought-bubble showing Bao's memory of floodwaters pouring down in front of Tu Di Gong's misshapen statue—leads Bao to ask Master Big Belly to teach him kung fu so that he can avenge the land and its gods. Master Big Belly's lessons involve a ritual in which Bao must write down the incantation "Power of Heaven, come down!" (87); even though Bao is illiterate, Master Big Belly tells him, "Imitate my strokes" (87). The ritual thus prioritizes ceremonial motions rather than cerebral knowledge or "belief"— a characteristic Mączynska identifies as prominent in postsecular fiction: by "foregrounding the role of religious ritual," postsecular fiction "moves beyond a Jamesian understanding of 'religion' as individual experience towards an alternative model based on the concept of performativity" (78). To complete this ritual, Bao must then burn the parchment, eat its ashes, and exhale "until all that is left is perfect nothingness" (89)—through these actions, he opens himself to be inhabited—one might even dare to say "possessed"—by the spirit of an opera god who wants him to purge the land of all foreigners.

The emphasis on ritual above cognitive knowledge continues through Yang's depiction of Bao's ignorance about the identity of the mysterious, black-robed god into whom he transforms. Despite his opera obsession, he does not recognize this figure at all, but he still accomplishes the god's will. In the early scenes involving the black-robed god, Bao fuses so completely with him that Yang shows only the figure of the god wielding the sword and stabbing imperial soldiers with it (*Boxers* 114–117); Bao completely disappears. Bao is indeed performing the motions of the god after him—*as* him. In a later scene, Yang depicts the god hovering as a presence behind an empty-eyed Bao, who delivers a nationalistic speech with words flowing through him from an outside source. It is these words that finally point to the god's identity; the literate Mei-wen, who becomes Bao's love interest, identifies the speech as belonging to Ch'in Shih-huang, the first emperor of China. When Bao does not know the god's identity, he performs more fluidly in his stead; once he gains knowledge of him, his cosplay as Ch'in Shih-huang becomes more conflicted.

The embodied performance of another subjectivity, combined with ignorance of that subjectivity's identity, is what makes Bao a postsecular cosplayer. According to Matthew Hale, typical (what I would call "disenchanted") cosplay "describes a performative action in which one dons a costume and/or accessories and manipulates his or her posture, gesture, and language in order to generate meaningful correspondences and contrasts between a given body and a set of texts from which it is modeled and made to relate. It is a somatic, material, and textual practice" (8). In this disenchanted cosplay, the general assumption (though there are exceptions, especially in the cases of actors or professional cosplayers)[4] is that the cosplayer knows the text he or she is performing, and that he or she chooses to perform that text, often because of some physical or psychological similarity to the character chosen.

When asked why they cosplay, cosplayers often express a "specific desire to become the characters they liked and a 'desire to change' (*henshin ganbō*)" (Truong, par. 19). In other words, they intentionally seek transformation into another subjectivity, but they exercise their own subjectivity through choosing the identity into whom they will transform. As Alexis Hieu Truong explains, "Characters taken from anime, manga and game narratives were said to be inspirational representations of transformational power, as the characters themselves often changed from regular people to extra-ordinary beings in their storylines. In these characters, participants seemed to be able to find experiences they recognised, wanted to acquire or felt like they had lost" (par. 19). Cosplay is the buffered self's attempt to recover at least a pretense of porosity. True porosity, in this disenchanted cosplay, is not possible: Ellen Kirkpatrick argues that, "because of corporeal limitations," cosplay, in the usual sense, does "not effect transformation [in which the cosplayer *becomes* another subjectivity] but rather what I term embodied translation, that through these processes both cosplayer and character become lost and recreated in translation" (sec. 2.3). This emphasis on boundaries between bodies and between subjectivities defines disenchanted cosplay; in contrast, Yang's depiction of cosplay questions these safeguards of modernity. Yang portrays Bao as genuinely transforming into Ch'in Shih-huang, without knowing who he is or anything about him. Bao may choose to enact the ritual, but he at first seems to be wholly taken over by the god he has unwittingly invoked. Yang's depiction of Bao *as* Ch'in Shih-huang suspends disenchanted disbelief and prods readers toward acknowledging the possibility of porosity. That Bao really transforms into an opera god, however, does not diminish the fact that he performs that god's identity with the modern fundamentalist motive of bringing back the enchanted past.

As Bao's narrative progresses, we see him both arguing with Ch'in Shih-huang and committing violence of his own accord—indicating that, in Yang's view, acknowledging our porosity to the spiritual world does not free us of buffered personal responsibility. The first time Yang depicts Bao killing a civilian—a European missionary reciting Psalm 23 to his trembling flock of Chinese Christians—he very clearly shows a panel in which the spirit of Ch'in Shih-huang leaves Bao's body before Bao slaughters the missionary (*Boxers* 187). The implication is not that Ch'in Shih-huang would disapprove of Bao's action—in fact, quite the reverse, as in the subsequent scene the god lambasts Bao for allowing the women and children among the converts to live. But the visual depiction of Bao himself performing the action, in his own skin, both reminds readers that he is morally responsible for his own actions and shows the ways that, even without Ch'in Shih-huang literally inhabiting him, he has taken on the god's vengeful, nationalistic identity. In subsequent panels, there-fore, whenever Bao kills civilians, we see him in the foreground, with Ch'in Shih-huang's demanding presence behind him. Even when Bao changes to the extent that Ch'in Shih-huang tells him, "You are not the same as before... . You will no longer become me when you perform the Ritual. You will become someone new. A new god for a new dynasty" (293), the god still harangues him and eggs him on to further violence. Bao may have a false sense of independent subjectivity when he becomes the "new god," but he still destroys all that he loves in the name of Ch'in Shih-huang's vision of a unified, pure "China." As he lies wounded, apparently dying, at the end of *Boxers*, a large panel shows "vivid bits of color" (323) disappearing into the sky. "The Gods of the Opera are fleeing," Bao concludes (325). Bao's world is now fully disenchanted; and readers feel the loss of that colorful world, at the same time that they mourn the actions that Bao has taken in the name of preserving those "vivid bits of color" in his life.

Bao's counterproductive attempts to re-enchant the world link him to fundamentalism, especially Habermas's definition of fundamentalism as reli-gious movements that, "given the cognitive limits of modern life, nevertheless persist in practicing or promoting a return to the exclusivity of premodern religious attitudes" (Habermas 151). As Habermas and others explain, how-ever, fundamentalism is itself part of the modern, disenchanted impulse. Yang's cosplay analogy brings the fundamentalist impulse home for young readers who may have felt modernity-induced nostalgia and sought to exer-cise it, albeit in less violent ways. Bao's narrative in *Boxers* thus destabilizes any clear distinction between "porous" and "buffered," "secular" and "funda-mentalist," "us" and "them."

Mei-wen and Vibiana: Reading and Performing the Text of the Holy Body

While Bao's actions represent the negative possibility of fundamentalism within postsecular cosplay, Yang offers more positive examples of cosplay involving Mei-wen in *Boxers* and Vibiana in *Saints*. Mei-wen, like Bao's other rebels, initially transforms into an opera goddess when she fights: Mu Gui-ying, "the legendary woman general" (*Boxers* 166). Mei-wen gives up this identity after a crucial scene in which she reads a story to Bao in the library, a story that becomes her new cosplay text. The tale is the legend of the Princess Miao-shan, who, after sacrificing her eyes and hands to make a potion necessary to heal her father, becomes Guan Yin, the "Goddess of Compassion—the goddess with one thousand eyes to look for suffering and one thousand hands to relieve it" (280). After the reading of her story, Guan Yin appears behind Mei-wen and Bao, but in a way apparently only visible to the reader, rather than to the two teenagers; Mei-wen and Guan Yin do not completely fuse, unlike Mei-wen and Mu Gui-ying.[5] Still, even without directly witnessing the apparition, Mei-wen enacts Guan Yin's identity through her compassion for Bao.

Mei-wen makes this embodiment more concrete when she tends to the wounded after a battle, carrying out Guan Yin's actions while bearing Guan Yin's symbol: an eye painted on her palm. When Bao asks about the symbol on her hands, Mei-wen confesses, "It … it helps me in my work" (300). Bao is incensed when he discovers that she is also tending wounded Christians. Mei-wen, like Bao, has been changed by her cosplay. Mei-wen's story, though, seems to promote acquiring knowledge about the spiritual forces one encounters and then putting that knowledge into practice. The "China" that she defends is thus very different from the "China" in whose name Bao kills. When Bao later sets fire to the library in which he and Mei-wen read the story of Guan Yin, he claims, "I did it for China" (312). Mei-wen responds, "For China? What is China but a people and their stories? And now you've burned them both to ash" (312–313). Bao's ritual to become a god, after all, involves burning a piece of writing he cannot even read—in essence, he performs the same action as he sets the library aflame.

Mei-wen's embodiment of Guan Yin involves inscribing a story onto her own skin. As Bethan Jones argues, fan tattoos are a form of cosplay that operates "at a deeper level than simply clothes or accessories can demonstrate" (sec. 1.2). Fan tattoos not only serve as a personal reminder of one's affinity for a particular text; Margo De Mello writes, "Except when worn in private areas, tattoos are meant to be read by others. For this reasons tattoos as identity markers are not merely private expressions of the need to 'write oneself,' but they express the need for others to read them in a certain way as well" (qtd. in Jones, sec 5.3). While Mei-wen's painted eyes are more of a personal reminder to help her embody Guan Yin's compassion, Yang also draws attention to the fact that Bao does not have the interpretive code to "read" Mei-wen's body markings; he slept through her recounting of the story of Miaoshan/Guan Yin. Mei-wen dies while attempting to retrieve books from the burning library; in essence, she is martyred for her belief in the transformative power of stories, knowingly embodied.

Mei-wen's embrace of Guan Yin's story also ultimately provides the interpretive key for the kind of postsecular cosplay readers encounter in *Saints*. On the whole, the protagonist Vibiana's relationship to cosplay combines aspects of both Bao's and Mei-wen's, but her journey is more focused on interpretation itself: how exactly to translate the cosplayed text into her life. Vibiana's (or Four-Girl, as she is called until she later takes on the baptismal name of Vibiana) whole life is focused around reading symbols as markers of identity, in large part because her interpretive community reads her birth circumstances—the "fourth daughter, born on the fourth day of the fourth month" (Yang, *Saints* 3)—as symbolic of death (because "four" is a homonym of "death" in Mandarin). When she accidentally breaks the Tu Di Gong statue in their home, her grandfather denounces her as a "devil," and she resolves thenceforward to make her face and actions fit that identity. She contorts her own face into a cross-eyed grimace that she thinks expresses the identity "devil" and wears this face in public. She thus enacts a form of cosplay motivated by her own self-loathing—not imagining herself as different from what her society has declared her to be, but resolving to fit that image to a tee, since getting others to read her differently seems impossible.

Vibiana's form of cosplay thus perhaps resonates most with twenty-first-century teen readers, who feel similarly pressured to conform to roles given them by others. As Dorothy Karlin explains, "Young adult literature often showcases ideological interpellation on a general scale, as adolescent characters become aware of social power structures and learn how to operate within them" (72–3). Karlin further adds, "ideological interpellation has a strong corporeal element" (73): as Vibiana is hailed by the identity of "devil," she seeks to reify it through her bodily performance. However, Vibiana's desire to make her outward appearance conform to others' labels for her actually leads to her transformation and gives her a new identity. When she sees the French priest smash the statue of Tu Di Gong (the same scene witnessed by Bao in *Boxers*), she recognizes the same action she had inadvertently committed and vows to become a "foreign devil"—a Christian.

The same catalyst launches Bao and Vibiana toward their very different roles, and like Bao, Vibiana encounters a spirit—once again portrayed matter-of-factly by Yang—that tempts her to embrace a kind of fundamentalist modernity. In the forest, she meets an evil spirit in raccoon form,[6] who urges her on to become a "true devil" (43), prompting her to take revenge against her family members. Yet the raccoon is displeased when Vibiana announces that she will complete her transformation into a devil by becoming a Christian; he warns Vibiana that the Christian acupuncturist will "leave [her] a husk of [her] former self" (19). The raccoon wants Vibiana to express her "self" through violence, not through conversion. Vibiana's narrative indeed shows the ways that religious conversion, like cosplay, is both a gaining and a loss of "self." While Vibiana's acceptance of the role of Christian (with no real knowledge of what that role entails) links her to postsecular cosplay, the raccoon's warning aligns him with a view of subjectivity characterized by Seligman et al. as representative of a modern worldview prioritizing "sincerity" over "ritual." Seligman et al. also link this contemporary preference for "sincerity" to the rise of fundamentalism, which "understands the religious act—and, all too often, the religious act as politics—as the vehicle for self-expression and self-fulfillment" (10). Even if fundamentalism claims to act in the name of some abstraction like "the nation" or "religion," in practice it most often is a quest to reinscribe the modern "self." Unlike Bao, Vibiana is not seduced by the fundamentalist vision of subjectivity, because what she longs for is not the preservation of a "pure" identity but the gift of a new role—a genuine transformation.

With Vibiana, as with Bao, cognitive religious knowledge does not effect her transformation. Readers see successive panels of Vibiana dozing through the stories of Jesus from the Gospels. She is unimpressed by doctrine; she wants to embody a new identity, and the Church promises her "sins forgiven … and a new name!" (62). During the period of her catechism, Vibiana begins receiving more apparitions in the forest—not from the raccoon, but from a young foreign person in armor who, in fact, roasts and eats the raccoon. Like Bao, Vibiana is initially completely ignorant about this armored spirit's identity, through the French priest Father Bey recognizes her from Vibiana's description as Joan of Arc. Vibiana knows next to nothing of Joan's history, but she sees Joan's face when Joan receives her calling from the archangel Michael. As Vibiana reflects, "At the time, I couldn't understand a word they spoke to each other, but a look came over Joan's face … a look I desperately wanted. Her face was utterly free of regret" (56). Vibiana wants to cosplay as Joan, but not at a superficial level—she wants to take on her face, her *habitus*—the dispositions with which she responds to the world, dispositions shaped by habit and ritual.[7] As Bainbridge and Norris argue, "cosplay is an embodied practice because cosplay is as much about assuming the habitus of the character (the way they act) as it is in wearing the clothes" (par. 11). Vibiana's desire to embody Joan thus connects her to Mei-wen's imitation of Guan Yin, an identity inscribed on her body both through her drawing of Guan Yin's symbol as well as her repetition of Guan Yin's acts of compassion.

As Vibiana struggles to perform her new role, Joan continues to appear to her from time to time, but Vibiana still cannot make these images of Joan match her own reality: Joan seems more like a fantasy hero Vibiana feels no hope of imitating. Joan, dressed in shining armor, receives honor from royalty and leads troops into battle, while Vibiana washes the laundry of the orphans in the village and prepares their meals. When Vibiana first hears of the impending threat from the Society of the Righteous and Harmonious Fist (or Boxers), she thinks she finally can interpret Joan's apparitions. As she tells a former mercenary, "God wants you to help me defend our home against the Society of the Righteous and Harmonious Fist! God wants you to train me into a MAIDEN WARRIOR!" (Yang, *Saints* 103). The spiritual beings appearing to both Bao and Vibiana have the potential to lead them into nationalistic violence; Yang's postsecularity goes beyond merely suggesting that religious fundamentalism and violent nationalism are linked—he treats realistically the possibility that spiritual forces are at the root of nationalistic violence.

Vibiana later begins to question her own interpretation of her calling to perform as Joan when she hears her cousin Chung, who has now joined the Boxers, utter the same phrase that she has heard Joan declare in an apparition: "We will make our nation whole again!" (127). If Vibiana embraces Joan's militaristic nationalism, it could lead her just as easily to take up arms "for China" against the foreigners as it could lead her to defend her Christian village against the Society of the Righteous and Harmonious First. Neither Joan nor God seems to offer Vibiana any interpretive help as the Boxers advance. She does encounter maiden warriors, but they are fighting on the side of the Boxers. The Red Lanterns (to whom Mei-wen at first belongs) appear "like characters out of some ancient, terrible tale" (140). Their violence, unlike Joan's in Vibiana's visions, has no sheen of glamor. When they gut a man with a spear, Vibiana, aghast, exclaims, "You murdered a man!" (140). The Red Lanterns justify their violence as bringing "justice to a secondary devil—a traitor to his own people!" (140). Though Yang does not show Vibiana explicitly reflecting on the parallel, it is clearly laid out for the reader: might Joan of Arc have used the same rationale for shedding blood?

Despite her horror, Vibiana still contemplates joining the Boxers, especially once Bao threatens to kill her if she doesn't renounce her Christian faith. Vibiana prays for Joan to appear to her one last time, promising, "I need to know for certain. Just say the word and I'll join them! I'll be just like you! I'll raise a sword high over my head! I'll fight against the foreigners! I'll make my country whole again!" (153). Only at this point does Joan finally appear to Vibiana again after her long absence—not in resplendent armor, but with her head shaved, her face sweating, and tears pouring down her face as she is burned at the stake. At this point, readers realize what really they already knew from reading *Boxers*: that Vibiana is to embody Joan's calling not through fighting as a hero against her enemies, but through dying an inglorious martyr's death. Joan does not speak to Vibiana at this point; her gaze points in the other direction, as she cries, "Jesus!" (153). Jesus, in white robes, then appears to Vibiana and, instead of answering her question, launches into recounting the parable of the Good Samaritan. Vibiana responds in frustration, "I don't need stories right now! You know what I do need? A straight answer!" (155). Jesus concludes the words of the parable, but the image on the page changes from pre-crucifixion Jesus to that of the crucified Jesus: his "straight answer" is an image inviting embodied imitation.

Vibiana may be illiterate, but she is capable of "*lectio domini*," "meditating on Christ's body as text" (Smith 608). As in medieval hagiography, the depiction of the saint's meditation on Christ's body extends toward the reader; "proper reading of the hagiography will allow [the reader] access to the body of the saint" (Smith 609), and ultimately this reading will culminate in the reader's imitation of the saint, which is, by extension, imitation of Christ. The text of *Saints* becomes a ritualistic object, inviting readers to read Christ's body as Vibiana does.[8] In three successive panels, the wounds on Jesus' palms open to display an eye, the same eyed hand used to represent Guan Yin in *Boxers*. The next page shows the resurrected Christ above the empty tomb, surrounded by many eyed hands, and he finally speaks directly to Vibiana: "So, please, Vibiana. Be as mindful of others as I am of you" (158). The clear visual parallels between the image of Guan Yin in *Boxers* and the image of Jesus in *Saints* reinforces the commonality of their messages of compassion, undermining the supposed clash of religions and cultures that drives both colonialism and the Boxers' violent resistance to it. Visually, Yang reinforces that cosplaying as Guan Yin might look a lot like cosplaying as Jesus, and vice versa. Only the readers see the visual symbols that imply this similarity, suggesting that it is more a message for Yang's twenty-first-century readers than it is a truth realized by any of the characters within the narrative.

As with cosplay, the performance takes on meaning because readers recognize the identity the cosplayer is embodying, and the reader's ability to recognize "depends on the amount of subcultural capital [knowledge of the text from which the character comes] that the reader has" (Jones, sec. 5.2). Yang gives his readers the subcultural capital that his characters lack, which gives them a sense of satisfaction and completion. At the same time, it reminds us that, in a disenchanted world, this sense of divine meaning infused into life often seems inaccessible. Or at least it should seem inaccessible—as in most postsecular fiction, those with certain interpretations about the religious figures they are performing are those most to be feared. Both *Boxers* and *Saints* uphold the role of mystery in postsecular cosplay.

Even without assured interpretations, it is still possible to enact divine compassion, still possible to perform as Jesus or Guan Yin. Vibiana responds to this encounter by showing compassion to Bao, teaching him the Lord's Prayer—"the only thing I could think of to give you," she says (161). When Bao gives her one last chance to renounce her faith by telling him her Chinese name, she responds, with gritted teeth, "My ... name ... is ... Vibiana!" (161). She holds fast to her new identity given to her by the Church. She may have little cognitive knowledge of Jesus and his stories, little orthodox Christian "belief," but she knows that she has been given the chance to perform a new identity, and she plants herself on that ground. Vibiana's stance thus in some ways mirrors McClure's description of the protagonists of postsecular fiction. She too is "compelled to navigate without any reliable map of the cosmos or of history, any full diagram of divine power or comprehensive census of supernatural beings"; yet, unlike them, she does find a "secure dwelling" in her new identity (McClure 6).

Just as Yang powerfully dramatizes why a teen might get caught up in violent fundamentalism, he also shows why a teen might give up everything for the identity that has freed her from the past. In declaring her name, Vibiana does not realize how she is also performing the role of her namesake; she chooses her baptismal name simply because she likes the sound of it and remains ignorant about the original Vibiana's story. In fact, no one knows much about the original Saint Vibiana except that she was a virgin martyr who lived and died in the third century. Though Saint Vibiana is the patron of Los Angeles, her remains were discovered only in the nineteenth century; as the *Cathedrals of California* web site puts it, "She stands for all of us, the insignificant ones who will never be written about in history books. Our lives may not be widely known, but they are known to God, who has called us each by name from before the beginning of time" (qtd. in Fusaro). Yang's Vibiana may seem like one of the insignificant ones, especially in comparison to Joan of Arc. But she enacts the martyr's strength when death arrives on an ordinary day of doing orphans' laundry, and her act of compassion has consequences beyond her knowledge. Though Vibiana's narration concludes with, "And that was it. That was how I died. Unable to protect anyone" (*Saints* 162), Yang shows us an epilogue from Bao's perspective in which he, having survived the battle at the end of *Boxers*, tremblingly recites the words Vibiana has taught him in order to convince the British soldiers that he is not a Boxer. By enacting the role of compassion, Vibiana unwittingly saves Bao's life.

That Vibiana's act of compassion is to teach Bao the Lord's Prayer—a seemingly futile gesture, yet one that saves Bao's life when he recites the words, even without knowing their meaning—reinforces the postsecular role of ritual in *Saints*. In fact, ritual becomes an interpretive tool for making sense of a simultaneously enchanted and disenchanted world. Péter Losonczi explains, "That is why ritual is so important: it does *not* do away with the tragic and fragmented character of life and the social and individual ambiguities of lived life, but contributes to a complex strategy for living together with these conditions" (714). "Belief" may seem diminished for those who demand a fundamentalist certainty and sincerity, but the rituals of postsecular cosplay transform those who perform them and lead them to read the world anew.

Conclusion

In both *Boxers & Saints*, Gene Luen Yang's characters enact a postsecular cosplay in which belief is deemphasized in favor of performance. This shift is no naïve return to what Charles Taylor, in Pierre Chanu's words, characterizes as the premodern "*religion du faire, non du savoir*" (Taylor, *Secular* 63). While Yang depicts the existence and agency of spiritual beings real, he also dramatizes the disenchantment that twenty-first-century readers often feel—the disenchantment that seeks outlet in cosplay and other forms of fantasy, not to mention perhaps in religious fundamentalism. Yang makes fundamentalism simultaneously comprehensible and reprehensible; at the same time, he upholds the religious performance that would lead one to suffer martyrdom. Thus he is not merely reenacting the usual postsecular preference for "weak religion," which sets "aside ideas of transcendence, eternal life, and absolute truth" and "makes a conversion to charity (rather than an anticipation of judgment and eternal life) the core of its message" (McClure 13). While Yang demonstrates more interest in charity and compassion than in doctrinal differences between Christianity and Buddhism, there is nothing weak about Mei-Wen's and Vibiana's religious performances. They demonstrate the fervor that is possible even without fundamentalist (whether "religious" or "secular") certainty. The felt lack of certainty and the ultimate separation of devotion from nationalistic violence makes Mei-wen's and Vibiana's religious performances profoundly postsecular—more truly postsecular, in fact, than most postsecular fiction, which still remains wary of anything powerful enough to die for.

Like both postsecular fiction and cosplay, *Boxers & Saints* emphasizes the kind of community produced by embodied performance, a community centered around rituals and symbols—in other words, a religious community, whether it is recognized as such or not. As Bethan Jones writes, "fans can become part of communities or clans which are not familial but nevertheless can represent a civic family and can find meaning from within the clan and their affective relationship to its totem" (sec. 1.4). Even though cosplay takes part in what Charles Taylor calls the culture of "'expressive' individualism" (Taylor, *Varieties* 80), it also, like most forms of consumerist expressions of identity (e.g., fashion), requires an interpretive community: "It matters to each of us as we act that there are others there, as witnesses of what we are doing, and thus as co-determiners of the meaning of our action" (Taylor, *Varieties* 85–86). Yang's use of the graphic narrative genre positions readers as part of this interpretive community and invites us to participate in reading itself as a postsecular ritual, a ritual that re-reads a disenchanted world.

NOTES

1. In an interview, Yang makes this contemporary application explicit, stating, "Early on in my research, I was struck by the parallels between the Boxer Rebellion and current events. The Boxers have a lot in common with many of today's extremist movements in the Middle East. Little Bao would probably be labeled a terrorist if he were real and alive today. I tried to make him understandable, but not justified. The Boxers were defending a culture under attack. Yet—within my story, at least—their view of their own culture was incomplete" (Mayer).

2. According to Bainbridge and Norris, "game designer Takahashi Nobuyuki coined the term *kosu-pure* (costume-play)" in 1984 to describe the practice of these performances, which often occur at fan conventions (par. 3).

3. The passages in single quotation marks are from Charles Taylor's *Varieties of Religion Today* (116).

4. "Even if actors declare that they were unaware of or not fans of superhero comics before they chose to undertake the role, as both Christian Bale as Bruce Wayne/Batman and Heath Ledger as Joker did of their performances within Christopher Nolan's rendering of the Batman mythos (although both Ledger and Bale read the comics and immersed themselves in the Batman mythos to prepare for their performances), it may still be cosplay. Even recreational cosplayers are not required to know or like their chosen characters" (Kirkpatrick, sec. 5.3).

5. Patricia Karetzky mentions that several real-life young women in China were celebrated for performing as Guan Yin: "The transformation of virtuous local women into incarnations of Guanyin is one of the ways in which Chinese society dealt with those who did not conform to the prevailing morality" (55). "Becoming" Guan Yin gives Mei-wen a counternarrative to resist the "prevailing morality" of the nationalistic Boxers.

6. I have not seen any explanation of why the evil spirit is a raccoon, specifically, but I hypothesize that Yang chooses the raccoon (as opposed to, say, a panda) because it is an animal native to North America rather than China. Neither of the competing voices influencing Vibiana is "Chinese"; her conflict is not between a Chinese identity and a Western identity but between an identity seeking revenge and an identity exercising compassion.

7. Pierre Bourdieu's influential concept of the habitus appears in *The Logic of Practice*. Essentially, the habitus acknowledges the role of the body's habits—rather than mere cognition—in shaping our responses.

8. Yang previously invited readers to use his text as a devotional object in *The Rosary Comic Book*, which invites readers to either "*Read* it as you would a regular comic book" or "*Pray* with it, using the panels in place of the beads of a traditional rosary" (8).

WORKS CITED

Bainbridge, Jason, and Craig Norris. "Posthuman Drag: Understanding Cosplay as Social Networking in a Material Culture." *Intersections: Gender and Sexuality in Asia and the Pacific*, no. 32 (2013). http://intersections.anu.edu.au/issue32/bainbridge_norris.htm.

Bourdieu, Pierre. *The Logic of Practice*. Translated by Richard Nice. Redwood City, CA: Stanford University Press, 1990.

Fusaro, Darrell. "Blessed Are the Nobodies." *i-Italy*. January 6, 2013. http://www.iitaly.org/35077/blessed-are-nobodies.

Habermas, Jürgen. *Religion and Rationality: Essays on Reason, God, and Modernity*. Cambridge: Polity Press, 2002.

Hale, Matthew. "Cosplay: Intertextuality, Public Texts, and the Body Fantastic." *Western Folklore* 73, no. 1 (2014): 5–37.

Jacobs, Alan. "Fantasy and the Buffered Self." *The New Atlantis*, no. 41 (2014): 3–18. http://www.thenewatlantis.com/publications/fantasy-and-the-buffered-self.

Jones, Bethan. "Fannish Tattooing and Sacred Identity." *Transformative Works and Cultures*, no. 18 (2015).

Karetzky, Patricia. *Guanyin*. Oxford: Oxford University Press, 2004.

Karlin, Dorothy. "How to Be Yourself: Ideological Interpellation, Weight Control, and YA Novels." *Jeunesse: Young People, Texts, Cultures* 6, no. 2 (2014): 72–89.

Kirkpatrick, Ellen. "Toward New Horizons: Cosplay (Re)Imagined Through the Superhero Genre, Authenticity, and Transformation." *Transformative Works and Cultures*, no. 18 (2015).

Losonczi, Péter. "Modernity, Postsecularism, Fundamentalism." *Philosophia*, vol. 44 (2016): 705–720.

Ludwig, Katherine. "Don Delillo's *Underworld* and the Postsecular in Contemporary Fiction." *Religion and Literature* 41, no. 3 (2009): 82–91.

Mączynska, Magdalena. "Toward a Postsecular Literary Criticism: Examining Ritual Gestures in Zadie Smith's *Autograph Man*." *Religion and Literature* 41, no. 3 (2009): 73–82.

Mayer, Petra. "*Boxers & Saints* and Compassion: Questions for Gene Luen Yang." *NPR*. October 22, 2013. http://www.npr.org/2013/10/22/234824741/boxers-saints-compassion-quesions-for-gene-luen-yang.

McClure, John A. *Partial Faiths: Postsecular Fiction in the Age of Pynchon and Morrison*. Athens: University of Georgia Press, 2007.

Rozema, Robert. "Gene Luen Yang on Iconography, Cultural Conflict, and His New Graphic Novel, *Boxers & Saints*." *Language Arts Journal of Michigan* 29, no. 1 (2013): 5–9.

Seligman, Adam B., et al. *Ritual and Its Consequences: An Essay on the Limits of Sincerity*. Oxford: Oxford University Press, 2008.

Smith, Rachel. "Language, Literacy, and the Saintly Body: Cistercian Reading Practices and the *Life of Lutgard of Aywières* (1182–1246)." *Harvard Theological Review* 109 (2016): 586–610.

Taylor, Charles. *A Secular Age*. Cambridge, MA: Belknap Press, 2007.

Taylor, Charles. *Varieties of Religion Today: William James Revisited*. Cambridge, MA: Harvard University Press, 2002.

Truong, Alexis Hieu. "Framing Cosplay: How 'Layers' Negotiate Body and Subjective Experience Through Play." *Intersections: Gender and Sexuality in Asia and the Pacific*, no. 32 (2013). http://intersections.anu.edu.au/issue32/truong.htm.

Vallely, Paul. "Leave 'Martyrdom' to the Jihadists." *The New York Times*. July 29, 2016. http://www.nytimes.com/2016/07/29/opinion/leave-martyrdom-to-the-jihadists.html?smid=tw-nytopinion&smtyp=cur&_r=1.

Yang, Gene Luen. *Boxers*. New York: First Second Books, 2013.

Yang, Gene Luen. *The Rosary Comic Book*. New York: Pauline Books and Media, 2003.

Yang, Gene Luen. *Saints*. New York: First Second Books, 2013.

Sight, Blindness and Identity in Gene Luen Yang's *American Born Chinese* and *Boxers & Saints*

SHIH-WEN SUE CHEN

In an interview with NPR books in 2013, graphic novelist Gene Luen Yang described his stories using YA author Marsha Qualey's equation, "Power + Belonging = Identity," explaining, "my characters long for power and belonging because they're figuring out their place in the world, their identities" (Mayer). Both writers highlight a keyword in young adult literature: "power." It has been argued that the main difference between texts for children and fiction for adolescents is the issue of power (Trites). Roberta Seelinger Trites states,

> adolescents must learn their place in the power structure by experiencing each of three interrelated issues: They must learn to negotiate the many institutions that shape them, they must also learn to balance their power with their parents' power and with the power of authority figures in general, and, finally, they must learn what portion of power they wield because of and despite such biological imperatives as sex and death [473].

What Trites's article does not consider is the relationship between the adolescent and a "higher power" in the religious sense of the term. In a postsecular world, where the religious coexists with the secular and the boundaries and definitions of the two terms are being redefined, young adult literature has been recognized as a genre that provides opportunities for explorations of the relationship between faith and identity. As Paul T. Corrigan notes in the introduction to this collection, "Postsecular young adult literature not only reflects the postsecular as a contemporary phenomenon in our society but also facilitates the postsecular as a process for readers, not by giving answers but by enacting questions" (20).

Sociologist Meredith B. McGuire observes that in the contemporary practice of religion in every-day life, "extensive religious blending and within-group religious heterogeneity are the norm, rather than the exception" and "challenges the Western image of a religion as a unitary, organizationally defined, and relatively stable set of collective beliefs and practices" (187). Yang's graphic novels, which draw upon religious texts, traditions, and beliefs to explore the complexity of adolescent identity formation, also present the relationship between young people and religion as complex, unstable, and heterogeneous. Yang's texts reflect religious blending of Christianity and Buddhism because Yang's experience with Catholicism is influenced by Buddhism. In an interview, Yang recalls his mother bringing back pictures of Buddha's journey from Catholic retreats because the people there talked about both religions together. He explains, "It's just part of how I understand religion. I don't think it was necessarily something bad" (Morton). This explanation reflects attitudes in post-secular society where religious blending is one of the characteristics of postmodern religious identity. As Thomas E. Reynolds puts it, "*religious traditions are not single dimensioned and monophonic wholes, but richly complex, polyphonic, and tension-filled entanglements of multiple conversational threads*" (171, emphasis in the original). The religious worlds of Yang's texts are multidimensional and complex, containing elements of not only Christianity but also Buddhism, incorporating both "Western" and "Eastern" belief systems.

This essay examines the interplay between religion and identity in *American Born Chinese* (2006) and *Boxers & Saints* (2013). The former, which features Chinese American teenager Jin Wang as he struggles to fit into his new suburban school, also includes a retelling of the Monkey King story from the sixteenth-century Chinese classic *Journey to the West* by Wu Cheng'en that is interlaced with Christian references. For example, the visual depiction of the Monkey King bowing before baby Jesus demonstrates the blending of Christian iconography with Wu's novel, a tale about a Buddhist monk's pilgrimage to bring back sacred Buddhist texts to China. The latter, which considers both sides of the Boxer Uprising (1899–1901), deals directly with Christianity during the anti-foreign and anti–Christian movement that erupted in Northern China at the turn of the twentieth century. *Boxers*, narrated by "Little Bao" Lee, presents the Boxers' viewpoint, and *Saints*, narrated by Four-Girl (later baptized as Vibiana), focuses on the Chinese Christians' perspective. Bao and Vibiana's stories converge in the summer of 1900 at the Siege of the Peking Legations, when those trapped for months in the Legations were finally rescued by an international force known as the "Allies" on August 14, 1900. When Bao confronts Vibiana, offering her the opportunity to renounce her faith in exchange for her life, she refuses, choosing her faith over nation and fulfills her purpose in life by teaching Bao a prayer that would save his life when he pretends to be a Christian in front of foreign soldiers. This closure suggests that only Vibiana's Christian God can save.

Yang utilizes both verbal and visual elements of the graphic novel format to explore identity formation. I argue that by employing varying motifs of sight and blindness *American Born Chinese* and *Boxers & Saints* implicitly advocate for belief in a monotheistic Christian God and emphasize the importance of internal transformation of the heart over a corporeal transformation. I will use positioning theory to analyze Yang's characters' identity struggles. According to Fathali Moghaddam and Rom Harré, "Positioning theory is about how people use words (and discourse of all types) to locate themselves and others" (2). While Dan McAdams and Claudia Zapata-Gietl define identity in relation to the "roles" people play and "the traits they consistently display" (85), positioning takes into account the dynamic aspect of identity and the possibility of multiple "selves" that can shift over time. Explained further by Bronwyn Davies and Rom Harré, positioning is a "discursive process whereby selves are located in conversations as observably and subjectively coherent participants in jointly produced story lines. There can be interactive positioning in which what one person says positions another. And there can be reflexive positioning in which one positions oneself" (48). Phillip L. Lammack Jr. also highlights "the role of language as the mediational mechanism through which identity develops" (13). The importance of words and stories in the formulation of identity is evident in Yang's texts. Most of Yang's characters' actions are motivated by how they think others see them and position them, reflecting the idea that, as Michael P. Jensen puts it, "the self can only be described with reference to the selves surrounding it" (10). Positionings can fluctuate according to context. Yang's characters initially try to challenge or assert their positions through bodily transformation. However, what Yang's texts suggest is that how other people see you is not as important as how a "higher power" (God) sees you. In other words, what matters is one's position in relation to God rather than one's position in relation to humans.

"My eyes have seen all your days": Eye Motifs

American Born Chinese, Boxers, and *Saints* all contain numerous references to eyes, seeing and visions. Yang, a practicing Roman Catholic, explains, "there is an idea within Christianity of intention behind your identity, that there is this outside agency that actually intended you to be who you are" (Woan 80). This "outside agency" is represented in the texts as a powerful being with the ability to see into the lives of every living being. In *American Born Chinese*, Tze-Yo-Tzuh ("I am"), who represents the Christian God, emphasizes his omniscience by telling the Monkey King, "My eyes have seen all your days" (*ABC* 80), an allusion to Psalm 139. This phrase provides an ironic contrast to the opening description of how the Monkey Kings's eyes "flashed rays of light deep into the sky" (*ABC* 9). Although his eyes illuminate bright light, he is figuratively blind to the existence of Tze-Yo-Tzuh. Although monkeys "frolicked under the watchful eye of the magical Monkey King" (*ABC* 8), the Monkey King did not realize that he had always been under the watchful eye of Tze-Yo-Tzuh and would never escape his reach (*ABC* 70). Thinking that he had flown "through the boundaries of *reality itself*," the Monkey King revels in his victory, using a speech act to order Tze-Yo-Tzuh to "get out of [his] sight," only to discover that he had never fly out of the palm of Tze-Yo-Tzuh's hand and was always being watched (*ABC* 77). The Monkey King initially rejects his positioning as "little monkey" and Tze-Yo-Tzuh's position as his creator. He is spiritually blind until he completes his "Journey to the West" to see baby Jesus. Thereafter, the Monkey King has "stood in his holy presence" and readily takes up the position of emissary of Tze-Yo-Tzuh (*ABC* 215). The hand and eye motif can also be found in *Boxers* and *Saints*.

In *Boxers* and *Saints*, Guan Yin and Jesus are represented literally with eyes looking over the protagonists. In *Boxers*, the Goddess of Compassion Guan Yin is described as "the goddess with one thousand eyes to look for suffering and one thousand hands to relieve it," although she is literally blind after sacrificing her own eyes to save her ailing father (*Boxers* 280). In literature, the physically blind are often represented as having more spiritual insight and wisdom than those who can see, and Guan Yin is a prime example because she sees those who are oppressed and helps relieve their pain. Bao's love interest Mei-wen positions herself as a Guan Yin–like figure when she starts a makeshift infirmary for the wounded and Bao notices that she has "painted eyes on the palms of [her] hands" (*Saints* 300). Both Guan Yin in *Boxers* and Jesus in *Saints* are depicted in full-page panels with yellow backgrounds filled with hands with eyes in them (*Boxers* 282; *Saints* 158). The light that emanates from them symbolizes their holiness and truth. The difference between the two panels of Jesus and Guan Yin lies in Vibiana's awareness of Jesus' presence, with her eyes wide open, while Bao and Mei-wen are unaware of Guan Yin because their eyes are closed.[1] In addition, the eye motif appears in *Boxers* when Master Big Belly opens his robe and reveals that his belly is "FILLED WITH MYSTIC VISION" (*Boxers* 108). Shocked by the big green eyeball that emanates light from Master's bellybutton, Bao screams "My eyes feel like they're bleeding!" (*Boxers* 109).[2] The visual imagery evokes the Freemasons' all-seeing-eye and readers see Bao's eyes becoming green like the eye he saw on Big Belly whenever he is in Ch'in Shih-huang mode. However, the irony is that instead of having a clear vision, Bao is blind to the consequences of his actions. These numerous references to eyes highlight the limited vision of characters such as the Monkey King and Bao in contrast to the all-seeing divine powers.

Sight, Performativity and the Relational Character of Identity

Raised in non-nurturing family environments, Bao and Four-Girl's motivations for becoming a Boxer and a Christian are strikingly similar: both feel "unseen" and neglected; they both long for a sense of belonging and purpose in life. In *American Born Chinese*, the main characters also struggle to be acknowledged. At the beginning of the story the Monkey King's reflexive self-positioning is that of a superior being, on equal footing with the deities. That is why he is shocked and angered when the deities in heaven refuse to admit him into their fold because he is not wearing shoes. After the conversation with the guard at the dinner party, the Monkey King has been positioned as an inferior "other." Similarly, Jin's classmates ostracize him for being different, refusing to see him as one of them. He is left alone in the playground after a bully labels him "Bucktooth" and positions him as a dog-eater in the speech act "stay away from my dog" (*ABC* 32–33).

According to positioning theory, "not everyone involved in a social episode has equal access to rights and duties to perform particular kinds of meaningful actions at *that* moment and with *those* people" (Harré 193, emphasis in the original). In their social interactions with others, whether at school (Jin), at home (Bao and Four-Girl), or in heaven (Monkey King), these characters are denied certain rights to act or even speak, causing them to feel insignificant. Their conceptualization of their identities is affected by the uneven power dynamics in their social circles. Considering that physical markers of identity are most easily seen by others, it is not surprising that these characters attempt to transform themselves outwardly in response to these negative social episodes. That is, they try to change their position.

These characters' interpretation of self-identity is defined by a transformed body, which they think will affect their position in future interactions. Physical transformation occurs throughout *American Born Chinese* as Elisabeth El Refaie and others have analyzed in detail.[3] For example, the Monkey King tries to be acknowledged as a deity by wearing shoes and Jin perms his hair curly like his Caucasian classmate Greg. In *Boxers*, too, physical transformation is present: Bao strives to fit in and be taken seriously as an adult by learning the kung fu strengthening exercises taught by his mentor Red

Lantern Chu, a member of the Society of the Big Swords. The most striking example is found in Four-Girl's storyline. Yang explains that in writing *Saints*, he "took inspiration from American autobio comics" (Mozzocco). A convention of autobio comics is the focus on the body. According to El Refaie, the autobiographical comic genre places

> a lot of emphasis on the importance of the body in constructing and maintaining a person's identity. Self-identity is typically represented as something that is constantly shifting and changing and which often threatens to fracture into multiple parts [*Autobiographical* 222].

The beginning of *Saints* reflects Four-Girl's concern with her body as well as her desire to express her identity through her outward appearance. She grasps onto the "devil" label that her grandfather hurls at her after she accidentally chops off the head of the family's Tu Di Gong (Earth God) statue in a failed attempt to please him. As the patriarch, her grandfather's words have a deep impact on her because of his powerful position in the family. Because he positions her as occupying the lowest order in the family, she does not have the right to challenge his authority, so she decides to "embrace [her] devil-self" (*Saints* 13). In other words, she actively takes on the position assigned to her in a literal way.

At night, Four-Girl practices her "devil-face" by poring over her reflection in a pool of water and distorting it in various unattractive ways (mirrors are a common feature in autobiographical comics). The ripples further distort her reflection, symbolizing her fragmented identity. Working on her look, she tries to determine how she wants others to perceive her: ugly, evil, and repulsive. She says, "It took me hours to perfect my devil-face, but I finally did" (*Saints* 13). The final result features a cross-eyed Four-Girl with a scowl. The fact that one of her irises is up while the other is down means that she's unable to focus, which implies that her vision of the world is distorted while she has her "devil-face" on. Her definition of self is determined by her perceived relationship with the Chinese community around her, or her social identity, which lacks clarity. It is a horizontal relationship rather than a vertical one and focuses on "performing" a certain face only when others are watching, as evidenced in the four panels on page 18. The implied reader sees her normal resting face in the first three panels as her mother and aunt converse about the acupuncturist Dr. Won with their back towards her. However, when the adults turn their heads around, she immediately distorts her face again. These examples suggest that her identity is performed.

Four-Girl tries to forge her identity by repeatedly taking on the position of "devil." Postmodern ideas of identity, according to Karen Coats, suggest that it is "fundamentally discursive and performative, and thus any appearance of sameness over time is merely the result of the repetition of certain kinds of performances" (110). Judith Butler and others have theorized the relationship between identity and performance. Butler argues that gender identity is "instituted in an exterior space through a stylized repetition of acts," and that "the effect of gender is produced through the stylization of the body" (179). Four-Girl repeatedly puts on her "devil-face" in public—an identity that she performs when others are looking: "I wore it whenever I was around other people, to warn them that they were in the presence of evil" (*Saints* 14). The word "wore" is significant because it suggests that she uses this face as a defensive mask. When Bao catches a glimpse of her at the beginning of Boxers, he describes her face as being "just like an opera mask" (*Boxers* 9).[4] Anselm L. Strauss's idea of masks and identity is applicable to the case of Four-Girl, for he posits "Everyone presents himself to others and to himself, and sees himself in the mirrors of their judgments. The masks he then and thereafter presents to the world and its citizens are fashioned upon his anticipations of their judgments" (11). Because Four-Girl's grandfather judgment of her is that of a "devil," she decides to present this mask to the world.

Although Four-Girl is unsuccessful in her attempt to become a "devil" after Dr. Won "cures" her, her desire to transform her body physically has not been quashed. Instead, she decides to become a "foreign devil" after seeing Father Bey destroying a Tu Di Gong statue like she did: "I'll become so devilish, my skill will lose all its color! My nose will swell to the size of a melon! My body will grow hair, and my chin will sprout a beard so long it will drag on the ground!" (*Saints* 31). She revels in these descriptions of the monstrous Caucasian body, anticipating an exaggerated bodily transformation as the answer to her identity crisis. What Four-Girl fails to realize is that no matter how much her physical appearance changes, her identity will not be secure until she finds belonging in God, which occurs after she has a mystic vision of Joan of Arc asking her to share a meal. Inspired by this mystic encounter, Four-Girl becomes more serious about exploring Christianity and decides to get baptized. Father Bey's declarative speech act "I baptize thee in the name of the Father—and the Son—and the Holy Ghost" proclaims a new identity for Four-Girl. His second speech act "I present to you the Church's newest daughter" firmly positions her as a member of the Church family (*Saints* 68). Furthermore, her new identity is signified by a new name: Vibiana.

The act of changing names is an important one, and often occurs when characters try to re-position themselves because there is an important link between one's name and self-image (Strauss 18). St. Vibiana is known as the "Patron saint of nobodies" (Fusaro), so the name suits Four-Girl, since she is considered a "nobody" in the eyes of her family and village. The role of language and its impact on Four-Girl's sense of identity is evident from the first page of *Saints*, where she explains the origins of her name: she is the fourth daughter, born on the fourth day of the fourth month. Because the Chinese word for "four," si, sounds like "death" in Chinese, Four-Girl is seen as bad luck. Four-Girl's name change to Vibiana is a rite of passage that symbolizes her shedding off her identity as an unwanted, unloved, "unlucky" child to someone whose identity is in Christ. Name changes also occur in *American Born Chinese*: the Monkey King renames himself "The Great Sage, Equal of Heaven" after mastering the twelve major disciplines of kung-fu (*ABC* 60) and Jin becomes "Danny" after transforming into a Caucasian boy because "a new **face** deserved a new **name**" (*ABC* 198). However, the Monkey King's self-positioning as "equal to heaven" is rejected by Ao-Kuang, Dragon King of the Eastern Sea, who laughs and calls him "little monkey" (*ABC* 62).

While the Monkey King uses violence to try to affirm his position, he later learns that instead of constantly transforming himself into a larger-than-life deity, humbling himself before Tze-Yo-Tzuh brings true freedom (*ABC* 215). The best example of someone who accepts his positioning is Wong Lai-Tsao, a follower of Tze-Yo-Tzuh, who exemplifies what it means to "walk by faith, not by sight" (2 Corinthians 5:7 NIV) and understands that faith as "the assurance of things hoped for, the conviction of things not seen" (Hebrews 11:1 NIV). He tells the emissaries "I accept whatever plans Tze-Yo-Tzuh has for me" (*ABC* 140) and the Monkey King that "If it is the will of Tze-Yo-Tzuh for me to die for your stubborness, then I accept" (*ABC* 146). Davies and Harré state that

> Once having taken up a particular position as one's own, a person inevitably sees the world from the vantage point of that position and in terms of the particular images, metaphors, story lines and concepts which are made relevant within the particular discursive practice in which they are positioned [46].

After humbling themselves before Tze-Yo-Tzuh/God, Wong, the Monkey King, and Four-Girl see the world from the vantage point of a follower, which is why Vibiana refuses to renounce her faith in front of Bao.

While Vibiana finally finds inner peace as a devotee of Jesus, Bao believes that he can be a god himself. He takes up the position of Boxer and sees the world through the lens of an opera lover and foreigner hater. Like Four-Girl, Bao's identity as a Boxer is also performative. He repeats the Boxer ritual many times: first he bows to the bean garden, then he writes the incantation "Power of Heaven, come down!" on parchment, burns it, swallows the ashes, and exhales (*Boxers* 89). He declares to his Brother-Disciples, "we're the ones who are gods! The foreign devils are mere humans!" (*Boxers* 180). This statement reveals that not only he does not believe in a monotheistic God, but he also positions himself reflexively as one of many gods, reflecting the influence of Chinese polytheistic folk religions on his worldview. Blaming the foreigners for his poverty and suffering after his village was devastated by floods then famine, Bao wants to banish the foreign presence in China, blind to the fact that these "mere humans" have powerful weapons and bullets. As the Siege of the Peking Legations begins, he narrates, "in every section of the city, the Gods of the Opera arise" (*Boxers* 291). Bao interprets his life by drawing on stories from his favorite Chinese opera performances, reflecting sociologists' research about how story making guides identity development (Lammark 24). He dreams of becoming a hero like the ones he sees on stage and imagines that the people will "write operas about [him]" (*Boxers* 92).

The fact that Bao is an opera lover is an important detail because, according to Paul Cohen, "In matters of dress, as in their boxing and trance behavior, the Boxers imitated the martial arts performers they had so often seen in village operas" (39). Ch'in "chose" Little Bao to act as his medium, and commands him through speech acts to behave in violent ways. The Siege of the Legations marks a turning point in Bao's journey as Ch'in informs Bao, "you will no longer become me when you perform the Ritual. You will become someone new." The new identity is that of a god of a "dynasty of fire" (*Boxers* 293). The visual image of the new Bao is more closely associated with the colorful Chinese opera masks that he is familiar with. This illustration reinforces the idea that Bao interprets his life through opera stories and identifies with the characters. Bao's desire to be immortalized by operas about him suggests his sense of pride and focus on self-glorification. Although Bao seems to become physically stronger after his rituals, his visions at night leave him unsettled, suggesting that some visions can be dangerous.

Visions and Blindness

Both Vibiana and Bao have visions at night but these visions affect the two in opposite ways. Four-Girl's mystic experience occurs in the forest at night. Patty Campbell explains that the form of mysticism that often appears in young adult literature can be defined using American philosopher William James's definition: "the feelings, acts, and experiences of individual men [*sic*] in their solitude, so far as they apprehend themselves to stand in relation to whatever they may consider the divine" (qtd. in Campbell 77). Her visions are depicted in warm yellow hues, signifying Joan's holiness. Because the limited color palette of *Saints* is subdued and almost monochromatic, the readers' eyes are drawn to the figure of the "Maid of Orleans." Later, Four-Girl sees a much younger Joan praying in the forest. Despite her ignorance about the words exchanged between Joan and the angel, Four-Girl notices that "a look came over Joan's face ... a look I desperately wanted. Her face was utterly free of regret" (*Saints* 56). Joan's peaceful expression reflects her trust in God and her sense of security with her identity as a "Daughter of God" (*Saints* 56).

This encounter suggests to the implied reader that an inward change will be reflected outwardly. Four-Girl desires to take up a similar position as Joan because of this vision, suggesting that a common verbal language is not always necessary for communication: visual imagery can be powerful as well.

Whereas Vibiana feels more peaceful after seeing Joan, Bao wakes up in terror after talking to Ch'in Shih-huang. At first, the illiterate Bao is unable to identify the "black-robed god" he transforms into because he has never seen this figure in a Chinese opera (*Boxers* 113, 129). He lacks a frame of reference to interpret the meaning of these visions. It is only after speaking to Mei-wen, the daughter of an elite Hanlin scholar, that he learns about Ch'in Shih-huang [Qin Shihuang 259 -210 BC], the first emperor of China. What Bao does not know is that Ch'in was notorious for burying scholars alive and burning books. When he is in Ch'in Shih-huang mode, Bao can inflict violence without mercy, wielding his big sword to chop off the head of a foreign solider (*Boxers* 184), commanding all the men on a train be murdered (*Boxers* 189), killing a young foreign woman even though he claimed to believe Boxer edict #4: "Have compassion for the weak" (*Boxers* 192, 229) and burning down a church full of women and children (*Boxers* 249).

At first, Bao prides himself in following the Boxer edicts but gradually turns a blind eye to them as the voice of Ch'in comes to dictate his life. Bao's recurring nightmare is about drowning and being unable to help the people he loved or killed who call to him from an island. Each time he is about to take action, Ch'in drags him to the bottom of the ocean. The water imagery represents Ch'in's power, as he explains to Bao: "Every dynasty draws its power from one of the Five Elements. Mine is **water**" (*Boxers* 237). These dreams reflect Bao's anxiety and guilt about the many deaths associated with him. Bao becomes increasingly disturbed as Ch'in's nightly visits become more horrifying, with the large black-robed figure looming over the boy, telling him that he had "ordered his own father's death" for the sake of China (*Boxers* 193).

Considering Yang's religious beliefs, these descriptions of Bao's disturbing encounters with Ch'in suggest the dangers of allowing demonic powers to possess oneself. It also warns against "emptying" oneself "until all that is left is a perfect **nothingness**" (*Boxers* 89) because it is like "forfeiting your soul." As the herbalist's wife in *American Born Chinese* warns, "It's easy to become anything you wish ... so long as you're willing to forfeit your soul" (29). Ch'in could be interpreted as a demonic force in Bao's life, threatening to take over his entire being, especially in a scene when Ch'in strangles Bao, yelling "the words from my lips **define** good and evil!" (*Boxers* 210). This is a powerful speech act that positions Bao as a powerless boy who is only able to occupy the subject position of someone who follows orders.

Although they initially placed emphasis on physical markers of identity, the Monkey King, Jin, and Four-Girl come to realize that an internal change in their heart is more important than a corporeal transformation. Yang's texts convey the Old Testament message that "People look at the outward appearance, but the Lord looks at the heart" (1 Samuel 16:7, NIV). The Monkey King tells Jin that after his failed attempts to be recognized as a deity, he has learned "how good it is to be a monkey" and it is implied that Jin comes to accept his Chinese American identity (*ABC* 223). As Pinti puts it, "Yang represents the Monkey King's understanding of his true identity as inherently relational, and even vocational, vis-à-vis a Christian conception of God" (240). The Monkey King initially desires power and personal glory, and wishes to be seen as important in the eyes of the dominant majority. However, when he discards his shoes, the Monkey King lets go of his previous identity to embark on a journey to find his true calling in the will of God (Stratman 493–500). However, it is unclear at the end of *Boxers* whether Bao has this revelation. Although readers don't know whether Bao will turn to Christianity or not, it is implied that he has a chance at redemption.

Conclusion

American Born Chinese and *Boxers & Saints* are richly complex in their depictions of young people's religious and spiritual experiences and how they relate to identity formation. Yang's characters, who have free will, represent different stages of the faith journey from a Christian perspective. The texts illustrate various attitudes towards belief and faith in a monotheistic Christian God and employ themes of sight and blindness to demonstrate the journeys on which characters with different religious convictions travel as they take up different positions in their interactions with others along the way. In *American Born Chinese*, the Monkey King is a polytheist with a dramatic conversion to a monotheistic Christian God, while Wong Lai-Tsao is a mature believer who leads him on his way. In *Saints*, Four-Girl is a seeker who has a mystic experience with Joan of Arc; and in *Boxers*, Bao is a folk religion follower turned possessed-Boxer leader. A common motivation for their turn to religion is the longing for power and belonging.

Yang explains that both Bao and Four-Girl "want wholeness, a completeness of identity, but they go about getting what they want in very different ways" (Mozzocco). Thus, Little Bao tries to find his niche in the Boxers, believing he has been chosen by Red Lantern Chu to lead the Boxers and chosen by Ch'in Shih-huang to fight for China to make it whole again. Unfortunately for Bao, listening to Ch'in leads to disastrous outcomes. Four-Girl takes her grandfather's words literally and becomes a "secondary devil," finding her belonging in the small Catholic community, leaving behind her identity as a cursed girl when she takes on the name Vibiana. The "outside agency" at work in her life is Jesus Christ, who communicates with her through her visions of Joan of Arc. Her identity as a Christian never wavers even in the face of death. Although Yang's texts implicitly promote a Christian message, the novels are not overtly proselytizing, and they do not suggest that having religious faith will guarantee a trouble-free life. Instead of prescribing answers, Yang's texts prompt the implied young adult audience to ask questions and think about how religious faith can shape one's identity. His inclusion of Buddhist images alongside Christian ones challenges the stability of the boundaries between different religions and spiritual practices, placing his graphic novels in the realm of postsecular YA fiction.

NOTES

1. Yang explains that his inspiration for the images came from a painting of the Chinese goddess Guan Yin that he saw in a museum which featured her "surrounded by a halo of hands with eyes in them," which struck him as being similar to hands with holes, linking the image of Jesus's nail-pierced hands with Chinese cultural symbolism (Mozzocco). This statement is an example of the influence of Buddhism in his understanding of Catholicism. The figure of Guan Yin in *Boxers* is of particular interest because Guan Yin is the Chinese name for the Bodhisattva of Compassion, Avalokitsvara, who was transformed from the masculine to the feminine by the Chinese (Yu 1–2). The Chinese drew on the Indian Avalokitsvara for their own needs, and the Chinese American Catholic Yang uses Guan Yin to understand Jesus. In an interview, Yang draws a parallel between Guan Yin and Christ: "Guan Yin is a Christ figure. Or if you're a devotee of Guan Yin, you could say that Christ is a Guan Yin figure. Both their stories exemplify self-donating love. They show the importance of self-donating love within all human culture" (Mozzocco).

2. Yang based Master Big Belly on "an itinerant martial arts master who Esherick describes in his books. Rumor had it that he had a mystical eye in the middle of his belly" (Mozzocco).

3. See for example, El Refaie, "Transnational Identity as Shape-shifting"; Doughty; Hathaway; Song; Munson.

4. This statement also points to the influence of opera stories on Bao's interpretation of the world around him, a point which will be addressed later in the essay.

WORKS CITED

The Bible. New International Version. Colorado Springs: Biblica, 2011.
Butler, Judith. *Gender Trouble: Feminism and the Subversion of Identity*. London: Routledge, 1999.
Campbell, Patty. *Spirituality in Young Adult Literature: The Last Taboo*. Lanham, MD: Rowman & Littlefield, 2015.
Coats, Karen. "Identity." In *Keywords for Children's Literature*, edited by Philip Nel and Lissa Paul, 109–112. New York: New York University Press, 2011.
Cohen, Paul A. *History in Three Keys*. New York: Columbia University Press, 1997.
Davies, Bronwyn and Rom Harré. "Positioning: The Discursive Production of Selves." *Journal for the Theory of Social Behaviour* 20, no. 1 (1990): 43–63.
Doughty, John. "More than Meets the 'I': Chinese Transnationality in Gene Luen Yang's *American Born Chinese*." *Asian American Literature: Discourse & Pedagogies* 1 (2010): 54–60.
El Refaie, Elisabeth. *Autobiographical Comics: Life Writing in Pictures*. Jackson: University Press of Mississippi, 2012.
El Refaie, Elisabeth. "Transnational Identity as Shape-Shifting: Metaphor and Cultural

Resonance in Gene Luen Yang's *American Born Chinese.*" In *Transnational Perspectives on Graphic Narratives: Comics at the Crossroads*, edited by Shane Denson et. al, 33–47. London: Bloomsbury Academic, 2013.

Fusaro, Darrell. "Blessed Are the Nobodies." *i-Italy.* January 6, 2013. http://www.iitaly.org/35077/blessed-are-nobodies.

Harré, Rom. "Positioning Theory: Moral Dimensions of Social-Cultural Psychology." In *The Oxford Handbook of Culture and Psychology*, edited by Jaan Valsiner, 191–206. Oxford: Oxford University Press, 2014.

Hathaway, Rosemary V. "'More than Meets the Eye': Transformative Intertextuality in Gene Luen Yang's *American Born Chinese.*" *ALAN Review* 37, no. 1 (Fall 2009): 41–47.

Jensen, Michael P. *Martyrdom and Identity: The Self on Trial.* London: T&T Clark International, 2010.

Lammark, Phillip L. Jr. "Theoretical Foundations of Identity." In *The Oxford Handbook of Identity Development*, edited by Kate C. McLean and Moin Syed, 12–26. Oxford: Oxford University Press, 2015.

Mayer, Petra. "'Boxers & Saints' & Compassion: Questions for Gene Luen Yang." *NPR.* October 22, 2013. http://www.npr.org/2013/10/22/234824741/boxers-saints-compassion-quesions-for-gene-luen-yang.

McAdams, Dan P., and Claudia Zapata-Gietl. "Three Strands of Identity Development Across the Human Life Course: Reading Erik Erikson in Full." *Oxford Handbooks Online.* June 2, 2014. http://www.oxfordhandbooks.com/view/10.1093/oxfordhb/9780199936564.001.0001/oxfordhb-9780199936564-e-006?rskey=LstO6K&result=1.

Moghaddam, Fathali and Rom Harré. "Words, Conflicts and Political Processes." In *Words of Conflict, Words of War: How the Language We Use in Political Processes Sparks Fighting*, edited by Fathali Moghaddam and Rom Harré, 1–27. Santa Barbara, CA: Praeger, 2010.

Morton, Paul. "The Millions Interview: Gene Luen Yang." *The Millions.* July 8, 2010. http://www.themillions.com/2010/07/the-millions-interview-gene-luen-yang.html.

Mozzocco, J. Caleb. "Interview: Gene Luen Yang on Boxers & Saints." *School Library Journal.* September 19, 2013. http://blogs.slj.com/goodcomicsforkids/2013/09/19/interview-gene-luen-yang-on-boxers-saints/.

Munson, Todd. "Transformers and Monkey Kings: Gene Yang's *American Born Chinese* and the Quest for Identity." In *Comic Books and American Cultural History*, edited by Matthew Pustz, 171–183. London: Continuum, 2012.

Pinti, Daniel. "Theology and Identity in Gene Luen Yang's *American Born Chinese.*" *Literature and Theology* 30 (2016): 233–247.

Reynolds, Thomas E. *The Broken Whole: Philosophical Steps Toward a Theology of Global Solidarity.* Albany: State University of New York Press, 2006.

Song, Min Hyoung. "'How Good It Is to Be a Monkey': Comics, Racial Formation, and *American Born Chinese.*" *Mosaic* 43, no. 1 (March 2010): 73–93.

Stratman, Jacob. "'How Good It Is to Be a Monkey': Conversion and Spiritual Formation in Gene Luen Yang's *American Born Chinese.*" *Christianity & Literature* 65, no. 4 (September 2016): 490–507.

Strauss, Anselm L. *Mirrors and Masks: The Search for Identity.* Piscataway, NJ: Transaction, 2009.

Trites, Roberta Seelinger. "The Harry Potter Novels as a Test Case for Adolescent Literature." *Style* 35, no. 3 (Fall 2001): 472–485.

Woan, Sunny. "Interview with Gene Luen Yang." *Kartika Review* 1 (Winter 2007): 77–88. https://issuu.com/kartikareview/docs/kartika_issue01.

Yang, Gene Luen. *American Born Chinese.* New York: First Second, 2006.

Yang, Gene Luen. *Boxers & Saints.* New York: First Second, 2013.

Yang, Gene Luen. "Festival of Faith and Writing." *Humblecomics: The Blog of Gene Luen Yang.* April 15, 2010. http://humblecomics.com/blog/comments.php?y=10&m=04&entry=entry100415-011419.

Yu, Chun-fang. *Kuan-Yin: The Chinese Transformation of Avalokitesvara.* New York: Columbia University Press, 2001.

About the Contributors

Fatema Johera **Ahmed** is a literary and cultural studies MA student at Monash University in Australia. Her dissertation examines the role of humor in fictional Indigenous Australian literature. Her research interests include Australian literature, diasporic writings, and feminist theory.

Susan Leigh **Brooks** is a professor of English at Bethel University in Minnesota, where she teaches literacy education and young adult literature. Her research includes how literature helps readers make sense of the world and how teachers can facilitate this process.

Katelyn R. **Browne** works as the Youth Services Librarian at the University of Northern Iowa. Before coming to UNI, she worked as a school librarian in a PK–12 school. Her research revolves around Quakers in fiction and queer representation in young adult literature.

Shih-Wen Sue **Chen** is a lecturer in literature at Deakin University in Australia. She received her Ph.D. in literature, screen and theatre studies from Australian National University. She is the author of *Representations of China in British Children's Fiction, 1851–1911* and has essays in multiple edited collections and journals.

Paul T. **Corrigan** is an associate professor of English at Southeastern University in Florida. He has published on religion and literature in various journals. His dissertation at the University of South Florida looked at the postsecular in contemporary American poetry.

Patricia F. **D'Ascoli** teaches Academic Writing and Foundations of Argument at the University of Hartford. She received her MS in English education at Southern Connecticut State University. She published a literary journal, *Connecticut Muse*, and is the author of two essays on themes in *Huckleberry Finn*.

David S. **Hogsette** is a professor of English and director of the writing program at Grove City College in Pennsylvania. His interests include Romantic literature, Gothic literature, science fiction, fantasy, college composition, and technical communication. He has published numerous articles on literature and is the author of two books.

Jeremy **Larson** is an assistant professor of English at Regent University. He earned his Ph.D. in English at Baylor University. His essays and reviews have appeared in *Pro Rege*, *Christ and Pop Culture*, *Christianity and Literature*, *Modern Reformation* and *Mythlore*, among others.

Rizia Begum **Laskar** teaches English at Manohari Devi Kanoi Girls' College in Dibrugarh, Assam, India. Her research includes children's literature, Indian English literature, crime and detective fiction, film studies, and queer literature. She has studied Indian English children's literature and has published various journal articles.

Carrie **Myers** earned her Ph.D. in English and American literature from New York University, has taught at several colleges and universities, and is a faculty member at City Seminary of New York. She is a writer, poet, and spiritual director-in-training.

Erin Wyble **Newcomb** teaches literature in the English department at SUNY New Paltz. She earned her doctoral degree in women's studies and literacy education at Pennsylvania State University. Her publications include feminist theories and theories of disability in young adult literature.

Carissa Turner **Smith** is a professor of English at Charleston Southern University, where she teaches American literature. She is working on a book about saints and posthumanism in children's and young adult fiction.

Jacob **Stratman** is an associate professor of English at John Brown University in Arkansas, where he serves as the Chair of Humanities and Social Sciences. He is the author and editor of various essays and journal articles about literature and faith, as well as disability in young adult literature.

Index